SALTMAKER

Also by Bob Reiss

Divine Assassin
The Casco Deception
Summer Fires

SALT

MAKER

Bob Reiss

VIKING

VIKING
Published by the Penguin Group
Viking Penguin Inc., 40 West 23rd Street,
New York, New York 10010, U.S.A.
Penguin Books Ltd, 27 Wrights Lane,
London W8 5TZ, England
Penguin Books Australia Ltd, Ringwood,
Victoria, Australia
Penguin Books Canada Ltd, 2801 John Street,
Markham, Ontario, Canada L3R 1B4
Penguin Books (N.Z.) Ltd, 182–190 Wairau Road,
Auckland 10, New Zealand

Penguin Books Ltd, Registered Offices:
Harmondsworth, Middlesex, England

First published in 1988 by Viking Penguin Inc.
Published simultaneously in Canada

Grateful acknowledgment is made for permission
to reprint an excerpt from "The Hollow Men"
from Collected Poems 1909–1962 by T. S. Eliot.
Copyright 1936 by Harcourt Brace Jovanovich, Inc.;
Copyright © 1963, 1964 by T. S. Eliot.
Reprinted by permission of Harcourt Brace
Jovanovich, Inc., and Faber and Faber Limited.

LIBRARY OF CONGRESS CATALOGING IN PUBLICATION DATA
Reiss, Bob.
Saltmaker/Bob Reiss.
p.   cm.
I. Title.   II. Title: Saltmaker.
PS3568.E517S2   1988
813'.54—dc19   87-21454
ISBN 0-670-80247-6

Printed in the United States of America by
Arcata Graphics, Fairfield, Pennsylvania
Set in Electra
Designed by Jeff Ward

For Choochie Le Bop

Very Special Thanks to

The Bread Loaf Writers Conference, Betty Bumpers, Kathryn Court, Samuel Dash, Alan Dershowitz, Fred Downs, James Grady, Ann Hood, Jamie Kostos, George Murphy, Esther Newberg, Ruth "the Wizard" Ravenel, Jerome Reiss, Ira Rosen, Howard Rosenberg, Curt Suplee, Susan Neiburg Terkel, and R. Kenelly Webster of second base.

SALTMAKER

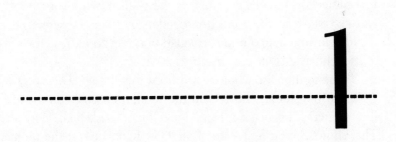

1

"**Y**ou can see why I'm not worried," DeLavery said. "Saboteurs can't get in here." The only reporter not writing—the skinny one with the tape recorder—never stopped watching DeLavery's face. It was 2 a.m., and they were in a glass office three quarters of a mile under Cheyenne Mountain, Colorado. DeLavery would have to stay on guard. The sabotage question had been easy, but the big one remained unasked. DeLavery guessed the reporters' strategy. They were waiting for him to relax.

The name plate on DeLavery's desk read "General." He was one of five men in North America empowered to launch a nuclear war.

Rising briskly, DeLavery grinned. "You want to know what goes on here while the country sleeps? Let's take a walk."

As he opened the soundproofed door, the hum of computers hit them. They stepped out onto a steel catwalk ringing the control room of NORAD, the joint U.S.–Canadian nuclear command. Below the glass office in a huge hexagon-shaped room, they looked down on rows of consoles. Bathed in greenish light from the screens, operators talked into headphone microphones.

"The whole mountain is hollowed out," DeLavery said. "We have forty-nine buildings here, built on steel springs. Explosions topside can't damage us. There's steam heat from natural hot springs. We have our own electrical system if there's an emergency."

Footsteps echoing, the dozen journalists followed DeLavery along the catwalk. Although the computer operators talked softly, there was a sense of activity below. DeLavery indicated six twelve-by-twelve-foot projection screens dominating the walls. SOVIET SOUTHERN DEFENSE ZONE, read white electronic letters on the main screen, below a softly glowing map outline. TURKISH DEFENSE ZONE, read the screen to its right. WESTERN U.S. DEFENSE ZONE.

"We monitor the whole world from this room," DeLavery said. "We can transfer anything from the smaller consoles up there. See that corner? The black screen, looks like a basketball scoreboard? That shows the current state of alert, DefCon Five at the moment, the lowest." Several reporters kept glancing at their skinny colleague, who hung back slightly. His name was Gardner. Robert Gardner, columnist for the *Daily News*. DeLavery had a feeling the big question would come from him.

They reached a narrow steel staircase and began to climb. "The similar screen in the left corner shows the classification level of information showing up front," DeLavery said. "Unclassified now. It's okay for reporters to be here." The *Times* man smiled; DeLavery had found the pushover. "The clocks show the time around the world," he added.

Robert Gardner broke in, he had a surprisingly deep voice for such a thin man. "Isn't it true there were three false alarms last year? That bomber crews were actually dispatched to their planes because of computer error? How close did we come to war?"

They had reached DeLavery's command post, an elevated bank of consoles, in a long desk which overlooked the room from its steel platform. There were red phones and orange phones and blue phones. The screens seemed immense from here, filling DeLavery's vision.

"We never came close to war, Mr. Gardner," DeLavery said. The number-two commander, Colonel Choyke, was manning the command post. DeLavery was a stocky blackhaired man with flattened features like an Indian's. "There never were any false alarms—not really. Here's what happened.

"See, lots of phenomenon can trigger our warning systems but we know that. The system is supposed to be sensitive. We know a warning doesn't mean we're being attacked, it just means there's reason to check." Inside the maps, little blips glowed in clusters, or alone. "Colonel Choyke, magnify Russia midsection, will you?"

The Soviet borderline rushed at them. The reporters stared at the overblown, pulsating blips. DeLavery knew they were fascinated. They were "seeing" Soviet missiles.

"Six thousand Russian ICBMs," he said. "Since we know outside factors can trigger the computers, we plan for it. Our whole warning system is based on independent methods of verifying attack. We're not plunging into any accidental war. I'm sure you've read that congressional report on those incidents, that's why you're here. You're dying to ask me about them, so go ahead, let's get that out of the way before I explain why you can sleep safely tonight—or tomorrow morning, if you have a schedule like mine."

Gardner stepped to the front. "My understanding is that someone accidentally put a war games program in the computer and the screens showed an attack. We almost went to war."

DeLavery grinned. He liked tough questions. "Absolutely. But that happened five years ago. War exercises are carried out in a totally different building now. Different computers. Different circuits. Impossible for that kind of mistake to happen again."

The woman from CBS held up her pen, but DeLavery wasn't finished. "And even on that occasion we didn't actually come close to war. You see, four separate command centers receive information from our warning systems: NORAD, which is us. The Strategic Air Command in Omaha. The Pentagon War Room. And Fort Ritchie, Maryland. There's an alternate NORAD there in case this one ceases to function. And folks, the point is that *none of those other war rooms signaled an attack that day.* Which meant the alarms weren't going off because our detection satellites picked up real launches. No. They were obviously being triggered inside our own computers. No danger. Let's go down to the main floor now."

The CBS woman was blond with fleshy arms and a green pants suit. As they moved down the stairs she asked, "But SAC did send out the bomber crews to the planes?"

"Standard practice," DeLavery assured them. "In nuclear war we have thirty minutes to get those bombers off the ground, maximum. Planes aren't protected by silos like Minuteman missiles, they're not hidden in the sea like subs. Just because you send men out to warm up planes . . . that's standard. The planes never took off. Turned out a forty-nine-cent computer chip malfunctioned."

DeLavery leaned forward conspiratorially.

"Ladies and gentlemen," he whispered. "We replaced the chip."

The reporters chuckled. This was more like the mood DeLavery wanted. Soon he would get to his own pitch, but he would have to time it right. "We're constantly checking and rechecking and *re*-checking these circuits," he said. "Using Army engineers. Private companies."

They stopped by the first console, the one closest to the command post. "Son," DeLavery addressed a blond corporal in a swivel chair, "you're new here, aren't you?"

The boy stood. "Yes, sir."

"Where you from?"

"Portland, Maine, sir." The boy didn't look at the reporters.

"No rooms like this in Portland, hey?"

"This is an amazing place, sir."

Reporters liked it when you talked to enlisted men. Conscious of the scribbling press, DeLavery said, "You're damn right it's amazing, but we're in control all the time. Thank you, Corporal." Then, to the reporters, "Any more false alarms you want to bring up?"

The *Washington Post* man looked more like a lawyer than a journalist, with a gray Brooks Brothers suit and brown tortoiseshell glasses that exaggerated the size of his eyes. "That Congressional report said a Soviet military exercise triggered an alert," he said.

"Good, that's the last one, and you're correct. In 1984 the Russians set off four SBLM long-range missiles during troop maneuvers in Siberia. One missile turned the wrong way, we went to DefCon Four." The reporters glanced automatically at the electronic board in the corner. In red digital letters it read DEFCON FIVE.

"Four is a low-level, standard alert," said DeLavery. "That haywire rocket was brought down by the Soviets before it left their airspace. Even if it *had* left Soviet airspace, its trajectory would have taken it into the sea." A sergeant came up to them with a mess tray. "Can I interest anyone in some radioactive coffee and cherry danish?" DeLavery joked.

The reporters laughed. All but Gardner took a Styrofoam cup. The columnist said with quiet persistence, "What would happen here if a *real* Soviet launch occurred?"

Sweeping his arm toward the giant screens, DeLavery turned serious. "A real Soviet launch? We'd know it in a minute. Our satellites would pick up infrared heat from the engine. Next line of detection—radar in mid-Atlantic or Pacific. A dozen stations, Greenland to Antarctica. Then coastal radar. And if, *if* after we got all those independent confirmations of attack, on different circuits, on different computers, in different locations . . . *if* after NORAD and SAC and the Pentagon and Fort Ritchie had all conferred, if we were still unclear about what was happening for some reason, and I can't imagine what that reason would be . . . we would still have one more system of verification left. A means of knowing instantly if a missile has hit anywhere in the U.S."

Up on the Turkish Defense Zone screen, he noticed a blip where none had been before. There were thousands of blips in the world. DeLavery had been here so long he knew them all.

"Like in the movies?" asked the *Times* man eagerly. In every group there was a nuclear-film buff. "You get on the phone with someone in the target area? You wait to see if they're still on the line afterwards?"

DeLavery bit into a cherry danish. The new blip wasn't moving. He supposed the Pentagon had added another Soviet installation to the map.

He said, "Well, suppose the phone lines are out that day, there's a short. Or suppose the enemy missile hits but it screws up, excuse me ladies, and lands two hundred miles away. Your man on the phone is still there. He thinks nothing happened, but he's wrong. No, it's more scientific than that. We've got seismic monitors in the ground, all over the country, to register shock." He grinned. "Like when my daughter calls and says she's out late with her boyfriend. The monitors go off near my house."

He had them in a good mood now. Robert Gardner leaned against the console. "Can the satellites show ground photos from Russia? Peasants walking, close-up stuff?"

"No, that equipment exists, but we don't have it here." DeLavery eased into the tricky part, the reason why the interviews had been granted. "We'd like to. It would be another verification system. It's hard to believe our equipment is over twenty years old, but that's the case. Meanwhile, weapons have grown more accurate, more powerful."

The *St. Louis Post-Dispatch* woman jumped on that one. "You mean your equipment is obsolete?"

DeLavery finished his danish. "Hardly. Not if we maintain an active program of updating. The Pentagon needs appropriations. And our nuclear forces should get priority. I hope you'll write that." He leaned forward, earnest now. "It's inconceivable almost," he said. "If a mess sergeant at Fort Bragg needs a computer to count his beans and we need one to help strengthen our data collecting, he gets priority if he asked first. We've got to acquire the sort of equipment that would give us the edge."

The *Times* man was going for his third danish. DeLavery rose and headed toward the exit. The reporters seemed tired and satisfied, although he wasn't sure about Gardner. He might hear from Gardner again. "I don't know if any of you have ever worked nights," DeLavery joked. He shook his head in a mirthful plea for sympathy. "My wife calls me . . ." He paused dramatically. "General Dracula."

The *Times* and the *Post-Dispatch* were writing. Jokes were good color. DeLavery said, "In fact, we have a whole circle of friends who shop at night on our days off, swim at night in the summer, ski, breakfast at night, play softball under . . ."

Two consoles away, a corporal said, loud enough to be heard over the fun, "Uh oh."

The big screen shifted pictures up front. SOVIET NORTHEAST ATTACK ZONE flashed on.

One of the little blips began to pulsate.

A woman's voice, clearly computerized, announced over the loudspeaker, "We have a launch detection, Soviet launch detection. This is not a test."

There was the briefest of pauses as everyone absorbed the words. The *Times* man gasped. Gardner said, "I guess we get a demonstration now?"

DeLavery said easily, "Now you'll see how it works. That's Bunnie, our computer voice." He was visibly calm, but a hot pain sliced through his belly. No matter how many times he presided over a nuclear alert, the feeling was just as sharp. He thought, is it only an alert?

The new blip he had detected a few minutes ago had been in Poland, not Russia. There couldn't be a connection, or could there?

Colonel Choyke met him at the command center. Activity in the room was picking up, soldiers seemed to have materialized out of nowhere. The SOVIET NORTHEAST ATTACK ZONE remained fixed on the central screen, but the pictures on the other big boards were shifting rapidly as the computers automatically scanned other Soviet areas for launches.

"Colonel Choyke, check with SAC and the Pent . . ." DeLavery broke off. The blip on the central screen had become five blips. The alarm horn wailed OOOOO-GA. Bunnie announced, "Five Soviet launch detections. Eight warheads apiece. Estimated arrival time twenty-seven minutes."

DeLavery said, "Go to DefCon Four, Colonel Choyke." The range light came on along the wall. If the alert didn't stop soon he would have to clear the reporters from the room.

The *Washington Post* man was cleaning his glasses with jerky, agitated bursts. "There's no provocation," he said, more a question than a statement. "Nothing's going on."

The reporters fell silent. Watching. None of them writing. "FIVE INBOUND MISSILES. WE HAVE GREENLAND CONFIRMATION." The blips were over the North Atlantic now.

Colonel Choyke said, "SAC and Fort Ritchie are getting them too."

DeLavery blew out a long stream of air. "DefCon Three. I'm afraid you reporters will have to wait in the coffee lounge." The security-status board was flashing CLASSIFIED MATERIAL in red. DeLavery ordered, "Sergeant, escort our guests down the hall." To the reporters, "I'll join you in a few minutes and explain what happened."

But as he spoke, white dotted lines sprouted from the blips. Each line broke into five more lines. A bouquet of forty computer-predicted flight paths arced toward the United States.

DeLavery heard Robert Gardner, surprisingly calm and still behind him, "Let us stay, General."

"Sergeant, I told you to move them!" DeLavery's console operators spoke to each other below on their headphone microphones.

"I have two bluebirds over the Northwest Territory."

"Target areas identified . . ."

"Switch to base power," DeLavery said. "Seal us off, Colonel Choyke. Get the planes up, defensive missiles only." Up top, the gates would be closing electronically. Horns would be sounding. Soldiers would be driving or running along the long underground tunnels to the ten-foot-thick steel vault door to the main war room. Within minutes the base would be closed off from the outside world.

On the big screens luminous circles began blossoming. Target areas.

DeLavery thought, No alert has ever triggered this many systems.

"My sister . . . my sister lives there," DeLavery heard a soldier repeating. "My sister . . ."

He was always amazed at how fast the whole system worked. Fourteen minutes had passed. He envisioned the frantic preparations he had ordered around the world. In smaller underground vaults throughout the United States and Canada, two-man missile launch teams were opening blue steel boxes, reading launch codes, inserting activation keys into their launch computers. They were arming missiles.

Steam was rising around missiles in silos. Roofs were being winched back.

On tarmacs at Andrews Air Force Base in Washington, in Minot, North Dakota, in Omaha, in the Philippines and Germany and Greece, the first bomber waves were taking off. They would fly to predetermined areas near Soviet airspace and turn around as the next wave approached. Bombers would keep circling until DefCon One sent them all in for the kill.

Colonel Choyke kept saying, "They're still getting it, they're get-

ting it, too." On Polaris and Trident submarines in the North Atlantic, off the Philippines, off Japan, off Denmark, captains were
opening envelopes containing attack orders. They'd received computer instructions to ready for launch.

And in a room like this one near Minsk, Russia, if the Soviets
weren't attacking, if, praise God, this alert was some crazy accident,
a Soviet air marshal was watching all the U.S. activity on his screen
and ordering Soviet Alert level three equivalent himself.

But then DeLavery's heart sank and he knew this was no false
alarm; this was the real thing. Another screen had shifted pictures to
show MID-ATLANTIC DEFENSE ZONE. Delaware. Maryland. Virginia.
North Carolina. The little blips were off Virginia.

"WE HAVE A SOVIET SUBMARINE LAUNCHING," Bunnie announced.
"NINE MINUTES ESTIMATED ARRIVAL TIME."

DeLavery heard himself say, "DefCon Two, Colonel Choyke."

"THIS IS NOT AN EXERCISE," Bunnie said.

The government had empowered DeLavery to launch with or
without presidential okay. Only a minute had passed since he'd placed
his call to the White House, yet it seemed much longer. Waiting
for the President's voice, which he knew he would hear momentarily,
DeLavery had a flash of the little house in which he had grown up
in Alexandria, Virginia. There was a red-and-blue plaster-of-paris
jockey on the lawn. He flashed to his wife and teenage daughter. It
took less than a second. I'll kill her if she comes in late tonight, he
thought.

Normally at 6 a.m. DeLavery climbed outside and walked in the
December snow. It was clean and sometimes he saw deer.

He grew aware of the new boy, the Maine corporal just below
his command post. The boy was hunched over his console, punching
in information. As DeLavery moved down behind the boy he stretched
his cord so that his earphone remained in place. Reflected over more
blossoming blips on the screen, DeLavery saw the boy's frightened
white face and his own Air Force tunic.

First day on the job, the boy had told DeLavery.

He placed his hand on the soldier's shoulder.

"Beginner's luck," he said.

Nose down, perfectly aimed and targeted, the football descended into the arms of Mark St. Johns. Madden was dreaming.

It was Thanksgiving Day, 1950. The players wore army boots, fatigue pants, and long johns against the cold. GIs cheered or booed on the sidelines. They'd each bet fifty dollars on the game.

"Last play. My wife's birthday present rides on you, Lieutenant," growled a Georgia lineman. They were a hundred yards from the Yalu River as part of General MacArthur's victorious Third Army. They'd pushed the North Koreans all the way to the Chinese border and they expected to go home soon. MacArthur had even flown to Japan for dinner.

Madden and St. Johns had enlisted together after high school. Madden told his old friend, "Do the little sidestep."

As they moved into formation, the cheering grew huge. They were playing on a wide, treeless tongue of earth that extended into the frozen river. At their backs the meadow sloped with iced-over patches two hundred yards to the crest of a hill. Four hundred yards south, beyond Madden's squad's stacked weapons, there was evergreen forest. The meadow led off to a bend in the river.

China, Madden had thought, surprised when he first saw the slate cliffs and fir forest, looks like western Massachusetts, like home, at least here.

At the hike Madden's makeshift defense line, the biggest soldiers he could find, fell back, battling. A gigantic Minnesota radioman with a beard rushed him. Twenty yards downfield St. Johns was a pair of retreating boots. As Madden released the ball the Minnesotan slammed into his hip, knocking him over. An odd whistling filled the air. In sleep, Madden shifted, recognized it. In the dream he screamed with horror, "Incoming!"

Nobody heard him over the cheering.

The football neatly landed in Mark St. Johns's hands. Winning touchdown.

Madden was already on the ground from the tackle. The earth rose up beneath him. On the sideline a head disappeared off a soldier's shoulders. He heard more whistles. Hot air swept over them and the earth filled with more roars. The whole division was caught, helpless, hugging the earth.

In the dream Madden remembered. "Into the shellholes," he yelled. He crawled toward the stacked weapons on the side of the field. He might be hit, but he needed them. He knew what would happen when the bombing stopped. Fountains of earth pelted him.

The dream shifted. A human wave of black-coated Chinese was coming. In the shellhole Madden's men kept up steady fire. The Chinese charged through shellholes and around corpses of American troops. Their bayonets gleamed in the setting sun. Madden yelled, "Cover fire, left! Left!" The man on his right grunted and slumped over, forehead in the earth. Madden sprayed the lead attacker and the man was blown backward, off his feet. The sky was blotted out. Spread-eagled, a Chinese was leaping down on him.

But the dream shifted again, and they were running in the forest. Madden's breathing seemed loud; no one was talking, and he carried a wounded sergeant on his back. They ducked low-hanging branches. Somewhere behind them were the Chinese. The dull rumble of artillery echoed in the forest. It was hard to know where it came from.

"Lieutenant, listen to me, he's slowing us down." The complaining corporal had a Boston accent. He was still bleeding from a shrapnel cut on his cheek. "Lieutenant, he'll die anyway, leave him here."

The corporal was the same man who had urged Madden to surrender after they'd beaten back the first Chinese attack and learned on the radio that the Americans were retreating. Two hours ago the front had already collapsed and the main army was two miles behind them.

The corporal had said, "We killed plenty of them. At least in prison camp we'd be alive."

Madden whispered, "Get ready to hit them." It was dawn now. Through the mist at the edge of the field they saw the Chinese encampment, the slow-moving men by the morning fire, the alien smell of new kinds of food. The truck.

"There are fifty guys there minimum, Lieutenant. We can't take them, forget the truck."

The gunfire faded and Madden was in his office, shaking hands with a Korean in a suit. Beaming, the man said, "Mutually beneficial to our peoples." But the Korean was shaking Madden's shoulders, not his hand.

A voice was saying, "Wake up, Mr. President."

In the dark, Madden looked into the white, oval face of his bodyguard. The man was supposed to be outside Madden's bedroom at his duty station. Why is he in here? Madden thought.

Moonlight flooded in through the French windows of the East Wing, tinged red and blue by the big Christmas tree outside.

"The Russians are attacking," the bodyguard said.

Madden hurried toward the Situation Room in the subbasement of the White House. Half a dozen men in military uniforms waited outside the room in the hallway, and one man in white bathrobe and slippers. The military men were night liaisons with the branches of the armed forces. The man in pajamas was a Georgetown University linguistics professor who worked as White House translator at night. His red hair was mussed, he ran his fingers through a Vandyke beard.

Madden was in pajamas too. They'd been a gift from his daughter-in-law in Evanston. Cute lettering on the sleeves that read MR. PRESIDENT.

The professor seemed dazed and frightened. None of the men had entered the Situation Room; only the President could invite people inside during a crisis. That way extra people would not distract the decision makers.

"Professor Shinitzky." Madden nodded briskly to the linguist, indicating he should follow Madden into the room. He left everyone else outside except his "doomsday aide," a Navy ensign who followed Madden everywhere, carrying the nation's nuclear codes in a briefcase. Madden wasn't about to waste time going through the papers, but he wanted the aide close by anyway.

The Situation Room seemed huge without lots of advisers inside. There was a twenty-seat redwood conference table with water carafes and crystal ashtrays. Chandeliers hung above both ends of the table. A strategy map filled the with red arrows showed the Ethiopia-Somalia border. The last meeting here had focused on Soviet arms aid to

Ethiopia and nobody had changed the map. There were no windows.

With the door closed, Madden moved to a speaker phone at his end of the table. Shinitzky's face was composed, but the sleeves on his bathrobe were shaking. Madden, who had a politician's memory for personal details, needed Shinitzky calm.

"Score any goals Sunday, Professor?" Madden asked. Despite his frail appearance, the professor was a talented polo player.

"Two." It did the trick. Shinitzky smiled slightly, as if to indicate he'd calmed himself. Madden waved him into a chair and turned back to the speaker phone. If the White House operator had done his job, the people to whom Madden needed to speak would be waiting on the conference line.

"General DeLavery, you there?" DeLavery's affirmation was crisp and monosyllabic. He'd met the General at NORAD and at a White House ball. "Admiral?" Jeb Tunney, a gruff, white-haired veteran of three wars, chaired the Joint Chiefs of Staff. Page Edwards was secretary of defense. The chairman of the National Security Council had not been reached yet. The operator was looking for him, but he wasn't answering his beeper.

All three men on the line besides the President carried gold codes cards, which empowered them to launch nuclear missiles and listed the codes by which the weapons could be fired. The Vice President also had a card, but Madden did not automatically include him on the crisis list.

"General, what happened?"

Madden's silver hair was mussed. He smelled sleep off the professor over the furniture-polish-and-leather odor of the chairs.

He asked DeLavery in rapid succession, "How many missiles? Launched from where? Are they MIRVed?" That meant, how many warheads did they have. "Arrival time? Any word from the Russians?" He forced himself to ask the most difficult question. "Targets?"

"Jesus Christ," Shinitzky breathed when the answer came.

"Any chance of mistake?" Madden asked. This had to be a mistake, he thought. But the general said, "Always a chance, but it's small. We have satellite and radar pickup both. Two tracks have gone off the screen—we figure they've ditched in the sea. An electronic error might knock off one circuit, but not two."

"Suggestions. Admiral?"

Madden poured a drink of water. The hoarse voice of the Joint Chiefs chairman was loud in the room. "Hand it to us, Mr. President." Madden saw Tunney in his Reston, Virginia, bedroom, sitting on the side of the bed, talking into the phone on the night table. Knowing he was about to die. "Get yourself out of there," Tunney said.

Despite the tension Madden smiled and said, "General?" and forgot the suggestion. There was no way out of the White House in six minutes. A bomb shelter under the East Wing could not withstand a hit on Washington. Madden didn't want to go. Anyway, a Carter plan to evacuate the President by helicopter had been proven impossible years before. The helicopter had been "vaporized" while on the ground during a simulated attack.

Tunney's real intention was to get Madden out of the decision-making process. Madden remembered a conversation they'd had years ago, when Madden was just a congressman. "Presidents screw up the military," Tunney had said. "They did it in Vietnam. They did it back in Madison's day. He tried to lead the defense of Washington in the War of 1812, and the British burned the city."

"General DeLavery?"

"The next few minutes are crucial, Mr. President. Once their missiles hit, our communications are out. You and the admiral and all you people in Washington . . . Our birds may be blown up in their silos. We've got to believe the machines, that's what we put them there for. Launch."

The secretary of defense could barely be heard over static suddenly coming over the line.

"I would wait . . . verification, Mr.——President——until you're sure."

"What's the matter with the phone?"

"I'm in a booth—the car phone's broken."

Madden snapped, "What are you doing driving around at four o'clock in the morning, for chrissakes?" He ordered, "Professor Shinitzky, get Menkes." He'd named the Soviet Premier. There were four minutes left, but he could start a launch in thirty seconds. Shinitzky rushed into a side room, a new addition Madden had had built. It contained two deep leather chairs, a bare table, and a red phone. The hotline. Until Madden's administration, the hotline had been a teletype machine in the Pentagon, not a phone like the public thought. Madden had added the phone. Shinitzky, going through a Pentagon operator, could activate the hotline with a special code. There was almost simultaneous link-up with Moscow.

Admiral Tunney said, "Mr. President, they will lie to you."

But Madden told DeLavery, "No launch until verification. You have planes up, right? Defensive action only. Where will the Russians hit first?"

"Grady Creek, Montana."

"What the hell is there?"

"Well, Minutemen seventy miles away. The Russians are sloppy."

Madden squeezed his forehead. His eyes burned. For no reason he smelled eggs. He hated the smell of eggs, but it wouldn't go away.

"We wait for confirmation," he told DeLavery.

"Yes, Mr. President."

The second hand of the wall clock jerked, moving from point to point. The Situation Room seemed warmer than usual. The door to the hotline was open; Madden heard Shinitzky talking forcefully in Russian. He wondered if there was anything else he should be doing. The top of the table was damp with sweat where his palm had rested.

Since the President was always the last person in the chain of command to be informed of possible nuclear attack, the inverted logic of the age had decreed that the man who would give the final go-ahead to fire would have the least amount of time to consider options.

"Civil Defense," Madden said. "Has anyone contacted Civil Defense?"

"Three minutes," said DeLavery.

Shinitzky called out, "I . . . I have the Russians, but they say Menkes is out, he's walking his dogs or something."

Tunney growled, "He doesn't have dogs. It's a trick."

Static on the speaker phone: the secretary of defense was trying to say something, but the only word discernible was "dogs."

"A Marshal Tomsky is on the line," Shinitzky called. "He wants to know why their screens show us on alert."

"Tell him it's Menkes I want to talk to. Tell him it's an exercise."

Tunney snapped, "The Japanese were talking peace when they attacked Pearl Harbor!"

Shinitzky said, "Someone's telling Tomsky *we're* attacking. Someone's urging him to launch."

The room was really hot. "Tell him I need to talk to Menkes. Repeat, it's an exercise."

"Tomsky says if it's an exercise, what are you doing on the hotline?"

"Tell him, Christ, tell him the truth. Tell him our screens show an attack. We're not retaliating until we get verification."

Tunney shouted, "He doesn't have dogs!"

"There's a big argument going on there," Shinitzky said. But now there was nothing to do but wait. If there really were missiles coming, they would trigger the seismic monitors in Montana when they hit, and those monitors would broadcast the news to the war rooms. Madden told himself the Russians couldn't be attacking, it was unreal. Impossible. There was no particularly intense crisis going on. Menkes had to know the two countries would destroy each other. Didn't Menkes know that? Or had someone else ordered the attack?

Madden's arms ached, and his neck was itching. He said, "Keep repeating, we're not doing anything." The words "Mr. President" looked stupid and trivial on his sleeve. He envisioned the secretary of defense in a Georgetown phone booth, looking out at the late revelers. Shinitzky wasn't visible, but he heard the man's rapid-fire Russian.

Tunney said, "They'll launch now even if they weren't before. They'll launch because you told them we were thinking of launching. You don't have time to wait for confirmation."

Then Shinitzky said, "Premier Menkes is on the line, Mr. President," and Madden reached for the other red phone beside Shinitzky.

2

Forty minutes later, Morgan Rittenhouse rolled over in bed and opened his eyes. His wife breathed peacefully beside him. Embers glowed in the fireplace, otherwise the house was still.

Rittenhouse slid from under the quilt, careful not to wake Ginny. A weak bladder roused the Vice President twice a night, and when he finished emptying it he lingered by the bedroom window. Washington looked quiet and beautiful outside.

Half an inch of fresh snow covered the Naval Observatory grounds. Beyond the shrub garden and lawn, floodlights shone down an embankment toward the iron fence. Woods partially blocked Rittenhouse's view of Massachusetts Avenue, but above the treetops he saw the missile-shaped minaret of the Islamic Center half a mile south.

Rittenhouse pulled absently at the fold of flesh hanging between chin and Adam's apple. He loved Washington best before sunrise. It was the combination of silence and expectation. He felt the powerful people stirring in sleep, preparing for the day's battles. And Rittenhouse liked to consider himself a thirty-year veteran of some of the biggest. He'd been a four-term Texas senator. Chairman of the Ways and Means Committee and Senate whip. Beaten by Madden early in the presidential primaries, he'd accepted the vice-presidential slot.

As usual, with the day's first thought of Madden, Rittenhouse felt a tug of irritation. Casting back, he saw himself in Madden's hotel room at the Houston Oaks Plaza during the convention. He saw himself and Madden shaking hands like a couple of boys' softball team captains after a game. Madden had needed help to win the South, and Rittenhouse could provide it. The offer had been couched in the usual expediencies: Madden's vice-president would have a "big role" to play.

"I'll put some backbone into those Harvards you keep around," Rittenhouse had laughed. News photos had shown them embracing amid a sea of red, white, and blue balloons. And Madden had even invited him to a couple of cabinet meetings—until it became obvious every time the Russians came up, Rittenhouse would fight him on military cuts or proposed treaties.

I'll be president in a few more years, Rittenhouse thought.

In the dark the phone rang, a fluty, birdlike sound. Ginny jolted awake. Someone died, Rittenhouse thought. He moved swiftly despite his bulk. One of his old campaign lines came to him: Presidents are remembered more for how they handle the three-o'clock-in-the-morning phone calls than how they run the country day to day.

But whoever he expected to hear on the other end, it was not Madden. He was astonished to recognize the flat, bitten-off New England consonants of the President.

"Slight problem here, Morgan."

Rittenhouse's first thought was, shit, the Israelis must have bombed Bagdad again.

Then he heard what the President was saying. Rittenhouse sat down on the bed. He whispered, "For the love of Christ. You surrendered?"

The room tilted, seemed to grow warm. Ginny was mouthing over and over, "*Who is it?*"

"I told them we wouldn't fight, Morgan," Madden said dryly. "*That's* what I told them. Thirty seconds later we found out there wasn't any attack. Maybe it was a computer malfunction, or sabotage. We're both backing down off alert. DefCon Three in twenty minutes, then Four. So far it's working."

As a boy Rittenhouse had rodeoed in Texas. When you were thrown from a steer you lost vision and the breath went out of you. But you had to get out of the way fast.

He started to laugh. "They weren't even coming and you *surrendered?*" He felt sick. "You gave up to them?" It was the worst nightmare Rittenhouse had had during the campaign against Madden. He'd never been tough enough. Rittenhouse shouted, "What did you do? Couldn't you wait? Why'd you do it, for Christ's fucking sake!"

Ginny was waving her hands to get Rittenhouse's attention.

Madden seemed calm, weary. "Morgan, you weren't there." There was a long pause. "But they'll be at our throats now, if they think I won't fight them. I can't stay on after this. You'd better come in and talk about the transition."

Seconds elapsed before Rittenhouse realized he still held the humming receiver in his hand. Lines of heat seemed to run down the sides of his face and onto his neck.

A voice in his head said "President Rittenhouse."

Already he heard sirens out on Massachusetts Avenue, and the roar of cars sweeping up the driveway. The new, bigger Secret Service detail for the President-to-be, he thought.

Ginny was saying, "What happened? What's going on? Morgan?" When he tried to explain it, she clutched him. He soothed her: the Russians weren't really attacking. Madden had made a mistake. The crisis was over.

But inside he knew it was just beginning. He rang downstairs to ask the stewards to put on coffee. "Madden was right about one thing," he told Ginny, buttoning his shirt. "They'll be coming at us a hundred ways. Nicaragua. Angola. What the hell is Thatcher going to think?" he groaned. "The allies."

Sweat ran down his neck. He was pulling on his pants. He felt sick. Humiliated.

The gray suit changed Rittenhouse's appearance: he looked like someone unequivocally in charge.

Rittenhouse said, "He was always too lenient, I told him but he wouldn't listen." Ginny got out of bed, "That coward!"

With the lights on, the room showed her expensive taste for things

Oriental: Chinese rugs and lacquered tables, Korean ebony chests. There were fresh bird-of-paradise flowers the stewards changed each morning.

She said, "It should have been you all along, Morgan. Just like him not to call you until it's over."

His fingers shook as he tied his tie. "Honest to God, they only respect strength."

Ginny walked barefoot over the soft pile toward her dressing table. She switched on the ring of soft lights around the mirror. She began sorting through her makeup. She would make an entrance when the newsmen arrived. Smiling coquettishly, she said, "Mr. President." His sudden elevation made her randy. "If those Secret Service men weren't waiting downstairs I'd unbutton that shirt right now."

Then she thought of something else and grew serious. "They'll be out for his blood. You'll have to go along with it."

Rittenhouse flashed back to the Texas state house, to a pair of black shoes dangling above an overturned chair. He had been a lowly page then, a boy with aspirations. He still remembered the scuff mark on the right shoe of the disgraced senator.

She said, "It's for the country's good. You don't owe him anything."

Rittenhouse was combing his hair.

"Ford pardoned Nixon and was never elected again," she said.

Rittenhouse snapped, "For God's sake, let me think!" He would help crush Madden, but he didn't have to like it. Losing the presidency was enough. He could show no sympathy, no kindness. Madden had just turned himself into the greatest pariah of the twentieth century.

3

The country was waking up. In Vermont the livestock farmers were switching on radios in their barns. In Key West the shrimpers heard the news as they chugged into the Gulf of Mexico. The all-night truckers told each other on their shortwaves. In the subways of New York early commuters listened on earphones of their pocket sets, stunned. Traffic seemed slower on Washington's Beltway. In the San Fernando Valley phones were ringing as easterners woke their relatives in the west.

In Chicago it was snowing. Josh Madden lowered the volume on the kitchen radio and shook his head, incredulous. "Meteors did it?"

The announcer's deep voice said, "Scientists at the National Meteorological Center are supposed to notify authorities of sightings but neither group contacted the other during the alert."

Josh couldn't help it. He started to smile. "My father sure screwed up this time," he said.

The announcer said, "The meteors triggered early-warning satellites designed to detect infrared heat from Soviet missiles. Radar stations in Greenland and Halifax confirmed the approach. When one meteor struck eastern Montana, it triggered seismic monitors."

"The White House confirmed Kremlin reports at four-fifty."

"Meteors!" Josh repeated, incredulous.

His wife, Stephanie, hung up the wall phone and wrapped her robe around her more tightly, even though the room was warm. "It's still busy," she said. She looked dazed. She fell into a chair and stared in horror at their son, Danny, drowsily spooning Cocoa Puffs from a bowl. The red cape on his Superman pajamas brushed the oak plank floor.

She whispered, "Oh God. He's only four."

They'd been up for two hours, glued to the radio. The TV was in the shop again.

The kitchen was filled with hanging ferns and smelled of wood cabinets and chicory coffee. Wind rattled the panes.

The announcer said, "Leaders of both countries issued assurances that no fighting had taken place. In a speech twenty minutes ago Premier Menkes said, 'The peace-loving peoples of the Soviet Union would never begin a nuclear war.' "

Josh came around the table and squeezed her shoulder. She was a plump, curly-haired blonde, plain looking in an open, girlish way. "There's nothing to worry about. We've been over this. The alert was canceled an hour ago."

Her knuckles were white around her coffee mug, which was full but no longer steaming. She did not take her eyes off Danny. "Melted in his sleep," she said.

Like his father's, Josh Madden's most notable features were his slate gray eyes. A thick auburn beard obscured the lower half of his face, imparting a bearish quality. More long hair fell over his forehead. Unlike his father, and at age thirty-four, he had a small paunch, visible beneath the corduroy jacket.

Stephanie told Danny, "Honey, drink your juice."

The little boy glanced away from the bowl. "Mommy, don't cry." With his free hand he reached across the corner of the table and patted her wrist. "Superman will protect you."

Josh said, "Danny, you want to go sledding this afternoon? Why don't you check Rosebud, make sure there's no rust on the runners."

When he left, Josh switched off the radio. "You'll scare him."

"I know I'm being silly. But I keep thinking, it was so close."

"Steph, the bottom line is *nothing happened*."

Stephanie dried a wet spot on her cheek with her index finger.

She'd been a nurse before Danny was born, and she planned to go back when he started preschool.

They heard a thump upstairs, probably the boy turning over the sled to look at the runners.

"Meteors," she said, closing the Cocoa Puffs box, "fly through space. Nobody knows when they're coming. How can anyone say it won't happen again?" Josh said, "Stephanie." The edge grew in her voice. "We were sleeping. He was in that room, all by himself. It isn't right, things happening when you're sleeping."

The phone started ringing. Ignoring it, Stephanie said, "The funny thing is, he's been asking weird questions all week. He brought home that sparrow. 'Is this dead?' 'Why did it die?' 'Did someone kill the chicken we ate for lunch?' "

Josh rubbed his forehead, "It's amazing how my father can mess things up for me when he's not around."

He grabbed the phone on the seventh ring, heard the perpetually cheery voice of his mother. She was in her study, looking out at Pennsylvania Avenue. "Are you all right?" she said. "Don't worry about your father, he's fine. He wanted to phone himself, but he has so many things to do."

"Sure. Why should today be any different?"

Breezily, she said, "Well, I just wanted to check in." She paused. "Josh, I was scared last night, I'll tell you!" Her voice lowered. "Your father did a brave thing. But not everyone might see it that way. It would be good for him to hear from you."

For her sake he said, "Steph's been trying to reach him."

When he hung up, he went back to the table, leaned toward his wife. "There wasn't any war after the Cuban missile crisis or Vietnam or Afghanistan. I used to think it would happen when I was in college. It never does. Reporters exaggerate. You know what they're like. Talk to them for an hour, say one bad thing, that's what they quote. Steph, the people in charge are too smart to let war happen."

No response. He tried, "God won't let it happen." He tried levity. "If it hits, I hope we go fast." He told her, wearying of her mood, "Block it out, there's nothing you can do about it anyway. Damn that phone!"

This time it was another female voice, hard edged and triumphant. "Professor Madden? Amy Duncan, *Tribune.* You heard about the surrender. Have you spoken to your father this morning?"

Keeping the irritation from his voice, Josh said, "I haven't spoken to him, but whatever he does, he has good reasons."

"Do you think he had a breakdown?"

"I'm in the middle of something. I can't talk," Josh said. He hung up. "Change the number again."

The phone started ringing. He unplugged it.

"Maybe we should go to Washington," Steph said. "He needs you." Her maternal instincts were swinging wildly, needing a focus. Josh's mouth grew hard. "He always does fine by himself."

She pushed back from the table. At the sink, she scraped eggs off a plate. "But he must feel awful. Look what might have happened last night."

Josh said dryly, "What's really bothering you? It wouldn't be that time of month, would it?"

"Why is it whenever I get upset about anything you ask if my period is here?"

He snapped, "Because that's the excuse you use when you don't want to talk!"

They both stopped, sheepish. Josh poured more coffee, blew away steam. His mug said, "THE PROFESSOR." He said, "Sorry. Look, I didn't want to tell you. Henderson is quitting the department. You know what that means? If I can finish the Chaucer essay and get it to the publisher, I have a shot at taking over. Head of the department, Steph! More money and everything! I'm under a lot of pressure."

He kissed her on the cheek. "I have to finish my grading. I have a class at ten." It was eight-thirty.

They heard the thump of running feet upstairs. The boy's excited cry came. "SUPERMANNNNNN!"

"I know I'm being emotional," she said. But a vision had come to her. It was Danny sleeping. She saw his tiny fist by his face, framed against the white pillowcase. She saw the shiny redbrown hair over his forehead. It was the picture she carried of Danny at his safest, and normally it filled her with choking love. Today she felt only terror. She'd never been this frightened. In the vision, it was like something else was in the room with her son. Something horrible and out of sight. Something she should have known about all along, except she had ignored it.

She tried one last time, groping. "You father's in trouble."

Josh put his hands on her shoulders. "Listen, if my father murdered someone it would turn out to be Hitler. Everything he touches turns to gold. I've watched this for years. He's got plenty of people around to help him. Now I have to get upstairs." He stroked her face. "You'll be okay?"

The tears were back. "I feel so helpless."

"One person can't do anything. You'll see, in a week everything will be back to normal."

He was wrong. There are moments that change people forever.

She said, "I just wish I could do something."

As he mounted the stairs, Danny ran by him, into the kitchen. The boy's voice floated up to him. "Mommy, if I die, who will play with my toys?"

4

At six that afternoon Madden stepped up to the podium in the East Wing press room of the White House. Reporters filled every seat and stood packed against the walls. The television lights glowed off Madden's silver hair. In the huge silence he seemed calm, but the hands holding the single page resignation speech shook.

"My friends," he said. "Last night danger threatened the American people. I did my best to avert it, to bring us through it safely. I take full responsibility for what I did. In the end, perhaps history will show lives were saved because of it."

Madden looked directly at the reporters and away from the speech.

"It is clear today from the reaction at home and abroad that my act may be misconstrued as weakness." A voice in back shouted, "That's for sure!" Madden continued, "As a sign the American people have lost their love of freedom, and will to fight for it. *Nothing could be further from the truth.* But I feel I can no longer serve my country best as president after last night."

Madden looked into the cameras. "I am stepping down voluntarily. One of a president's great tools in foreign policy is his own unpredictability, and I have lost that edge." Madden looked down for a moment. "I have every faith in the strength of the American people, and I ask you to give unqualified support to your new President, Morgan Rittenhouse. The coming months will be crucial."

There was no visible reaction to the resignation. Over thirty senators had called for him to step down or be impeached today. In the third row, Robert Gardner made sure his tape recorder was spinning and wrote, "Although the immediate threat has subsided, the question is, will Madden's surrender *cause* a war? State Department sources say the Soviets will increase activity in Africa and the Mideast. At least Madden has spared the country an impeachment fight."

Madden ran one hand down the top of the lectern. "Well, the resignation is signed," he said.

Ignoring the shouted questions, he left to cross the east lawn, hand in hand with his wife, toward a waiting Marine helicopter. Madded asked the pilot to circle the White House for a last look. The crowd on Pennsylvania Avenue was roaring. As they rose, the beating of voices was audible over the slashing blades of the machine.

TRAITOR, read dozens of signs visible from the air. A few said, DON'T GO!

Madden watched the White House recede as they headed toward Andrews Air Force base and his waiting plane.

"Christ, Rittenhouse!" he told Catherine. "He'll blow us up."

5

He was a simple gardener, the visitor said, come to deliver
a message. Nervous, rubbing his hands on his knees, the Oriental
kept glancing out of the picture window. Manhattan was ninety stories
below. He might have been unaccustomed to being up this high in
a building. He might have been memorizing the view, to describe
it to someone else.

Mark St. Johns, chairman of the Global American Bank, moved
out from behind the desk of polished mahogany to seat himself across
a glass coffee table from the man. The word "Chasŏng," whispered
in his ear by his secretary, had terminated his meeting with his vice-
presidents and hurried him back to his office.

St. Johns tried to put the messenger at ease.

"You're from Vietnam?"

"Cambodia." The pressed white French suit was ten years old,
the English perfect.

"When did you come to the United States?"

"Fourteen years ago. He brought me out."

"He?"

"President Madden."

With the utterance of his old friend's name, St. Johns felt the pulse beating in his throat. If Madden had sent this man he was safe. But a thousand questions assailed St. Johns.

A *Times* column, open between them on the glass table, read:

> Is he dead? Hiding? Rumors and accusations fly. He has been sighted in the Bahamas, no, in New York City, no, at the Idaho mansion of a millionaire friend. He is ill. He has had a breakdown. White House spokesmen claim he is "recuperating" and will return to Washington for hearings, but where is the proof?

St. Johns had not been able to accept the wilder theories. That Madden had defected. Or had been paid to surrender.

"He's at the lake cottage in Lyle," the Cambodian said.

St. Johns sat back, and reveled in the brilliance of the hiding place. Madden was right under the reporters' noses. He was twenty miles from where he'd grown up, from where he and St. Johns had played football together, drank beer, and dated the same girls. Catherine Madden owned the lake cottage but nobody knew about it. The Maddens had purposely never used the cottage during his presidency.

Two weeks short of his sixtieth birthday, St. Johns had lost little to the years. He remained solid and athletic looking, more like a college fullback than the end he had been. Flanking his dome shaped pate, which imparted power rather than age, his hair began in steel-colored streaks at the temples and receded into white wings. His eyes were steel colored as well. He was not the first person people noticed when they entered a room, but he was the one they generally remembered.

St. Johns said, "Is he all right?"

An expression of pain twisted the gardener's flat features; he wavered between loyalty and truth. "He looks old. I saw soldiers like him in Phnom Penh. They'd run from battle. They wouldn't look you in the eye. But Madden wouldn't run. He must be afraid war will start because of what he did. War won't start, will it?"

"I don't know," St. Johns said. It was the same question everyone was asking.

The man leaned forward earnestly. His own story would be proof of Madden's good intentions. "The Communists would have killed me. I was a gardener at the embassy. I was engaged to a girl from Lyle. He was a senator then. He got me out."

The Cambodian told St. Johns he had been caretaker of the lake cottage for years. No one in Lyle thought it odd he went there now. He brought the Maddens food and cooked for them. His grateful brother-in-law, the police chief, had closed the dirt road to the place, not that anyone used it anyway.

"That airplane looks so small down there." He looked out the window again, fascinated or afraid. "Those clouds are almost touching the river. Are they gas? They're moving fast."

St. Johns rang for tea. "Only steam," he soothed. "On cold days the air above the Hudson condenses." He prompted, "The message."

"He says come."

Through his relief and anxiety St. Johns found himself amused at the effrontery. Madden was summoning him as if he still remained in office. As chairman of Global American, St. Johns had dealt with four presidents, had dined at the White House and raised money for campaigns, had run informal errands when official channels of communication were blocked.

But the amusement faded. On the wall over the Cambodian's head, he glimpsed a photograph of himself at a banquet with Global American's biggest depositors, Saudi and American oil men who could withdraw billions if the chairman displeased them. Already, in the two weeks since the surrender, the dollar had plunged, and frightened clients were transferring assets to Switzerland.

"The President said to give you time to answer. He said I should answer your questions or leave a phone number."

"Did he say why he wants to see me?"

"No."

"Did he tell you anything else?"

The man wavered, looked down. "The President said he hoped you and Mrs. St. Johns were feeling better. He said you lost a son. I lost a son in Cambodia. I'm sorry."

"Thank you." St. Johns felt the pain start up inside. "Yes, I'll come. You can spend tonight at my apartment if you like. We have plenty of room."

"I told my wife I'd be back." The man looked outside again, and St. Johns knew he hated the city, the bigness. The Cambodian splayed his fingers and pressed his hands together in a well-wishing goodbye.

After he left, the burning pain in St. Johns's stomach grew worse. *I'm sorry about your son.* Two months ago his son, Weber, an amateur pilot, flying his Cessna to Nantucket, had lost his way in a fog bank and crashed into the sea. St. Johns's eyes picked out a faded spot on his desk, and he imagined the photograph that had once rested there. He saw Weber's curly black hair, round glasses, and zestful grin.

He had a vision of forty years ago. Madden, black hair tousled, on the big rock overlooking Pohl Reservoir. Madden in high school, ripping the top off a bottle of frothing beer. Talking about Catherine.

Then he saw Madden in a dark wool coat, right hand raised at his inauguration. The shame of Madden's surrender made St. Johns sick. What had happened that night?

The buzzer screamed on his desk and his secretary Willa's voice said, "John Gillespie's here for the four o'clock, Chief."

St. Johns pushed Madden from his mind as the door opened. Gillespie was St. Johns's protégé, slated someday for a bank vice presidency himself. He looked elegant in a charcoal Savile Row pin-striped suit. He wore a white shirt and narrow burgundy tie. He seated himself opposite the big desk in a familiar but respectful way.

"Lots of decisions today, Chief."

Neither of them admitted openly that since Weber's death St. Johns had been less energetic at the bank. Gillespie did much more of the work. He probably made most of the decisions, and these regular meetings gave St. Johns a last chance to change them. Currently the bank's assets exceeded four trillion dollars. Global American employed sixty thousand people in thirty-five cities around the world. St. Johns was king.

Although Gillespie affected a tough street manner, he was a graduate of Harvard and Wharton. "The Alvos people want another extension in Buenos Aires. They're making default noises again."

He glanced at another color photo on the wall. It showed St.

Johns and Madden in deck chairs on a boat. They both wore bathing suits in the picture.

The unspoken message was, everybody thinks they can get away with things now.

"How long an extension?" St. Johns asked.

"Six months. They also want two hundred fifty million more. For tanks and Exocet missiles."

St. Johns raised his eyebrows and leaned back in his chair. Gillespie counted on his fingers, making points. "They've always paid us back. If we say no, they default. If we turn down the extra money, they go to Chase next time. If we say yes to both, we ought to send someone to supervise the investment. Bingo, Chief. We're in the arms business."

"Do it. What else?"

"You were right about Sir Rupert. He's been stealing half a million at a time, investing in metals. Marty Lazarus says London Global American is short three million."

St. Johns felt the anger as a tightening in his neck. "Give Marty a bonus. Nobody else knows, I take it?"

"Want me to go to London?"

"I'll fire him myself. Rupert's been with us twenty-five years."

"Are you feeling all right?"

"I liked him, that's all. What's next?"

"Juicy opportunity. Two loan applications from Colorado railroads. Bad risks, but I think we should take a harder look. Colorado Western and Western Shipping Alliance. Both might fold, but whichever goes first, the other picks up rolling stock and business. We back the right one we can make money. Western Shipping's offering a place on the board."

"Okay. That it?"

The last problem was local. After a rash of robberies in Harlem branches of the bank, the architecture department wanted to seal the tellers behind walls and have business done through slots in the walls. "Teller and customer would see each other on TV," Gillespie said.

"The cost?"

Gillespie rolled his eyes.

"Do it anyway."

"The tellers hate the idea. They say they'll feel like they're in a cage. We have a turnover problem up there already."

"We also have two dead tellers. Do the remodeling, but try to make them happy. Plants, music. Find out what they want. Make it the best conditions in the city."

Gillespie was writing on a pad. Other than St. Johns's wife, Nicki, he was the only person he could trust with secrets.

"I heard from Madden," St. Johns said. "He wants me to come."

Gillespie whistled. He glanced at the door, making the connection between the Cambodian and the invitation. St. Johns told the story and Gillespie said, flatly, "Bad idea, Chief. It's dangerous."

"Why?"

"Oh, you know why. Just want me to say it, eh? Okay. We have seven hundred million from the Saudis. Nobody knows what really happened to Madden, and they're jumpy enough without you associating with him. The Houston guys are red, white, and blue. You have a chairman fight in a month and a half, and the Sir Rupert disclosure will make things bad enough. The world might blow up tomorrow, but it's business as usual for us."

He smiled wryly. "You taught me to be a rough tough banker, Chief, but I'm curious what you're going to do. I know you and Madden are close."

"I think I'll take tomorrow off," St. Johns said. "You take care of things."

"Bravo."

Jackhammer noise hit him when he reached the street. St. Johns walked home three miles each night. PRO AND ANTI NUKERS CLASH IN SAN FRANCISCO, screamed a *News* headline at a kiosk. SOVIET ADVISORS IN ETHIOPIA, roared the *Times*. CHARGE MISSILES INSTALLED IN NICARAGUA.

Up until now, the century had been marked by distant wars fueled by major powers. The idea was to avoid major conflicts by funding little ones. St. Johns had been reading about combat in these little places for years, but in the weeks since Madden's surrender the faraway wars had seemed to go out of control, to build.

He passed a Madison Avenue television store showing four rows of screens in the front window. An unusually quiet crowd of Christmas shoppers watched the new president, Rittenhouse, bang his fist on a podium. Rittenhouse's words carried on a blast of hot air from the packed interior of the store.

"To those who have charged we will no longer protect our allies, I say we must be tougher! Vigilant! I am asking Congress for more arms for . . ."

Traffic was blocked on Fifty-eighth Street by a river of chanting demonstrators holding pictures of Madden. "ARREST HIM FOR TREASON!" they cried.

On Fifth Avenue, near Trump Tower, more picketers marched outside the Aeroflot office with signs that read MADDEN'S YOUR MAN and WE'RE NOT AFRAID TO FIGHT. More churchgoers than usual were exiting St. Patrick's after five o'clock mass.

Shoppers seemed more subdued. They hurried through the streets, backs bent, like children expecting punishment. No one looked at the sky.

Passing Lord and Taylor, St. Johns joined a crowd outside the Christmas display windows. Little mechanical dummies moved in circles inside. Women carrying parasols rode a steam-engine locomotive. A man with a pencil mustache and tuxedo escorted a woman in a hoop dress from a carriage to an opera house. The dummies seemed fragile, breakable.

St. Johns heard the clanging bell of a Salvation Army volunteer. He folded a hundred dollar bill so the denomination was not visible. Usually he gave less. He dropped the bill in the can.

Just before reaching home, he stopped at his favorite fruit stand on Third Avenue. Beneath a plastic awning, bright oranges and lemons were arrayed in rows. St. Johns liked to bring fresh fruit home for dessert each evening. Looking over the grapefruit, he grew aware that someone had materialized beside him. It was the shop's owner. He'd never met the Korean but had frequently seen him haranguing a stock boy inside. The shopowner shyly held up a bag bulging with grapefruit.

"You buy every day. I give for Christmas, yes?"

St. Johns took the bag, surprised, and watched a grin widen across the man's face. "Sweet," the man said. He hurried back into the shop.

Strolling easier, smelling the citrus aroma escaping from the bag, St. Johns thought it impossible suddenly that any of the bustling human activity around him could end. The brooding expectation of the afternoon was gone. Only weeks later would he realize the significance of the seemingly innocuous gift of fruit.

He was pleased to hear light music, "The Blue Danube," coming from the penthouse. Nicki was putting gladiolas into a long-stemmed vase. She was cheery these days when she threw dinner parties, but most of the time he found her on the couch when he came home, curled up, staring out the french windows, a blank pad beside her.

Smiling, humming, she kissed him on the cheek, regarded the gift of fruit with a delighted laugh, and announced, "General Cader is coming." Cader was a retired military man who lived in the building and liked to tell war stories. "And Robert Gardner. He's back from Washington, I ran into him in the laundry room. Do you know he was one of the reporters at NORAD last week? Susan Henry's coming too."

It was clear tonight's discussion would be the Madden surrender. Susan Henry was a Washington sculptor who was gaining a following in New York. Her father had been appointed special prosecutor looking into the Madden case.

"Who knows?" Nicki said. "Susan and Robert?"

She paled and dropped her hands to her sides when he told her about the Madden invitation. "Don't go," she said. He brought her to the sofa; her eyes were wide with fright. His fingers touched the back of her neck, her black hair. Their knees touched. He'd met her at a fundraiser in New York, back from Korea. He'd fallen in love when he'd heard her husky voice. After thirty-five years of marriage she remained attractive to him, with her Rubenesque figure and jet black hair. She filled the apartment with flowers and music. Surprisingly, at age fifty-seven, she'd turned to writing successful children's books.

"He only wants to talk," soothed St. Johns, not knowing what

Madden wanted at all but certain the President had a reason for everything he did.

"Talk?" she shot back. He thought she might cry. "You know why he's hiding as well as I do. They'll kill him because of what he did. They'll never let him live."

"Nicki, you're getting carried away."

"You know it's true. Bill Madden will be shot dead within six months and you know it." She burst into tears. "Anyone with him, it will be the same."

She'd not removed Weber's picture from the piano. There were Pissarros on the walls and potted palms by the patio doors. There were *Travel* and *Forbes* and *Fortune* magazines on the cedar coffee table. *Wall Street Journals*. A round free-standing staircase led to the master bedroom and study.

She was weeping. "I'm so afraid. I'm afraid when I wake up, when I cross the street. I'm afraid when you're late from the bank."

"Baby, baby, it's okay."

"I couldn't stand to lose the two of you." Her cheeks were fiery. "Everything's going crazy. Everything's breaking up."

At length she wiped her eyes. "Look at me," she joked. "Some kind of psychotic. Laughing. Crying." From the kitchen, they heard Hilma, the cook, singing "New York, New York." Outside the window and a half-mile north, the red and green lights atop the Empire State Building switched on.

She said, "He came to Weber's funeral, he didn't have to do that." She kissed St. Johns on the mouth. "Of course you have to go." It was a graceful surrender to the inevitable, but she was not good at keeping fear off her face. "Promise me if he asks you to do something, you'll think about it. Will you do that?"

"Nobody will know I've talked to him. They don't even know where he is. He only wants to talk."

She smiled wryly and rose to finish setting the table. "He's never wanted to 'just talk' in his life. Put on a fresh shirt," she said. "And shave before the guests arrive."

Showering, he knew she was right. Someone would assassinate the President who'd surrendered. He would never be allowed to live. For the thousandth time since Madden's surrender St. Johns tried to figure out how he felt about it. He started to get a headache. Hot water stung him. He tried to keep Madden out of it. How would he have felt if a different president had surrendered?

In Belgrade a year ago he had witnessed a military parade. Goose-stepping soldiers. Soviet tanks. He saw the tanks in Gramercy Park, outside his building.

It wasn't right to surrender, no, not without a fight.

But St. Johns told himself a different president hadn't surrendered. Madden had. The headache grew worse.

At dinner St. Johns carved beef Wellington at the table and announced, "I know what's on everyone's mind, so rules of the table, no holding back. What do you think of the Madden situation?" Even as he said it, he knew it wasn't a "situation." It was life and death.

He looked over the guests leaning forward, ready to argue. Madden was all anyone talked about, and no one could get enough. At seventy-two General Cader was straightbacked with cropped steely hair. His wife, Georgia, porcine and brilliant, taught history at Columbia University. Susan Henry was the human centerpiece of the table. Her face was a stunning mix of delicate, high-cheeked bone structure and contrasts in color: jet black hair, red lips, alabaster skin. She wore a clinging evening dress of black velvet which showed her model's figure; the bodice plunged and thrust her small breasts outward. She wore thin gold triangular earrings and a Roman numeral watch.

"Madden," said Robert Gardner, sitting next to her, cutting his beef. He sounded disgusted. "The paper finished a survey today, a thousand people. Did Madden do the right thing? Eighty percent said *they didn't know.* He didn't have to give up so fast, they said. He could have waited another minute."

He had been drinking gin steadily since arriving. St. Johns respected the journalist, but the man was a stranger. He'd spoken to Gardner in the grocery, had seen him in the elevator with women or with traveling bags. Bachelor workaholic, he'd thought, and a liberal to boot. Nicki had disagreed. "He's been hurt," she'd said when they saw him alone in Gramercy Park one day.

"You don't know him. How can you say that?"

She'd nodded with mysterious feminine superiority. "I know."

Gardner speared a piece of meat with a fork. "Nobody wants to deal with it, everyone wants to talk, but nobody has opinions." General Cader smiled with a combative gleam. Gardner challenged him diagonally across the table. "If Rittenhouse had been in the White House that night, there'd be a hole in space instead of earth."

Cader sat across from Susan Henry and beside Nicki. He supplemented his retirement pension giving lectures on military history to veterans' groups. He always spoke slowly, as if in a public hall. At a dinner party this made him sound condescending.

"Robert, we weren't even being attacked. Let's separate the issues, shall we? We avoided war, but we did so because he ran away, yes, ran, and he knows it. That's why he's hiding." Cader leaned back and looked from guest to guest. "The best I can say about Madden is that I pity him. He was unequal to the job he convinced voters he could do." He smiled. "The *best*."

Incredulous, Gardner said, "He's destroyed himself to keep us alive."

"I've seen men in battle destroy themselves for others, and running into the woods wasn't the way they did it," Cader said.

Across the table Nicki sat straighter, stared hard at St. Johns. She was asking him not to go to Madden.

St. Johns addressed Gardner. "Humanitarian motives, eh?"

"That's right, that's exactly right. In a hundred years if we survive this insanity he'll be a saint. It's not the same in the nuclear age. Hit back and everybody dies."

"Dear, in a hundred years people might not remember the facts." Georgia Cader touched her lips with a napkin. She had a deliberate way of speaking, like a professor. "World War Two began because of appeasers. Neville Chamberlain handed Hitler Czechoslovakia to keep the peace and seven years later twenty million people were dead. You call Madden humanitarian for cowardice? That betrays the people who died for their country."

She'd cut her meat into small pieces and arranged them on the plate. "Journalists don't fare well behind the Iron Curtain. If the Russians had really been attacking, or if the surrender had gone through, you'd be dead or on your way to a prison camp. You think he made a phone call, that's all, so what is everyone so excited about?

But Madden shattered a fifty-year-old balance of power. He's endangered our nuclear equilibrium. Huge forces have been unleashed, and they swing in the balance." Her cheeks colored. "He's got to be smashed. He'll try for power again, like Nixon. The Russians have to be shown the end of Madden."

"This certainly is delicious, Nicki," Susan Henry interrupted. "Can I bribe you for the recipe?"

"Oh, I'll give you that."

St. Johns realized Susan had purposely changed the subject, sensing Nicki's distress. Gardner emptied his glass and reached for the bottle.

"This wine is spectacular," said General Cader. "What is it, French?"

"Chilean."

"Delicious."

The maid set down plates of fruit and cheese. The argument would break out again soon. St. Johns saw Gardner's furrowed forehead and Cader's tightened jaw. Cader concentrated on his plate. Nicki asked who'd seen what movies. St. Johns told the story about the Korean giving him the fruit. That lightened the mood a bit, and the conversation broke into smaller groups. Nobody thought the peace would last.

"You get pretty excited about things, don't you?" Susan Henry said to Gardner. When she smiled, one side of her mouth rose slightly. Her eyes were bright with amusement.

"That was nice, what you did for Nicki," he said. They were leaning close. Gardner was dressed quietly and well in a dark suit; the jacket wide at the shoulders. He had curly black hair. He said, peeling an apple with a knife, "I didn't hear what you thought about Madden, though, being our Washingtonian here."

"Oh no!" She was laughing. "I leave the politics to you and the general. Or my father."

Gardner chewed awhile. Another noncommittal vote. He was aware that she kept watching him. He could see the white of her forearm on the table and one hand, devoid of jewelry and oddly mannish, rough. He could smell her perfume.

"I saw your show at the Max Protetch Gallery," he said. "What was the, uh . . .?" He traced a fluttery tower in the air with his hands.

"Prometheus."

"No kidding. Prometheus! I should have known. Prometheus used to come to my house when I was a kid. It looked just like him."

She was laughing.

"He showed up on hamburger nights. He liked to stay up late and watch dubbed Italian movies. Hercules."

"Steve Reeves," she said. She had a dark freckle above the cleavage of her dress. He said, "Well, I went to the opening and you were surrounded by admirers. I'm surprised you didn't get an escort out of it. For tonight, I mean."

She bit into a piece of cheese. "Which should I have taken: the divorced doctor who kept talking about his ex-wife? The married stockbroker who wanted to whisk me off to Southampton? Or the painter who suggested I try heroin?"

She spoke matter-of-factly, without bitterness or malice.

"Which got the most excited about things?" said Robert Gardner.

General Cader exclaimed, "Absolutely not!" across the table, and the Caders and St. Johnses broke into laughter.

Gardner was conscious of Susan's legs disappearing under the table. "No strong opinions on politics or escorts," he said.

"Oh, I have my passions." He remained silent. "Babies," she said. "Having babies." She had never given this answer to anyone. She had simply decided to tell him.

"How many babies do you have?"

"So far? None."

Robert Gardner lost all expression. She said in the same bantering tone, "Should I have said Acapulco or the south of France?"

He touched her wrist, the sensation jolted her. Two of his fingers remained, warm. He said, "I like what you said." His voice had gone gentler. She saw with surprise, because there'd been no hint before, that he was hurt.

"Coffee, anyone?" St. Johns announced. "Robert, what *should* Madden have done, then?" His interest seemed more than casual.

Gardner removed his fingers from Susan's wrist, leaving two fading white marks. "He did the right thing, exactly the right thing."

The general pushed himself back from the table with a violent shove. Gardner said, "What was the point? Hitting back and killing everybody?" Cader started to say something, but Gardner held up a hand, talked over him. "The whole point of nuclear weapons is *not* to use them. *Not* fighting back was courageous. We have to change the way we think in the nuclear age, new definitions." On the table, the tendons on his hands were stretched. He was flushed. "Einstein said it."

"Oh, 'new'!" said Georgia Cader. She was growing annoyed with his thickheadedness and the length of the argument. It was clear this would be her final word on the subject. "You journalists and we historians use the word 'new' in opposite ways. To you 'new' means unique in all history, the furthermost point in the evolution of an idea." She drank coffee. "I use 'new' to call something old. I'm writing a book about Napoleon. I call him the nineteenth century's 'new' enfant terrible, which only means that era's version of an old idea. Courage doesn't change. It hasn't changed in a million years, since the first caveman stood up to a charging mastodon."

The clock was chiming ten. Frowning and drawn to the argument despite herself, Nicki said, "What about General MacArthur? He left the Philippines when the Japanese were coming. A man who gives up rather than letting his troops be slaughtered . . . knowing when to give up, nobody calls General MacArthur a coward."

Gardner nodded. He was on his sixth glass of wine. St. Johns was certain something was eating at him, and it wasn't the conversation. "That's what Madden did," Gardner said. "There was no way to win, only to limit casualties."

The Caders were gathering themselves at the table, ready to go. The general said, "I hope you won't take this the wrong way, Robert, but were you ever in the military?"

"No."

"Ah." Cader's face cleared. He stood up. "Delicious dinner, Mark, Nicki. Old soldiers never die, they just go to sleep early."

"What would have been the wrong way to take it?" Robert Gardner said.

"Excuse me?" The general had been turning. Gardner's gaze was placid and unwavering. He repeated the question. Cader said, "Well, civilians have different sensibilities."

"Frightened sensibilities?"

"Let's just say they have the luxury of ignoring certain realities about the world."

"My father was a pilot in Vietnam," Gardner said in the same calm tones. "Killed during the last week of the war, when everyone knew it was over. That was the reality, that the war had ended."

General Cader was the one who seemed offended. A dead soldier deserved better than a pacifist's argument. "That doesn't excuse you," he said.

Exiting the elevator in the main lobby twenty minutes later, Susan Henry ran into Robert Gardner. He'd excused himself after the Caders left. She'd chatted with Nicki, surprised he had not waited for her or arranged to meet her later.

Gardner was dressed in a sheepskin coat and carried two bouquets wrapped in white paper. He'd gone back to his apartment for them. The doorman swung open the heavy glass-and-wrought-iron door. Flurries blew outside, and a dog passing and pulling on a leash wore ear muffs.

"Twins?" asked Susan Henry. He realized she would always look amused, no matter what her private emotions.

"Birthday party." It was eleven at night, and he didn't look festive but drawn. She wore a full-length black fur coat. The wind lashed at them, and she pulled the collar tight.

She said, "You're going to call me?" It was a statement, and the closest she would publicly come to vulnerability.

He recited her Washington number. "Max Protetch gave it to me at the gallery," he said.

She watched him walk off toward Third Avenue with the bouquets. It was very cold and he seemed alone. From the back he had a slightly bow-legged walk, like an athlete's. He swayed a bit. The wind blew against him. As he rounded the corner, the streetlight hit the bouquet, and the wind ripped off petals and blew them back. He didn't notice.

She didn't think he was going to another party, yet she believed what he'd told her. She liked that much contradiction; it made him a little mysterious. She was glad that she'd told him about the babies. She'd had enough of the other type of men. She thought his curly hair would feel rough under her fingers. She thought she would like kissing him very much. She wondered how long it would take them to become lovers.

Riding back to the Plaza Hotel, in the back of a cab, she turned her thoughts elsewhere. She wondered what Robert Gardner would do when he found out what her father was planning for Madden.

At three a.m., lying beside Nicki and unable to sleep again, Mark St. Johns missed Weber terribly. Fathers should never outlive sons, he thought. Nicki breathed lightly beside him. Their fingers touched.

Maybe tonight would be the last night. Lately, staring through the slit in the curtains at the night outside, a vision had started coming to him. Maybe tonight the fireball would come. He had been told for years that one day it would come and maybe it would come tonight. He'd read that if you tried to cover your eyes with your hands during a blast, you could see through your skin to your bones, like an X-ray.

Before Weber's death, St. Johns had never been prone to morbid thoughts.

At five he slipped from the bed, made coffee, and left enough brewing so Nicki would have her customary two cups. He phoned for the Continental. The doorman had it outside when he reached the street. His heart was beating crazily in his chest. Gramercy Park was empty and white. Steam billowed from a manhole cover. A garbage truck went by.

In the end, millions of people would be affected by what St. Johns was about to do. Now he thought only that he had lied to Nicki. A white lie, so as not to worry her. Madden was a doer, not a talker. Madden had a reason for everything he did, and if he had summoned St. Johns it was for a purpose. The only other possibility was that the President had suffered a nervous breakdown and if that was the case St. Johns would be forced to watch another demise.

When he turned the ignition key, the sudden terror filled him. He saw the buildings crumble and the flames reach high. He thought, Dear God, don't let it happen. He felt his prayer diffuse into tiny particles and disappear with his frosting breath.

St. Johns turned the car north and pushed down on the accelerator. The pilgrimage had begun that would change his life.

6

St. Johns pulled the Lincoln off Route 8 in Winsted, Connecticut, and steered into the parking lot of the Flood Cafe. He was
just reaching the Berkshire Hills. At eight a.m. ice crusted the small
New England town, and the sky was light blue like the cold had
sucked deeper color from it.

He was twenty miles from Lyle and Madden, but the ride and
lack of sleep had fatigued him. Driving north at dawn, he had passed
a line of parked-for-the-night moving vans, part of the exodus from
nuclear target New York. The news on the radio had continued to
be bad. "Bombs exploded last night at American embassies in Paris
and Cairo." A talk show guest on another station had said, "With
Madden's surrender, terrorists have declared open season on Americans. We look weak."

He shut the engine, but the radio kept playing. He was horrified
to realize the sort of advertisement he was hearing, even here in
Winsted.

"Listen, Joe," a friendly-sounding man was saying. "There are
more ways to protect your loved ones than with fire and home insurance. No one wants to think about bomb shelters, but can you
afford not to? Why don't we walk over to New Basement at 34 Main
Street in Lyle and . . ."

St. Johns shut it off. Outside, the cold made his teeth ache and his eyes water. Maybe if he would start taking some kind of pill he wouldn't get up at three o'clock in the morning all the time.

But the cafe bustle, the bacon smells, clatter of dishes, and rough laughter of breakfasting workmen dispelled his gloom. The Flood was the only coffee house between the Interstate and Lyle. "Mark St. Johns!" boomed a woman's voice. "What a nice surprise!" She was white haired and moon faced, and she vastly filled the space behind the cash register. In an instant she had him at a table near a series of forty-year-old eight-by-ten black-and-white aerial photographs on a wall.

"Sit by your picture," she ordered. She had to be at least eighty, but her mind was unimpaired, her rosy face cheery. She signaled a waitress to work the register and seated herself across from him. In seconds coffee steamed before him.

"Here you are piling sandbags," she said, jabbing at a tiny figure on a levee by a foaming river. In 1946 the Mad River had overflowed, and Winsted had offered cash to anyone who would help build the levee. In the photo St. Johns wore a stocking cap and lifted a sandbag, bent with effort. A line of booted men passed more bags toward him.

"You boys saved this place," she said. "I'd just bought it."

"I'd have gone anywhere for fifty cents an hour those days."

"You were the hardest working kid I ever met. And you were on the road crew up in Lyle too, after school."

"That's right." Her pleasure in showing off her memory made him happy.

"And your daddy drove the plow up there."

"In the winter," he said. The coffee warmed him. "Rest of the time was shooting deer or casting for pickerel." St. Johns shrugged. "A good man, but he had no use for money."

"Ann Marie, get him another cup! Eat those eggs, I'll be back!"

Forty-two years later, St. Johns still felt the cold of that spring, smelled the rushing water with its mill effluence, experienced the ache in his shoulders as he piled bags, ecstatic to have work that day. The Flood Cafe filled him with peaceful nostalgia. A trip to Lyle could condense forty years of living into a flash of yearning.

On school nights he'd been a handyman in a bowling alley. With his father out hunting or fishing, St. Johns had paid most of the bills. Summers he'd done yard work and carpentry for wealthy Bostonians vacationing in the Berkshires. One employer was a banker who wanted an extension built on his turn-of-the-century Victorian mansion. The music room had contained two grand pianos. The dignity of the man's life style had triggered something powerful in the boy hammering nails in the backyard. When St. Johns had screwed up enough courage to ask the banker for a recommendation to Columbia University not only had the man complied, he had arranged St. Johns's first job at Global American, in the bonds department. That had been the first step in the steady climb.

Stopping at the cafe, St. Johns was like a deep-sea diver pausing as he moved between one world and another.

But now he glanced right and the coffee went sour in his stomach. He'd made a mistake stopping here. He should have known reporters would be searching for Madden and a familiar one sat twenty feet away. A black-haired man from the *Times* smoked a cigarette at a corner table by the window and gazed disinterestedly at the parking lot outside. That didn't mean he hadn't seen St. Johns. The man had interviewed him when the bank refused New York City a loan for new subway cars. He'd asked about the friendship with Madden, because the administration had wanted New York to get the cars. St. Johns had explained there were times when business interests won out over friendship.

St. Johns left a big tip and walked out of the restaurant. As he put the key in the Lincoln, he felt the man's eyes on him. He glanced at the cafe window. No one was there, and the front door was opening.

A yellow Honda followed St. Johns out of the lot.

St. Johns hated the cloak-and-dagger aspect of dealing with politicians. There were always passwords and secret meetings and journalists sniffing around. Why an intelligent man would choose as a profession the currying of approval from strangers was beyond him.

Going back toward New York was impossible. If the reporter had seen St. Johns arrive at the cafe, a retreat back the way he had come would confirm the man's suspicions. St. Johns headed north, toward Lyle, the yellow Honda behind.

Route 8 curved up into the wooded Connecticut hills. He passed white birch patches and roadside stands locked for the winter. He drove through ice-crusted valleys, purple-striped fields. He drove beneath a series of hazy rounded peaks. The Honda stayed behind. St. Johns began stopping at real-estate offices to inquire about summer homes. He had no interest in summer homes, but the reporter would check after him. St. Johns even let one agent drive him to an A-frame house near a ski area. As the agent praised the resort, St. Johns did not mention that the bank's money had built it. The yellow Honda did not follow the agent's car, but when they got back to the office St. Johns saw it in a 7-Eleven lot across the road.

The strategy was backfiring: St. Johns was bringing the *Times* man closer to Madden. He entered Massachusetts and the road widened to climb through blasted-out sections of the Berkshires. Thick blue-white ice waterfalls were frozen solid over gray granite cliffs. Otis, Massachusetts, was a few clapboard homes by a rural state intersection. He bought gas in East Lee. The damn Honda never gave up.

Seething with frustration, St. Johns got on the Massachusetts Turnpike at Lee and headed away from Madden, east toward Boston and New Hampshire. It was past noon. Finally he looked in the rearview mirror and the reporter was gone. He was thirty miles from Lee. Once, as President Carter's envoy in Brussels, St. Johns had changed cars to elude a French magazine reporter. Running into the Honda by accident back in Lyle would be a disaster. He left the Lincoln in a service station for a tune-up it needed anyway. In a rented Ford Tempo he headed back the way he had come.

Ten miles out of Lyle he caught sight of the Honda idling in a roadside overlook. Instead of facing the scenery, the Honda pointed at the road. The *Times* man had staked out the highway on the off chance that St. Johns would come back. Heart pounding, St. Johns drove past the Honda.

He passed the Episcopal Church where Madden's uncle had preached every Sunday. He passed the state park where he'd kissed his first girl.

In the Lyle town square St. Johns idled the Tempo across from a bronze statue of a Revolutionary War soldier. He knew the inscription by heart: "To Lyle's Beloved Sons Who Died for Their Country in the Great War of Independence. To Joseph Madden, Colonel of the Western Massachusetts Minutemen."

The Minutemen had been local militia who repelled a British attack on Lyle in 1773. Joseph Madden had been the great-great-granduncle of the President.

As St. Johns passed the high school, he saw a granite bust of Joseph Madden over the double doors. The football team St. Johns and Madden had led to the state championship had been called the Minutemen.

Then he was out of town and driving along a two-lane blacktop and an iced-over dirt road. He grew fearful of what he might find ahead; the Madden questions were back now that the reporter was gone. The Tempo skidded. Birches, maples, and oaks crowded out the sun. After dealing with four presidents, St. Johns had come to expect the almost immediate aging process that overtook the retiree. Minor physical ailments grew more pronounced when presidents left office. There was no truth to the myth that retirement improved their dispositions. Stepping down exacted an enormous physical toll. They had been bred from birth not only to grasp for power but to surrender it when their time was up. This was an unnatural state of affairs, the voluntary giving up of influence. Successful men in other professions, like banking, were not required to do it. St. Johns had seen president after president at their inaugurations, flushed with victory, glowing with triumph. And he had seen them four or eight years later, defeated, broken, or ignored. Now he knew all he had witnessed was nothing compared to what lay a few miles up this road. No disgrace exceeded Madden's. No fall had been swifter or more pronounced.

Startled, he braked hard coming around a bend. The Tempo slid sideways and stopped four feet from a yellow bulldozer. His hands clutched the steering wheel at the near-miss, he was astonished to find anyone this close to the President. But when the three forestry workers approached the Tempo St. Johns saw the walkie-talkie earplugs and recognized Madden's Secret Service detail.

"Mr. St. Johns, sorry," said a red-haired agent in a workman's green parka. St. Johns had met the man before. His name was Huff.

"We're supposed to stop anyone coming through." He grinned. "Nobody does, though. The police chief is pretty thorough. I thought you drove a Lincoln."

"It broke down. I rented this."

The dozer backed out of the way. Two hundred yards later the track spilled him out of the forest. The agent must have radioed ahead, because Catherine Madden waited outside the cabin. It was a low timber structure built in Norway and shipped here piece by piece. Catherine's father had been a well-to-do Lee surgeon who bought the cabin because he liked to fish and because the only other building on the lake, on the far side and now closed, was a privately funded clinic for cancer.

Catherine had become a patient there when she was fourteen, and a lump had been found in one of her ovaries. Six years later she had been pronounced cured.

He was not close enough to see her features, but he recognized her lustrous gray hair. At fifty-nine she was still a famous beauty.

The years had molded the oval of her face into bolder angles which imparted stateliness and elegance. The seagreen eyes were usually bright and joyful. She liked small turquoise jewelry and tight clothing that showed her slim figure advantageously. In the woods her taste ran to jeans and largish lumberjack jackets.

When he had first seen her they were both sixteen. He had wanted to ask her out, but had been intimidated by the illness. All the boys except Madden had been scared off by the sickness. She'd been blond then, the rich hair and thin brows golden. The story of the Maddens' courtship had been published during the campaign and had probably secured Madden thousands of votes. It was included in a book called *Three Crossroads*, an account of the great instinctual leaps of Madden's life: his marriage over parental objections to a dying girl, his winning of the Congressional Medal of Honor in Korea, and his initial startling move into politics. Each crossroad had brought fame and success. With the fourth, Madden had pitched himself into disaster.

Madden had never been garrulous about his enthusiasms, but with Catherine it was different. She rode horses. She was a great cook, loved to take drives, to listen to all kinds of music. All her senses seemed to be magnified. And when in the locker room one day the obnoxious front lineman had cupped his crotch and leered, "What kind of senses we talking about?" Madden had broken the kid's front tooth against the locker.

In the White House she had banished the formal French look favored by the previous first lady and created a happy eclectic mood. Bright pillows. Flowers everywhere. Catherine Madden had worked with the blind, the crippled, the aged, and infirm. She'd headed funding drives. She'd gone on the road speaking in favor of Madden's nuclear missile building programs. She'd sponsored citizens' committees to improve housing and public transportation for the elderly. She'd visited orphanages overseas. Testified in Congress on the status of refugee children in Asia. Even critics of the Madden administration had admired her efforts, knowledge, and preparation for every fight.

To one television interviewer who had called her "the President's conscience," she had retorted, "He doesn't need my conscience. He has his own."

As she and St. Johns approached each other across the snow, he saw a smile of welcome but a stretched quality beneath it, a tautness. He did not think she could ever look old, but this was as close as she would come. Lines pulled at her mouth. The cords on her neck stretched with the effort of simple greeting.

"Oh, Mark, good to see you, good." Was he all right? She and Bill were "resting at the cottage. You forget how peaceful the world can be. This quiet is heaven. How's Nicki?"

"Not working. Weber."

· "Do they know anything more about why the plane failed?"

"No," said St. Johns unhappily. "He may have misjudged the landing in the fog."

"Well, you come in, it's freezing out here. Bill spends hours outside. I'm just a cold-blooded reptile. I should hibernate in the winter, like a snake."

The warmth hit him when she opened the cabin door. He felt a wave of fatigue. The dark timbered living room was flooded with light from overhead bubble windows cut into the roof. She'd chosen furniture of dark leather. Snowshoes hung over the fireplace and flames added gold to her face. The sugary, rich cocoa invigorated him.

She was fine, she told him for the second time. Bill was tired but well. Josh had called this morning to say hello. St. Johns knew father and son had not gotten along for years. "This is the kind of thing that brings families together," she said. He doubted it.

"Bill's not here," she added, seeing him glance around. They sat by the fireplace, St. Johns had removed his coat. "He's walking, probably by the lake again."

"Is he really all right?"

"You mean ill? Broken down?" She went quiet, firm. She might have been addressing a courtroom. "We were asleep. His aide Steve Bauer came into the room. 'The Russians are attacking,' he said.

"Mark, you never really expect to hear those words. I read Churchill in college. He said wars just start. Things go along and then one day wars just begin, not particularly for any reason. Everything in the room remained ordinary. The fire was glowing. I had the most bizarre thought: 'Let's eat prime ribs tomorrow night.' Of course I'm describing a fraction of a second. Bill had his robe on. He kissed me and said, 'Call Josh.' Steve Bauer kept looking at him like a boy watches a father, like Bill might stop it. Broken down? Bah! We had five minutes maximum at that point. We'd been told Russian missiles take nine minutes from sub launch, so maybe we had five. I didn't phone Josh. He'd be asleep when it hit. For him it might be peaceful."

Wood snapped in the fireplace, showers of sparks erupted. "Then I remember we were in the hallway. The night staff was hurrying downstairs. No protocol for fleeing to a shelter. A butler ran out, out of the building. What was going on underground all over the country, where the soldiers are?

"After a while Steve Bauer appeared in the shelter. He had a funny grin on his face. 'False alarm,' he said. He made a joke. 'We can play the piano again.' He threw up.

"I hadn't any feeling in my legs. It was hard to stand up. Dave Huff helped me upstairs. I was crying when Bill came back. He didn't have any color, but his voice was strong. Do you think people make love more after what happened? I do. I think people are happy they're alive. Around dawn I woke and the bed was cold beside me. I saw his back at the window. It was snowing outside. He must have felt me looking, because he turned. 'I gave up to them,' he said. He said it matter-of-factly, but I felt the misery in him. 'I picked up the phone and told Menkes we wouldn't fight.' "

"What else could he have done?" St. Johns said, uneasy with his own words.

"Drink that cocoa, it's getting cold."

"He really couldn't have done anything else," St. Johns said.

St. Johns picked his way through the forest, toward the lake. At dusk the sky was purpling and the Berkshire wind sounded like a river. The cold lodged inside his lower lip and his knees. Where matted dead leaves didn't cover the frozen earth, deer and rabbit tracks were preserved and frosted over. Dark lichens covered fallen logs and the ubiquitous sharp-edged and flat-faced New England rocks.

Through a gap in the birches he made out the gray snow-dusted oval of the frozen lake. Then he glimpsed Madden. It was a shock. The trees had already obstructed his view, but the figure had looked old, too old to be possible. Even at a distance the apparition had been stooped. Madden's normal posture was almost military. The figure's arms hung lifelessly. The Madden St. Johns knew was filled with energy. St. Johns recoiled at the vision of dejection. Maybe it wasn't Madden. Maybe somebody else was here.

Then he rounded an oak and Madden was there grinning, striding forward in a sheepskin coat, hand outstretched. "Aha!" It was Madden's most familiar, most imitated phrase. "We were worried about you. Thought you'd be here earlier." The handshake was strong. The dejected figure was gone like it had never existed. The familiar features glowed, rosy and confident. St. Johns looked over the flinty hard jaw, corded at the cheek, the pale blue eyes and bushy eyebrows. Cartoonists still loved the eyebrows. Madden's gray hair, whipped by the wind, fell over his high forehead or stood up in back. He had the tousled look of a farm boy, the gaze of a general, the voice of a radio host.

St. Johns explained why he was late, and Madden laughed heartily at the part about switching cars. "We ought to have a fleet of old

Chevies at the White House for that." He lifted his right hand high, a quarterback holding an imaginary ball. "Kill 'em, crunch 'em, use that might!"

St. Johns finished: "Minutemen, Minutemen, fight, fight, fight!"

"Nicki started to write again yet?" Madden said.

"She's getting a little better, I think."

Madden looked at him piercingly. "Global American going to fund those Colorado railroads?"

As always, St. Johns was astounded at the reach of Madden's information, especially here.

"Good," Madden said. "Colorado needs that line. We would have had to bail 'em out if you didn't." Madden stood six inches taller than St. Johns. "Ah, to hell with politics. Up here it's too beautiful to think about that. Know what I was thinking before you came? About the reservoir."

He was talking about how he had met Catherine. Back in the 1940s the big summer recreation spot near Lyle had been the Pohl Reservoir. The kids parked pickups and Packards along the high dam wall, spread blankets on the steeply sloping grass banks, and ate picnics or swam.

That day, six football players from Minuteman High had been sunning themselves when St. Johns had felt a nudge in his ribs. "Look at that," Madden had whispered. The most beautiful blonde either of them had ever seen was lying on a blanket with her parents forty feet away. Gutsy Madden had walked right up to them. When the girl sat up, something was odd. She seemed to lean sideways as if in pain. Smiling, she stood to go into the water with Madden, and St. Johns realized, from the limp way she moved her arms when Madden took the elbow, that she was sick. Both sets of parents would oppose the marriage.

St. Johns remembered Madden's mother at the dinner table. "Do you want to take care of her while she gets worse?" she had said. She'd been a lean, ambitious woman with Madden's hair. "Sure she looks pretty now, but her hair will fall out, she'll lose her figure. You want to walk her across streets, wheel her around in a chair at parties? She's a nice girl, but what if you have children and they get it too?"

Now St. Johns said, "She looked good on that blanket."

Madden took St. Johns's arm and they walked along the edge of the lake. Madden entertained him with a vivid and amusing anecdote about a congressman who had been caught sleeping with a senator's wife. He told a funny story about the French prime minister's allergy to the White House Labrador retriever. Even as a boy, Madden had possessed the ability to make people feel better, to make them feel strong.

St. Johns began to think Madden had summoned him for no other reason than to talk. The former President was lonely and needed a friend, that was all. But a ticking inside told him the coming request would be big. Madden was spending extra time setting the mood.

Light was fading, the cold seemed sharper. Madden was telling a story now about a fight between the White House and the Senate to push through an energy bill. One senator had voted for the bill because he'd lost a bet on the Super Bowl.

Half-listening to Madden's voice, St. Johns ran through more of Madden's history. Back from Korea, Madden had finished law school. He'd been snapped up by a wealthy Pittsfield firm. At age thirty-two he'd become a partner. That year the governor announced an investigation into the finances of highway companies around Massachusetts. A Republican was needed for the investigatory committee, a man from the western part of the state. The governor asked Madden. But unlike the other committee members, who met merely to approve reports, Madden took a personal hand in the inquiry.

He uncovered a payoff scheme between the Republican party chairman and one Boston company. The governor tried to convince him to drop the matter. The chairman would resign quietly and the state would switch business to another company. That way the public interest would be served, but the party would remain undamaged.

Madden had gone public with the charges. The chairman and the highway company president had been jailed. Madden had been publicly hailed as a comer and privately notified his political career was over. Two weeks later, a delegation of Democrats had proposed to Madden that he switch parties and run for Congress.

St. Johns thought, I'm trying to figure out what he's going to do but part of him has always been hidden.

He heard Madden say, "I'm wondering if you'll talk to some people for me."

"Who?"

Madden laughed. "The British. The French." He paused. "Russians."

St. Johns's heart pounded. "I need to know more."

Madden nodded. He'd expected the question. More earnestly he said he'd experienced a moment of clarity before the surrender. He wanted to share it with other leaders. "They have to know what it was like, those last two minutes. This time we saved ourselves, but what about next time? You travel all the time. You can contact them." He squeezed his fists. "I *have* to tell them."

Immediately St. Johns suspected Madden knew of his impending London trip. Madden said, "I'll go to them. I'll meet them in secret. I'll write a letter, you can take it with you. I'll talk to their representatives. I'll talk on the phone. That's the way we can do it with the Russians."

St. Johns repeated, "The British. The Russians. Everyone who has nuclear weapons." Sarcastically, he added, "Is that all?"

"Yes, all of them, the people who count. I want to tell them what happened to me. Ah ha, I'm having a little trouble getting them to return my calls."

"And what will come of all this?"

Madden said, "When they know, maybe we can change things."

"How?"

Madden sighed. "I don't know."

St. Johns grew angry. "You're asking me to risk my reputation and the bank's for a whim, is that it?"

Madden's narrow face assumed a smile of genuine amusement.

"I'm offering an opportunity to participate in a chance for peace. You can't pull out a calculator now and figure odds before you make a move. It's late in the day for that, my friend. This is private conviction. I still wield a little power as the old President. I know Comrade Menkes will try to twist my offer, make me a symbol of weakness and take advantage. 'World! Look at disgraced Madden crawling to Moscow to beg for peace!' Or he'll sponsor a conference, offer to make me a star performer. I won't do it if that's the case. But not to try is to let a potential opportunity go by. That's the bottom line. Tell me, Mark, how many opportunities do we have left?"

It didn't sound like the whole reason. "That's easy for you to say," St. Johns said. "You have nothing to lose."

"Not exactly nothing. In a week I'll be paraded back to Washington like a monkey in a cage, and the circus will begin. 'Ladies and gentlemen! In ring number one, the coward of the worst kind! Tell us why you did it! Tell us that you're sorry! Beg for mercy so the world sees how tough we are!' It's necessary, Mark, truly it is. But what do you think will happen to me if the inquisitors find out I'm talking to the Russians?"

"I didn't see that."

"No matter. Two weeks ago, if the former President had announced he was trying to contact Menkes I would have yelled bloody murder. You're ruining foreign policy! And I'll tell you more. I liked being President. You think I wanted to give it up? When you get up there on stage on convention night and you've been nominated . . . when the lights are on you and the whole room, the whole world, it seems, is screaming your name, when that wave after wave of adoration washes over you, well, that is a pleasure! And then your every personal whim is satisfied for years. Great leaders meet with you. You feel the might of the nation in your veins." Madden's eyes were bright. He leaned forward. He whispered, "You love it."

He straightened. "I played the game for thirty years to win the prize. I made deals like any politician. I maneuvered and fought and won. And who knows? Maybe I'm fooling myself. Maybe I need to play one last game for that great big presidential ego."

"You're arguing against yourself."

"No, I'm admitting all the possibilities you already know exist. You've always had a good sense of things, and you'll see the truth, whatever it is. You work from logic and I from instinct. What does your logic tell you, Mark?"

"It tells me perhaps this is an inopportune time for us. Perhaps after the hearings, when the pressure dies down a little, wouldn't that make more sense?"

Madden shook his head. "What was that line from Eliot? 'This is the way the world ends, not with a bang but a whimper'? We all tread down our little personal lanes and one day we disappear? We may not have time to wait for an 'opportune moment.' I'm responsible for what is about to happen. I . . . I caused it. I can't just sit and do nothing. At least I've got to try to tell them what it was like. Two minutes to go. And the missiles coming. How did we get to that point, Mark?"

The initials carved in an old oak read "C&B." St. Johns traced his gloved finger in the overgrown bark. So that was what Madden wanted: a crusade. "You said you'd be dragged back to Washington in a week. How do you know? I've heard nothing in the news."

"I asked Rittenhouse for three weeks on my own. To collect myself, I guess. I was in shock. I've always trusted my feelings, allowed my reason to catch up. I needed time alone."

"Has the outcome of the hearings been arranged too?"

Madden smiled ruefully. "No, but ha, ha! They can't impeach me! I left first." He shivered. "Let's go back to the house." He took St. Johns's arm again. Light snow began to fall. The sun was an orange glow above the hills and below the oncoming darkness. The lake was out of sight. On the snow dusted path Madden fell behind St. Johns.

"Mark, you put yourself in an uncomfortable position even coming here, and I appreciate it. Don't hesitate to say no. Or if you take it on and you don't like it, stop. I know I'm asking you to compromise yourself. It's dangerous. I don't want to damage the friendship."

St. Johns remembered the dejected apparition by the lake. He had to go to London anyway within a week, and he could easily get Madden's request to Whitehall with a phone call. But Madden wouldn't be satisfied with just the British. He wanted to talk to the French.

He wanted to talk to the Russians.

You have a chairman fight coming up, John Gillespie had said.

And Nicki. *Anyone associated with him will be killed.* What else had she said, last night, before bed? *No one can do anything about the situation. We're powerless, all we can do is sit and wait.*

That was all she did all day, sit and wait for Weber.

Oh, Weber, he thought, overcome by fatherly longing.

His thoughts were jumping from one topic to another. He told himself nothing in the world was innocent and any talks, no matter how casual, would have to be paid for, but how?

Overhead, three jet fighters roared east, leaving thin trails. Madden's rich voice mingled with their noise and the crunching of footsteps. "They're out of Hamstead. Different targets every day."

St. Johns said doggedly, "What does my position at the bank have to do with this, and why ask me instead of one of your Washington people?"

"You're a trusted friend and diplomat. It's no different from before. Besides, the Washington people are watched by reporters. And they have to stay for the hearings."

St. Johns realized he'd lost feeling in his face. He touched it; it felt crusty. "But by involving ourselves with the Soviets, aren't we jeopardizing Rittenhouse's plans? I heard your speech. Support him, you said. 'Diplomat' is an official word." St. Johns regretted he had to wound a friend. "You're not President now, face it."

Evergreens swayed from side to side in the wind. Madden drew himself up, the thick eyebrows rose. He pursed his lips as if amused. The regal posture seemed to say, *"I can say I'm not President, but to you I will always be President."*

The smell of smoke announced the cabin's proximity. St. Johns was touched by Madden's courage and loved his old friend at that moment. He said, "What did Rittenhouse say when you told him what happened that night?"

"Morgan has his own agenda," Madden said simply. "He's trying to get us back on course."

The feeling of danger was huge. St. Johns said, "I have to ask one last question."

"I know."

"Why did you give up to them?"

Madden looked straight into his face. "I saw the end of the world," he said.

The confident veil slid from Madden's eyes. Fear and torment so powerful washed out of him that St. Johns felt physically ill. The potential, the unspoken, the partially true responses lay between them in the winter silence. Because I didn't want to die. Because I could not destroy the earth. Because I believe in peace. Because it was the middle of the night and I was frightened. Because I didn't think. Because it was arranged.

Suddenly St. Johns was terrified Madden was going to ask, "Do you think I was a coward?" But the former President's face had returned to normal. In the moment of truth St. Johns saw Madden suffered the same questions.

With the look Madden had absolved himself of complicity with the Russians. Madden had accepted doubt as part of existence. Help me search for answers, he was saying.

There was no embellishment. It was a moment of naked honesty. I need help, St. Johns thought. Weber died and Nicki sits all day doing nothing.

He was startled by the realization that one reason he had come here was that Madden had always been able to make him feel better. Maybe this personal mission was what he'd been asking for.

Lately, St. Johns had begun envisioning nuclear catastrophe as millions of parents lying awake at night seeing dead offspring. It was crazy, because parents wouldn't survive either, but that was the way he saw it. All the personal and professional dangers of becoming Madden's envoy were very clear. They were two old men flailing about in international affairs. No bank backed St. Johns in this, and no country stood behind Madden.

Nevertheless, a surge of powerful benevolence and affection rose up in him. And defiance of the cautious business interests of the bank. The bank would be destroyed if the bombs fell anyway. He'd run other errands for other presidents. He'd always managed to keep them secret. Why should this one be any different?

He saw that from the beginning he had intended to help Madden.

"I'll go," St. Johns said.

Catherine Madden swung around on the couch as they entered. She said, "It's bad, Bill. You'd better watch this."

On television, a neat elderly man in a tweed jacket addressed newsmen in a law office. The United States Capitol was framed in the background window. St. Johns recognized James Henry, Susan's father and special prosecutor in the Madden case.

"Madden has been located in Massachusetts. We should contact him within the hour. Our inquiry will be vigorous, and any wrong-doing will be punished to the full extent of the law."

By the roaring hearth, a table was set for three, brightened by daisies. There was an open bottle of Madeira.

A reporter wearing glasses said, "Are you seriously saying you would push for the execution of a former President?"

James Henry adjusted his bow tie. "He will be treated like any other citizen, like you or me."

Catherine Madden said, "I thought Morgan gave you *three* weeks."

Madden frowned. "Well, that's just a little extra trouble. I guess he could only hold out for two." He seemed mildly contemptuous. "Pressure," he said.

Madden laid a hand on Catherine's shoulder. Their fingers twined. He told her, "What can they do, Cats? Send me to jail for bad judgment? It's theater. They'd have to trump up evidence for any chargeable offense, and I hardly think anyone is about to do that." He grew thoughtful. "But James Henry, that's odd. I would have thought the attorney general could handle it. Special prosecutor, well, I guess they need to distance themselves from me. Mark, you okay?"

"Don't worry about me."

"Good. Better take a rain check on that dinner. You don't want to be here when Torquemada's men arrive."

As St. Johns drove away, he watched Madden and Catherine in the rearview mirror. They stood in the lighted doorway, waving. They seemed small, the darkness around them immense.

He reached the bulldozer. Huff was still there, drinking from a steaming Thermos. The agent bent to the window. "They'll crucify him, won't they, Mr. St. Johns?"

St. Johns bumped off the dirt road and turned onto Route 8. A quarter-mile ahead, blazing lights in the sky shot over a rise, became the shadow forms of two helicopters rushing toward Madden. A safari of speeding vehicles, police cars and TV news vans, came next. James Henry was overdoing it.

St. Johns pressed down on the accelerator, and the broken center line in the road moved faster, became solid.

On the radio, James Henry's measured voice was saying, "Anyone involved with Madden will be called to account."

Nicki was waiting up at home. There were no secrets in their marriage. Their lovemaking was fierce and lasting. When St. Johns awoke in the morning he was astounded to realize he felt rested for the first time in months.

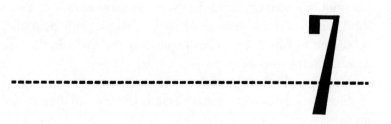

7

Stephanie Madden pulled the Volvo to the curb, shut the engine and began to cry. She draped her arms over the steering wheel. At least nobody would see.

She'd set out for the Safeway to buy cake mix and chocolate lettering for Danny. But she was thinking about last night.

Stephanie remembered lying on the bed, surrounded by recipe books. For coconut cakes, cherry cakes, lemon cakes, fudge cakes. Josh had laughed at her. "He can only eat one, he'll love it. Don't worry."

She'd burst out, "It could be his last birthday."

The day was bright. She'd parked on an oak lined Evanston street. Across from a row of Victorian houses and a Northwestern University dorm, students passed, changing classes, bundled against the cold. She heard them joking with each other. Heard rock music from the dorm.

This morning Danny had risen to leave the breakfast table and Josh had said, "Pal, say 'May I be excused, please?'" She'd said, "When will he use it?" after Danny had gone.

She started at a rapping on the window. A boy in a blue stocking cap looked in. "You all right, ma'am?"

She started the car. Her headache was back. At the DrugFair, buying papier-mâché streamers, she thought she might burst into tears again. Danny was at a friend's. Josh would pick him up later. She decided not to go home yet. There was something she needed to do.

She drove south, on Lake Shore Drive. The highrises of North Chicago rose on her right. Motherhood had changed her. She did not want to switch on the radio. News bulletins were bad. Yesterday she'd tried to get the news and heard, "Extra security personnel are being sent to American embassies all over the world in the wake of a rash of terrorist bombings."

She slipped a Vivaldi cassette into the stereo.

She pushed down on the accelerator. Music filled the car, violins, flutes.

The doctor was tall with black hair and he came around the desk, frowning. "Are you eating well?" he asked Stephanie. "Taking medication that might have caused the headaches?"

They were in a highrise overlooking Lake Shore Drive. Dr. Heinemann was seventy, blue eyed, with a steady reassuring voice. Autographed comic strips from newspapers hung opposite his Stanford medical degrees.

Stephanie said, "I'm not on medication."

"Well, you're not the kind to imagine things, or get this upset either. Blood pressure's fine. X-rays show a healthy girl. Anything changed at home? How's Danny and Josh?"

The story spilled out. She said, "I don't want to depress my family. I don't want to spoil the time we have left." Heinemann listened gravely, leaning against the desk. "I need a pill, that's all. To sleep. I'll feel better if I sleep."

Heinemann closed her chart. He'd delivered her thirty-two years before, and he still called her "Princess." He drummed his fingers against his medical jacket. "You're the fourth patient come in like this," he said. She looked up sharply and he nodded. "It's true. Regular patients too, people who don't get carried away."

One comic strip showed Beetle Bailey pointing at a man who looked like Heinemann in medical whites. Beetle Bailey said, "To the kitchen, Heinemann!"

Heinemann said, "I'll tell you what I told them, although so many of you are coming in I'm doubting my advice." He leaned backwards to open a drawer and extracted a card. "Here's the name of a doctor you can talk to," he said.

"A psychiatrist?" She colored. "I'm not crazy." She laughed. "Well, maybe a little, but it won't last."

"I'll give you Dalmane to help you sleep, but a one-time prescription only. If you're still upset after, come back."

"The pills will do it. I'm probably nervous because I can't sleep. You get tired. Everything seems worse."

The lake below was blue, vast. More slowly, Heinemann said, "Princess, have you ever thought of doing political work?" He'd surprised her again. Even though he kept photos of his family on the desk, she never thought of him as having a life beyond the office. "I belong to a group, Physicians for Social Responsibility. Heard of it?"

"No."

"Well, it's just a bunch of old doctors. But there's a march Saturday, in the Loop. For disarmament."

"A march?" When he put it that way, used the word "march," it sounded silly, ineffectual, something students might do. Or Josh fifteen years ago. She was Madden's daughter-in-law. She wasn't supposed to "march." She envisioned Heinemann with his stethoscope, stomping up Michigan Avenue. She wanted to giggle, but he looked serious.

"We're taking Danny to my mother's Saturday," she said. But the pressure had lifted. Turning him down, she'd given herself power. And other people were upset too, Heinemann had said. She would be able to sleep with the Dalmane. The headaches would go away.

Outside, she grew aware of the blue sky again. By the time she reached Evanston, she felt normal, cheery.

She frosted the cake and hung streamers. Set the table with red paper plates. The phone rang. Her neighbor Michelle sounded like she was holding back tears. "My brother didn't join the army to fight, he joined to learn electronics. I don't even know where Somalia is!"

Stephanie went upstairs to pack Danny's old summer clothes. His room smelled of bath powder. The bed stood on stilts. Danny used a ladder to reach his "spaceship." In a cavity underneath were plastic aliens and a ray gun that ran on batteries.

Kneeling, she removed a blue pastel jacket from a chest. It was small on Danny, she would pack it for the next child. She folded a pair of dungarees.

Michelle had said, *He's leaving tomorrow.*

She felt the pain returning between her eyes. Every time she started to feel better, news pushed her down.

No time for another baby, she thought.

I'll give the clothes to Goodwill.

The doorbell rang.

Party time.

"Stop fighting," Stephanie ordered. The giggling in the backseat ceased. She raised her index finger so the last two children to be dropped off, a serious blond girl named Annie and her chubby brother, Frederick, could see. She said in a high pitched voice, "I'm Finger Man. Able to leap tall buildings and do magic tricks."

"What tricks?" the little girl asked.

Stephanie turned off Dempster Street onto a quiet road lined with small homes. Although Josh bore the brunt of her depression she worked hard to keep it from everyone else. "Finger Man can walk through walls and make string beans disappear without eating them. Also, I'm a ventriloquist. Know what that is?"

"What is it?" asked the chubby boy. Stephanie pulled into the driveway of a Tudor home. "It means I can make you think someone else is talking when really it's me. For instance, see the lady driving this car?"

"That's you," the boy said.

"No." She held the finger higher. "*This* is me. I said the lady, Danny's mother."

"You're Danny's mother," said the boy.

"Frederick," the girl said. "Let her do the trick."

"Trick? What trick, it's science," said Stephanie. "You think Mrs. Madden is talking, but it's really me, Finger Man, making you *think* it's Mrs. Madden."

"Oh gawd," the little girl said. Remembering her manners as she opened the door, she said, "Thank you for a lovely party. Frederick!"

"Thanks, Mrs. Madden."

With the children gone, Stephanie slumped from the effort of entertaining. What happened next surprised her. Back on Dempster Street, through the cars ahead and under the glow from a Mobil sign, she caught sight of a hitchhiker. A tall, broad boy in a parka. One foot on the curb, one insolently thrust into traffic.

She never picked up hitchers. She rode past them, staring straight ahead, feeling guilty because she was too afraid to stop. Last year the *Tribune* had published articles about a hitchhiker who robbed his drivers.

But the boy looked so frail and cold. A thought came into her mind: *Danny's helpless.* One thing had nothing to do with the other, yet benevolence overwhelmed her natural caution. It seemed such a small gesture to stop. Looming at the window, the boy seemed much older. He wore a button that said NO NUKES.

"You picked up a hitchhiker? Don't you know what he could have done to you?"

"Nothing bad happened, so drop it."

Stephanie and Josh lay in bed, reading. Josh held *The Canterbury Tales*; Stephanie's finger marked her page in *Life After Nuclear War.*

His frown seemed to be growing permanent. "I don't know why I did it," she snapped, because he was staring. "It made me feel better, okay? I was feeling bad and doing something nice made me feel better."

"Would you have stopped if Danny had been in the car?"

It wasn't worth answering. He reasoned, "Was it any less dangerous for you?"

She hated the desperate sense of unraveling. She didn't want to fight. "One time!" Her voice was low with suppressed fury. "What do you want me to say, I shouldn't have done it? You win! No more! I helped a boy who was freezing!"

She snapped open her book. He said, "You know that's not the point." She heard him breathing. He said, "I'm worried about you, that's all." She wore a white flannel nightgown. Makeshift wooden shelves lined one wall, held up by bricks. Josh's novels filled the space. Dickens. Trollope. Hugo. James.

After a period of silence he tried to change the subject. "What do you think of the timesharing idea in Colorado?"

Her book said, "After the war the expected loss of medical personnel and large number of casualties will dramatically change the doctor–patient ratio."

"We put in a couple thousand every year," he said. "Five years and the condos are finished. We have our own place in the Rockies." He waved his hands eagerly. "Three weeks a year, skiing. Or the summer if you like. The rest of the time we rent it out."

"Five years?" she said slowly. "*Five* years."

"Look," he said. "I've just about had it with you. What is this, the sixties? Snap out of it." He sighed. He would try one last time, one more subject. "You fill out those insurance forms we were supposed to mail?"

They split house duties. She said, "Oh, I was working on the cake. I'll do it now." When he put his book on the night table and turned off his light and rolled away from her, she said, "I just wanted to do something for someone. I feel helpless, Josh."

"So drive around and pick up more hitchhikers. Jesus."

She was still awake when he fell asleep, although drowsiness was starting to overtake her. What kind of peacemaker couldn't even have peace in her own home? she thought. Josh's words kept going through her mind.

She sat up and smiled. She knew what to do.

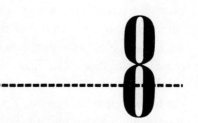

J ail to the Chief
(beat)
Jail to the Chief

Madden let the curtain drop back across the window. He could not see the demonstrators but their chanting grew huge. Outside it was night. The image of the White House still filled his mind, beyond the protesters below and across Lafayette Park. "Lots of death threats," Huff had said. "We'll need extra men at the hotel."

He was in Washington for hearings which would start in twelve hours. A gong started up outside, beating time with the cries. The sitting room of the newly renovated Hay-Adams Presidential Suite seemed smaller than the Oval Office. The double mahogany doors to the bedroom remained closed; over the chanting and the crackling from the fireplace he heard Catherine sliding hangers on the other side. An oil portrait of George Washington dominated the room, above the marble mantel with its bronze eagle. Washington's eyes followed him as he moved toward an open rolltop desk in a corner. An immense chandelier hung above a dark leather couch and a coffee table. Under his slippers, the burgundy pile felt soft and deep.

But the room faded. He saw the Princeton class ring on his aide's finger as the man shook him awake. He saw Professor Shinitzky in the Situation Room, trembling in his bathrobe as he picked up the hotline.

Madden wrote, *I did the right thing.*

He slipped into the past. The chanting changed to "Kennedy! Kennedy!" Balloons tumbled from the ceiling; a thousand signs bobbed above the screaming, jubilant crowd. The images that came the most surprised him; they were not from his own presidency. He was in the Los Angeles Coliseum, vice chairman of the Massachusetts Democratic delegation. His first convention, at thirty-one. The loudspeakers boomed "The next President of . . ." and the lights went out for Kennedy's entrance. Trumpets played "Fanfare for the Common Man." Thousands of flashbulbs turned the delegates' faces to silhouettes. Suddenly Madden's throat seemed to be rising; his chest grew huge. In the dark the specific issues of the convention lost importance. He saw he was in one room with all the people who had nominated the next President of the United States. Governors. Ice cream vendors. Mothers on welfare.

It was a moment of purity. And then he saw more. He was in one room with all the people who had ever nominated any president. His emotions embarrassed him until he saw others wiping their faces. Then the lights came on and the convention turned political again. He would always remember the jowly face of Chicago's mayor streaming tears across the aisle.

In his mind it was two a.m. and his breath frosted. He thrust his hands into the pockets of his long wool coat. The night before President Ronald Reagan's inauguration, he walked Pennsylvania Avenue in front of the White House. Senator Madden had driven in from McLean, Virginia. He loved late-night walks.

Columnists were already calling him the next Democratic candidate. Viewing stands had been erected along Pennsylvania Avenue. In twelve hours they would be packed with people. A pickup truck slowed to allow its driver a look at the White House. A policeman walked an explosives-sniffing German shepherd in the stands. Otherwise, wide, grand Pennsylvania Avenue was empty.

Madden's heart began beating fast. He'd been in countries where tanks began their protective rings around the president's residence a quarter-mile away, where the lowliest cook needed bodyguards when he left the grounds. He'd been in countries where brown coated soldiers slept in barracks near their presidents to keep them safe, and on that night, in front of the White House he thought, My God, tomorrow a government will fall, a President will be exiled. I don't see a single soldier outside this house.

Madden wrote, *I have never kept a diary before. Politicians keep journals to boost their reputations, or to give themselves a private place in which to confess.*

By surrendering, he'd been prepared to give up his grandchildren's opportunity to experience moments like that convention, he thought. He'd surrendered two hundred years of history. Surrendered every person he saw on the street: teachers, television repairmen, mothers with strollers.

Woooom, went the gong outside. *Wooom woooom wooom wooom.*

He'd sentenced the industrialists to prison. Given up the bounty of the farms. He'd agreed to the placement of Soviet troops in every town hall in America and every court. He'd signed an execution order for thousands of patriots who would privately take up arms against the foe.

A voice on a bullhorn outside, clearly police, ordered, "Move back from the entrance of the hotel!"

Madden said furiously, "Do something!" He ripped the words to shreds. The room seemed smaller. Flames turned the paper black.

In his memory the briefings room at the Brookings Institution looked like a high school classroom, except congressmen filled the desks, not teenagers. A fat man in a blue suit paced before a blackboard. He wiped his forehead with a handkerchief. He spoke with the shrewd, calculating tones of a high paid military consultant.

"What would you do if the Soviets dropped a bomb on Buffalo, just one, and stopped?" he asked. "Options! Suppose they decimated Erie, Pennsylvania, to threaten us, make a point. Isn't that what we did in Japan? No mass attack. Just take out two cities. Suppose they destroyed an unpopulated area, part of Nevada?"

"We'd fight," muttered a Milwaukee congressman in a powder blue leisure suit. They'd all muttered the words, indignation flooding their faces.

I thought I would fight.

Madden sat at the desk, head in his hands. Madden in the time capsule. Madden at fifteen. A handsome boy. A boy classmates marked as confident, self-possessed. A boy even teachers confided in. A boy who never complained. A boy who loved sports and parties. A boy who many thought exceeded expectations in Lyle, Massachusetts. Most popular boy. A boy like a million other boys in high schools that year.

I wonder if Mark has contacted the Russians yet?

His political career had begun with the speech announcing results of his graft investigation. He'd gone on radio despite the governor's entreaties to quiet down. In the Senate he'd worked hard. His manner with seniors remained respectful but not subservient. He was not afraid to speak his mind, yet only did so when he had thought carefully about what he was going to say. He allied himself with powerful interests without giving up to them his free will. He survived Josh's arrest for possession of marijuana. The country swung to his views at proper moments. He helped start the Urban Job Corps and Jupiter space project. He was like dozens of other senators.

There had to be more to reach the presidency, even for someone of his superior abilities. Each President had a special trait, Madden had found. Hunger, like Nixon. Luck. Family, like Kennedy. Fortune. Savagery. Brilliance. Connection.

He had those attributes in pieces, but an inner certainty had made him President. This was the central mystery, even to him. It was his spark, his extra. Four times the sureness had come upon him: a sudden and immediate change in the boundaries of his universe. Not a wrenching, not a surge. The sense of walls falling away, dissolving and realigning themselves so that instantly the world looked different. This was his special talent: instinctive decision making in a flash of clarity.

Whatever action followed, appearing to others as brave or daring, was to him so natural it was devoid of choice. As he acquired experience and honed his capabilities, the nature of the certainty never changed. It asserted itself at crucial junctures. Feeling sure, he had defied his parents and married Catherine. With quiet certainty he had led the attack against the Chinese. He could not predict when the feeling would come. It had never lasted longer than a minute. He could not manufacture it. He wished for it now.

Madden had been thrust into a place no human had ever been. There had been other presidents but none had surrendered the country. All he had known seemed to be receding like a planet in the porthole of a rapidly climbing space craft. He was left with a hellish suffocation or a sense of out-of-control speed.

He whirled as the door clicked open behind him.

Framed in the doorway, Catherine looked stunning in high heels and a midnight blue gown. Her bare shoulders were milky. She wore her silver hair loose.

Trying for light tones she said, "Good news from the warden, darling. You're out of solitary. You can even go to a party tonight."

"Good God, what time is it?"

"You could use a shave." She crossed the room diagonally, skirting him. In public they remained as loving as ever but they would fight tonight: the strain had been building, and it was due to erupt.

"If you do not move back," the bullhorn voice announced outside, "we will have to move you!"

She sat down and crossed her legs. He was seven feet away, back to the fire. Under her calm, direct scrutiny the Chinese ambassador had once remarked, "When she looks at me like that, I swear she knows what I'm thinking."

"Shave later," she said.

From outside, the comic, wavering tones of a trumpet joined the mocking rendition of "Hail to the Chief."

"We can get a room on the other side of the hotel," Catherine began.

"They don't bother me."

"You don't have to fight every single fight. Give yourself a break." She shrugged. "Then stay." Moving rooms wasn't going to be the point of the argument anyway. With the double doors open he saw the canopied bed they had shared in silence the last two nights. A crimson and an emerald evening gown, rejects for tonight's party, lay on the covers. Tonight would be their first public appearance since the surrender.

She said, "We've turned into a couple of strangers in a hotel room, talking politely and going crazy inside. Three weeks is enough, don't you think?"

Madden couldn't help smiling. Sure it was enough, but from this obvious point the conversation would unravel.

She said, "I've been patient because I know what you're going through, but you have to start talking to me."

He had that feeling of the world receding again, getting far away. Nancy Reagan had grown anemic as the President's wife. Betty Ford drank.

She went over old ground. He meant everything to her. To her he had always been a great man. She was furious that the public for whom he had worked so relentlessly had abandoned him. The hysteria in the world would pass.

The bullhorn boomed, "THIS IS YOUR LAST WARNING!"

A vague shattering sound came from below. Catherine stared into his eyes. "I'd be the first to tell you if I thought you did wrong, you know that. I've never held back. The people against you now will be the first to cheer you later. Or they'd be crying out no matter what you did."

He had to turn his back on her to reach the curtain. Something out there drew him. Don't stand against lighted windows, Huff had said. But standing to the side, he could still look down. Seven stories below a line of police motorcycles advanced toward the demonstrators. More police, on horseback, remained immobile behind the cyclists. There was a jagged rotor sound from above. A blue searchlight from the helicopter impaled the retreating masses. They were running into Lafayette Park. They were not just students but veterans, young people, housewives, lawyers.

More mounted police, in two lines, converged on the park from north and south. There would be police snipers on the roof.

Beyond the park the White House glowed blue-white. He saw parked limousines in the driveway beyond the spiked gate. He saw blazing windows in the ballroom of the East Wing. Men and women in tuxedos and gowns disappeared into the White House.

"Seeing Stacky and Neuman, that'll be good," he said absently. They were old friends who would be at the party.

"At least you'll talk to someone." She winced at her complaint. She had not come here to nag him.

"Honey, we're on safe ground. No one's going to charge me with treason, never mind what James Henry says."

"Oh Bill, it's not treason I'm talking about and you know it. You lock yourself in here to think, but you're not alone. Two hundred years of Madden ghosts are with you." When she brushed against him, he smelled her perfume, his favorite French scent and an invitation to bed. They linked hands.

She said, "The rose bushes need pruning." Despite the mood the reference surprised him into laughter. During the Korean War they'd invented a code, used it to hide intimate words from the army. "Rose bush" meant "I want you inside me." "Blueberry Pie" was "Wear that nightie." "The Otis fair, I loved it" meant "I'll chase you around the house all night."

The code had institutionalized the private language of lovers. For years they'd joked about the army's response. Madden had been continually called into the censor's office in Seoul by one cigar-smoking major. "What the hell does this mean," the New Yorker would demand, waving Dutch Masters stubs at the love letters, " 'Bobby Saunders is building a bowling alley.' " ("I love the smell of you during sex.") "In eighteen straight letters! What are you, a spy?"

The code had kept them close when they were far away. Closer, she was saying, than they were now.

Madden said, "A little more time."

The massaging hand jerked away. "What about me? Who's taking over my projects, my kids! You think I didn't have a job? Thirty-five years ago we made a deal because I didn't want to come to Washington, so we wouldn't end up like those other couples! Divorced! I believe in you, even if you're having a lapse! Christ," she said. "Listen to me, begging for affection."

What was he supposed to say? That they had opposite ways of dealing with the problem? Men were different; it was harder to talk. He didn't care if it was genetics or training. He slid the curtain closed. The police had stopped; for the moment the protesters were contained. Her shoulders felt narrower. Her eyes glistened. He told her he loved her, but the words sounded hollow even to him. Her skin was so soft. His heart was breaking. As lovely as she had been when he met her, she had grown into her beauty as the years passed. He stroked her face. "If you trust my instincts, trust me to figure this out myself."

He kissed her on the mouth. She did not respond and then she did. There was desperation in it. She shuddered with passion, grief, and self disgust. The argument had spent itself for the moment. It would erupt later, they both knew. On the canopied bed she threw herself into lovemaking. Her perfume surrounded him. She liked to feel his teeth. She'd taken to wearing high-collared dresses last winter and the women's magazines had proclaimed "The 1890s are back." The truth was, at age fifty-eight she was hiding a hickey.

Afterwards they showered together. When they stepped out of the elevator into the lobby, Secret Service men surrounded them. A woman in a white fur registering at the front desk cried, "God bless you, Mr. President." If you let the friendly ones raise your spirits the others brought you down, but he couldn't help it. Outside, the crowd seemed bigger. Demonstrators had spilled into the street again and strained against the linked arms of the police. Beyond the crowd, Madden made out the star atop the White House Christmas tree.

A Cincinnati hardware store owner would be arrested for what happened next. The limousine pulled up, and as Huff reached for the door, Catherine's scream jerked Madden's head left. A big man in a dark raincoat was bursting through the police line. The gun loomed, a black circle in his fist. Madden hurled himself at Catherine. The finger yanked the trigger twice. Something hit him hard, on the right. He was going down. It took less than a second. He thought, "I can't be shot, he was on my left." He had never been shot, even in Korea. Some wounded men told him you didn't feel it right away. Others said you knew instantly. Madden realized the blow had been Huff hitting him out of the way. He yelled, "Catherine!" but other voices drowned him out.

"It didn't go off!"

Madden was yanked to his feet. One of Catherine's high heels was disappearing into the limousine. The backseat rushed up at him, slammed into his face. Huff was on top of him, shouting "Go!"

Then Madden regained his senses. Huff was strong, but Madden pushed him off, commanded, "Stop!" The lurch of braking threw them forward. The rage beat in his head, he could hardly hear anything else. Huff grabbed his arm but he threw open the door. "Take care of her," he barked. Wind lashed his face. He marched up the driveway. Ahead, police wrestled the man on the ground. Running footsteps sounded behind him and Huff yelled, "There could be more of them!"

The demonstrators had dropped to the ground but now people were rising, staring. Police regrouped to protect him. The blue parka had ridden up past the attacker's waist. Heavy calves showed beneath his trouser cuffs.

As Madden looked down, the face turned toward him. Time seemed to stop. He stared into a wedge-shaped, dough-colored face. He'd seen faces like this a thousand times in crowds. The black eyes focused in recognition. The man fought against restraining police. "He died for you!" he screamed.

"Who? Tell me?" Madden bent over. But it wasn't important whether the man answered or not. The important thing was that Madden had not fled.

As the Secret Service men pushed him back into the limousine, the man yelled, "Someone will get you!"

Then they were speeding onto Connecticut Avenue, sirens blaring. More squad cars converged on the hotel from the other direction. Catherine's thighs shook, but she did not seem injured. Madden gripped her wrist. "You're all right?"

She whispered, "He could have shot you." Madden held her in his arms. "It's fine," he said. But the peacefulness between them was gone.

The limousine descended into the Dupont Circle tunnel, and Madden saw police looking down from the rail. Huff's voice from the front seat was flat with anger. Madden shouldn't have walked back to the crowd. "We should get you to the hospital, sir. That wrist."

Madden hadn't felt it, the torn cuff and scratch. "Not necessary," he said. Exuberance filled him. For the first time in weeks he felt triumphant. He asked the driver to drive to the Potomac, to give

Catherine time to calm down. After a while he said to Catherine, "Want to go to the party now?" Ten minutes later he asked again. He ordered the driver, "Foxhall Road."

Chauffeurs stamped in the snow to keep warm. Idling limousines lined the driveway, and the thirty-room Tudor mansion blazed with light. Ken Goldman opened the door himself, his lean, patrician face flushed with relief.

"Thank God! We saw it on TV." He drew the Maddens into the house as if fearful more attackers lurked outside. He was a tall man in a tuxedo, a squash player with silvery hair. He'd resigned as Madden's White House counsel when Madden left office, but unlike others in the administration, had stayed away when Rittenhouse asked everyone to return. Catherine said, "Ken, darling." She said, "Jill, you look beautiful."

Madden was eager to see his friends. He had been eating badly for days and he was famished. Guests gathered at the edge of the sunken living room burst into applause. Goldman said, "You didn't go to the hospital? Dr. Zeer!" he called.

A neurosurgeon friend of Goldman's took them upstairs. "You look fine," the bald, cheery doctor said, "but you ought to get checked out." Now that the emergency was over, Madden started shaking. He borrowed a sweater. He joked, "Happens whenever someone tries to shoot me." But he was back to normal when they returned to the party, although Catherine had become very quiet.

A string quartet played Mozart in a corner. The roaring fireplace was piled high with logs. As the crowd pressed close, Madden looked over faces and his appetite died. He recognized no one. Goldman had packed the party. The Democratic party chairman "had a cold," Goldman said, his embarrassment evident. The attorney general "might stop by later." Goldman introduced Madden to a Bethesda lawyer and a Roslyn pharmaceuticals lobbyist. The blond wife of a Wisconsin congressman pumped his hand and said she was appalled at how Congress was treating him.

Madden worked the crowd, joking and telling stories, asking people about themselves. Catherine seemed to be doing the same thing across the room.

"There's someone you want to meet," Goldman said. Madden followed the pointing finger and said, "Well!" The Constitutional law expert was a woman, no more than thirty-two or thirty-three. A slim, tanned brunette in a red gown gestured animatedly to Jill Goldman by the fireplace.

"Diane Medaglia," Goldman said. "Top talent at Harvard. Won the Webster case last year." Webster had been a Navy captain charged with selling radar secrets to the Russians. Medaglia had uncovered the real spy, an enlisted man in his office. She'd also defended the governor of Alaska, Goldman said, against an impeachment charge.

"I'm keeping good company these days," Madden said wryly.

Up close her age surprised him and he upped his estimate to forty. Her face struck him with its contrasts. Beneath black eyes the nose seemed stubby, puttylike, an ugly afterthought. The mouth dipped in a hard line. In this face the mouth absorbed all the pressure. The posture was easy, loose. She had the shiny hair of a twenty-year-old, jet black and swept back from her forehead, cut stylishly above the nape of the neck.

Everyone else had mentioned the shooting or hearings. Medaglia offered her hand and said, "You got yourself in a mess, didn't you?" She had a low, smooth voice, like a radio host's. There was private amusement in her look that went beyond the law.

Goldman led them to his second-floor study, a low-ceilinged room in mahogany and leather. While Madden crossed his legs on the couch, Goldman started a small fire in the fireplace and mixed drinks. Medaglia chose to stand. There was no smalltalk.

Madden sipped his Jamisons on ice. "Give it to me straight, Diane. I'm not an expert on treason, but Ken's concerns are exaggerated, don't you think?"

"Straight?" Her gown matched her lipstick. "I think you will be indicted."

Goldman stiffened with shock behind the desk. He'd been unrolling his tobacco pouch. Medaglia qualified herself. "I'm a trained pessimist, paid to come up with worst-case scenarios. The government might not indict, but they have grounds."

Madden let out a breath at the word "government." Medaglia

sipped at her gin and tonic. "The rock pile," Madden joked. "Ah ha! You'll have to smuggle me a file, Ken."

"You can paint stripes on the tennis courts," Medaglia said bluntly. In an odd way, Madden thought, she seemed angry with him, although he was unsure why. His levity did not fool her. Her whole manner implied that she knew him, understood him. With a jolt he realized she might.

Medaglia said, "Treason is the only criminal law defined by the Constitution." Her red nails tapped the tumbler, focusing her memory when she recited, "Treason consists of waging war against the United States or giving aid and comfort to the enemy. No one can be convicted without testimony from two witnesses or a confession in open court."

Goldman leaned forward. "He didn't wage war."

The firelight played on her ankles. " 'Aid and abet' is the problem. Two witnesses saw the surrender."

Goldman lit his pipe, immediately the room smelled of tobacco. "He made a phone call, that's all. The Russians never took it seriously."

"You don't have to complete the act for it to constitute treason," Medaglia said. "During the Civil War a man named Greenhouse bought ships for the Confederacy. He was arrested before he could deliver them. Treason."

Madden concentrated on Medaglia. Goldman said, "Oh, it's not comparable." He waved the pipe. "What happened to Greenhouse?"

"They hung him." Medaglia added, "Treason is foggy. For two hundred years the courts have stuck with obvious cases. This one isn't clear. Fewer grounds exist for dropping it. And James Henry," she pronounced the prosecutor's name with the first sign of reverence she'd shown, "will find a way to get it to trial."

Madden swished the whiskey in his glass. "How do we fight if you're right?"

She leaned back on her elbows against the fireplace. This was the part she'd waited for. She seemed eager now. "Background," she said. "English law is the basis of ours. We're back in 1351. If a British subject commits an act that in any way weakens the power of the king and country to face enemies, that's treason. Keep that in mind.

"Now us. The Court said, in 1861 . . ." The fingers tapped the glass again. "Acts of injury to, or the destruction of property of the United States is giving aid and comfort to the enemy, if the acts are performed with the intent to . . ."

"No intent!" Goldman hit the desk with his fist. "That's clear this time!" The quartet began an arrangement of a Bach aria downstairs.

"Sorry, Ken. Intent is hard to prove. How does the court know what goes on in someone's head? It doesn't, so it gets around the problem." She began pacing in front of the fireplace. "Justice Duval said, '*If the act is treasonous, the intent is automatic.*' If you know your act will damage the country and you commit it anyway . . ." She trailed off. "If it makes you feel better, most experts agree with you."

"Automatic, eh?" Madden said.

Goldman said, "It's farfetched. You can't stretch that rule in this instance."

"Why not? You think farfetched things never happen?" She balled her hands into fists and exploded them. "The surrender was farfetched, wasn't it?" Madden saw her, all intense, in front of a jury.

The finger started tapping again. "No person, even from religious motives or other fundamental beliefs, may aid the enemy without being liable for treason." Her voice drove at them. "Again the court was dealing with Confederates. They were fighting for another country, they said. How could they be prosecuted for treason against the United States?"

A burst of laughter came from downstairs. She said, "The justices didn't buy it. The court defines motives, not defendants. Ken, I could use another drink."

Gloomy and shaken, Goldman went to the bar. Medaglia addressed Madden. "You'll say you were commander-in-chief. You made a judgment call, part of the job. Why you did it stays out of it, we ignore the argument you saved everyone."

Goldman whirled at the bar. "Absolutely not, this time!" He waved ice tongs. "We'd be dead, for chrissake."

"No, no, no, no, no! We're not arguing for the history books. Dreyfus lost his treason judgment in France and ten years passed before he was vindicated. You want to put nuclear war on trial? You think a jury wants to vote on that? We play it on presidential powers, period. Besides," she added with relish, "we can drag the whole Defense Department into court; companies, engineers. DeLavery told you the Russians were attacking, didn't he? What do you mean, no!?"

Madden was shaking his head. "That's not the way I want to win it," he said. His technique was to listen, then reach his decision. She started to protest. Madden held up his hand and she stopped. Suddenly Madden was emanating quiet force. "No DeLavery," he said. "No engineers. Your argument about presidential powers, I like that."

Medaglia looked at Goldman, waiting for him to join in against Madden, but the former White House counsel knew his boss. She persisted, "It's the death penalty." Madden said, "Whatever happens, they won't do *that*." She came close, the blackness of her pupils huge when she sat on the hassock.

"The Defense Department will survive no matter what, Mr. President. And if they have to clean house, so? You don't understand the danger to you."

Goldman smiled. She'd started calling Madden "Mr. President."

"Why do you want to defend me?" Madden said.

She drew back at the personal question. She seemed to consider and gather herself. She said, with much bitterness, "I have a thing about scapegoats." Madden understood something horrible had happened to someone she loved. He thought, a crusader.

She said, "I don't know if you did the right thing that night but I know what they want to do to you." She leaned forward. "I know how scapegoats sabotage themselves. How they *need* trials." Her voice grew low with challenge. "They have so much faith in their precious systems they don't believe they've been accused by mistake. They don't fight, not hard, not like they should. They don't call DeLavery to the stand. Part of them wants to lose."

Goldman said, "Diane!" Madden waved his hand to dismiss the protest. She went silent. Passionate, her mouth seemed fuller. The hard line was gone. Madden said, "You're just what I need. But my way or not at all."

He sipped the Jamisons. Medaglia stood up. She went to the

mantel. She was breathing hard and then she changed, the emotion left her face. She said, in the old impersonal tones, "Henry will claim the surrender assisted the enemy. He'll say even though the Russians never accepted or came here, our position in the world has been weakened anyway, endangered by you. He'll say there are different treason standards for a President."

Goldman thought she was like an animal reined. She said, "He'll have experts testify you acted prematurely. Cowardice led to treason, he'll say. He'll be implying punishing you is necessary to show the Russians we're strong. He'll make a guilty vote into a patriotic act. I studied under him. He's a genius. Assuming you want to prepare a . . ." Diplomatically she avoided the word "defense" and said "strategy." ". . . may I ask questions?"

"Go ahead," Madden said. Her analysis was worse than anything he had imagined.

"You had no intention of siding with the enemy when you surrendered, correct?"

"Yes."

"You had no prior knowledge the early warning system was faulty. You never took gifts or money from the Soviets."

"This is ridiculous!" Goldman protested.

Madden sipped his drink. "No."

"And of course you've had no dealings with the Soviets since the surrender."

"Attorney-client privilege?"

He told them, in brisk, factual tones, of Mark St. Johns's mission. Color drained from Medaglia's face. Goldman urged, "Mr. President, call him back."

"I don't want to call him back," Madden said calmly. "Perhaps some good can come of it."

Diane Medaglia laid one finger on his shoulder. When he'd been President, strangers had never presumed to touch him. "We want to avoid a snowball reaction," she said. "It will happen if people find out about St. Johns."

Madden said, "Any more questions?"

The finger withdrew. "In ten years we don't want everyone feeling sorry for what they did to you," Medaglia said.

"Aha! You're not so pessimistic if you think we have ten years."
It was a dismissal. After she left, Madden said, "We'll use her. But
I'm not dragging the Defense Department in to save myself."

Goldman advised him again to recall St. Johns. Madden said,
"Shouldn't we be getting back to the party, Ken?"

He did not phone Mark St. Johns. At three a.m. he walked the
streets, Huff behind. Catherine's quietness had persisted all the way
home, but the moment they'd reached their suite she'd exploded.

"You could have been killed!" she cried. "I could have! I can't
believe you stopped that limousine. You're turning into another
person!"

Wearily he said, "Cats, that was two hours ago. Let's go to sleep."

"Two hours because I held it in, worried about you! Who were
you thinking about when you stopped the car?"

Madden threw his jacket onto a chair. This wasn't the way he'd
envisioned the evening ending. But the anger was rising in him too.
He knew the argument wasn't her fault. He said, "This mood started
when the doctor was examining me." He felt cruelty coming out, it
wasn't what he wanted to say. "When I got sick, the minute I showed
weakness, you got quiet. You want me to tell you things, but you
don't want to hear them. What did you want me to do, run from
that man?"

She was crying. "By all means invite him to dinner tomorrow."

He'd turned away from her, knowing she wanted him in her
arms, knowing what she needed and refusing to give it. Dried up.
Dried out. Both hurting. He'd gone back to the window. The White
House floodlights glowed white. The party had ended there, the
windows were dark. Behind him she cried, "Don't do this to us!" He
did not turn back and when he did she was in bed.

Now a scarf covered his mouth and he wore a hat and long gray
coat. He was unrecognizable.

The snow had stopped. Powdery remnants advanced in windswept
lines across streets. Frost turned windows of parked cars opaque.

He had never needed much sleep; he was energetic and he liked
to work. In the past he had enjoyed a sense of intimacy with the city.
For three years he had determined its character even in the most

minor ways. Thousands of appointees had moved here to do his bidding. Jazz musicians had become popular during his stay. Italian rather than French restaurants had flourished. Blue-striped ties had become prevalent in offices because he wore them. Sunday sermons had revolved around his Job Corps and space-station program. Madden walked away from the lights of downtown. He felt the passage of history in the city's wintry indifference, in its continuity without him.

At the Lincoln Memorial he wondered again whether St. Johns had contacted the Russians. Maybe Medaglia had been right. Madden approached the statue with reverence. Spurning surrender, Lincoln had overseen the bloodiest conflict in the nation's history to preserve unity.

It wasn't nuclear, he told himself.

A lone German tourist with a camera asked the American with the scarf around his face to snap his picture. The German tried to start a conversation about the surrender. "I don't think your President was a coward. I think he is kind."

Descending the steps, Madden glanced at the sky and his bowels froze. A flash of white sped across the horizon behind the clouds. Too fast to be a jet. He braced for explosion. After a moment Huff materialized beside him, shaken. "Jesus Christ, Mr. President! I thought that was it."

Filled with sick relief, Madden drew away from the monument, walking toward downtown. Another meteor. He still saw the speeding light in his head. The wedge-faced man lunging through the police line . . . Diane Medaglia's fingernail tapping on her glass. He saw Catherine's hair spread on the pillow, her face turned away, toward the wall. He could not believe he had exposed her to attack.

His back sweated, his feet grew cold. They were approaching the Organization of American States building, all brightly lit. Over the years Madden had read about trials of famous men, men who had divorced their wives when the trials were over. Madden had always assumed these couples had been on the brink of divorce anyway. They only remained together as strategy for a better verdict. Now he understood the trials had driven the couples apart.

"Mr. President," Huff called. "You're shivering." The cab driver who picked them up spoke with a clipped West African accent. Tinny reggae crackled from a Sony swinging from the dashboard.

"The Hay-Adams Hotel, ha ha! President Madden is there! I don't know what the big fuss is about him anyway." The driver addressed Madden in the rearview mirror. Since he drove customers around the Capital, he felt his job included political commentary.

"I'm from Ghana," the driver said. "We have drought for the last five years. You know how much money Congress will spend on Madden's hearing? They'll talk about what he did and do nothing. They could save lives in Ghana with that money. Or Kenya or Somalia. Build dams, plant seeds. But they're talkers. They don't care about people. You look a little like Madden," he said.

"I am Madden."

The driver pulled to the curb and turned and studied Madden. A huge grin lit his face. From laugh lines around his mouth Madden saw he was a happy man. "You're his double or you're him. Rough on you now, I tell you! I get congressmen in this cab sometimes! They're out to get you. But the other people, the tourists, they're not so sure. And in my country you're a hero. Start a war in Washington and Accra burns to the ground. So thank you from me, Kwame Nkrumah. I'm named after the first president of my country and he had guts. He was the first to go against the British, the old way of thinking. Maybe you are the Nkrumah of North America. Or of the nuclear time. No charge for the ride, Madden." He used the West African form of address, last name first. "And God be with you because you're about to walk in the desert. The first to do anything is a lonely man."

Madden was buoyed by Kwame Nkrumah. Catherine was naked under the covers when he slid in. Her breathing was irregular, he knew she was awake.

"Look," he said, "I was stupid."

After a moment one hand slid across his chest. Her finger curled the hair above his nipple. He thought, too many shocks. He rested his palm on her thigh. He thought, I'll keep it calm, it's going to be better. The contours of their bodies molded in the dark.

The phone rang.

It's St. Johns. Catherine jerked, her finger accidentally yanking his hair. Madden's throat tightened. The last time the phone had rung so late had been the night of the surrender.

"President William Madden, please," said a professional sounding operator with a British accent.

"Yes."

"Dr. Charles Pound calling from London Anglican Hospital." The voice was loud enough so Catherine heard it and groaned. Madden knew no Dr. Charles Pound. The pain stabbed back into his shoulder.

"Mr. President?" Another voice now, respectful but assured. "Charles Pound here. I'm calling about Mark St. Johns."

There were no covers on Catherine's shoulders. Madden's heart beat very fast.

"Mark. Where is he?"

"I'm afraid there's been a bombing," said Dr. Charles Pound.

9

"James, James, you don't seriously think you'll convict him!" the attorney general argued. On their third circuit around the deck of the White House pool, the two men paused by a rolling silver bar topped with an ice bucket and glasses. A huge splash forty feet off indicated President Rittenhouse had started another lap. The punch made a clicking sound when it hit the ice. Pieces of lemon peel and apple slices floated in the pitcher.

For the past half hour, tactful, embarrassed, anxious, the attorney general had been explaining to the special prosecutor how he'd been tricked.

James Henry refused the drink. "Oh, I'll convict him," he said. He was cradling the President's gray Angora cat Louis, and ran his index finger down the animal's belly. Louis swatted playfully at him but subsided when it seemed James Henry might put him down. Louis seemed to feel James Henry's approval was important.

He'd been called "the Magician" in court, "the Conjurer." He'd won more cases during his career than any other prosecutor in history.

President Nixon had said, in awe, "James Henry could make a hostile jury see ghosts in the rafters."

He wore brownish suits and freshly laundered white shirts, with antique silver cufflinks. The burgundy bow tie revealed the subtle dandy beneath. Reading glasses lent sternness to the flinty face, but his smile could create instant warmth. His hair was brown and peltish, brushed back. As he listened, his attention remained inscrutably fixed on the attorney general. They started strolling again. Either James Henry was totally absorbed or the attorney general wasn't getting through. He urged the President's messenger on with nods or light, one-syllable "hmmms." His "no"s were gentle head shakes, more like statements than confrontations. His whole demeanor was one of severity with the rest of the world but warmth with you.

As he petted the cat, he said in his soft, cultured voice, "He committed treason, Arthur. The penalty is death."

The tension kept rising. The attorney general was short, in a gray suit and striped blue-and-white tie. He moved his small hands in jerks. His anxiety was reflected in a tendency to keep glancing at the swimming President. He said, "The Justice Department checked the facts before giving anything to you. I did. No treason."

"Then why appoint a special prosecutor?"

"Ah ha ha ha," the attorney general laughed. The tile walls gleamed, Mediterranean blue. Louis snuggled deeper into James Henry's arms. The attorney general touched the knot of his tie. "How do you keep from sweating in here?" He grew earnest, pulled two folding chairs close. "You want me to spell it out?" They sat by a corner of the pool. Two lanes separated them from the President, who swam with smooth, bearish pulls. He said, "Look at the President's view. The Russians are all over him. Peace conference proposals on one hand and troops on the other. You hear about Indianapolis last night? Two dead, thirty in the hospital. A YMCA Peace Dance, fighting breaks out. It's the mood, James. Plus an election next year."

He grew brotherly. "We're both Democrats. You know the only way to win is get clear of Madden, resolve the thing. Who's going to believe me if I drop the issue? I used to work for him."

"That's right," James Henry said. "You did."

The attorney general poked his palm with his left index finger. "Corrigan and Maserati and Street," he said, naming the party's powerful conservative senators, "said nobody would doubt you. But it was an act! You weren't supposed to bring charges! I'm sorry we didn't tell you. This is embarrassing, but nobody thought you'd go after him. There's no grounds! You can still stop! James, you've always been a team man."

"What is the temperature in here anyway?" James Henry said. "Eighty?"

The attorney general grew imploring. "We have to get back to the way things were. Before he made that phone call. Drop the case. Do us all a favor and forget it. You haven't filed yet. It'll take twenty years to repair the damage. Remember what Carter did to the CIA?"

Henry tapped the cat's nose lightly. Louis wrapped the prosecutor's finger in his paws and shook it side to side. He said, without looking up, "The problem is, he did commit treason."

The cat leaped from James Henry's arms and ran toward Rittenhouse, who was climbing from the pool. "You boys work it out?" the President called boisterously.

The attorney general dropped his voice. "You don't know anything new, do you, that we don't?" The President reached the rolling silver bar and poured punch into two glasses. The attorney general pressed on. "Believe me, it was a judgment call. He was a coward. Let everybody forget." The President was padding toward them with the glasses. He had a side-to-side gait.

"There's real mango in here, James!" Rittenhouse called out. "It's not alcoholic. Shit, you'll die of heat prostration in here."

James Henry leaned toward the attorney general; he looked down over his reading glasses into the pale blue eyes. For the first time his voice grew harder, angry. "It's because of my daughter, Arthur! Susan, you know her. That's why I'm going after him. That's why he has to die."

As James Henry accepted punch from the President, Sergeant Bartholomew Price, age twenty-two, picked his way along a foot-wide rocky mountain path six thousand miles away. The Somalia heat felt like a blast furnace. The desert was hard earth, cobble and boulder, six hundred feet below. Brown. Endless. For the last two days.

"*Keep low. There could be snipers in the rocks,*" the lieutenant had said. The valley remained wide at this point, over a mile across. Above the hazy, dun colored cliffs opposite, the sun descended in a ball larger than anything Price had seen in the United States, even in Key West, where he had grown up, where sunsets were famous.

"Prr-iccccccce," hissed a low, nasal voice ahead. The two Somali scouts waved for him to catch up. They wore Somali army shoulder patches on their American-made uniforms. They were in superb shape, and Price still felt a little jet lag. They looked like tough fighters. He was thinking that landscapes were supposed to look this desolate after wars were over, not before they start.

Within twenty-four hours the whole world would know of Bartholomew Price.

"You're an advisor. No shooting," the lieutenant had ordered. During the briefing Price had finally learned where they were. The desert was named Ogaden and the valley Mehta. Mehta meant prayer. The valley's shape resembled a Danakil tribesman's hands at prayer, wrists close, palms apart. It ran for twenty miles like a funnel to a pass Price could not yet see.

Rubble crunched underfoot. Price grew aware of a vague pressure in his ears. He stopped. It was almost a humming, somewhere between sound and silence. A sound about to become audible. An odd pulsating that made him feel fear. He fought it off. He began rounding a boulder. He thought, *is it Russians?* The chalky rock smell became tinged with another odor, more fetid. He'd smelled it before, humid and dank. The pressure in his ears kept growing.

Price had heard of Somalia in high school, but only a week ago he'd learned it was in Africa, near Egypt and Ethiopia. Four days ago he'd been in Fort Tucson, Arizona. The plane rides had taken a day and a half. A train had brought them into the desert; then half-tracks had picked them up and set off where there weren't any roads. Price knew the driver and had sat up front. He'd seen two hundred kinds of nothing. First there was sandy, clay colored earth with bluish, foot high scrub. The land had become browner, and he'd seen dust devils swirling in the distance. Then the ground had grown hard and big rocks lay all over, except Price couldn't figure out where they came from.

Once, when the half-track chugged across a dry riverbed, he'd seen something that would not go away in his mind. A camel lying on its side, heaving, with ragged packs still tied to its hump. Two men digging in the sandy earth for water, on all fours, not even bothering to look up. Women wrapped in black staring at their men. And vultures close to another partially eaten camel, its ribs exposed, the carrion birds the only ones paying attention to the vehicles, flapping their wings to get away, too gorged to lift into the air.

"There may be Russians with the Ethiopians," the lieutenant had said. *"Count the weapons and men."*

Price had raised his hand. What do they want with this godforsaken place?

"How do I know? It's the border."

Price paused as a wave of jet lag hit him, but he kept going. They had been hiking for five hours. He rounded a boulder and the valley spread beneath him. Sure enough, the high walls abruptly came together and funneled a few miles ahead into a steep pass already bathed in night shadow. The setting sun had touched the opposite cliffs. The two Somalis had settled into a niche in the rock, off the footpath that hugged the side of the cliff. Price eased down alongside them. He gasped. The most incredible sight he had ever seen lay below.

It was a city, a steel city, he thought at first. Thousands of tin roofs threw back the waning sunlight. Then he saw the animal-skin huts too, and the people dressed in white. Little cotton forms with black limbs, tiny and sluggish below. Price told himself a city was impossible. There were no roads to get here, no rivers, no airport, no train tracks. The temperature had to hit 140 degrees down there at noon. Price pulled at his binoculars.

What kind of army is that? he thought.

Then he sucked in air because he saw it wasn't any army. In the round binocular O he saw a boy lying on the ground in the shade of an animal-skin hovel, waving flies from his face, his arms as thin as twigs. He saw a woman shaking an infant, holding it away from her face and screaming at it, but the baby was limp. He saw two tiny Red Cross jeeps and a long line of men holding bowls.

It was the most incredible, awful sight Price had ever seen. He could not tear his eyes from the binoculars. He heard a voice he recognized as coming from the smaller Somali scout.

"They walked here for water. River dry."

Now the smell hit him again and he realized it was sewage, human sewage, and he understood the murmur he had been hearing for the last mile was the life of this camp. A scout poked him. The small Somali was shielding his eyes, looking south toward the pass. A new sound came to Price over the camp noise. Clanking. He swung the binoculars left, toward the pass. At first he saw nothing. Then the shadow moved and the first tank emerged into the dusk light. The Soviet star grew visible for an instant, then the tank was suffused in the red glow.

The tank wheeled and stopped. More troops were coming out of the pass, in jeeps or on foot. They didn't seem to be interested in the tin-roofed city, just in setting up camp. Half an hour later, when, Price had estimated a hundred Ethiopians had driven tents into the ground, and as evening fires began flickering in the convoluted air, they rose to leave.

But the smaller Somali caught Price's arm. He smiled. He pulled his American made .45 from his holster and waved his fingers to indicate Price should move back a step. If the man fired, everyone in the valley would know they were here. Instead, he used the tip of the gun to pry loose a flat piece of shale. Price started, because he had been sitting on it, and the scorpion beneath was two inches in length. Yellow. Price had never seen a scorpion before. The stinger went up, and he figured the insect would run. Instead it viciously charged the .45 and began striking it with the stinger. He could hear the tinny sound again and again.

A hyena howled in the valley. Lots of fires flickered below.

The Somali's teeth shone in the rising ash-white moon. "Ethiopians," he said as he crushed the scorpion with his boot. "Now we go."

His expression died and Price heard the erupting shots simultaneously. The Ethiopians had come over the rise silently; they were above Price and moving down, flame spurting from five machine guns. Figures were running and dropping in attack. Price had his M-16 up. He raked the ridge. He saw a shadowy figure blown backwards, off its feet. The scream echoed with the shots. The small Somali had slumped to his knees. His forehead gently touched the rock. His fist stretched and clenched. The second Somali was yelling in Arabic, firing, belly on the ground, sliding back along the path.

Price realized one of the attackers was white. Russian bastard, he thought. He directed his fire toward the man and something plowed into his shoulder. He felt multiple slithering impacts cross his chest. His head seemed to float. A wave of pain knocked him backwards. He heard the crunch of his back striking the rock. In Key West at dusk the town gathered in Mallory Square to watch jugglers as the sun went down. He wondered if there were more scorpions beneath him. He couldn't hear shooting anymore.

FIRST AMERICAN ADVISOR KILLED IN SOMALIA, the teletype machines clicked out to the world.

Lunch at the White House was open-faced sandwiches on thinly sliced German rye. Smoked pheasant. Roast beef. Shrimp. Turkey. The Oval Office was cooler than the pool. A television on a redwood shelf broadcast midday news. James Henry put a bit of pheasant on his finger and offered it to Louis. The cat sniffed it.

On screen, a red-haired man in a blue suit stood at a rostrum, below a banner: REVEREND JIMMIE MACK AT NOON. The man crooned into a microphone to row upon row of packed churchgoers.

"The *law* should be the *will* of the *people*. We are not *in*terested in *leg*al subtleties and *eva*sions. The man should be in jail. The man should feel the wrath of an angry *people*. The man who tried to give everything away should be locked away. He must not *do more damage*."

"Two million viewers every day," Rittenhouse groaned. "And he's signed up six more stations as of Wednesday. Chicago and Seattle." Rittenhouse speared a dill pickle with a party fork. The food was spread out on a tablecloth on his desk. He seemed irritated at the attorney general for letting the meeting go so long, but he remained courteous to James Henry. Ultimately, he had the power to fire him.

Louis jumped onto the shelf beside the TV, where the scene showed the parking lot outside Jimmie Mack's Virginia church. Worshippers were emerging to see two lines of men and women carrying placards. FASCIST! LEAVE OUR TOWN!

The three men could hear the chanting of demonstrators on Pennsylvania Avenue.

Fights were starting on screen.

Rittenhouse flicked the automatic control and the room went silent. A shaft of sunlight streamed through French windows. The cat moved inside it, rolled belly-up on the blue pile and purred.

Rittenhouse said, "Start a trial and we'll need troops in the cities." James Henry said, "Hmmmm." Rittenhouse said, "You don't seriously think he intended to commit treason, do you?" James Henry said, "That's what the indictment will say, Mr. President."

Rittenhouse bit down on a sandwich and wiped his mouth. "I'm taking a lot of time with you today because I want to convince you," he said. He came around the desk. He said, "I don't like what he did either, but you'll never get it to trial, not in the end. Even if a grand jury hands you an indictment the judge will throw it out of court when Madden's attorney asks for it. No grounds."

"I'll take my chances."

Rittenhouse exhaled. "Even if the judge *does* go for it, the Supreme Court will get it before it reaches trial. Do you have any idea of the long odds you're talking about? You'll never do it."

"Then why are you so worried?" said James Henry.

Henry wiped his mouth. He walked to the window. Outside, the Rose Garden was crusted with ice and the sun formed dazzling patterns. Cloud shadows shifted across the lawn, toward the Potomac. He watched a blue jay on a maple.

"It's Christmas in a week," Henry said. "My daughter, Susan, is in love. She hasn't told me, but I can tell. She walks different, you know, light steps. Laughs at nothing. We have dinner once a week."

They didn't interrupt him. He said, "It's a beautiful thing to see, your daughter in love. She was wild." He laughed. "I was worried all those years. Paris, Caracas." He made a face. "Mr. President, you should have seen the men she sent me pictures of."

The attorney general said, softly, "James."

"It relates. I understand what you fear. But you know what I'm afraid of? Susan dying. I'm seventy-one, but what about her? You met her, Arthur, remember? She's never married. Never been a mother." He walked away from the window; there was passion in his voice. "Don't you feel it, every day, unraveling a little bit more? It's because of him. You're right, Arthur, we have to go back to the way it was. But your way won't do it. Madden'll come back. Become strong again."

James Henry had reached the center of the Oval Office. Louis rubbed against his ankles, begging to be picked up. Henry said, "Leave him alone? So he can go home and write his memoirs and give speeches? Stand out as a symbol of how we reward people who give up?" His eyes, through the reading glasses, had gone hard. A *New York Daily News* appeared in his hand. "You read Robert Gardner?" There was disgust in his voice. "People like him won't leave it alone. Goading. Opportunists. They'll try to make him big again. Don't wait until it's too late, Mr. President. I know what you're saying about the Defense Department, but it was treason. I'll prove it and the jury will know."

Rittenhouse blew out air noisily. He said, "I'm taking a piss." The instant he left, the attorney general pulled his chair close. The muscles in his face seemed bunched, but his voice went soft. It was time for the carrot, the sweet.

"I know what it's like not to work," he coaxed. He placed his hand on James Henry's sleeve. "One time, after I left Lythe & Futter, I was out of work for two months. Never again. I hated it. People like you and me *need* to work. Retirement, well, not for me, thanks."

James Henry nodded. The attorney general said, "Not that Madden isn't a good cause but let's face it, if you drop the case you go back to nothing. It's tough to retire. Hell, who says seventy-year-old men have to retire anyway?" His voice dropped further. "I can't promise anything," he said. "I haven't talked to the President about this. But Ireland is opening up in June when Ambassador Sabonjian retires. I have a little influence. What do you think, James? You think an old warhorse prosecutor could be happy in Dublin?"

"Dublin?" James Henry said.

"I haven't mentioned it to him, but he may go for it."

"In June," James Henry said musingly.

"Trout fishing," the attorney general said, "is great in Ireland."

James Henry broke into a broad smile. "That's wonderful. The trial should be over by June."

YOU BASTARD I HOPE THE REDS SHOOT YOU IN THE BELLY. THAT'S WHAT
THEY DID TO MY SON JONATHAN IN VIETNAM.

Wearily, Robert Gardner dropped the letter in his wastebasket
and picked another off the pile.

"Take care, Mr. Gardner! What you're doing is brave, but the
people who tried to kill the President will come after you!"

He pushed the pile away. He tried phoning the Hay-Adams Hotel
again. "Sorry, Mr. Gardner," the hotel manager told him, "President
Madden isn't giving interviews. I'm sure he knows you're on his
side."

"But did you pass on to him what I want to write? I won't change
his words, I'll print the whole thing. Anything he wants."

The voice grew irritated. "I heard how you tried to get in here
yesterday. The maintenance worker who rented you his uniform has
been fired. Don't try it again!"

Robert Gardner listened to the receiver buzz. He reached for a
half filled Styrofoam cup but put it down when he saw the blue film
coating the coffee. He said, "Probably cold anyway."

Beside him, white against the blue screen of his word processor,
a column was taking shape.

```
How did we reach this point? The engineers who
designed the weapons were not unfeeling. The
politicians really cared. The voters were never
ignorant. The Soviets never wanted nuclear war,
no one wanted it. No one wants it now. Why are all
the well meaning components malfunctioning? How
has the mere presence of these weapons funneled
the best the race has to offer down a forty year
schizophrenic episode about to fail? Or has Mad-
den shown us a way out, a way of saying no?
```

"Words," he said, disgusted. The anger was rising in his temples.
It never seemed to go away, it just simmered and erupted. From his
temporary partitioned space in the *Daily News* Washington bureau
on Pennsylvania Avenue, the gray Executive Office building was
visible through half-raised blinds. He was in Washington to cover
Congressional hearings on the surrender but the real story was
Madden.

Even at his desk Gardner felt the witch hunt mood building

around the city, by the hour: in the marble hallways of the Senate, at the lunching holes of the powerful, Sans Souci or Cantina D'Italia, at Georgetown cocktail parties, in the stiff, righteous prose of Pentagon spokesmen, in the Massachusetts Avenue think tanks.

War fever. Not the way he would have imagined it, not a rabid crying out for combat, but a back and forth motion, fear to anger, fury to fear. Always escalating, always wondering: What is the other side doing? What are they thinking? And always the metallic taste in his mouth, the sense that something had to be done, fast.

He shut the machine. His heart beat faster when he saw the Colorado postmark on the next envelope. He exhaled softly and pulled a bottle of Johnny Walker from his desk drawer. He poured a little into a clean Styrofoam cup. The sharp anger was turning to excitement.

IF YOU WANT TO HELP MADDEN SO MUCH WHY DON'T YOU FIND OUT WHAT REALLY HAPPENED AT NORAD THAT NIGHT?

No signature. No return address. Two other reporters were joking beyond the partition, near the door. One said, "So the parrot says, 'I don't know, mister. I got a hard-on and fell off the perch.' "

Laughter erupted. There was an old Remington typewriter beside the word processor. He'd tacked photos of his sister's two little girls on the cork partition.

Gardner opened the top drawer and extracted another similarly addressed envelope, already open but postmarked two days earlier. In both letters the lower loop of the lower case *E* was missing each time the key was struck. The letter contained a single sentence typed in the center of the page:

"No one knows the whole story of what happened at NORAD!!!!!!!"

The walls faded and Gardner was back at NORAD. The Pepsi machine in the coffee lounge glowed blue-red. The room seemed narrow for eight people and a guard blocked the door, broad-shouldered, boots spread. The woman from CBS ranted, "Let me call my family! It's real, isn't it, not a test! Oh God, my kids!"

The loudspeaker above the Pepsi machine remained silent, although Gardner knew all other squawk boxes on the base were erupting. The woman quieted down. They heard coffee gurgling. "Help yourself to donuts," the guard said. "Blueberry's good." The room was so soundproofed Gardner could only imagine he heard the soldiers he knew had to be running past outside. He wanted to scream with frustration. He studied the guard. When the guard glanced at the donut box, Gardner stood up and the soldier said, "Don't sir. There are two more in the hall."

The *Post* man ate a donut. *I don't want to die in a coffee lounge two hundred feet underground,* Gardner told himself. He wrote in his notebook, I don't want to live the rest of my life here, either.

"Will we feel it down here, if missiles hit?" he asked the guard.

"Don't exactly know, sir. The buildings are on springs."

He remembered being hustled along the steel corridors hours later, out the quarter-mile-long tunnel linking the installation with the surface. "Snow! Still here!" The CBS woman was running, kicking snow. She shouted, "Snow!"

Now Gardner sipped his Johnny Walker and dialed a number in Reston, Virginia. "Don't call me anymore on this story," a furtive-sounding man's voice said. "Rittenhouse isn't telling us anything, and frankly, I don't want to know. Any leaks on that night and they'll hunt down whoever did it and probably send them to prison with Madden."

He tried a number near Rockville, Maryland. "The company stands by our satellites, Bob," a cheery voice told him. "They were supposed to pick up flying objects, and meteors are flying objects, right? In fact, if you think about it, the system operated perfectly. If the President hadn't surrendered prematurely, everything would have been fine."

He called a bar near Capitol Hill. The Senate aide's voice sounded slurred. "You're chasing a nothing story. Everybody knows what happened. The satellites picked out the meteors. NORAD shifted to private electrical power and blew out a computer. The computer signaled the submarine attack. The committee's been over it ten times. What else could have happened? You playing poker Thursday, or you'll be back in New York?"

"I'll let you know." He drank more Johnny Walker. In his mind he was in a phone booth at a Colorado gas station near NORAD, in the mountains. His editor's voice was saying, over the line, "We got the story an hour ago. Moscow released it, the White House confirmed it. Guess they couldn't deny it with our man on the scene held prisoner in the coffee lounge, ha ha ha!"

As Gardner flipped toward N for NORAD in his book, Susan Henry's name stood out. His chest tightened. He would have called her after St. Johns's dinner, but by the time he'd reached the East River that night his grief had overwhelmed his desire for her. He remembered watching the sun rising over the river in the morning. He remembered the tugs chugging against the current and the wind blowing around his face. By morning all he could think about was Julia.

DeLavery was "touring the base," a Hispanic-sounding operator told him from Colorado. "He got your other messages. Have you tried the public relations office?"

Ten minutes later, Gardner was walking along Pennsylvania Avenue toward the Mayflower Hotel to pack for Colorado when a car began honking at him. Her face was framed in the window of a cream-colored Mercedes. His heart beat fast, and he felt the blood rushing in his wrists. When he leaned into the car, he smelled the warm air and a fragrance like tulips.

"This is a kidnapping," she said. "Get in."

"I knew I shouldn't have given my bodyguard the day off," Robert Gardner said.

"Do what I say and you won't get hurt." Classical music, light Mozart, played on the stereo. Susan Henry said, "Our leader, El Shabib, wants to talk to you."

"Aren't you going to blindfold me?"

She seemed small and lean in the black coat and dress. Her leg muscles moved beneath her sheer stockings as she worked the brake and clutch. She drove with fluid motions, moving north along Pennsylvania Avenue toward Georgetown. Her face was more beautiful than he remembered. Office workers were going into restaurants or stopping at hot-dog stands on corners, laughing and joking on lunch hour. The Mozart changed to Handel.

Gardner caught her eye at a light. "My good luck, running into you like that."

"Oh, I was coming to get you. I heard you were here." She used the same detached tone as before, understated yet direct. Her long, slim fingers wrapped the steering wheel. Neither of them mentioned he had not called. Even when he looked straight ahead, he was conscious of the black hair falling about her shoulders.

On Rock Creek Parkway and across from the Watergate, she turned into a small parking lot by the Potomac. A boat ramp was visible along a walkway and beyond bare trees.

"Where's El Shabib?" Robert Gardner asked.

"I'm El Shabib. And it's lunchtime."

She took a picnic basket and blankets from the trunk. Wind blew off the river; the joggers wore ear muffs or stocking caps. Off to the side of the path, fronting the river and spread along a retaining wall, was an area frequented by picnickers in the spring, a grassy knoll then, hard and bare now.

"El Shabib likes your winter," she said. "In El Shabib's country it is hot all the time. El Shabib desires a snownik."

She held up a blanket and he saw she was fiddling with an electronic control. "Battery," she said. "Feel." It was hot. "They make them in Israel, on a kibbutz," she said. She spread it on the ground.

There was hot Irish coffee from a Thermos. Hot clam chowder and cold lobster bits. Hot mulled wine. Each time she reached for the food, he saw her shoulder blades working under the black coat. She wore the same small triangular gold earrings she had worn at St. Johns's dinner.

He liked jazz and played the trumpet in jazz sessions in New York. She loved riding and took packhorse trips out west. He'd gone to college in Chicago. She'd lived in Paris and Venezuela and liked Robert Redford movies. He preferred Marilyn Monroe.

There were strawberries for dessert. Her legs were tucked beneath her. The sun glowed on ice patches in the Potomac. He felt his nerve endings alive. When she was near him, he felt his clothing rubbing against his skin. Four hundred yards away, in the middle of the river, they saw the bare reaching branches of the trees on Roosevelt Island.

She said, "My first sculptures came from the Potomac. Look at the currents, the shapes. There's an owl. Oops, it's gone. People used to say, '*Where do you dream these up?*' " When she stood she wrapped her coat close. "I stole them," she smiled.

He had a thought that he was in love with her. She said, "This river is my favorite. When I was a girl you could see your reflection in it sometimes. My father told me all the reflections went to the bottom and met each other and had fun. You could swim in the river then." Gardner pictured the stern federal prosecutor. He'd called James Henry "Rittenhouse's hit man" in his next column.

She said, "We'd anchor in the sailboat and my father would read history and my mother read medicine. She was a doctor. I think rivers bring pieces of lives to you, things people throw away, things they lose. They bring people to you." Their shoulders were touching. He felt the bad memory come into his mind and he hated himself and tried to make it go away. She said, "All the great capitals should have a river. The Thames and the Seine and the Danube and the Potomac. Did you grow up near a river?"

"Air Force brats grow up lots of places. But in Maine there was a river," Gardner said. "I fished for pickerel there."

"What else do you remember about Maine?"

"I remember when my father took me up in his fighter. He wasn't supposed to do that, but he used to sneak my mother up. One day he just said to me, 'Let's go.' I remember the seat pressing against my back when we took off. It was loud and then it was quiet. I'd never been in a plane before. We flew over the coast of Maine."

"It sounds beautiful."

"I still think of it when I take off in a plane. He said to me, 'You have a talent, son, use it for good.' I know it sounds corny. But I think that's why he took me up there, to show me something bigger than myself, to show me what he wanted me to do. Does that sound silly?"

"No."

"That was the last time I saw him." Gardner laughed. "When we landed, the military police were there. '*Christ, Captain, you're not supposed to take up the kid!*' But pilots did what they wanted. They're sociopaths in their own ways. The Air Force gets them to do what it wants by giving them planes."

He drew away an inch. "So, El Shabib. Isn't it customary for the kidnapped man to pay a ransom? What would you like?"

She glanced back at the Watergate. "First the hideout," she said.

When she swung open her apartment door ten minutes later she said, "The ransom is, suffer my etchings." In contrast to her all-black clothing, the huge studio apartment was utterly white. He closed the door behind him, heard the lock click into place. There seemed to be less air in here. He remembered New York and thought he was the worst person who had ever lived. The room was bathed in sunlight, and her sculptures rose and twisted in a forest of plaster and marble from the oak floor. Walls had been removed. The space was a semicircle, its outer wall the wall of the Watergate, curved, with an almost continuous French window visible behind white lace curtains. The bed was king-sized with brass posts.

He had a sense of things happening fast. She took off her high heels and went to the refrigerator. She opened a closet. The high heels lay overturned on the floor by the bed. There were lots of big blue pillows on the covers. The room smelled of plaster and tulips, always tulips. There was a color photo of Susan and a blond woman on horseback on a wall, with mountains in the distance. Both women wore western button-down shirts. Another photo showed Susan with her father, but this James Henry lacked his famous reading glasses and smiled so warmly that at first Gardner thought he was another person. Father and daughter were on chairs on a beach. She wore a white bikini and her hair was in a bun. More photos showed a dark-haired man with sunglasses and his arm around Susan's waist.

She was turning and carrying glasses toward him. The last photo was black and white, of an older woman. She lay on a lawn chair and waved to the camera. She looked like Susan. He decided the mother was dead because the hairstyle was old and there were no more recent photos.

The sun struck the bedposts and formed long bar shadows on the floor. A clock was ticking. His throat was dry. He didn't taste whatever she gave him to drink, although it made the thirst go away. He wanted to leave, but he didn't. The sadness came back to him. He heard an airplane droning outside. She placed the tips of her fingers on his shirt, over his nipples. The touch was electric. The tulip smell grew strong. He slid his index finger down her cheek.

She said, "I do want the babies. With you. Not today but afterwards."

He said, "You have to know something. There's something I . . ."

"Men say that in movies," she said. "I want to marry you. It's bold and admirable when a man says it. Do you think it's bold and admirable for a woman?"

"Yes," he said after a moment.

"Are you going to kiss me now?" she said.

Something was breaking inside him. Then he was kissing her, and then he felt his shirt sliding down his arms. He was free of it. He was free of the material. Her ribs, under his tongue, were small, and he felt her heart pounding beneath them. The inside of her thighs tasted like salt. Her fingernails were sliding across his scalp. She spoke his name. Her stomach tasted like clover. Her fingernails slid down his back and legs. She was ripping into him from behind. He felt the curtains on his back. He loved the shape of her lips. She gave a little gasp and locked her legs around him and thrust forward. Undressed, she was thin, curling around him in a frenzy, her head shaking, her hands, her legs. He felt the skin snap on his shoulder when her teeth broke its surface. Someone screamed. He heard the bed scraping when it moved. He moved faster.

Later he slept, head and upper back bare above the covers, one arm splayed loose over her azure blue pillow. She stood a little bit off from the bed, among the sculptures, watching. Plaster dusted the tops of her bare feet, and her toes pressed into the wooden floor. Her hair fell to the middle of her back, stopping above the swell of her buttocks. Her breasts were small mounds. Her pubic hair was shiny, black, and tangled, reaching in all directions. She cocked her head. The river outside looked cold, but it was warm in the apartment. Her right leg lifted, pointing at the tallest sculpture. She lifted her arms so her wrists rose above her ears. With Gardner asleep she glided, dancing.

In the White House, nobody was smiling anymore. The President had returned. The attorney general scowled and shook his head. "I'm sorry, James, but you don't understand. We're going to have to fire you."

The cat dozed on the sofa, beside James Henry, who looked from the President to the attorney general. He said softly, "I see." He seemed sad as he nodded. "I'm afraid you're the one who doesn't understand," he said. "Go ahead, announce I'm out, and try getting elected again, Mr. President. You'll be finished, like Ford after Nixon."

In the silence James Henry rose and said, "Thank you for the delicious lunch, Mr. President. I don't know where you got the turkey, but it's the best I've had, and I love turkey!" The attorney general was reminded of his old family doctor in Tennessee, leaning close with a paternal smile, positioning a painful injection.

"Look at it this way," Henry said quietly, and the cat stirred on the couch. "If I lose, I look foolish. If I win, you get the credit for appointing me, Mr. President! You can't come out badly. I'm old. I have plenty of money." He was walking toward the door. "I'm doing what I want. There's no way you can stop me, Mr. President, although . . . Irish ambassador! Well, that's tempting!"

He left the two men staring at each other.

Hours later he was putting the finishing touches on his speech to the grand jury, which he planned to convene tomorrow. Since he lived alone, he preferred to work at his favorite restaurant, Joe & Mo's on Connecticut Avenue. A shadow fell across the table. He looked up and removed his glasses and said, "Beautiful, as always." He stood and said, "On time, too, and a woman in love is generally on time for only one person. Two old fashioneds," he told the waiter. And to Susan, who was dressed in black: "Tonight you're telling me his name or you're not leaving."

10

St. Johns spotted the Soviet envoy through the crowd, across the ballroom. Thirty feet away, a tall man with a beard like Lincoln's clinked glasses with an Oriental woman in red high heels. The man's eyes settled on St. Johns. Wait a few minutes, they seemed to say. St. Johns had the urge to leave.

It was hours before Madden would learn of the bombing but St. Johns had known since this afternoon the Russians would contact him tonight. There was no other reason why he should be asked to the Christmas party of a man he'd never met, a British peer with Soviet sympathies. Some friends would love to talk to you, had been scribbled beneath the gold-leaf invitation. The problem was, St. Johns had made no effort to contact the Russians yet. If they were initiating talks with him, his mission had leaked. Already what had begun as a straightforward message relay for Madden was changing into something far more dangerous.

Who else knew he represented Madden? He felt exposed, vulnerable. He wondered whether Madden had asked the Russians to contact him. Learn what they want, he thought. But he decided after tonight, his work for Madden was over.

St. Johns was twenty miles south of London in an Elizabethan manor house in Surrey. An all-woman Dixieland band played "Bill Bailey" beneath a two-story tapestry of British battle scenes. Howling Sikh swordsmen charged British redcoats, who fired back. The British were outnumbered. They held their ground.

Front paws raised, marble lions flanked four immense fireplaces. The sweet smell of burning cedar permeated the room. Massive oak tables were loaded with turkeys, puddings, champagne cup, and lemon sorbet.

St. Johns took his plate and stood beneath an oil portrait of the first earl. A plump Fleet Street publisher with a red cummerbund joined him. "Merry Christmas, Mark. Your problems in Africa seem over."

The publisher wolfed sponge and cream trifles. "Ivan's offered to pull out if you will. Let the wogs kill themselves over their bloody desert."

In the portrait, the first earl looked like the current one: same hatchet face, downturned nose and ice-blue eyes.

"The Russians say they'll leave?" St. Johns said. "That's the first I've heard of it."

A House of Commons Laborite wore a gold Rolex and tuxedo with tails. "Rittenhouse has pulled it off. A firm hand, that's what Menkes respects."

The sense of disaster had been building since he'd accepted Madden's offer. Nicki had grown quieter by the day until she hardly spoke to him at all. *He never tells what he really wants,* she'd said when she'd seen him off at the airport.

He'd argued with Sir Rupert at the bank. The head of London Global American had admitted taking the three million. Then he'd made threats.

St. Johns had passed Madden's message to the British labor minister, an old friend. The British had showed no interest in meeting with the ex-President. They'd asked lots of questions about his mental state. In their maddeningly polite way, they seemed to be wondering about St. Johns as well.

Now St. Johns made small talk about the strength of the dollar. His mind was someplace else. He tried to find out about the U.S.–

Soviet deal to phase out troops in Africa, but no one knew anything. Presidents always thought they were indispensable, always tried to hold on.

A low, musical voice said, "Mark St. Johns." He looked into the Lincoln face. The smile was warm, the hazel eyes merry. St. Johns had seen Ivan Van Pelt at parties at the UN, presenting the Soviet case over canapés and cocktails. Swede by nationality. Converted Jew. Investment banker. Millionaire who'd made his fortune buying wheat for Moscow or selling it when the Russians had a surplus.

A two-humped mole marred the bridge of Van Pelt's nose. "The library is magnificent here," he said. "Original Tolstoys and Jameses." He touched St. Johns's wrist. He smelled of Paco Rabanne. "Have you seen it?"

St. Johns didn't know if that room had microphones so he said, "I need some air."

They strolled away from the house, past a sculpted garden where bushes were giant rabbits, across a hexagonal lawn and toward woods. Van Pelt chatted about the weather. Behind them, chauffeurs stood by Bentleys and Rolls-Royces, each man more than mere driver, hiding Uzis or Berettas beneath bulletproof glass and armored steel.

For three hundred years the Forsyth family had given Christmas parties here. Once the soldiers guarding their interests had been posted at the edges of the Empire. Now they watched the house.

The mist played tricks with St. Johns's vision. The oaks seemed to recede, slide farther away. Van Pelt told a joke about a cow voting in the House of Lords. He grew serious. "I want to tell you how much I admire President Madden," he said. He stood taller than the banker but took more leisurely strides. He kept his hands in his pockets. "It took courage, what he did. He deserves better than he's getting."

Startled, St. Johns wondered whether the offer was defection. The wind made "aaahing" sounds in the trees. "Premier Menkes was shaken up by the President's phone call, by what almost happened," Van Pelt said. "You know, he's always been interested in greater arms control." Now the Russians planned a great peace conference. Prominent men and women would be invited from all countries, to talk about the nuclear threat.

A woman's high-pitched laugh came to them from the party. Doctors would attend, Van Pelt said. Teachers. Philosophers. St. Johns wondered whether directional microphones pointed at them from the trees. The Soviets were even inviting the United States to co-sponsor the event. Might Madden consider attending? Van Pelt asked. Who better than he should deliver the keynote address?

The damp air made St. Johns's scalp itch. His shoes were wet, as were the cuffs of his trousers. *I'll never go to any Soviet conference,* Madden had said. But St. Johns had a vision: Madden thirty years ago in his book-lined study in Lyle. *I'm a Republican, Mark.* St. Johns saw him three weeks later, running for Congress on the Democratic ticket.

He counterproposed Madden's suggestion: a private talk with Menkes over satellite phone. The Swede stretched his thin fingers. His hands seemed independent of the rest of his body. "What if the premier came to the opening of the conference? He and the President could talk together and Madden could give the speech. What you want is what we're offering. The whole world should hear President Madden's experience."

St. Johns started coughing, the chill was in his chest. He saw that he had fooled himself. Carrying messages for Madden was not helping a President. He wished Van Pelt would stop saying "President." He was a businessman, not a diplomat. He didn't even believe in the cause. Everyone had a plan for Madden. Prosecute him or elevate him. Trick him into going to a conference. No one was going to talk to him. Not the British, not the Russians. What was the point of even being here if the United States and the Soviets had reached an accord?

The weather had been foggy like this the night Weber died. When St. Johns looked at the house, the lights seemed fainter, the night more dark. He glimpsed the red splash of the battle tapestry through a three-story window. Van Pelt promised to pass on Madden's request.

The whole game had taken less than fifteen minutes.

Leaving, St. Johns leaned back in the soft leather of the Bentley's rear seat. In the headlights oaks slid past on both sides of the driveway, and rain began to fall. The cold feeling in St. Johns's chest grew. He was angry at himself. Ten minutes ago St. Johns had been ready to drop the mission. Why was he disappointed now? It made no sense, even to him. They turned onto a two-lane country road; the driver sped up. You could know a man for decades and not really know him at all, St. Johns thought. Sir Rupert had taught him that.

He flashed back to the Englishman on the terrace of the bank's apartment. Sir Rupert drank Tanqueray and tonic, he wore a dark wool coat against the cold.

"I should have known better than to try to fool you," Sir Rupert chuckled. The head of London Global American resembled a jolly German shopkeeper more than a British aristocrat. His chubby burgomaster's face was veined red; his fingers were swollen like sausages. His hair remained full and white, the bachelor's pride.

"Money can be put back. Nothing's lost," Rupert said. St. Johns thought, It's adventurous to him. He likes being caught.

"Besides," the Englishman said, "I've made you more than I took just this month. Mark, we've been friends twenty years."

"You're out, Rupert."

The Englishman drained his glass and snorted. "Oh, don't get carried away! So I have a bad habit. You never asked how we landed the Gambia contract. With bribes! Or don't you want to know even now?"

He looked down at the Thames from the railing. "I always liked the view here. Always admired your American mentality. Compartmentalization. Everything I touch is dirty, it's why we make so much money."

He added, reaching for the short-necked bottle, "A few thousand people are killing themselves in Africa with guns we made. The whole world might blow up. We funded the missiles. We bankroll murderers and thieves, we're pimps in bowler hats and you worry about a pickpocket."

Then he grew friendly, the old bachelor who brought roses to Nicki and Havana cigars to Mark. Once when Weber was ten Sir Rupert had taken him to the zoo. He said, "You have the evidence. I'm not going anywhere. Think about it."

"Rupert, I don't have to think about it. Next time you take a step into the bank you'll be arrested. Get out."

Sir Rupert had picked up his hat, twirled it with one finger at the door. "You should be more tolerant, Mark," he said. "The others would let me stay but for you." He winked. "You're the one I hold responsible for this."

St. Johns looked at his knuckles, on his knees. When had they grown so old? The car was quiet except for the smooth Bentley purr. Headlights rounded a bend half a mile ahead. He closed his eyes. He felt gray with fatigue. The old feeling of futility made St. Johns's shoulders ache.

Then it happened. A new sound came to him. Hissing. Like water dripping onto a hot wire.

He'd barely registered the sound came from beneath him when the driver jerked the wheel, slammed on the brake, and yelled, "Get out of . . ."

It was too late. There was a flash of light. St. Johns felt something sharp strike his chest sideways. He was lying on the side of the road but did not know how he had gotten there. The weaving headlights were coming closer. The limousine doors lay on the wet grass. The driver stared at him, still in the front seat. Flames turned his face orange. Rain washed down on St. Johns.

He struggled to his feet, staggered to the car. "Get out of there, Marty," he said. He reached to pull the driver out. There wasn't any hand on one of his wrists. Blood poured onto the white padding protruding from the shredded seat.

Fighting nausea, St. Johns tugged at the man. The driver toppled out of the car, severed from legs pinioned under the collapsed steering wheel. One shoe remained pressed on the brake.

St. Johns backed away. The treetops were whirling. He heard screeching brakes and a door slam. Someone shouted, "Get into town, Harry, quick!" St. Johns wondered why his wrist didn't hurt. He fell backwards. There was a splash, the rain pummeled his eyes and mouth. A voice was saying, *Hurry*. A voice was saying, *The other one's dead. Do something, do something. He's dying.*

Mark St. Johns felt the darkness, the speed. He could see nothing, the velocity was in his throat. There was no wind yet but he knew he was moving. He was calm. Unafraid. It was like he was being sucked forward, hurtling through space.

Up ahead he saw a tiny golden light and the light grew bigger. It suffused him. It was warm. He was standing on a meadow and it was summer. There were lots of roses and the trees were green. From out of the oaks Weber walked toward him in his flying clothes, his red flannel shirt and oil-stained trousers. He grinned. His blue eyes were merry, magnified by strong lenses. He said, warmly, like a host, "Dad."

St. Johns embraced him. The edges of the meadow were fuzzy. He was dizzy with delight. "Where are we?" he asked. Then he felt a tug behind him. He'd never seen the meadow before. The tug came again, harder, to pull him away. He said, "Your mother will be happy." This time he was jerked away. He grabbed at Weber, but it was no use. Something was pulling him. Weber shrank, smaller . . . smaller.

Weber was gone.

St. Johns followed Madden, at a crouch, through a smoking Korean village. Madden fired into a hut. A Chinese soldier with a red star on his fur hat toppled out of a doorway. A dead peasant lay half in rubble; the huts were on fire. The peasant's arm stretched toward a dead chicken. Everywhere there was a rotting smell. The peasant's mouth opened. He said in Weber's voice, "I'm dead, are you?"

St. Johns groaned. He wanted to be the dead man, not Weber. He would take Weber's place. He reached to pull Weber from the wreckage, but his son sat five feet away, in the driver's seat of the burning Bentley. Weber cried in a ten-year-old voice, "Dad, help me. It hurts! It hurts!"

St. Johns tried to reach him, but he moved so slowly. He cried, "No, son, it's only a little shot." He reached Weber and tugged, but Weber toppled sideways. He saw Weber's shoe still on the brake pedal. He backed away, but suddenly he was in Gramercy Park. The steel fence was broken, knocked flat. People in black sat on benches. He saw Nicki high up on the penthouse patio, reading. The sky turned red and orange in bursts. Heat blasted his face. Nicki stood, a speck in the red. Then she was gone, swept away by the wind. When he tried to get into the building, Sir Rupert stood in the doorway in the doorman's uniform, gin and tonic in hand. Sir Rupert smiled. "Pimps in bowler hats," he said. "We bought the hardware."

St. Johns thought, *Madden knew this was going to happen.* He had to find Madden, but the President was gone. He wandered New York streets, searching for Madden. It was night. Red steam hissed from manhole covers. Shadowy forms looked down at him from windows in apartment buildings that were still whole. Other structures had been truncated. The bank tower was jagged; red oozed down the side. Wild dogs disappeared around the corner of Third Avenue. The phone booth was shattered, so he could not phone Madden. The heat kept growing. He groaned from the heat. Ivan Van Pelt came out of the Korean grocery carrying a bag of grapefruit. The Lincoln beard caught fire. The flesh peeled from Van Pelt's face. The Swede kept screaming. Mannequins were melting in Macy's window.

Up ahead, through smoke and erupting gunfire, he saw Madden running across Forty-second Street in his lieutenant's uniform. Madden fired into a doorway. He ran very fast.

St. Johns couldn't catch up. Madden disappeared into a subway. St. Johns started down after him; it was dark down there. Huge round things were rubbing in the blackness. Alive. Weber's voice carried out to him: "It's warm in the subway, Dad. Come down, Dad." He smelled dirt from the subway. Two red eyes stared up at him, started to rise, started to come to the street, victorious, hungry, zeroing in on St. Johns.

At the precise moment his pulse began to fail, St. Johns screamed in the operating room, "You're right! You're right! We have to stop it! Now I understand!"

The gray North Atlantic slipped by and became the green western coast of England. Madden looked away from the airplane window to where the stewards were cleaning up in first class. In his mind he saw a different beach, white, with gray breakers. He sat on a rocking couch on a screened porch. St. Johns swung on a hammock, hairy legs protruding from rolled trousers. The women clattered dishes inside the house. Weber and Josh built sand castles thirty yards away, by the tide line. Smooth limbed ten-year-olds in bathing trunks, hair falling over their foreheads: Weber's work a masterpiece, turreted and spired, Josh's a pathetic overturned pail of sand, crumbling too close to the water.

"To the next senator of Massachusetts," said St. Johns, taking the sweating pitcher of lemonade from Catherine. Nicki served a plastic tray of cucumber sandwiches, crust cut off the edges.

"You didn't touch your dinner, sir. Anything wrong?" the steward said.

"Watching the weight, son."

St. Johns was alive, but barely. "They're operating," said another voice in his head. Madden pictured the British ambassador, gaunt and dignified, in the suite at the Hay-Adams Hotel. They drank strong coffee. The ambassador looked embarrassed.

"The prime minister won't, er, stop you from coming, Mr. President, but he would prefer that you follow Mr. St. Johns's progress by phone. We'd supply constant reports. You could talk to the doctors. When Mr. St. Johns wakes, you would be in instant communication. Please understand. The security. President Rittenhouse hasn't visited us yet. We'd like good relations with him, just as we had with you."

The ambassador had visited the White House frequently during Madden's presidency; he'd come to Camp David for tennis and riding. He said, "When your status is, er, cleared, the prime minister would love for you to be his guest."

In Air Force One Madden had liked to work in the private bedroom. As the plane came in low, the bodyguards seemed restless. They looked out the windows and listened to the white radio receivers in their ears. Maybe they thought someone would fire a missile at the jet, but touchdown was uneventful. Madden was hustled off the plane.

Unmarked police cars preceded and followed him into London. The route was familiar, but he'd never seen it without cheering crowds. He remembered St. Johns, bareheaded, in a black wool coat, in a seaside cemetery in Nantucket, Massachusetts. Mourners huddled, backs to a white picket fence, near stones worn thin by centuries. St. Johns supported Nicki. Gulls screeched overhead.

Now the hospital rose through the fog, two stone towers beyond a sweeping lawn probably filled with convalescing patients in the summer. A light went off in a fifth-story window.

Be all right, Mark, Madden thought.

Don't go. They'd all said it except Catherine. The State Department. Diane Medaglia. In his mind she wore a severely cut blue business suit, skirt below the knee. She balanced a manila folder on her lap in Goldman's study. She'd been grilling him for hours.

"Did you belong to any leftist political organizations in college, peace organizations? How about Mrs. Madden? What organizations *did* you belong to? Was anyone accused of communism in those organizations?"

"You're getting carried away, Diane. James Henry isn't Joe McCarthy."

"Answer, please." She was rigid with anger over the trip, but she'd learned argument was useless. "Who knows what angle he'll use."

The building smelled like any hospital. Antiseptic. A photographer with a blue cap and lots of cameras around his neck saw Madden and grabbed into the tangle of equipment. He was too late, but as the elevator doors closed he ran for the phone.

"So much for the secret visit," murmured one bodyguard to another.

On the porch that day in Massachusetts they'd sung "Happy Days Are Here Again," and St. Johns had agreed to raise funds for Madden's Senate campaign.

They exited the elevator and the police guarding St. Johns stiffened in the corridor. Madden saw a red-headed nurse run into a room with a bottle of plasma. He saw Nicki through the tiny glass window of the door to the waiting room. She was alone, on a brown couch. She looked lost. Open magazines lay scattered on a coffee table, swatches of bright color. She'd always been a careful dresser. Her disarray struck him almost physically. Her peach-colored dress and jacket were crumpled. He smelled sweat when he pushed open the door. Empty Carlton packs lay jammed in an ashtray. She'd stopped smoking years ago. Her look was glazed, her mouth a hard, downturned curve of misery.

He said, "I'm sorry," and stretched out his hands.

For an instant he wondered whether she recognized him, her eyes were so blank. Then suddenly she was flying at him, fists up, face twisted. She pounded his chest. He was stunned. "How could you come here?" she ranted. "I told him not to go! You did this, you!"

The blows rained on his chest. If it helped her to hit him, he would take it. She backed off as if catching her breath for another attack. She hissed, "You use people. You always got him to do what you wanted." She'd been sitting here, stewing. In that instant her face reminded him of the man who had tried to shoot him in Washington. She said, "Everything you got was because of him. Even back in the old days, even back in high school. What do you want now? He won't wake up. Get out!"

"I'll come back in a few minutes," he said. In the hallway Secret Service men looked the other way. They'd heard her yell *You did this* and undoubtedly they would relay the words to their superiors. They were probably wondering what he had to do with the bombing. The police would ask him soon.

When he'd first become President, a TWA jet had been hijacked in San Francisco. Madden had ordered the FBI to storm the plane. Two college students had died in the shootout.

Madden glimpsed one of their fathers, a Nevada sheep rancher he'd invited to the White House. He'd told the parents of their children's bravery. Issued civilian medals. The rancher had been half shaven, his grizzly face wet with tears. He'd said to Madden, "I'm only here, you son of a bitch, to say you killed Willie."

The intercom called, "Dr. Pound, Dr. Pound to 334."

In the White House, Madden had spent hours looking at photos of the dead students. The boy had wanted to be an engineer, the girl a newscaster. A New York author wrote a bestseller about the incident called *Killed for No Reason;* the movie rights sold for half a million dollars. Madden had never regretted his decision. No more hijackings had occurred during his presidency.

When he reentered the waiting room, Nicki would not look at him. They sat opposite each other across the coffee table. Over her head he saw a painting of a blond girl on a swing in a meadow. The swing lifted high, the girl's skirts flew up to show white knees.

Tears crinkled the pages of Nicki's magazines.

He'd told Diane Medaglia, *When you send a man out and he gets hurt, you go to him.*

He was President, and no one could take that away. The President had to make hard decisions and live with them. The President had to look at the big picture. These were things he might have told the dead boy's father, but fathers have a right to feel grief. The President doesn't have to explain himself, Madden thought. The President is king.

He was aware of the door opening. A strong medicinal smell came into the room with Dr. Charles Pound. He was thin and balding with light blond hair. Madden realized three hours had passed. The doctor's teeth shone very white when he smiled.

"Now I believe in miracles," Dr. Pound said.

Nicki flashed Madden a look of triumph. You lost, she seemed to say. You tried to kill him. I have him back. You were never his friend. Leave now.

She started for the doctor, grabbing her purse.

But something in the man's face stopped her. Dr. Pound spread his hands. He could see trouble in the waiting room. He looked from Nicki to Madden. His grin turned to embarrassment.

"He's asking to see Mr. Madden," the doctor said. Nicki's mouth was opening, but no sound came out. Dr. Pound addressed Madden. "He has something to tell you." Nicki looked like she was screaming, but the only sound in the room was the tick of a clock. Dr. Pound said, "Alone."

"We never saw the explosion. It happened too far away. The fallout started two days later. Pink and beautiful. It coated cars and treetops. We were proud the government had tested the first bombs near us. Nothing important ever happened in Nevada. Even us kids felt important."

The woman was a lean, attractive fifty-year-old in stylish jeans and a soft yellow cashmere sweater. Her legs were crossed casually; she rocked one brown boot up and down as she spoke. A discarded auburn wig lay beside her on the arm of the easy chair. She was completely bald.

"We played in the fallout," she said. "Pretended it was snow. If my mother made me wash before dinner, I would. Otherwise I'd eat with the stuff on my hands."

Catherine Madden listened, transfixed and aghast. She was in Stephanie's living room in Evanston. Light shone on the delicate white skull of the woman, and faint blue veins were visible beneath the skin. Red and blue throw rugs lay scattered on the wooden floor near the long couch and coffee table. Catherine was spending Christmas with the family while Madden was in England. Josh was teaching during the meeting this afternoon, Danny had been sent to a friend's.

After the initial stir over Catherine's presence, Stephanie's group had gone back to talking.

The bald woman spoke with a slight southwestern twang. "I've had five operations for leukemia, but never mind me," she said. "I have sons in Arizona and if war starts they'll die too."

A lawyer and an exotic dancer and a third grade teacher squeezed together on the couch. A teenage girl in blue jeans and hoop earrings sat legs akimbo on the floor, looking fresh and blond like a cheerleader.

She said, "I came home from school and found my little brother in the basement. He's nine. He was hiding behind the couch. There'd been a power failure, and when the lights went off, he thought it was war. He wouldn't stop crying."

Catherine felt tears well. "I got them together after my doctor told me there were other people like me, scared," Stephanie had said. "I don't know why it makes me feel better when they're here, maybe I don't feel alone. Maybe I think we can do something."

Catherine took in the room. None of these people seemed like crackpots. For years when she'd looked out on Pennsylvania Avenue she'd seen the Nuke crazies in Lafayette Park. The women who lived out of shopping carts. The men who never cut their hair. The signs screaming, NUCLEAR PARK and STOP NUCLEAR WAR. But this was a quiet living room near Chicago. These were her daughter-in-law's friends.

Something was building in this room, coalescing.

Even Danny had said when she arrived, with that four-year-old frown she loved, "Grandma, is the world going to die?"

"Pal, don't talk like that," Josh had advised. "Those scary things."

"But the monster under my bed is scary and you said it was okay to talk about that."

Catherine had stroked his hair and read him a Nicki St. Johns bedtime story. *Weber's First Day at School.* She'd said, "No one is going to die."

But she felt the weight of the lie. She still dreamed about the man in the dark raincoat, bursting through police lines outside the Hay-Adams Hotel. In the dream the man had no face, just a dough-colored blob. The gun spit flame.

Cherry and lemon danish lay on the coffee table. Steam rose from the mugs.

The podiatrist said he'd decided not to charge his poorer patients fees this month. For a reason he did not understand, he worried less about war afterwards. He scratched his head. "Doesn't make sense," he said.

At a White House dinner Catherine had sat beside the wife of a slain civil rights leader. The woman traveled the country giving speeches. She'd told Catherine, "We knew they'd shoot him, it was only a question of when. Each day you had to tell yourself, not today. You savored every day."

Stephanie was saying, "I don't know why picking up that hitch-hiker made me feel better, either, but it did."

It was funny because once Catherine had been the doomed one. In her mind she was sixteen, strolling up Madden's walk to his house one July night. She heard crickets chirping. She smelled lilies. She stopped inside the rock wall entrance at the sound of Madden's moth-er's harsh Yankee voice. The woman was silhouetted against the kitchen window, timing her comments so Catherine could hear.

"Why do you have to marry her? She's going to be an invalid soon. You know that smell in Grandma's room? You're too young to have to deal with that, cleaning up. I like her. Date her. But other girls, you can build something with them. That Elizabeth Ravenel is pretty, James, don't you think?"

She still heard Madden's reply as clearly as she had forty years ago. "Want me to set the table, Mom?" Not challenging. Unthreat-ened. Even then going his own way. The silhouette had moved away

from the window, and Catherine's love for him had exploded in her
at that moment, so powerful she was sure it could drive out any
sickness. How could infirmity stand before such love?

And yet she'd known his mother was right. Didn't doctors tell
her what would happen? Catherine's father was a surgeon, he insisted
nobody fool his little girl. One day she would start to thin. Her hair
would fall out, her wrists would wither. Her breath would turn sour.
Her eyesight would fail. Her world would shrink to a bedroom. Maybe
it would happen in a year, maybe six months. She would be hooked
to machines. Wires would run like veins into her body. Sometimes
she would look at her forearms during a picnic by Pohl Reservoir,
or at a football game in Indian summer, while St. Johns ran full-tilt
across the high school gridiron and Madden's arm pumped back for
the pass, and she would see the faint blue of veins beneath the skin,
imagine wires hooked into her, imagine those points of color as the
junction of artificial life. She'd bat the fears away. The lake was
beautiful, the trees so green.

The real estate saleswoman wore a beige pants suit and drank cup
after cup of coffee. "I went to my school board," she said. "I told
them, *teach the kids about these bombs!* Why scare them? they said.
I tried the church, the pastor. *Too negative for a sermon.* But we
have to do something. It's not enough just to talk."

Catherine went into the kitchen and slumped against the sink.
Her heart could break from the effort of not thinking about him. It
was worse when the person you loved was in danger. What would
happen if he never came back from England?

She saw James Henry on the news, striding confidently into the
District Court building, fat briefcase bulging with accusations and
twisted bits of Madden's life. What had he learned? She saw their
old friends, the secretary of state, a Georgetown hostess she'd shopped
with . . . called into that building. What did Henry know? "Why
don't they tell the accused person what goes on in the grand jury?"
she'd cried to Josh the night before. "James Henry's not even calling
him to testify. How can you accuse someone and not even call him
to defend himself?"

Catherine put on more coffee. He needed to be in England.
Inactivity was the worst thing. She heard Josh in her mind. "He

never comes for Christmas, there's always a reason." She wondered how many people there were like the ones in Stephanie's living room. Quiet. Scared. Her thoughts were jumping. When they had sex, he liked to insert his fingers inside her while they moved. Once a reporter had asked her, "How often do you sleep with your husband?"

"Like Betty Ford said, as often as possible," Catherine had said.

She had a glimpse of herself and Madden in bed, talking. Lots of nights they stayed up late that way. "They balance each other perfectly," a *Times* editorial had said. "During the day he meets with senators and lawyers, people who draw up bills. She meets with the sick, the injured. Who knows how legislation changes because of the mix?"

When she went back into the living room, suggestions were coming fast.

They should organize more groups like themselves. They should start a letter writing campaign. They shouldn't do either of those things, because they never work. They should run a candidate for the school board. No, for Congress itself! They should ask Catherine for advice. They should forget about useless politics and do little things around the neighborhood. Friendly, helpful things like picking up the hitchhiker. Things to make them feel better. They should go to Washington right now.

The bald woman in the yellow sweater said, "Sometimes I think I'll throw away the wig. Let people see me like I really am. I was brought up a Quaker. Quakers believe in bearing witness. If people see something wrong, they do something about it. You have to make them see it, that's the hardest part."

The podiatrist cleaned his wire-rimmed lenses with his fingers. "Gandhi threw the British out of India that way. And Greenpeace is like that," he said. "Bearing witness. They get in those little speedboats and drive out and stop whalers from killing whales. We see it on TV and pass laws."

The lawyer wore a gray Brooks Brothers suit. "Whales," he scoffed. "How do you bear witness to nuclear bombs, go where they blow up?"

The ticking started in Catherine's head. She sat straighter.

The cheerleader said, "I heard on the news we're pulling out of

Africa. Everything's going back to normal. I don't think I'll be coming again. Stephanie, you're a lifesaver."

Stephanie thanked them all for coming. "Next week, same time," she said.

In Washington, the grand jury filed back into the hearing room. James Henry watched, heart pounding. Juries could turn on you.

The foreman stood.

He said, "We vote to indict William Madden for treason against the United States."

Mark St. Johns had slept and awakened. It was two days after the operation. Nicki stood stiffly beside the bed, near the TV and bouquets of tulips. Madden sat by the window. St. Johns lay half-raised, forearm resting on the blue covers, swathed in bandages that ended in a brown-stained stump. His throat was mottled purple. He'd suffered cuts on his shoulders from flying glass. He could see, outside the window and below, police vans blocking the parking lot and press trucks parked across the street, cameras on their roofs.

The Scotland Yard detectives had left. "We still don't know who set the bomb off," a red-headed captain with a hussar's mustache had said, "Three groups claimed credit. Christ, the things people want credit for!"

Sir Rupert had visited, too. "I swear I had nothing to do with it," the banker had said, white faced. "You believe me, don't you?"

St. Johns had told the detectives about Sir Rupert but not about his work with Madden.

Now Nicki was saying, "You can't be serious. You want to go again?!"

St. Johns held her hand. The burning pain was starting in the stump. He'd need more pills soon. His voice was still weak. He said, "It's crazy but losing the hand made me understand what Bill wanted. If he'd launched those missiles, I would have lost everything, not just a hand. And all those people . . ."

"You had a dream," Nicki argued. "It wasn't real."

"Baby, I'm not doing this because of a dream."

She wore a single strand of pearls over a blue pullover dress with a high collar. "If you're worried about losing me, *stay*."

"Just a few more people to try to talk to."

For the first time since the waiting room, she appealed to Madden. Her cheeks were hollow, and she needed extra blush to cover the pasty skin. "Stop him! He listens to you! Nobody's going to meet with you! Don't you read the papers? The troops are going home!"

Outside, at the entrance to the parking lot, police had surrounded a red car and were watching the driver open the trunk. St. Johns said, "Maybe the French will talk with you. Or the Chinese."

Madden watched the police allow the man back into the car. "Mark, you've already done enough," he said.

"That was very forceful," Nicki snorted. "I'm amazed how persuasive you can be."

When Madden left, Nicki sat close to St. Johns on the bed. She smelled like lemons. His favorite perfume. She forced her voice into softness but the thin edge of hysteria remained underneath. "We can have a good life," she said. "Even without Weber." Her breath smelled of cigarettes. St. Johns did not reply. She said, "I should have talked to you more. Now I know that."

She cradled his bandaged wrist. Her words came faster. "Ever since Weber died, I couldn't even think how to act. Me in that chair all the time. You had no one to talk to. I'll change."

She wept. "I couldn't stand it if something happened to you."

St. Johns stroked her hair. "It isn't because of what you said or didn't say. I need to do this. It makes me feel whole. Nothing mattered to me."

She dropped his hand. He said, "You know I love you, Nicki. But everything I worked for, the bank, I stopped caring. Since the accident I realized Bill is right."

"It wasn't an accident," Nicki said.

St. Johns said, "Thinking about going out for him, I feel like I felt that first day at the bank."

"He can't bring back Weber," Nicki said. "It won't change."

St. Johns said, "I need to hold on to this feeling. This feeling that I can do things."

She looked directly at him. "Well, I need to hold on to me. I'm going to go to the Cape a while."

"Alone?" The stump was throbbing badly. She had never gone to the beach house alone before.

She picked up her purse. "I can't stay here and wait for you to get well just to see you work for him again. Maybe I'll do some writing. A new Weber book," she said. *"Weber and His Father's Obsession. Weber and the Big Bomb."*

She was gathering her coat. "I can still smell him in here. I don't want to know what's going to happen. I don't want to know why he's right. I don't want to even hear about Madden. I want things like they were."

A nurse came and put a tray in front of St. Johns. There was orange juice in a green plastic cup and a bent straw so he could drink it more easily. There was a red pill on a blue napkin.

When the nurse went out Nicki said, "Look at me. I had you. All I thought about was Weber. I look so bad." She touched her hair. Her expression softened. "Remember that summer in Nova Scotia? When you wore that Red Sox hat the whole time? I hated it." She laughed. "Weber was nine then, right?"

"We got him the Schwinn for his birthday."

"He was a good kid. He liked that molasses, remember? On everything."

"I remember," St. Johns said.

"Things were nice then," she said. "That baseball hat. I think about that summer a lot. Do you think we'll ever go back to Nova Scotia?"

"Why not?" St. Johns said.

He felt a little hope then, but she buttoned the top of her coat. She turned. Nicki was gone.

11

The gate guard at NORAD said, "Uh oh." He reached for the phone and barked, "Somebody get down here quick." Five hundred yards ahead, where the access road met the aspen forest, a line of slowly moving cars emerged into view. Their honking slashed into Cheyenne Mountain's normally quiet morning air. No towns were up here, no parks or turnoffs.

The guard released the safety on his M-16 and went out into the cold to wait behind the electrified barbed-wire fence. He was nineteen, from Kansas City. He hoped help would get here soon.

The cars stopped thirty feet from the gate and regrouped, turning right or left until they blocked the road in four rows. Vans. Chevys. Toyotas.

Behind him, the guard heard the roar of jeeps, the screech of brakes. Troops in parkas formed a defensive line inside the grounds.

No one spoke while men, women, and children got out of the cars. One little boy carried a sign saying CLOSE NORAD. The guard heard the click of M-16 straps, the snap of safeties. Tear gas canisters scraped as they were pulled from wooden crates.

From the civilian side a lone man approached, crunching through the snow in an orange parka. Wire-rimmed glasses perched on his pale, narrow face.

From the NORAD side stepped a young major from the public affairs department. He too wore wire-rimmed glasses. The wind tossed his red hair.

The man in the parka spoke loudly, so his people could hear. "We demand to see General DeLavery."

"Sorry, sir, he's unavailable. Maybe I could help you." Despite the freezing cold, a bead of sweat trickled down the major's right cheek. "Could you please move those cars? We need a clear path to the gate. Then we'll talk, get some coffee. By God, it's cold out!"

To the dull grinding of gears, the Dolly Bakery truck chugged up the road and stopped, blocked by the cars. The driver poked his head out of the cab. He wore a black tractor cap. "Hey, what the . . ." he cried. "Move it! I got deliveries to make!"

The man in the orange parka turned sideways so both sides saw his profile. In the early morning the sky was blue. His voice echoed as he shouted theatrically, "We're not moving until the general sees us!" The guard realized the man was posing for a photographer who had emerged from the group to snap pictures.

The bakery truck began honking.

The man in the parka cried, "We're the Denver chapter of Americans for Disarmament. Our tax dollars pay for this place. We own it, we want to get in." A cheer went up from the protesters. The major tried to reason, "Sir?" but the man shouted, "Signs out!" One said, WE CHOOSE LIFE. Another, DISARM THE MISSILES. Coloring, the major said, "You have to clear a path." The bakery truck edged forward until its front bumper nudged a green Dodge van. One protester shouted, "Hey!"

"Reds," hissed the soldier to the guard's right.

The delighted photographer came up to the fence and snapped the angry troops.

The man in the orange parka announced, loudly and belligerently, "Madden was right! He said no to nuclear weapons and so do we! We have food and water. We'll block this road until you close NORAD. We choose life!"

"*We choose life!*" A chant went up behind him. The major cautioned, his politeness almost spent, "We have tear gas. Please, sir, there are children back there." That was when a Coke bottle sailed over the fence. It shattered harmlessly behind the soldiers, but the man on the guard's right fired. A muffled volley echoed through the mountains, causing snow clumps to drop from the trees. Tear gas obscured the aspens. It had all taken eight minutes.

The photo in the *Rocky Mountain News*, *The New York Times*, *The Washington Post*, *Der Spiegel*, *Pravda*, and *Le Monde* showed a tear gas canister striking a five-year-old boy in the face.

Robert Gardner ordered another Johnny Walker, furious at being taken off the Madden story. He hated his new assignment. He was at Joe & Mo's in Washington interviewing a professor who had written the book *How Trends Start*. At least he'd chosen a restaurant where he could spy on James Henry, two tables away. *You'll meet him tonight*, Susan had said this morning at her apartment. As Gardner watched now, an under secretary of state joined the prosecutor at his corner table. A waiter taking orders obscured the two men, but when he moved away, Gardner saw the under secretary give Henry an envelope.

"Delicious, delicious," crooned Professor Soja, pouring red wine. He was fiftyish, with long white hair and pasty skin. He gobbled his veal with greedy, childlike intensity.

"It's funny you called me, Robert," he said. "I've been thinking of writing an article on this new trend myself."

James Henry opened the envelope, unfolded a sheet of paper, donned his stern-looking reading glasses and scanned the page. His lips moved when he read. Gardner made out the word "President."

Gardner felt another flash of anger remembering why he was here. His editor's voice in his head said, "The problems in Africa are dying down, we'll be pulling the advisors out. You've been doing too many Madden pieces lately. How about something light for a change?"

Henry smiled at the under secretary as if the paper contained something he wanted.

"Now this is a weird little trend going on but it'll make nice reading," the editor said. "Benevolence." He went through the clips. More people volunteering for the Clean-Up-Harlem program. More people joining the tutor-slow-students in the schools. Chicago. San

Francisco. Wichita. Here's one from Los Angeles. The Central America adoption program is up four hundred percent in applicants for kids. Like the Me decade backwards." The editor had made a long mocking noise, like a spaceship landing. Newwwwww socialllllll consciousnesssss," he announced, grinning. "Here's an odd one, I don't even believe it's real but it came over the wire. A motorcycle gang cleans up a town in the outback, picking up beercans and shit. Hey Gardner, have *you* helped your neighbor today?"

Robert Gardner remembered how he had fought to stay on the Madden story. The editor's voice had hardened. "Take a break. Benevolence."

But then Gardner remembered what he planned to do tonight and he didn't care about even James Henry. His heart started beating crazily. Happiness flooded him. I'm going to marry you, he thought. I'm going to ask you tonight and you'll say yes, won't you? I hope you will. And we'll have years together and babies together. Lots of babies, oh, I love you. No one's made me feel like this for a long time.

He wanted to shout his joy, but he sipped his Johnny Walker and over the rim of the glass nodded and said, "Um-hmmmmm."

He saw her as she had been last night, legs akimbo on the floor, moonlight filling the hollows of her shoulders, purpling their half-finished bottle of wine. She was so self-contained on the outside and savagely wild in bed. An incredible, primeval turn on. Eyes rolling in her head. Body breaking into pleasure centers. Stomach. Legs. Breasts.

He wanted her now. His breathing quickened.

But then he remembered he was going to have to tell her his secret tonight and the joy froze in him and he was afraid. I'll tell you, I'll make myself, no matter what. Even if it makes you hate me. Even if you want to leave.

The professor said, "In a funny way, all these little kindly acts are aimed against NORAD and the new President. Madden started it."

Gardner wasn't sure he'd heard correctly, but his interest was piqued. "Excuse me?"

"Oh yes," Soja said, enjoying himself. *How Trends Start* had been a bestseller eight years ago and he had not written another book since. "Does it sound outlandish?" He chuckled. "Of course it does. Even my wife . . . after twenty-two years she's started making me breakfast again."

Gardner said, "I'll be back in a second." He started to get up. He was going to introduce himself to James Henry and try to get a glimpse of the paper. But the prosescutor folded the sheet and Gardner sat down. He would wait for another opportunity. Incredulous, he said to Soja, "You're telling me a bunch of lawyers go downtown to clean up abandoned buildings and it's a protest against nuclear arms?"

The prosecutor shook hands with the under secretary, who left. In his head Gardner argued with his editor. *I don't believe you, Africa's going to blow. The whole world could blow and you want these damn little articles! Didn't you see this morning's headlines?* MENKES AND RITTENHOUSE ACCUSE EACH OTHER OF OBSTRUCTING ARMS TALKS. *Everything's breaking down.*

The professor drank more wine. "Why do you think this all started right after Madden surrendered?"

"You're the expert. You tell me."

Soja leaned forward, reached for another roll, so that Gardner wondered, God, hasn't this guy eaten for three weeks? "Analogy," Soja said. "How do you think Christianity got started?"

Gardner smiled. "Christ had something to do with it, if I recall."

"Yes, yes, but it wasn't only that. The Romans had been running things for five hundred years. Brutally." He waved the bread like a pointer at a blackboard. *"The time was right for a benevolent revolution!* The Christians didn't even know it was a revolution at first. They just wanted to be left alone. It's the same today. People have had enough of nuclear arms."

Two tables away, Madden's old White House counsel, Ken Goldman, eagerly pulled out a chair next to James Henry. They looked glad to see each other. Shocked, Gardner told himself, I thought Goldman was Madden's friend.

He said skeptically, "If you want to protest nuclear arms, that's what you do. You don't start a soup kitchen."

"Ah! Compartmentalization." Gardner imagined Soja jovially addressing a class. "Do you think I could have dessert? Ice cream or cherry tart? Hmmmm. Big decision."

"A la mode," Gardner suggested, astounded at the man's capacity for eating.

"Yes, both of them." Soja lowered his voice. "Molly will never know. State secret." Gardner ordered dessert for Soja and coffee for himself. Soja said, intensely, "I'll start another way, I'll set the stage for our modern 'Christians.' Forty years ago something massive and incredible and terrifying happened. A bomb wiped out a whole city. Suddenly every human knew, logically and scientifically, that we could destroy the earth in seconds. Not only people but animals. Air. Cemeteries. Books."

"I know this," Robert Gardner said impatiently.

"Everyone knows it. I'm talking about pressure and what it does to people. The Romans put pressure on for five hundred years before Christianity erupted. The bomb's put pressure on people for forty years. How do you live day by day knowing you can be wiped out in the next second? The answer is, you divide up how you think about it." Soja bit into a piece of bread. "You decide even though war might begin at any time . . . isn't that what the politicians and the papers tell you every day . . . you decide to live *as if* the weapons don't exist." He laughed. "It's the only way! Pretend to ignore it! Invent excuses! Leaders are too smart to use the weapons! The big war could never happen! The bottom line is, the average person can't do anything about it. The weapons have to be maintained *because they exist*. Like the Romans. They won't go away. People know even if they protest, what can they ask? Reduce the stockpile? Big deal. We can still blow ourselves up. Sign a treaty? The basic problem is still there."

Goldman stood and shook hands with James Henry. Henry's eyes met Robert Gardner's. He winked. Gardner looked back at Soja, who continued. "But you can't live healthily suppressing things. How can you appreciate smaller forms of caring if you accept the idea of the whole world blowing up? Over the last forty years corrosion set in. Families fell apart. People became selfish for pleasure, have fun while you can. These are attitudes that always take hold when cataclysms are imminent. Wasn't there a moral breakdown at the end of the Roman empire? Now the threat has existed for forty years. The effects are systemized so we don't think them so severe. But they are."

Gardner said sarcastically, "How about the phone company strike? You going to blame that on nuclear arms too?"

Soja laughed as the waiter served his dessert. "Okay, make fun," he said. "What else can you do?" He took a spoonful of vanilla ice cream. More seriously, he said, "Madden's thrown our whole system out of whack. Up until now this has been the traditional . . . ha! . . . traditional nuclear crisis. One side throws up a challenge. The Cuba blockade. The Berlin Wall. War might begin. Some people get belligerent and others protest for peace. Most people, the numb ones, do nothing. After a while the crisis ends. The protesters go home. The middle ground goes back to sleep.

"This time it's different. I've been interviewing people, Robert. They've been depressed since the surrender. At a loss what to do. What they *really* want to do is destroy all the weapons, boom, knock out the Romans, so to speak, but that's fundamentally crazy to them. Wrecking the weapons threatening their lives is *wrong* to them, what do you make of that!?"

Robert Gardner realized, for the first time he was paying more attention to Soja than to James Henry.

Soja tapped his spoon on the table eagerly. His eyes were bright. He said, "They won't attack the real problem, but it makes them feel better to go after the symptoms." The spoon moved faster, creating a little rhythm on the table. "They're saying '*I care.*' All this benevolence is people waking up, trying to get back to where they were forty years ago, when nuclear weapons were unthinkable. At what point do people say 'I've had enough'?"

Gardner said doubtfully, "The surrender was critical threshold? I don't buy it."

"Who cares if you buy it! It's the *brink* of critical threshold." James Henry was getting up from his table, gathering papers. Gardner realized that the restaurant was emptying fast.

Soja said, "The great ideas are always around for years before they take hold. If the pressure keeps up, if those people in the middle stay riled, after a while little benevolent acts won't be enough for them anymore. Like those early Christians who started out peaceful and raised armies. We could have the greatest or most terrible crusade in history start during our lifetime. And Madden started it! We could have mobs sacking our nuclear installations! It's only random acts of kindness now, but it could tear the nuclear system to its foundations or blow us to kingdom come. If I were Rittenhouse, I'd pray to God Madden would drop dead. He's the danger, the one they might rally around, the one who could rouse them."

Gardner's head hurt from the argument. He envisioned Madden in prison blues, being led into a courtroom. He envisioned the ex-President stepping into a basement room with a chair in it, a steel chair with handcuffs on the arm rests and ankle cuffs near the floor. Electric wires ran into the back of the chair. The room went black and there was a humming noise and a crackle. A burning odor.

I will ask for the toughest sentence possible against treason, James Henry had said.

Would they kill him? No. Impossible.

Passing their table, James Henry said, "Hello, Dr. Soja. Robert Gardner, isn't it?" When he smiled, all the sternness went out of his face. "What a fine column this week," he said.

The big Huey helicopter swept over the rubbly ridge, angled toward the earth, and descended toward the Mehta Valley. Wedged between burlap sacks of rice, sugar, and coffee, Sergeant Dewey Beech of Oklahoma City, Oklahoma, sweated in a red cotton Santa Claus suit. He sang out in the heat, "Tomorrow! Home!"

Two privates cleaning their M-16s looked up and laughed. One yelled back to the pilot, "Donner, Blitzen! Speed this baby up!"

Beech picked at the white cotton beard glued to his chin. "Up yours, Grady," he said sourly.

He fell back against a sack. The coffee smell surrounded him. More soldiers checked the sacks, filled out lists.

"Can't we just give them the food?" Beech said. "They don't even know who Santa Claus is. They're not even Christians, are they?"

"Coptic Christians."

"Well, what the hell's that?"

Nobody could answer, so they fell silent, keeping their balance as the copter angled down. A stocky, muscular forty-nine-year-old, Beech filled out the suit. The beard itched. At least the lieutenant had let him wear his .45.

"Just make sure you watch *them* when we land, not me," Beech ordered. "Even with the truce there could be Russians in the camp. Or guerrillas."

"But we're bringing food," a private said. "No one's going to complain about that."

Beech snapped, "Just do what I say."

The thin New Hampshire private shrugged. "Okay, okay. Watch them. Not you. But relax. We feed 'em. They get the spirit of U.S.A. We fly home tomorrow, mission accomplished, sir! To Budweiser. Amy Irving. Boston Red Sox. Bettina Farkas in my Chevy."

The heat blasted in when they landed. The privates exited first, M-16s ready. In the cockpit the pilot flicked a switch. A cheery recorded chorus sang, "Jingle Bells" from loudspeakers atop the copter.

Beech cursed inwardly against whichever officer had thought up this stunt, forced a smile, hefted the sack of toys, and stepped into the blasting sunlight.

"Ho, ho, ho!" he cried. "Merrrrry . . ."

The word "Christmas" died on his lips.

All he saw were eyes at first, enormous, staring eyes. Huge. Round. Watery. Gaping. Eyes on skeletons that somehow managed to stand up. A baby cried. He heard buzzing. Flies crawled on the faces. The metallic ache began in his belly and moved to his head. He smelled the worst latrine odor he'd ever known. Soldiers briskly exited the copter carrying sacks of food, disappearing into holes in the crowd which closed behind them.

His brain screamed at him, Give out the toys!

A voice hissed, "Sergeant!"

But another image immobilized him. In an old *Life* magazine in his father's attic in Tulsa, he'd found a black and white photograph of Nazi death camp prisoners behind a barbed wire fence.

The singers chorused, ". . . on a one horse open sleigh!"

Beech bellowed, "Merrrry Chrissssstmassss!" The front line of walking cadavers retreated. The earth was so devoid of color even brown had been sucked from it. Beech laid the sack on the desert rubble. He came up with a blue and red steel robot with plastic pincers and a battery powered yellow flasher on top. "Mister Might" was written on its chest.

The only sounds were soldiers' footsteps as they carried supplies past him, into the crowd.

Beech swatted flies. He wished his sack contained hamburgers. Milk shakes, not toys.

But when he flicked the switch and Mister Might went grinding along the hard earth, light winking, and two of the skeleton children laughed and ran for it, and human language came out of their mouths, he thought, maybe toys are okay. Maybe toys are good for them. He was glad he had toys.

Then he saw the Russians.

Fifty yards ahead, over the crowd and against the background of dirty animal-skin shelters, an olive-drab jeep was stopping, throwing up yellow dust, a red star on its door. Five or six soldiers leaped out, their helmets shorter and wider than the Americans'. The sun glinted on AK-47s.

"I see 'em," said Grady, spreading his legs as if planting himself against trouble.

Guarded by their own men, two Soviets began pulling sacks, food or ammunition, from their jeep. A second Russian jeep arrived.

The Americans and Russians watched each other.

As Beech warily went back to giving out toys, the sun seemed hotter. Children surrounded him now, reaching. He could feel the eyes of the Russians. The crowd was splitting into two groups, gathering about the Soviets or Americans. The little arms brushing against Beech seemed impossibly skinny. The flies went for the moisture in his eyes. A low, cool voice cautioned, "Take it easy," and Beech realized the lieutenant had come out of the copter. He was young and competent and had black hair. He said, "They're allowed to be here, too. Easy."

Some insect bit Beech in the back of the neck.

An empty space separated the two sections of the crowd now.

"They got bullets in those boxes, I'm sure of it," said Private Grady.

"Maybe they do and maybe they don't," the lieutenant snapped. "Do your job." Beech was only aware the music had stopped when it started again, startling him as Nat King Cole boomed "A Christmas Song."

The last toy was a blue-eyed doll that said, "Put me to bed, mommy." A little girl who looked better fed than the rest snatched it and fled back to a woman in white. Beech noticed two men in the front line who had not been there before. Tall, skinny men in rags a grimy, oily color. Sometimes they looked at the bag, sometimes at the back of the helicopter. A forced blandness in their faces alerted him.

"Grady," he whispered, picking at the itchy beard. "On the right. Mustache. Hand going into the shirt."

Grinning, Beech called to the crowd, senses screaming danger, "Santa's out of toys, kids. Sorry!"

"EEEEEAAAHHHHHHHH!!" The scream came from the left, the other direction. Even as Beech swung to meet the threat, coming up with the .45, seeing the two men on the ground grappling, he knew he had been tricked. The fight was a diversion; his reflexes had betrayed him. The attack would come from the right. He flung himself toward the earth, glimpsing the privates doing the same. Grenades arced toward them, dropping through the blue sky. The crowd screamed, trying to flee, and Nat King Cole's melodious voice crooned about chestnuts roasting.

The first explosion blasted rice and pieces of wood out of the cabin. Fountains of grain. He couldn't see the Russians. "Hold your fire!" he bellowed, and, miraculously, no one shot into the panicked tribesmen. He had no idea who had thrown the grenades.

From somewhere ahead, high but discernible through the din, rose a lone male voice from the tent city. High. Fierce. Ululating. Triumphant. Beech knew the tone if not the language.

Mister Might lay on the ground, red plastic wheels rotating, pincers opening and closing, white light flashing beneath the shattered glass on top.

At length Dewey Beech rose at a crouch. He did not return the gun to its holster. Tentatively, a smaller crowd formed. He risked a glance behind him. The big helicopter lay partially on its side, one wheel blasted off, metal twisted and sharp in the doorway. He heard the crackling of fire and the whoosh of extinguishers inside.

"I will be one fucking happy man to get out of this hellhole," Private Grady said, holding the M-16 hip high, not looking away from the Ethiopians.

The flies returned as the dust settled.

Beech shook his head. He knew they wouldn't leave now. He had no formal schooling beyond eleventh grade, but wide experience in Vietnam had acquainted him with basic rhythms of deteriorating military situations. He would not have been able to predict that within three hours President Rittenhouse would be in the Situation Room in the White House with key advisors, reading the report on the wrecked Huey. He did not know other information arriving in Washington detailed increased Soviet troop "maneuvers" in Afghanistan and the Mediterranean as well as on the borders of Poland and Iran. He had never heard of the alcoholic CIA freelancer in Cairo who had passed on vaguely worded hints that the Russians were installing tactical nuclear weapons "somewhere in North Africa" and that these claims, while doubted, were too serious for Rittenhouse to ignore. He had no idea deep inside the Kremlin Premier Menkes was brooding over satellite photos of U.S. Navy ships unloading tanks and rocket launchers in Israel and Somalia.

Dewey Beech had no need to know specifics. Specifics would mold themselves to the general situation. "We're not going home tomorrow, not for a long, long time," he said. He saw the privates doubted him, which would make their disappointment later worse. "By tomorrow they won't be calling us advisors any more. Maybe we'll even move in some heavy equipment."

He was right.

Robert Gardner pushed down on the accelerator. The Porsche leaped forward and he felt more alive than he had in years. *I'll ask her after dinner,* he thought. The light snow had stopped. Under the yellow moon snow dusted fallow fields in northern Maryland. He swerved to avoid an ice patch, then increased his speed.

She wore a full-length black fur coat tonight, half-open to reveal the tight white dress. Her perfume was like a physical presence. She'd whistled admiringly when she met him at the Madison. "On a scale of one to ten," she'd said, eyeing the dark jacket and open shirt, "you're an eleven."

"Maybe I've got a surprise for you."

"What?"

He'd fought the urge to ask her right then. He wanted the mood perfect. He'd said, "Then again, maybe I don't."

He slowed for a village, a few clapboard homes and a darkened Shell station. She said, "Did you bring your jousting sword for my father?"

"I brought my bazooka."

He loved her laugh, the way she tilted her head sideways. "He's a sweetie," she said. "A big old bear." Driving, Gardner shifted to fifth and felt the letter in his pocket and the pulse beat strong in his ears. It had come this afternoon, postmarked Colorado. Same handwriting on the address. *You missed the real story while you were shut up in the coffee lounge with Corporal Morgan.* It could be the biggest story of the century. Only soldiers at NORAD knew the name of the guard in the room. Gardner had made plane reservations for tomorrow.

A big old bear? He envisioned another woman, also black haired, with a soft, finishing-school voice. A pretty woman in a high-necked Boston-lace cotton dress, blinking back tears over tea in a sitting room in Cape Cod. A woman who'd just learned her father had been convicted of ordering the murders of twelve union officials. Daughter of the biggest mobster the FBI had caught in years.

"He took me horseback riding," she'd wept during the interview.

Susan's perfume came to him in a wave and the joy flooded back. He pushed the problem of her father away, at least for the moment.

"Why did he stay a prosecutor all these years?" he asked, not to find out information, more to talk. She snuggled close. Henry had refused to give interviews since charging Madden with treason.

"Two more miles," she said. "He liked it, that's why."

She rested her hand on his thigh; he felt his muscles tighten, respond to her. The houses were small and white and set back from the road. PICK YOUR OWN APPLES read a sign near a deserted roadside stand. He had the sudden violent urge to take her in the car. She said, "Ambition was always different for him. His family had money, they were ranchers and they were rich. But they taught him to work." Her index finger slid along his thigh. "He was a defense attorney at first."

Gardner glanced at her with interest. The hand stopped moving as she nodded, losing herself in the story. "He could afford to be an idealist. He defended poor people at first. Indians. Drifters." She frowned. "Then he got a big case. A gas jockey, he worked at the Esso station, had been arrested for murder." They were on a straight-away and Gardner slowed so she would have time to finish the story. "The sheriff said he'd killed a woman with a baseball bat. The deputy had planted evidence on him. My father got him off. It was the first time he'd gone up against the real DA, not the assistant." She looked out the other window, suddenly subdued. "A week later the man killed a mother and two little daughters. He was still holding the bat when they found him. He didn't even know her. It was terrible." She looked back at Gardner, voice flat. "My father wouldn't take the case. He became a prosecutor."

Horrified, Gardner said, "He's been making up for getting that man off for forty years?"

"No, he's not like that. Maybe at first he felt guilty, but now he just likes the work. He hated retiring."

The driveway brought them past a barn and a polo field. The farmhouse had lots of gables and porches, and Henry's old Oldsmobile was parked in front. The weathervane, a two-foot-high bull, spun in the wind. The prosecutor opened the door himself, in a purple cardigan and reading glasses. To Gardner he epitomized all the forces gathering to destroy Madden. Henry shook hands firmly. Susan, who was not normally demonstrative in public, threw her arms around her father.

In the living room they chatted about baseball and car engines. The furniture was early American, lots of handcrafted silver and pewter on mantels. Portraits of Madison and Jefferson watched Gardner sternly from over highbacked sitting chairs. The paint was finely cracked with age but luminous, well preserved. Clipper ships had brought the rugs from China a hundred years ago.

After a suitable period Susan excused herself. They heard her in the kitchen laughing with the cook. Her presence had smoothed conversation. Now Gardner felt the tension rise, although Henry remained friendly, asking casual questions about the apartment crunch in New York. Gardner was thinking, If Madden hadn't saved everyone all your fine pewter would be molten now. The anger came, cold and hard. Beneath Henry's cultured exterior Gardner sensed the predator. He concentrated on the conversation. He was in the opposition's house, and that was a marvelous opportunity. He could not write what happened but there would be hints, leads. He could use them against Henry.

He told Henry in his mind, There's a new enemy now, bigger than the Russians. The Russians are dangerous, they're hungry and brutal and they're at our doorstep. But the weapons are too powerful. They cry out to be used. You and Rittenhouse and all the people who serve them have to be crushed.

Gardner glimpsed his father in the cockpit of the jet. He heard the voice in his ear. "Use your talent. Be a hero, I'll be proud of you."

When James Henry asked, "Do you shoot?," Gardner said, "I've done it once or twice." On their way to the skeet range Henry brought him through the study and the journalist in Gardner was thrilled: he paused, wanting to delay in this room, to see it. He'd hit pay dirt.

The study could have been part of a totally different house. The early American furniture was gone. There was a low modern couch, a black, furry throw rug, and shotguns in racks over the stone fireplace. Photos lined a wall, showing criminals Henry had sent to prison. Unaware he was being photographed, face twisted in hate, a congressman shot a middle finger at Henry. Tears streamed down the face of an electric-company chairman as federal marshals led him back to his cell, past the impassive prosecutor, who gazed disinterestedly in another direction. In a third photo marshals restrained a lean, bearded man with a butterfly tattoo on his shoulder as he tried to leap over a table to reach Henry. The prosecutor held his reading glasses with two fingers, looking the man in the face.

They're trophies, Gardner thought, delighted with the knowledge but not yet knowing how to use it. Every man has a secret chamber, said another voice in his head, his first editor's voice. It doesn't have to be a physical place, it can be a poem, a song. It's where he goes to be himself. It's how he defines himself. But if you learn who he thinks he is, you will have power over him, power to get things from him.

Among the legal books lining a wall, he spotted Sun-tzu's *The Art of War* bound in red leather. "Greatest lawyer's book ever written," Henry remarked. "The right information is worth ten thousand soldiers." Gardner saw biographies of Hannibal and Aratzu, a German barbarian king who had held the mighty Roman army at bay in Gaul.

Henry's heroes always defeated powerful enemies. On the wall, the prosecutor casually indicated a bare spot between a woman in a green dress and a former FCC chairman now serving time in Allenwood for taking bribes.

He asked, matter-of-factly, "Who do you think I should hang here?" And Gardner, feeling the letter burning in his pocket, knew suddenly how to get everything he wanted, to beat Henry, to break the story.

He said, "General DeLavery?"

"DeLavery?" Henry stared at him, perplexed. "DeLavery? Why?"

He's acting, Gardner thought, excited. *I'm right,* he exulted inside. He had the urge to show Henry the letter, to let the meaning register on the prosecutor's face. But he thought, *Not yet. I need proof.*

His glee was interrupted by Susan's laughter from the kitchen. *He's her father.* The only time he had argued with her had been because of him.

In his head she stood in her studio, on a ladder. Hair in a bun, dust on her lips and forehead and hand that held the hammer. Her chin jutted when she was mad. "He's not so different from you, writer. He prosecutes people in a court and you do it in a magazine. At least if he's wrong the jury tells him, but you can't lose. Don't be so hard on him."

Acting, he's acting, Gardner's senses screamed.

James Henry pointed to the door. "Deck's there," he said. He supplied shooting gloves and jacket from a closet. A side door led to a special addition on the house, a raised-deck skeet-shooting range, surrounded on two sides by thick glass, lighted by overhead white fluorescent tubes and overlooking a small man-made lake. The cold felt good after the toasty house. Henry explained how to adjust the manual launch mechanism. He tore open a cardboard box stacked with clay pigeons. He loaded the shotguns.

"Pull," Henry said a moment later. The first pigeon blew to pieces, black bits sprinkling the ice-covered lake. Henry said, "Try it?"

The shotgun felt heavy and unfamiliar against Gardner's shoulder. "Best out of five?" Henry said. The prosecutor launched the spinning target into the night, and Gardner pulled the trigger smoothly, the stock slammed back against his shoulder.

"Bravo," said Henry with real admiration. "Did you learn that in Vietnam?"

"I wasn't in Vietnam. Are you a veteran?"

He laughed. "A veteran weatherman! I spent World War Two in the Aleutians. Pull! Well! I must be lucky tonight."

He said, as Gardner loaded the next target, "She's very loyal when she loves something."

"I know."

"Are you? Loyal?"

Gardner, crouched on one knee by the steel arm of the launcher, looked up at the shotgun held sideways across the prosecutor's chest. "Sure," he said. He had a vision of her last night, on the studio floor, naked, faint rock 'n' roll coming up from the apartment below, the sculptures reflected in the candlelight in her eyes, rising around her in a forest of white. Especially the newest piece, hidden under a tarp, which she would not show him: an odd looking wide shape ending in two points, like horns, on either side. A sickle shape beneath the covering.

"Secret," she'd whispered when he asked. She'd touched his lips with a finger. He'd licked off the dust.

He saw her beneath him, clawing at him.

Gardner felt himself blushing. Henry said, "Pull." He hit.

Henry said, "She's like an animal, fierce. That's the kind of mother she'd be. Well! Another hit for you. You're the first one she's brought here. She's taken people to the house but not the farm."

"Then I'm lucky."

Henry fired and the target broke into two halves, plummeted.

Gardner hit the edge of the spinning pigeon, which disintegrated before it hit the ice.

"One more apiece, eh?" Henry said. He opened the breech and hot smoke dissipated between them. Gardner smelled cordite. "She had a pet raccoon, Elvis, she called it," Henry said, ramming in cartridges. "I hate that music." He stretched his neck, preparing for the last shot. "Now Brahms, *that's* music. She found Elvis near the lake. Raised him, but he wandered the property a lot. One night he got in a fight. Maybe with a dog, another raccoon. He came back chewed up. The vet said, 'Watch him. There's rabies going around.' You ever see an animal with rabies, Mr. Gardner?"

They were standing close together. James Henry's mouth was asymmetrical, the left side slightly higher. Gardner said, "No."

"Scariest damn thing in the world. The gentlest animal changes. Chest heaving in and out. Foam frothing. Just before it goes mad, something happens in the eyes. They change color, go yellow." He was moving the shotgun back and forth, swishing it. "She hid him. I think she knew he had it. We couldn't convince her to tell us where he was. Punishments, nothing worked. I was scared. You only have one daughter. You don't want to lose your daughter."

"Pull," Henry said. The target blew to pieces.

They looked at one another. Henry said, as if there had been no pause, "She had Elvis in the barn. I'd looked there, but she'd been moving him around. By the time the state troopers got here his eyes were yellow. He was weaving. She screamed, '*Don't shoot!*' They couldn't do anything because she was close to him. He was going mad and she wouldn't leave him alone. But the crazy thing was, Elvis was fighting it. I don't think he wanted to hurt her. He went for her and rolled up in a heap, biting himself. Stopping himself. He must have been burning up with fever. It must have been four hundred degrees in his little animal brain. He was in a ball, screaming. I shot him."

Clouds were moving in again, skimming the moon, and the wind picked up. Gardner felt it through his gloves.

"Pull," he said. He missed.

"That's the way we love in this family," Henry said. "It's the way I taught her to love. It's the way I loved my wife. I loved her when she was eighteen and she was the most beautiful girl in Arizona. I loved her like that when she was sick with cancer, when the bed was filled with vomit and excrement and I cleaned her up. I wouldn't take her to the hospital to die. That's what love is to us, loyalty. You buy into a situation and you don't change the rules later. I love my daughter like that. Can you love her like that? It's what Susan needs."

"I hope so," Gardner said, meeting the stare, fighting at the weakness inside because he was going to tell her his secret.

James Henry smiled. "One more shot," he said. After the blast, pieces of clay pigeon fell in the moonlight and sprinkled black against the snow.

The storm started again, wind lashed the car as they drove, pushed it from side to side. Susan said drowsily, "You see what I meant about him? He's just a gentle old bear."

Gardner coughed. "Sure. A grizzly."

He wanted to see her face when he told her. He pulled into a darkened Esso station in Darnestown. One light was on in a house nearby. The engine clicked as it cooled, and snow began coating the windshield, enclosing them.

She said with her amused look. "Oh, goody. Kissing in the car."

I don't want to lose you, he thought. He felt his heart beating in his throat, fast. He said, "Remember when I met you at the St. Johnses'? I went off somewhere afterwards?"

At once her smile dropped away and she grew still and expectant. "With flowers," she said. He thought that this was what she would look like were she ever afraid, just a slight widening of the eyes.

He'd never spoken about it to anyone. The grief rose in him, but he kept his voice steady. "That night was a birthday. For my kids."

He heard her quick intake of breath. He had a vision of her as a little girl, arms around a shivering raccoon, crying, "Don't shoot!" His shame burned him. He forced himself to continue. "I met Julia at the *News*. We lived together, we were going to get married. She . . . we got pregnant."

Somewhere in the back of his throat a dry ache started. "We

didn't want children, not yet," he said. How quickly they'd agreed on what to do. "We had our *careers* to think of," he said bitterly. "Photographer! Writer! Travel all over the world! Dance all night, New York's a big party." His breath frosted in a long line. "We went to a clinic in Manhattan."

In his mind he saw a tiny blonde girl in a calico peasant dress. He saw a gray stone building on the Upper West Side. Susan covered his hand with hers on the gear shift. At night he stared at her when she slept sometimes, wondrous she was so soft.

But the walls rose around him, still hateful in memory: the waiting room filled with fathers-who-weren't, slouched on brown couches, staring at magazines or not meeting each other's eyes. The girlfriends who'd come instead of boyfriends. The fifteen-year-olds with false IDs. The room was like any hospital waiting area, except here people waited for babies not to be born. Gardner's men friends had taken classes so they could help deliver their own babies in operating rooms. He'd never met a man who'd trained to stand by while the fetus was scraped from the womb.

Susan's eyes grew darker when they watered, and green flecks nestled against her pupils. Wind gusted against the car. The waiting room had haunted him afterwards, during the no-work days, the not-getting-out-of-bed, the empty-bottle-in-the-morning days. In one dream she'd run frantically around the waiting room in a green surgical gown, barefoot, screaming, battering the walls in search of a door.

He said, "While I waited, a social worker came out to do a birth control demonstration. Looked about fifteen. He had little wooden ovaries and sperm." Gardner's lips were thin and tight. Unable to stand the apartment some nights, he'd gone to the nighclubs they'd frequented, sat for hours drinking while the comics made drug jokes or the jazz musicians played sax. "Talk about timing," he said. "I think he figured no one there knew anything about birth control." Gardner's laugh was a hoarse bark. "Maybe he was right."

The snow on the window was very thick. James Henry had said, "Could you love somebody like that?" Gardner said, "After a while other women, they'd gone in before Julia, started coming out. I got worried. Nothing to be concerned about, the receptionist said. But she was really late. I pounded on the desk. I wanted to see a doctor."

He pulled his hand back. Susan's fingers curled on the gear shift, red fingernails, alone. In his head he was seeing a bearded man in a white jacket come through swinging doors. "A doctor came finally," he said. The emotion left Gardner's voice. "All three of them died."

"Three . . . ?"

"Twins," Gardner said miserably. "We never knew it was twins. I was in shock. I couldn't believe it. I kept saying, 'You're sure?' I asked questions, lots of questions. Like I could keep it from being true, like I could control it if I didn't shut up. After a while I said, 'Was it peaceful?' 'Peaceful,' he said. 'Yes.' Then he got mad. 'No,' he said. 'It wasn't peaceful. It was agony and I hate doing abortions. I'm quitting this place.' "

"Where did you go with the flowers after leaving St. Johns'?" she said when he had been quiet a while.

"It would have been their birthday, when they were supposed to have been born. Julia and I used to work by the East River. I threw the flowers there."

Now she knows. There was nothing more to say. He knew he had lost her; the animation had gone out of her face. He realized the heat had been off and it was cold inside the car. He was going to drive her home in silence and say goodbye. He would go back to the Mayflower and pack his bags. Tomorrow he would fly to Colorado, there would be lots of work to throw himself into there. In a curious way he felt lighter for having told her. But he knew the feeling was temporary because he loved her very much. Then the moment passed and he was amazed. She flowed toward him, crying, in the car.

She said, "What an awful thing to carry around!"

"Susan, you don't hate me?"

"I could never hate you." She was kissing his forehead, his cheeks and chin and lips. The wind hissed outside. He was drained.

After a while he raised her chin with one finger. "I want to ask you something," he said. And he asked her to marry him.

Her lower lip was twitching like a little girl's. "Do you love Julia?" she said.

"People you love are always part of you. I love you."

"Do you want to get married to make up for it?"

"No, I love you, that's why."

Crying openly, she said, "I love you so much." Then they were in each other's arms. At length she pulled back. She punched him lightly on the arm. "Haven't I been saying it all along?"

Then the tension broke and he was screaming his joy in the car, banging his fists on the roof, jumping around inside, hooting, singing, kissing her.

By the time they reached Washington, only a few cars moved on Wisconsin Avenue. They talked about children. Houses. They kissed with such emotion at a red light the driver of the car beside them honked indignantly, shouted at them as they laughed.

Just before they reached the Watergate, he remembered he had to go to Colorado. He told her about the letter, "Is it dangerous?" she said. "Going?" Gardner said no, but he knew it was very dangerous if his hunch was right. Something horrible had happened at NORAD that night while the soldiers stood guard in the coffee lounge. Something that had been covered up. Something the writer of the letter had been too frightened to mention.

"I'll miss you," he said. "I'll call every night."

He didn't tell her if his idea was right, he was going to send her father to jail.

12

Madden was alone. He could finally let the despair come out. He reeled around in the snow, drunk. He was at Antietam battlefield in northern Maryland. After testifying before Congress he'd ordered Huff to drive him here. If they won't talk to me, he thought, I'll find another way to beat them.

The sun was setting. On the ridge where he stood wind hissed into hundred-year-old cannon. It whistled past missile-shaped obelisks with bronze plaques, listing Union soldiers who had died. To the north, beneath the soft hump of Catoctin Mountain, barns and split log fences dotted meadows covered with snow and bare patches. These fields had once hosted the bloodiest battle of the Civil War.

Antietam, he thought. Where Lincoln saved the Union. In Madden's mind the scream of wind became the screech of shells. It was summer. In the baking heat cannons leaped on their wheels when they fired. Men in cornfields fell in bloodied rows, cut down as they advanced.

Behind him on the two-lane country highway, the sun glinted on a blue pickup barreling past and smeared the white box houses orange. Light caught the folds of billowing American flags.

A new wave of despair drove at him. The pressure built, steel in his chest, pounding in his stomach.

Madden saw Mark St. Johns's severed hand.

He'd dreamt about it on the plane, and each night for a week since he'd been back. With that hand St. Johns had caught Madden's long passes. Swung squash rackets and signed bank documents. Shaken hands. Poured cocktails. Started cars. Brushed his teeth.

St. Johns had phoned five days ago, starting this mood. "They'll let me out of the hospital soon," he'd said. "I get plenty of visitors. We argue politics and I lose."

The code meant; I've tried my contacts. Nobody will talk to you. Not the Chinese. Not the French. St. Johns had added, voice strong, "Whatever you decide, I'm in. I'll patch things up with Nicki."

Madden ran his gloved hand over the smooth barrels of the six-pounder cannon. Mark St. Johns's voice deepened and became Goldman's. *You won't be able to address the UN. Rittenhouse is blocking your appearance.*

Madden had asked, overriding his disappointment, "And the networks? When can you get me on?"

Goldman's voice had grown embarrassed. "Look, they're not going to let you make a speech, no speech. It's out. They'll put you on the news, and '60 Minutes' wants to do a segment, but they only want to talk to you about what happened that night. They're not interested in your opinions about what happens next."

"No networks?"

"They're scared, everyone is. The Russian fleet is heading for the Red Sea. They don't want to stir things up. They'll put you on for a minute or two if you give a press conference, but they want to screen everything you might say. I think Rittenhouse or Henry has been at them. National security. Henry's threatening them. If you talk treason, he says, he'll drag them to court too."

"Oh, for chrissake!"

Goldman had said, "In another few months everything will go back to normal. The networks will fall all over themselves to put you on."

Madden had felt the pressure grow. "We may not have another few months."

"Phone! Mr. President!" Huff called him from the car.

The parking lot was fifty yards across the ridge near a one-story park service headquarters where rangers were lowering the flag for the night. He leaned into the Buick, smelled the leather-and-booze smell. He saw himself in the dark raincoat reflected in the side-view mirror. The seat went in and out of focus. His head ached. Madden was surprised to hear the Georgia lilt of the White House operator. Then Rittenhouse boomed in on him.

"Bill! You sound great!" Sideways on the backseat, he saw a red-jacketed hardback book beside an empty Dixie cup. The title was *The Real Madden*. He'd bought it this afternoon after leaving hearings in the Dirksen Building on Independence Avenue. He could see the subtitle, *A Lifelong History of Betrayal*.

Rittenhouse said, "You're at Antietam? There's nothing there but snow and old cannons!" Madden heard splashing in the background. "Sorry I haven't checked up on you before," the President said. "Not enough hours in the day."

Opening the book on the ride to Antietam, Madden had read: "So Madden switched parties to run for Congress, turning his back on his Republican friends, who had invited him into politics and laid their careers on the line to get him started . . ."

Rittenhouse must have pulled away from the phone. He snapped at someone else, "What do you mean, Paris is signing a separate treaty with Menkes!?" He returned to Madden. "Assholes," he said. "By God, I'm snowed. And I'm sorry about the indictment. We never thought Henry'd indict. What a lot of crappy breaks. I ought to testify for you myself!"

Rittenhouse lowered his voice. "But it'll never get that far. The Supreme Court'll knock it out."

Madden said wearily, "Don't worry, Morgan. I won't tell anyone what really happened."

Rittenhouse didn't seem to hear. "I need a favor," he said. Madden imagined him in his blue boxer bathing suit, hair matted with water, on a folding chair by the pool. "It's the Denver problem, NORAD, actually." Wind gusted, so Madden heard only snatches. "Protesters . . . think you want them there . . . a couple words from you to clear the air." Last night Madden had seen the news report:

hundreds of new demonstrators camped outside the installation. He'd seen the gas canisters flying over the fence, the ambulances racing toward Denver.

Rittenhouse said, "Not to mention the strikers at the Ohio missile plant. Can you believe the leaders are telling them *you* want to shut it down?"

The sun was almost down. A station wagon pulled into the parking lot forty yards off, and Huff straightened to watch it. Madden knew every license plate from campaigning. This one was Michigan blue. Rittenhouse told him, "You know what to say." The boys in sheepskin coats got out and ran toward the cannons, followed by a heavy man in a stocking cap smoking a pipe. Rittenhouse said, "Stop them before there's real violence." A woman got out of the car, alone, looking bored.

Madden let out a deep breath. "No."

There was a beat of silence. Then Rittenhouse said, more quietly, "No?"

Madden rubbed his forehead. "I'm not so sure they're wrong anymore."

In a way, he was thinking, Rittenhouse was as much his legacy to the country as the surrender. He often disagreed with the man, yet he had chosen him as Vice President. Presidents, he thought, never believe they can die.

Rittenhouse's voice compressed into a hiss. "I don't think I heard that right, let's start over," he said. "There must be something wrong with my ears, because I thought you said no. I better get myself to a doctor."

Madden said thickly, "We were never in charge, never in control. The missiles controlled us."

Rittenhouse repeated, "Never in control." As Senate whip he'd been very much like Lyndon Johnson. Powerful. Forceful. A fighter who if challenged would dig in, unable to change course.

Now Rittenhouse said, low, so that Madden could tell he was trying to control himself, "They're inanimate. They can't get anybody to do anything. They're machines."

"Morgan, let me meet with you. I want to tell you what happened that night."

"You did tell me. You think because I see it differently I didn't hear you." All pretense of friendship dropped from Rittenhouse's voice. He said, "We both know what happened. You didn't wait because you were afraid."

One of the boys straddled a twelve-pounder cannon. His voice was high in the wind. He shouted at his brother, "I'm General Lee and you're McClellan!"

Rittenhouse's voice changed again, grew suspicious. "Are you drunk?"

"Drunk with sorrow, drunk with grief. Drunk in the hearts of his countrymen." Madden said, "I know we don't agree on things, but . . ."

The receiver hummed, the connection broken. Huff, who'd stepped away so as not to hear the conversation, crunched back. "It's cold, sir. You want a hat? Your ears are blue."

Madden had lost feeling in his ears. He looked the Secret Service man in the face. "Did you study history in college? Twenty-three thousand men died here."

"I know that, sir. There's Maxwell House in the car."

"Coffee? Who wants coffee? I want Irish." His head throbbed. "People thought twenty-three thousand was a lot. It took a whole day to do it, too."

Huff took Madden's arm, but Madden shook him off, walked back to the twelve-foot-high obelisk. The air smelled clean. A sickle moon was rising. Nixon had gotten drunk and prayed in the White House when he was losing his grip. Johnson had retired to his ranch to count visitors to the Johnson museum.

The tourist father was rounding up his boys, herding them back to the station wagon. In the dark Madden heard the phone ringing back at the Buick; probably a Rittenhouse flunky calling back to make excuses. The President is tired. He's overworked and he snaps at us, so don't think he singled you out. He's under pressure. He can't sleep, that's a secret between you and me. He asked me to tell you he'll call back. Think about what he said.

Madden looked at the swirly patterns the wind made on the snow. One long, curving line reminded him of a giraffe's neck, or the trajectory of a missile. As he started laughing the station wagon

152 ■ *Bob Reiss*

lurched out of the lot, taillights glowing red. "Meteors," he said to himself. What a joke. He couldn't stop laughing. "Meteors."

In Madden's mind Lincoln stepped toward him, in the dark, through the snow. He wore a black suit and carried his stovepipe hat. Close up, Lincoln had the heavily lined face of a brooder.

He said, "I saved the Union and you gave it up."

Madden told Lincoln, "It wasn't nuclear."

"Lots of people said I should let the South go, to save lives," Lincoln said. "I held firm."

Madden screamed at Lincoln inside himself. "It wasn't nuclear!" The words echoed. "Nuclearrrrrrrr!"

Madden and Huff walked into the bar. They were near Picketsville, Maryland, two miles from Antietam. Inside it was cool and dark. A man in a red tractor cap played skeet bowling on a wooden lane that cut the room in two. A man in old jeans nursed a Coors Light on a stool and punched buttons on a poker machine by the Slim Jim box, beneath tacked up signs on paper plates: TUNA SALAD SANDWICH 80 CENTS. KAHLUA AND CREME $1.20.

Above the bare pool table a printed handout tacked to the wall read: JOHN BIRCH SOCIETY MEMBERSHIP DRIVE. FOR PATRIOTS.

Huff had said, standing outside in the empty street, "I'm not sure this is a good idea."

Madden had coughed. "You're telling me we can't go into a bar? It's dangerous in a bar?" He'd squeezed his bodyguard's shoulder, muscular beneath the sheepskin coat. "I come from here. It's like Lyle. My people. I grew up here. Don't tell me I can't go into a bar."

They sat at a Formica table dwarfed by a twelve-foot-long floor-to-ceiling photo of the Anheuser-Busch Clydesdale horses pulling a beer wagon. The red-nosed driver seemed to be falling toward Madden.

"A Cutty on the rocks for me and Coors for my friend," Madden said. Huff changed the order. "Coke for me, please."

"Ah, yes," Madden said expansively. "The ever vigilant Mr. Huff is on duty. Assassins around every corner. Only he stands between me and the long pine box." To the waitress, standing frozen by the table, he said in a boozy campaigner's voice, "What's your name? I'm Bill Madden."

She had fluffy black hair and glasses with heart-shaped frames. "You're him," she said, staring. Madden said, "That Budweiser mirror, a classic, isn't it?"

All the way back to the bar she never stopped staring.

The jukebox clicked on. Linda Ronstadt sang "Heart Like a Wheel."

Shoulders hunched by the bar, three workmen nursed draft beers while an announcer on a TV game show cried, "Newlyweds say the darnedest things!"

Madden folded his arms on the table. He felt sleepy. "This is what I've been missing," he said. "Washington. Jesus! I used to speak in these places, five, ten times a day. Bars. Schools. Gas stations. Restaurants." He laughed. "Hell, a bus stop once. The bus was late and we were driving by. Later we got a plane. Mark St. Johns arranged . . ."

He stopped. He could smell the alcohol odor of St. Johns's bandage. He saw the stump with the rust-colored stain.

Glad Madden was talking, Huff prompted, "What about Mr. St. Johns? He'll be out of the hospital next week, won't he?"

The men at the bar were muttering. Two of them rotated on their stools so that, leaning back on their elbows, they could look straight at Madden. The leaner one, who wore a yellow undershirt under an unbuttoned red flannel shirt, ambled to the table. He was Madden's age but harder looking, and he had the swarthy color of a man who spends lots of time outdoors. Huff's chair scraped when he pushed it back. Madden was staring into his Cutty, but suddenly he looked up and gave the man a dazzling smile.

"What's *your* name?" he asked, sticking out his hand. "I'm Bill Madden."

The man's face seemed to float down with a kind of vicious, mocking expression. He pressed his hands on the table, his knuckles were white. To Huff, he said, barely swiveling his head from Madden, "The bodyguard, eh?" To Madden he said, "I voted for you." He spat on the floor. With low, quiet vehemence he said, "They'll never put you in jail, guys like you, important guys, you never go to jail.

You make a deal. Who do you think you're fooling with that trial act?" Huff looked between the man at the table and the men at the bar. The man said, "Lawyers. I'd like to take you outside and show you what I think of you, but you wouldn't go."

Huff started to rise but Madden silenced him with a chop of the hand. He said, "Well, I tell you, sir. I will go outside with you. Yes, I will."

He weaved when he rose. "This is the way we did things in Lyle," he told Huff. Extravagantly, he swept his hand low, so the man could pass in front of him. "After you," he said. "Huff, stay here."

Huff blocked Madden. "There could be others outside."

The man guffawed. "Sure! I need a whole team of killers to handle him. Me and Ed and Harry are Roosians, can't you tell by the accent?"

Madden put his hands on Huff's shoulders. He seemed happy in a way, relieved. "You're a good boy but come outside and I'll whip your ass too," he said.

After Madden left, Huff and the men at the bar eyed each other. It was curiosity; the men didn't seem to share their friend's mood. The man at the poker machine pounded the keyboard in delight. "Straight flush!" he cried. The TV announcer crooned, "For five points, where's the strangest place you and your husband made whoopie?"

Huff started at the thud and grunt outside. The back door jerked open. Huff was moving as the man in the flannel shirt strode in, took his place at the bar, and picked up his glass. Huff found Madden outside, leaning against the building in an alley. Madden's hands pressed hard against his stomach and he was half doubled over. Admiringly, he said, between gasps, "I saw it coming. I was too drunk to get out of the way."

They had to go through the bar again to reach the street. As they passed the man at the poker machine, he swung around and saw Madden for the first time. "Hey! Hey, everyone! You know who was just in here?" he was saying, when the door slammed and cut off his voice.

"Grandpa, are you a cow . . . cow-ard?"

"Danny, a what?"

Madden was at Josh's home. The kitchen table groaned under the weight of Stephanie's post-Christmas Christmas dinner. There were platters of string beans and salad and candied potatoes with marshmallows. Ferns lined the ceiling above the long cedar counters. The kitchen was the heart of Josh's house.

Stephanie said faintly, "Where'd you hear that, Danny?"

Danny said, "Jackie Rosen said you were a coward because you ran away from Russians. Did you, Grandpa?"

Madden had pictured the evening turning out differently. As a warm family gathering. Jokes exchanged. Photo albums pulled out. Danny's laughter as he opened presents. The easy, unthinking relaxation you can only achieve with family.

"Grandpa would never do that," Catherine said.

Josh had been sullen and antagonistic all evening. "I didn't get the department chairmanship," he'd announced almost as soon as Madden arrived. He'd glared at his father as if Madden had been responsible. Stephanie had seemed either overly solicitous, bringing him slippers and drinks and hors d'oeuvres, or about to burst into tears. She kept disappearing into the bathroom, where Madden suspected she was crying. Catherine was at her best, lively and full of stories. But the army of police outside bothered Madden. They reminded him how vulnerable his family was when he was near. At Huff's request the shades were drawn so they would not be targets. He pictured the blue and white squad cars outside, the beefy police lined in front of the house in leather jackets and powder blue helmets. The horse policemen. The plainclothesmen with radio receivers in their ears, at both ends of the block.

Secret Service men had always protected homes in which Madden had dined, blocking the streets, steering away cars and pedestrians. Only tonight he felt like a prisoner.

He'd decided not to tell Catherine about the fight outside the bar. His stomach still burned when he moved, but there were no visible marks. He told Danny, "No, I didn't run away."

"Eat your turkey, Danny," Stephanie said.

Danny needed both his hands to lift his Hires root beer. He wore Spiderman pajamas Madden had given him for Christmas. They were red and blue with the black outline of a web across the chest. Danny wiped a foam mustache from his upper lip. He frowned. "Jackie said the police would arrest you. Is that why they're outside, to take you away?"

"The police are our friends," Stephanie said. She wore jeans and a white sweater over her plump frame. "And Jackie Rosen talks too much. Grandpa was a hero, we're proud of him." She brightened. "Pop, leave room for your favorite dessert. Stephanie's homemade cherry pie."

Madden groaned happily. "No more." Josh looked sideways at Stephanie at the word "pie." "Leave lots of room," he said. "Nobody else likes cherry."

Catherine protested, "Josh, you know cherry is my favorite."

Josh's plate was heaped with second helpings. He reached for more mashed potatoes. Madden looked at Josh's stomach pushing against the table, but said nothing.

When Stephanie had said, earlier, "Dad, we're with you all the way," Josh had leered, "Things always work out for him. Don't worry about him."

Now she said, "I'm so glad Mr. St. Johns is all right."

"Yeah, no thanks to you," Josh muttered.

"Josh!"

"Sorry." Josh's fork was poised, dripping with cranberry sauce and mashed potatoes. He said, "I've been turned down for a job I should have gotten, that's all. It's not as important as what happens to him. It never is."

"Stop whining," Madden said.

"Why can't you two get along for a change?" Catherine said.

The knocking was too insistent to ignore. It filled Madden with apprehension. When Stephanie returned leading Huff, his anxiety grew. It had to be more bad news. The Secret Service man wore his sheepskin jacket with the collar turned up against his red hair. He held a fur hat in both hands. "The Russians have landed," Madden joked.

Huff looked embarrassed at interrupting the dinner. "I'm sure this will turn out to be nothing, but we've had a threat." Stephanie shot a glance at Danny, chewing carrots directly across the table. His eyes brightened at all the activity. Huff said, "It might be safer to move to the basement."

"Oh, great," Josh said. Catherine frowned. "The basement? What did the caller say?"

"That he had some kind of . . ." Looking at Danny, Huff spelled "R-O-C-K-E-T."

"Gun!" Danny burst out. "He has a gun!"

"He doesn't have a gun, honey. Mr. Huff spelled out 'cold.' The man who called has a cold."

Danny laughed. "He did not spell out 'cold.' 'Cold' starts with a *c*."

Madden said, "But 'gun' starts with *g*. G-U-N. See, he didn't spell 'gun.' "

Stephanie had gone white with fear. She squeezed her eyes shut. But when she opened them she forced a smile so Danny wouldn't be afraid. Madden sang to his grandson, "Hi ho, hi ho, it's off downstairs we go."

"It's just a precaution," Huff said. "Believe me, we have the house sealed. It's just that with these weapons . . ." He trailed off. He said, "Is there anything I can do to help.? You want help moving the table?"

Madden answered, "We can do it, thanks." Seeing Josh redden he realized his mistake. "Is that okay with you, Josh?"

"We can take care of it," Josh said.

Danny stomped up to Huff. The soles of his pajama suit made scraping moises on the oak plank floor. "Spiderman will help," he announced. He came up to the Secret Service man's thighs. "I can walk up buildings," he bragged.

Huff kneeled. "Guard your mom and dad. Grandma too." He'd been around Madden enough to leave him out of it. He said, "Make sure they stay in the basement until I tell you to let them out. Got it?"

Danny nodded importantly. His hair was tousled from wrestling with Josh before dinner. He tilted his head sideways and the web scrunched up on his chest. He said to Josh, as if coaxing a difficult child, "I'll play a *game* with you if you come in the basement. You can go back up later, I promise."

"Thanks, pal. What do you want to play?"

In the basement it was chilly. On his professor's salary Josh had never finished the room. They wore sweaters and sat at a card table draped with a red and white checkered tablecloth. Josh sat pressed back against a concrete wall. They used candles to avoid the stark overhead light. "Why," Catherine announced pleasantly, "this is just like La Traviata Restaurant!" The pipes trickled with condensation, and a low hum came from the boiler. Danny had insisted on taking his turtle, Elias, along. The odor of mildew came off the walls.

Stephanie piled old throw rugs near the boiler so Danny could spread the Twister board on the ground. The red light from a squad car flashed across the drawn shade every half second. Danny got everyone laughing, making them play. "Red, I'm on red," Josh cried, his feet tangled up with Catherine's. Stephanie fell on his back. It was more fun than upstairs until Danny announced, "I have to go to the bathroom."

Stephanie untangled herself from the group. "Hold it in," she said, more like a plea. The thin edge of panic touched her voice.

Danny shifted from side to side. "Can't."

Josh let out a long breath. "My house," he said. Stephanie looked up the stairs at the closed kitchen door. She might have been gazing at some faraway planet where she could never go. Then the fear slipped from her face. She crossed the basement to rummage through the drawers of an old cabinet. She pulled out a mason jar.

"Do it," she said, "behind the furnace."

"But I can't wash my hands down here."

In her mother's voice she ordered, "In the jar."

Everyone else stood in stocking feet on the Twister game. In his mind, Madden saw the rocket launched. He heard the explosion, saw the windows burst in, glass shards slashing. He saw chunks of wood and cement blown across the table, smashing the glass bowls, striking Catherine and Josh. There were so many alleys and trees outside that could shield an attacker. A rocket could be launched from half a mile away.

Lightly, he told Catherine, "We haven't spent a night at the Drake in a long time."

It was their favorite Chicago hotel. She said, picking up on the cue to leave, "Second honeymoon."

"Tenth honeymoon," he said. Across the Twister board her hand fitted nicely in his. Josh said, as the tinkling started behind the furnace, "Can't you take him up for a minute?" Stephanie turned to Madden and Catherine, her fists against her hips. "You're not going anywhere," she snapped. "You're staying right here. This is my house and nobody is making you run . . ."

Her hand flew to her mouth. "I didn't mean 'run,' " she said. "I mean, I know you're only trying to protect us, Dad."

"He knows what you mean," Josh said.

Madden grinned in the silence. "We'll *all* go to the hotel. My treat!"

It didn't work. Later, while they ate the cherry pie in silence, Huff came back and told them they could go upstairs. "We arrested the guy at a Dunkin Donuts. The waitress could hear him making calls. He was harmless." But Stephanie still wouldn't turn on the light in Danny's bedroom when she put him to sleep. Instead they played Spiderman Camps Out in a Dark Cave. Downstairs, Josh put on a George Winston record. Sipping amaretto in the living room, Madden told a funny story about taking Josh to a fishing tournament when he was thirteen. Josh had caught the biggest pike, but they'd fallen out of the rowboat on the way back. It was a relief to go to bed early.

Through the bedroom walls Madden and Catherine heard Josh arguing. "I don't care if they hear me," he snarled. Stephanie said, "You make me ashamed sometimes." Josh said, "I didn't know you had time to pay attention to anything besides your damn group, angel of mercy! You know why I didn't get the job? The donors didn't want his son, that's why."

Madden was thinking whenever he was with Catherine he would worry there might be another attack. He would spend as little time with her as possible.

Josh's voice, gruff with the old familiar anger, said, "I can never get away from him."

Madden rolled over. He looked Catherine in the face. "Maybe I screwed up," he said.

"I don't ever want to hear you say that! I love Josh, but he'd find something to complain about no matter what." All the hours he'd spent away from home working hung between them. She dispelled them with a look. "The time we have together," she said, "is going to be the best time possible."

"You look happy." He caressed her cheek.

"I have a lot to be happy about."

Before dawn they opened the shades, despite what Huff had said, and the moonlight flooded in on them in the big brass bed. Madden remembered something Josh had said. "What did he mean, that angel of mercy stuff?" he said.

She told him about Stephanie's group and their good works in the neighborhood. How it all seemed to stem from the surrender. How Stephanie had been getting worse lately, breaking into tears when Danny wasn't around. Catherine said, "Yesterday she told me, '*I need to do more but I don't know what.*'"

"She's never been interested in politics," Madden said.

"That's what I mean. Neither have those others she meets with." Catherine sighed. "Those are the kinds of people Martin Luther King and Gandhi reached. They weren't presidents but they got those things done, Bill. I know you're frustrated. It's what we need now, isn't it? A nuclear Gandhi."

Madden stared at her. Something was stirring inside.

She told him her idea.

Falling asleep later, he prayed. *When they kill me, let her be far away.*

At the same moment, two justices of the Supreme Court sat sipping sherry and playing chess in Georgetown, in Washington, D.C. They liked to stay up late and argue on Friday nights.

The town house was narrow, with plush, expensive furniture. As justices, they were among the most powerful people in the U.S. government, able to block Congress or even the President. They could tear down laws, send men to the gas chamber or save their lives.

They were the absolute bottom line of law in the most powerful nation on earth.

Lawyers liked to boast that the Supreme Court was a pure arbiter of law, unaffected by passion or politics. But the truth was the Court allowed popular sentiment to affect decisions from time to time. In the 1960s it had struck down laws other courts had allowed to exist since the Civil War. Laws requiring separate public facilities for blacks and whites. Laws requiring children in public schools to say prayers.

The chief justice had written at that time, plain and simple and never mind law, "Separate facilities are wrong."

Now the political climate had swung in the other direction. The last holdover from the progressive court, an eighty-eight-year-old Ohioan named Mason Land, moved a black pawn to threaten a white queen. He ran a liver spotted hand through a thick head of white hair. He told the chief justice, "It wasn't treason."

It was late and they were old friends. The new chief justice, who was younger, seventy-six, presided over an activist court where votes were often five to four against Mason Land.

A slim, bald Minnesotan, he moved his queen diagonally and took another sip of sherry. He said, "Check. Mason, I'm not talking about a conviction, just a trial. We're talking about two hundred and fifty million confused people. They need answers. They need a trial. That sort of thing. Can you really say the country was better off because Nixon got pardoned?"

"You might as well be the Pope, talking like that. Instead of chief justice."

The chief justice studied the board again. He was generally in a better mood than Mason Land. Then again, he generally got his way. "Look, if there's a conviction we'll probably get it back, decide if the grounds are there when it comes to us again. It's just a trial, Mason. And I think James Henry has good points."

"James Henry wants another trophy for his wall."

"Check. Don't worry. Madden will never hang until we review a conviction first. It'll never get that far, anyway. Believe me."

"Check yourself," Mason Land growled, moving his knight. "In fact, checkmate."

The court voted five to four to send Madden to trial.

13

Madden stepped out of the car and the roar hit him. It was the first day of jury selection, two months after he'd visited Josh. He extended his hand, drew Catherine into the open. I almost don't notice the crowds anymore, he thought. Police herded them through the mob. At 9 A.M. the moon was still visible above the courthouse, white and fading.

He glimpsed a man tearing a sign from a woman's hands. It read: RUN AGAIN FOR PRESIDENT! He saw two men fighting as police surged into the crowd. *The worse it gets in Africa, the worse for you,* Diane Medaglia had argued in the car. *You're the scapegoat. Let me put DeLavery on the stand.*

Madden looked straight ahead, but knew the view: the Capitol dome half a mile south, dominating the hill; the National Archives in the other direction, on Constitution Avenue; the white marble of the National Gallery's east wing, modern and angular, across the street.

A newsman shouted, "Will you run again?" Medaglia called, "No questions!" Madden was glad to be finally here, glad the trial was coming to a head. The old desire for combat stirred.

The crowd pushed them left and he drew Catherine closer. A triangular free-standing pillar marked the bottom step of Federal

Court. The marble fresco on it showed an early American courtroom scene: a bewigged judge and an Indian witness or defendant.

Madden saw James Henry and his group struggling toward the building, a few feet away.

Then he was inside. The marshals blocked off the doors behind him. The ground floor was surprisingly empty. A man in handcuffs stood, head bowed and flanked by marshals, in front of the elevator. Madden realized his trial wasn't the only one scheduled today.

No, I won't run again, he told the newsman outside, in his head. *It's not the way to win.* The elevator doors hummed shut, and Madden felt the answer inside him, rushing toward the surface. He gripped the elevator railing. But the thought subsided before making itself clear. It had been so close. Madden realized he was sweating. He looked up as if he had just entered the elevator and saw James Henry there too.

He smelled perfume and cologne. A walkie-talkie emitted static in a marshal's pocket. Diane Medaglia wore a blue suit and white cowl-neck shirt. She gripped an enormous square briefcase of black leather.

Henry reached across to his old student. "Diane," he said affectionately, taking her free hand. His tan raincoat fell open to reveal a brown tweed jacket, beige V-neck sweater, and knotted gold tie over a white shirt. He turned to his associate, a curly-haired young man. He said, "Doesn't look like she was in SDS, does she?" Everyone looked at Diane Medaglia.

Henry reminisced, "I remember you on that ledge at Harvard. That American flag patch on your jeans. 'Seize the building,' ha ha! 'Out the fascist swine!' " He patted her hand. Her long red fingernails extended out from under his puffy skin. Madden remembered the awe she had shown at Henry's name when they first met.

Henry said, "You've come around to my way of doing things. Good. But I see you still like these cockeyed causes."

The doors slid open. In the sixth floor hallway, the more privileged reporters, who had courtroom passes, surged forward yelling questions. Madden heard something about the Russian fleet in the Red Sea. A high-pitched woman's voice, which he recognized as a CBS reporter's, yelled, "Will it be war?"

Madden imagined Medaglia on a ledge at Harvard, short hair blowing. Her wide, angry mouth seemed suited to a bullhorn. She gestured a lot when she talked.

Medaglia stepped out of the elevator but turned to block Henry's path. He looked at her, surprised. The two lawyers were of equal height. As TV cameras rolled, she reached up and patted his cheek. The tension line of her mouth broke. Smiling, she seemed more sad than happy.

"I used to need a bullhorn," she told Henry. "You used to respect the law."

"Blumstein was wounded at the rifle range," said Private Grady. "He was finished firing. He thought his clip was empty, so when it went off he looked surprised, really surprised. I could see the bone in his shoulder, white, shiny. And this other stuff. Streamers. Like tapeworms spilling out of his shoulder. But there aren't tapeworms in shoulders, are there?"

"That's enough," ordered Dewey Beech. "Dig."

The soldiers leaned into their entrenching tools, earth flew, and sweat ran into their eyes. Their faces were brown from sun and dust, which coated everything. Chests. Shoes. Bare legs. They wore round canvas hats to dull the great heat.

"I'm changing my bet in the pool," Grady said. "It must be a hundred twenty, on the dot. Check the thermometer. Three more bucks."

All along the two miles between sandstone cliffs, troops dug in the desert. They rolled barbed wire with heavy asbestos gloves. They probed in the earth, implanting mines.

It was three o'clock, down six degrees. It was really cooling off.

"I saw a guy shoot his hand off," boasted Mendez, the willowy private who'd been born in Cuba. "He ran around holding the stump. The hand fell on the ground, twitching. What a dope, shooting his own hand."

"Dig," said Beech. "Bailey, that's a beautiful hole. There's the den and there's the bedroom. There's the tub and shower."

No matter how many times he saw a camp spring up, he was still amazed how fast it happened. Two weeks ago the wide end of the Mehta Valley had been desolate brown rock, desert, and scorpions, with maybe a camel train staggering in from the Ogaden bringing more hungry refugees who somehow knew there was food to be had two miles away, in the Red Cross camp. You could smell it when the wind blew from the west.

"Will they come straight up the middle, Sarge?" Grady asked. All the time they worked they were aware, whether they looked up or not, of the purplish triangular mountain jutting into the blue sky, huge even at twenty miles. At the far end of the valley, high ground at the Mehta Pass. Beech imagined the enemy gunners working their levers, lowering or swiveling guns. At noon yesterday he'd heard the familiar whine of a high flying aircraft, taking pictures probably, but for whom? "Water break!" Beech called. As the men hurled themselves toward the shade of the tent, a mammoth explosion split the air.

A reedy private from Mississippi jumped and then laughed at himself. It was only the engineers blasting howitzer positions into the sandstone cliffs flanking their position. The earth vibrated as boulders and dust fell. Beech felt sorry for the gunners up there. The fight would be bad enough on the desert floor, but the cliffs would be hell. The Russians would pour all their artillery fire into the cliffs.

To the rear more tents were going up. Bulldozers worked on a landing strip. Tanks and heavy artillery came in with the big planes. There were portable field kitchens and an underground headquarters held up by wooden beams.

A big Cobra gunship screeched overhead, diving in practice, missiles visible underneath. It roared sideways into the valley, receding into the narrower central portion, the demilitarized zone and refugee camp, where no soldiers were supposed to be.

Beech wished there were fighter planes too. F-15s and F-16s.

"I never saw a Russian tank," Grady said nervously. "Do they look different than ours?"

"They're lower, near the ground." Lately, Grady had gotten on his nerves asking questions. The private drank greedily from a ladle. Water ran down the edges of his mouth. "What about all those people in that camp?"

"What about them?" Beech said.

"It isn't right, it isn't Christian them being in the middle. There's kids there. There must be over a thousand people. Why don't we fly them out, make them go? What'll happen to them if shooting starts?"

Beech tried to smash a fly on the back of his neck, but it was gone by the time his palm struck flesh. "What are you, a baby, an infant?" he yelled. "I don't know! Stop asking questions! Because they're hungry and they'd rather take their chances where they know there's food. Because if we send guys in to get them, the Russians will think we're attacking. We're not allowed to go in there, remember? Drink up."

In his mind, Beech saw the Russian attack unrolling, the tanks spewing gasoline clouds and dust, the flames at the cannons, the screech of shells, the fountains of earth pelting them. He'd learned Russian strategy was to mass tanks and hit the line at one point. If the line broke, the tanks would cloverleaf around and wipe out survivors.

"Ten HUT!"

Beech groaned inwardly. The civilian standing beside Colonel Paquette was short and stocky in a white panama hat. Lesser civilians in light summer suits trailed him, taking notes. They were too formally dressed to be journalists. Beech guessed government. The Russians would be digging in, not sucking up to asshole VIPs. And this particular VIP's name was Chester A. Dancer, chairman of the House Armed Services Committee, said Paquette. Dancer had bravely come to the front to see the men, to talk to them. Fuck you and the horse you rode in on, Beech thought. I have to live here. I want to be ready when they come.

Beech figured the battle would develop like this. For weeks the two armies would dig in, bring in equipment. All you could do was to hope to outlast the enemy when the shit hit the fan.

Dancer stepped forward and said, "At ease." From his legs-apart stance, hands behind his back, Beech guessed he was an ex-officer. Regular officers were bad enough.

Dancer addressed Beech. "You're the sergeant was in that Huey that got blown up. You all right?"

"Yes, sir. Would you like to see us finish our foxholes, sir?"

The ploy did not work. Dancer rocked on his heels and looked

over the men. Flies buzzed. "Maybe you think you got a bad deal
out here," he snapped out. "Maybe you think nobody cares about
you back home." Grady coughed. Dancer used the slightly mocking
tone of an officer throwing down a challenge. "You're wrong if you
think that. There are places in the world that epitomize freedom.
Gateways to freedom, I call them. The enemy busts through those
gates and he's in our home. Well, you guard the gate."

His aides scribbled, taking notes. Dancer said, "The enemy is
going to test us here, test you. Test your willingness to fight. Test
your resolve. The whole United States, every mother, every child,
every worker, teacher, truck driver depends on you, and we're behind
you."

They all knew it was a lot of bullshit, a speech the congressman
had given a hundred times before. Maybe it was Dancer's stirring
tone, or his stance, or just that they wanted to believe, seeing that
they were stuck out here anyway with no way out, but as Dancer
spoke Beech saw the men straightening. A kind of light came into
their eyes. He felt a little tougher himself. To hell with the heat.

Dancer told them what American spy satellites had seen: Russian
ships unloading tanks in Ethiopia, Russian supply lines snaking through
the desert to the purple mountains beyond. If the name Death Valley
hadn't been used already, it would have been perfect for this hellhole.
Beech saw his old Tulsa neighborhood where he'd grown up. A
picture of the Manhattan skyline came into his mind, and the Golden
Gate Bridge. He saw Fort Bragg, North Carolina, and his little boy
playing on the grass.

No matter how smart you were, these speeches got to you. Flies
crawled near Dancer's eyes but he didn't even brush them away.
He'd been military for sure. "We'll back you in Washington," he
promised. "Send you anything you need, you're the front line of
America, so don't be shy, talk to me, tell me what you want and
don't be scared of *him*." He jerked his head toward Colonel Paquette,
whose icy grin told them he was waiting to remember the first man
who complained.

Cool as usual, Mendez drawled, "Girls."

The men laughed, but Dancer said, "We'll send you girls, a
USO. Why shouldn't you have girls? I'm reporting to the President

when I get back. He told me, Rittenhouse told me, *find out what they want.*"

"Air cover, sir," Beech said respectfully. There was a little silence, but Dancer swelled with pride. "Colonel Paquette asked the same thing. Well, a fighter base has been completed fifty miles from here, I'm pleased to say. And those Red ships I told you about? Our Sixth Fleet's in the Red Sea now too. We'll defend ourselves. Now let me ask *you* a question." His chin jutted. Korean War, Beech guessed. Dancer called out, "What are you going to do to the enemy if he tries to come through here?"

No one said anything. Beech, feeling the heat of the desert seep up through his boots, answered, "Kill them, sir."

Dancer barked, "All of you!"

"KILL THEM, SIR!"

Dancer stepped back and smiled at Paquette. "I think we have nothing to worry about," he drawled. Even the colonel seemed looser. Later, Beech's squad dozed in the shade and cleaned their M-16s again. They dined on beef stew which arrived in twenty-five-gallon cans which a jeep collected when they were through. It took the empties to a dump so guerrillas couldn't use them for mines.

At eleven p.m., under a bright quarter moon, Beech led them single-file through the mine field into the demilitarized zone, on patrol. Neither side was supposed to send armed men into the center of the valley, but everyone did it, otherwise you could be surprised by attack. Clouds scudded across the moon. There were lots of shooting stars. Some kind of animal kept coughing nearby. "Hyena, I bet," whispered Grady.

"I heard clanking," said Mendez, the point man, returning from a foray around three. "Tanks."

"Did you *see* tanks?" Beech asked, his skin crawling.

"I know what I heard."

They saw no tanks, but Beech included Mendez's opinion in his report. The information went from headquarters to the U.S.: the Russians might be running tank patrols in the Mehta Valley. The Joint Chiefs learned it in their morning meeting. Rittenhouse heard it that afternoon.

▬ ▬ ▬

Statues of Moses, Solon, Justinian, and Hammurabi stood on pedestals in the wall behind Judge Murtaugh. Madden sat with Diane Medaglia at the defense table. Four feet away, James Henry idly sipped water from a plastic cup.

"Bring in the next group," Murtaugh said.

It was the third day of jury selection. The huge Ceremonial Courtroom on the sixth floor was usually used for citizenship inductions. New judges being sworn in. The Watergate trial had begun in this room. The jury selection in the trial of John Hinckley, who had shot President Reagan.

Reporters and TV artists packed two sections of pews on either side of the room.

Forty prospective jurors, herded in through swinging doors, began seating themselves in the larger central area, hushed and awed at Madden's presence. They stared at oil portraits of judges covering the walls, men and women who had served the court. Judges in black robes, in repose. Judges with one hand on law books, faces luminous from paint. Bald men. Men with whiskers. Men with hands folded judiciously on their laps.

The somber, respectful mood lasted less than thirty seconds.

Murtaugh's low tones were given added resonance by loudspeakers flanking the bench. "Do any of you know the defendant, or have any reason to believe you might not objectively be able to sit on a jury?"

He had asked this question hundreds of times and was scrupulous to keep this delivery unvaried. For two days the lawyers had been following him up with: "Have you ever worked on campaigns for or against the defendant?" "Do you have a particular loyalty for or against the defendant's party?" "Do you or any member of your family work for the federal government?"

But before more questions could be asked, a short, well fed man in a blue sports jacket raised his hand in the second row.

"I have reason to believe the son of a bitch ought to hang," he announced.

The gavel came down to quiet the crowd. A thin, high voice

yelled from the back, "He saved your life!" The woman who jumped up wore wire rimmed glasses and a red scarf. It slipped back so Madden glimpsed her strawberry hair.

Four jurors still needed to be chosen, and two alternates.

"Jurors nine and eighteen," Murtaugh sighed when the yelling was over, "are excused."

The snowstorm formed a gray veil, obscuring the top of the hill. From the base of the lift Gardner saw her, a hundred yards up the ridge, shooting over a rise. Even from far away the first glimpse closed his throat. She was a small figure in black, building up speed, avoiding skiers who'd fallen, plunging into the almost vertical chute that ended the run. She turned expertly, he heard the ice scrape under her edges. She began to lose balance but righted herself, dug in her skis. She threw up a fountain of snow as she stopped a foot away, grinning under the tri-peaked hat.

Gardner held up an imaginary sign with both hands. "Nine point eight," he said. "The new champ."

"Hey, that's pretty good for the Czechoslovakian judge."

"Well, we like the way you Americans fill out your ski suits. No steroids too!"

When they laughed, skiers coming off the hill smiled at them. Lights came on in the lodge.

She stepped out of her skis. "Come on, I'll buy you a beer."

Gardner recoiled. "Trying to bribe the Czechoslovakian judge? Okay, you get a ten."

They were in Colorado, thirty miles from NORAD at a ski resort called Nugget. "You're going *again?*" his editor Edelstein had protested. "Wichita and Miami dropped your column yesterday. Another cancellation and I won't be able to help you."

Just looking at the flakes melting on her cheeks made his heart turn over. Her black hair fell in a long braid when she pulled off the hat. The lifts were stopping at dusk.

"Any luck?" she said hopefully.

Gardner's grin died. "Nothing. For three days, nothing." He blew out breath in a long bitter stream.

"He'll find you. I know it."

Gardner kissed her on the mouth and grinned. "I'm tired of writing the column anyway. I could get a job as a Czechoslovakian ski judge."

He saw Edelstein's glass office at the *Daily News. I know he's out there. I have vacation time coming,* Gardner had said.

But after three days he fought the feeling of futility. The ache in the back of his head when he stood around the ski lifts and bars, waiting for someone to look back at him. "Stop staring at me, faggot," a man in a blue turtleneck had snapped in the lodge lunch line today.

Two months ago he'd come to NORAD the overt way. He'd phoned and tried to see DeLavery, who had declined. Colonel Choyke, the number-two commander, was busy as well. Even the public relations department had refused a tour. Gardner had been reduced, when he came anyway, to trying to argue his way in, to making calls that were not returned, to buttonholing soldiers on leave in town, trying to learn information.

"I know where to find him," Susan now said, linking her arm in his. "Madame Veronica sees and knows all." She whispered, "Sedgewick's."

He remembered how he'd returned bitterly to New York to an Edelstein lecture on expense accounts. No more Colorado, he'd decided. A week later the letters started again.

"I tried to talk to you at Post's. They watched us."

His heart still beat faster when he thought about it. Post's was a bar where he'd buttonholed soldiers.

"Why aren't you here?" came next.

Driving back toward town, Gardner remembered how his stomach had turned over at the last letter. "Come. I'll find you. I'm scared." He saw he was helpless before the urge. The only time to stop had been at the beginning, before he'd committed himself.

"Our last night here," Susan said, turning on the radio.

His last column, really a note to the letter writer, had said:

It's good to remind ourselves the world can move along without us. I love to take my vacation every year at Midas Gulch, Colorado, the best-kept secret of a ski resort around. I throw myself into blissful routine. Ski till four on Geneva run. Then over to Sedgewick's in Midas Gulch for a scotch or two. Then the biggest steak you've ever seen at the Cow Palace, and back to Millie White's for the downiest, most comfortable most forget-about-problems mattress in the west.

"Listen to this!" she said, turning up the volume. An all-male group sang, with a heavy, martial beat,

> At the Dunkirk Camp at the top of the hill
> If the heat don't kill you the Russians will
> If you've come for war you'll get your fill
> At the Dunkirk Camp at the top of the hill

"Why do they call a place in the middle of the desert 'Dunkirk'?" Susan said.

"You know what Dunkirk was? A beach in France where the Germans cornered the British. No way out. *The New York Times* started calling our camp in Somalia Dunkirk first. The gunners are on top of a cliff. Nowhere to go, too, see?"

"I don't like that song, it scares me," she said.

He passed jeeps and four wheel drive vehicles filled with skiers finished for the day. Outside town they slowed behind a steer, lost in the snow and trotting, zigzagging on the road. They passed a brown pickup truck abandoned in a drift, and a kid in earmuffs on a balloon tire bicycle, pedaling hard.

Midas Gulch was a row of one-story storefronts with neon signs. A snow plow rolled toward them, red lights blinking. HONK IF YOU LOVE YOUR COUNTRY, read a bumper sticker on the side. Sedgewick's parking lot was packed. "Madame Veronica sees the past, present, and future," Susan said. She waved a hand before her eyes. "A man will contact you tonight. A tall blond. DeWayne."

DeWayne was the nickname she'd given a man watching them in the bar for the past two days. Last night Gardner had started to elbow his way toward him, but the man had fled into the crowd.

The clamor hit them when they pushed open the doors. After three days, every overfamiliar aspect of the place irritated him. He knew all the songs on the jukebox. "On the Road Again," by Willie Nelson, blaring from speakers overhead, was E-4. The maritime decor seemed better suited to a waterfront. The owner had sailed on the Polish tall ship the *Kukulka*. Beneath blue and red fishing nets and Japanese floats suspended from the low ceiling, a model of the ship filled a two foot long bottle behind the bar. Paintings on the wall showed sailors in a clipper's rigging battling a storm, sailors barefoot and dancing to an accordion.

Where are you, you bastard? he thought, heading for the bar. Don't you know I'm leaving in seventeen hours? "A Johnny Walker and a kir," he ordered. Amid the noise, two or three people stood alone at the bar, nursing drinks. Tap me on the shoulder. Phone the place. Christ! "Excuse me," he said, nearly colliding with a blond woman as he turned with the drinks.

He was looking down into the greenest eyes he'd ever seen. "Black diamond, right?" she said, smiling. Whatever perfume she was wearing, he would buy Susan a quart.

His heart was racing. *It's you,* he thought.

She let the press of bodies push her forward so that her cashmere sweater brushed his chest. "It's a game. Guess the kind of hill you ski. I bet you like tough ones." Her smile broadened. "Curves."

"That's right," Gardner said. "Black diamonds."

She noticed the two drinks. "For my fiancée," Gardner said, hoping it wouldn't make a difference. But the smile faded to a wistful pout. "You looked too good to be true," she sighed. "That's Gloria, she always meets them two years too soon."

He batted away sick disappointment. At the table, Susan concentrated, hunched over napkins she molded into shapes. Two mounds with a cleft in the middle, small versions of whatever she kept in her apartment under the tarp.

"Two mountains," he guessed. "No. Aliens. With pointy heads." She kept working. He said, "When are you going to show me what you have under that sheet?"

"Sheet?" she asked in the playful Madame Veronica voice. "I know no sheet." Then her eyes moved over his shoulder and she whispered, excitedly, "DeWayne."

He started to jerk around but she hissed, "He's coming here." They'd worked out what to do next. "I see an old friend," she said. "I know you want me to stay, but I can't."

A moment later he felt the man's presence and looked up into a tanned, triangular face. The short blond hair was brushed back above a high forehead and intense black eyes. The sleeves of his yellow and black flannel shirt were rolled to reveal powerful forearms. DeWayne placed a proprietary hand on the back of Susan's vacated chair.

"You're Robert Gardner, the columnist. I recognize you from your picture in the *Post*."

He sat down smoothly, without invitation. Gardner's heart was thumping, but he felt surprise. DeWayne seemed more self possessed than Gardner would have guessed, especially if the man had needed three days to build up his courage.

"Rich Jankerelli," DeWayne said, extending his hand. He plunked his draft beer on the table. "I always wanted to be a writer. Wrote in high school. Science fiction." Gardner thought, he's watching me. He *did* write the letters. Jankerelli zeroed in on the area of mutual interest. "No time for that stuff now. Up at NORAD they work my ass off."

"Oh, you work for NORAD?"

No reply. Gardner said casually, "What's your job there?"

"Punch buttons. Same old shit." Jankerelli shrugged. Interest came into his voice. "You working on a story here?"

Something's wrong, Gardner told himself. It wasn't Jankerelli's words but the measuring eyes, almost mocking. They reminded him of someone back in New York, but who? A woman at the next table brayed, "I'm not going home with you!" Gardner did not taste the scotch when he sipped it. "I'll write a story if you'll tell me one," he said. "Otherwise I'll stick to vacation."

"Skiing."

"That's right."

"Where? Nugget?"

"Beats the east."

Jankerelli slid down in his chair and spread his legs easily. The bright interest stayed in his face. "You'd be surprised how little skiing I get to do here, even living close to the slopes. Work. All the time.

I was even on duty the night they, er, put you guys in the coffee lounge."

When Jankerelli smiled, Gardner was suddenly back in New York, in a basement in the Bronx, ten years ago. The police beat. As a black man sat in a chair, two detectives, one white, one black, sat on the edge of a table, smiling, offering him a cigarette, chatting about basketball and big cars. Gardner hid the icy, delicious feeling that suddenly flooded him, driving out the anger. The frustration might have never existed. He made his face go stony, but inside he howled with glee.

He demanded, "How long have you been a cop?"

Jankerelli said, "Eh?" He stared blankly, then he laughed. "A what?" His grin broadened. "Are you talking to me or someone else?" He buried his face in the uplifted stein.

Gardner's hand was white on the scotch glass. "You have no right to follow me," he hissed. "To spy on me."

Jankerelli said placatingly, holding up his palms, "Come on, I was in here and I happened to see you. I wanted to be a writer when I was a kid."

"Bullshit! You've been watching us for three days."

Jankerelli eased a pack of Camels from his pocket. When he lit up, blue smoke obscured half his face. He said, "Caught." But he smiled. Gardner saw the meanness in him. His admission was a taunt.

Now that he'd confessed he pulled out his wallet. In the NORAD ID, Jankerelli's jaw thrust out. His voice went flatter; the friendliness was gone. "Mr. Gardner," he said wearily, sounding like the cops back in the Bronx, "what are you doing here?"

"Joining the merchant marine."

Jankerelli stubbed out the just-lit butt and shrugged. "You want to joke, that's fine with me," he said. "I get to drink beer on this assignment. I drive around outside the base. Stick around all you want." He stood up. "By the way, how come you spend so much time standing around the bottom of the lift? You'll never be a better skier that way."

The big man ambled back into the crowd. Gardner sank back into his seat as Susan appeared. His mind was working furiously. No wonder he'd not been contacted. "What did he say?" she asked. "You look horrible." Gardner growled, "I do? Good." He hoped Jankerelli was watching, thinking he was mad. He shoved her parka into her hands. "Let's get out of here," he snarled.

Outside, the plows rumbled by on Main Street, and music thumped across the parking lot from the bar. When he told her about Jankerelli, she drew in her breath. "I bet whoever wrote you has been trying to reach you," she said. Gardner said, "Right. But what do I do now?"

He asked himself, suppose Jankerelli had nothing to do with any cover-up? Suppose NORAD was simply curious why he was here?

Then he unlocked the Subaru and saw the folded yellow paper on the front seat and he had to suppress a laugh. For months you worked on a story and then it all broke open at the same time. "Don't read it, just hold it," he said, putting the car in gear, watching in the rearview mirror. When nobody followed them out of the lot, he said, "Keep it low, under the dashboard. Can you see what it says?"

"A New Yorker," she said. "I knew he was a New Yorker. He broke into the car."

She read, " 'Dave's Mobil, by the phone. Route 24. Ten o'clock.' "

"You know what? I'm starving suddenly," Gardner said. "A porterhouse with Worcestershire sauce. A baked potato with chives and salad. A couple of Manhattans. A French red."

"Don't starve yourself," she grinned.

"A fat piece of apple pie with mocha ice cream on top. A little amaretto."

"Let me guess where," she said. "The Cow Palace again."

Gardner smiled broadly. "We have to keep the schedule." Then he had a stab of guilt. "Listen," he began. "About your father . . ." But she did not let him finish. She whirled around. Her eyes got blacker when she was mad. "I told you, my father wouldn't do anything illegal and I'm not afraid of anything you'll find out."

"Sorry I brought it up."

"Sure you are."

"It's you I'm worried about," he said.

"I know," she said, softening. He saw she was crying. "I love both of you, what do you want me to do?"

"I want you to forget about your big dumb fiancé who won't leave things alone."

"My big dumb fiancé?" she said, brightening through the tears. "You mean you found out about the other one?"

With one hand on the back of her neck he brought the car to a stop in front of the restaurant, with its life-size plastic steer on the roof. She had her compact out and made little adjustments to her face. He said, "By the way, there were other ski prizes I forgot to tell you about." He told her now and she said, huskily, "Mmmmmmmm. I like that." Arm in arm they walked into the Cow Palace. It was six o'clock, four hours till he'd leave her. There are different kinds of countdowns, Gardner thought. He wondered which kind this was.

The undertaker whispered with the piano company customer-service representative. The beautician curled her index finger in her frizzy auburn hair. A gold medallion hung over her silk blouse. The actress broke a stick of gum in half and offered some to the secretary from Housing and Urban Development.

Madden knew facts about the jurors but most faces gave little away. The bus driver squinted antagonistically at Diane Medaglia. The chemist sat hands folded on his stomach in the center of the upper tier. He never took his eyes off Madden. His bland expression never changed.

Judge Murtaugh had moved the trial downstairs to his usual courtroom, number 2. It was smaller than the Ceremonial Court. Most of the newsmen had to wait in the hall now.

Only twenty spectators could be squeezed in for each session from the line that snaked off outside the door. The group present fidgeted and hoped something memorable would happen while they were here.

Murtaugh ran his hands through his hair. He kept a glass bowl of peppermint sucking candies next to the gavel on the bench. Taking a breath, he leaned sideways to instruct the jury.

"We are a nation governed by laws and not men," he began, setting the trial in motion. "Two hundred and twenty-five million people live in the United States, and none is above the law. The question you are to decide is whether this man broke the law."

In the grim, churchlike sanctity of the room, shut away from the crowds, there was the sense of the larger world removed, the feeling that new realities could be constructed here as easily as old ones could be defined. No portraits decorated this court, no statues. The walls were bare. An implicit demand for order existed: in the somber black of Murtaugh's robe, in the symmetry of the pews, in the solid, respectful colors the jury wore, no plaids or stripes. There was order in Diane Medaglia's heavy square briefcase by the defense table. In the clock. The quiet. There was the feeling that anarchy would not fare well in this court.

Defense and prosecution tables ran parallel to each other, lengthwise between the judge's bench and wooden railing separating participants from spectators.

Murtaugh told the jury, "In the coming days you will hear many claims here. Remember, claims are not facts. In this court only you decide what is a fact, and nothing is a fact until you say it is."

He let his words sink in. He nodded toward James Henry.

"Would the prosecution like to make an opening statement?"

All heads swung toward James Henry, who rose, eyes lowered, as if considering a last-minute point.

"Ladies and gentlemen of the jury," he began, walking back and forth before the box, "this is a very hard thing for me to do, and it is going to be even harder for you." He was the old warrior called from retirement to perform an unpleasant patriotic task.

"Our case involves the prosecution of a former President of the United States," he said. Despite his proximity to the jury, his low tones caused them to lean forward, straining.

"This is the only case of its kind in the annals of the country," Henry said. "Treason. No crime more excites and agitates the passion of a people than treason. And it is important that we deal with it properly, not only because of what has been done, but for what may happen to us in the future. I intend to prove that William Madden," he said, letting his voice rise, "surrendered this country deliberately, failing to utilize an entire defense system we have spent decades, and billions of dollars, building, not because he believed us in imminent danger but because he was predisposed to do so." James Henry's voice rang out. "Because he intended to surrender all along if attacked!"

The hubbub died by gavel. Murtaugh looked around sternly. Henry, dropping back to conversational volume, "The prosecution will prove, beyond a reasonable doubt, that when he was sworn in as President, William Madden took an oath to uphold the country and everything for which it stands. *But he was in violation of that oath from the day he made it.*

"Because he never intended to defend this country against aggression, armed aggression. Because he always intended to surrender. That sacred oath of office which he took was meaningless to him, even though he was aware of the vast, crucial aspect defense was supposed to play in his job, the job he never intended to carry out."

Hands on the railing, Henry moved down the jury box. "If he did not intend to fulfill that oath, he should not have run for the presidency. He should not have fooled the people by telling them he was prepared to fulfill *all* the obligations of the office, including the vital defense of the country. He didn't wait until the last minute, which any well intentioned President would have done. He knew he did the wrong thing, the treasonous thing, when he resigned."

Henry moved toward the lectern in front of the bench. Before he reached it he swung around, facing the jury again. "I will ask you to watch and to listen carefully to the testimony of the prominent people I will furnish as witnesses; I will ask you to look at documents I will furnish. And I will ask you to weigh the history of this man, established in this courtroom, and when you do, I am sure you will reach an unavoidable determination." His voice rose.

"That for his criminal act, the act of surrender, the refusal to use the armed forces of the United States when under attack, the attempt to turn over each and every person in this court to a foreign power, this man is guilty."

James Henry's voice shook. "I want you to tell him, and not only him but anyone in the future predisposed to let our country go, as well as the foreign powers watching these proceedings, that what William Madden did will be punished to the full extent of the law!"

The bus driver nodded, leaning forward. When Medaglia rose her black eyes seemed to emit light. The bladder shaped nose was like a blob pasted on her face. The driver leaned back, as if what she had to say was less important. She strode toward the jury, more formal than James Henry, stiffer.

"The defendant in this case," Diane Medaglia began in a voice that sailed across the courtroom, "is a man, formerly our President, who came into office committed to the welfare of the nation as a whole and of each and every one of its citizens. He has been charged with a crime we will show has been fabricated, invented by taking bits and pieces of isolated situations and weaving them into a patchwork of ridiculous claims purporting to show he is a traitor."

She was warming up. She carried a pencil and rolled it between her fingers. She seemed astounded that the case had come to court. If Henry would launch into emotional theatrics, she seemed to say, she would rely on plain, indisputable fact.

"Nothing could be further from the truth," she announced. "We will prove it by presenting witnesses, evidence and written documents showing that President Ma . . ."

"Objection!" Henry climbed slowly to his feet. He protested, in a reasonable tone, "The defendant is no longer President, so the use of his former title is inaccurate and prejudicial."

Diane Medaglia waved a hand as if Henry's notion were too silly to take seriously. "Your Honor, it is customary to address a former President by the title of 'Mr. President.' And he *was* President at the time the events took place."

Murtaugh thought about it. "I'll allow it."

Henry sat with a gracious nod. Medaglia turned to the jury and continued as if no interruption had taken place. "President Madden, from day one, had every intention of protecting this country and maintaining the health and well-being of every person in it. That is precisely what he said he would do, and *that is what he did.*"

She planted herself in front of the bus driver, who sat up straighter. "We will prove how the prosecution, by going to witnesses who can only be described as hostile to the President, not only now but even prior to his taking office, has been gleefully involved in trying to besmirch the record and reputation of a great man whom seventy-two percent of the voters chose as President of the United States."

"Objection," interrupted Henry. "The number of voters Mr. Madden tricked is irrelevant to the issue."

"I object to the word 'tricked,' " countered Diane Medaglia.

"Sustained. Both objections. Strike the last two lines."

Diane Medaglia continued. "We will show the problems that developed during those horrible seven minutes after President Madden was informed missiles were hurtling toward this country, when he knew that if he did not do something to preclude wholesale war, millions would die. We will show that had President Madden launched missiles, an alternative the prosecution apparently believes preferable . . ."

"Objection."

"Sustained."

"We will show that if those missiles had been launched, as well as the extra fifty thousand warheads that could have been released in a wholesale war, they would have decimated families, homes, massive structures. Our economy would have been devastated. Our climate would change. Governments would cease to exist. Extinction, human extinction, could have resulted. We will show the effects, not only the immediate effects of atomic war but the aftereffects of these terrible weapons, nuclear warheads and radiation." Diane Medaglia pounded the lectern. Her voice rang out. "The President made a judgment call. That was why he was elected, to make independent decisions, and that is what he did. You may agree or disagree with his act but it was not treason!

"We will show that President Madden thought he was doomed no matter what he did and could not have possibly been motivated by personal gain.

"We will show President Madden's belief that even if there was an initial surrender, no enemy could continue to control an area of our magnitude, and a people with our love of freedom, for long. Domination by a foreign power was the last thing the President had in mind during those seven minutes. The last thing on his mind was this ridiculous . . . was treason. We will show," she challenged the courtroom, "that President Madden's act was not only *not* treason but was an unprecedented act of extraordinary courage!"

The courtroom collectively exhaled as she sat down. "Good,"
Madden whispered to her. "You ought to run for office yourself."
Catherine watched them from the front row, hands in her lap. She
showed no expression. Murtaugh said, "We will adjourn for lunch,
and then the prosecution may call its first witness."

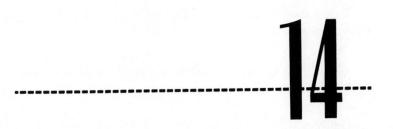

14

"When did you first meet the defendant?" James Henry asked.

Carl Stahlhaber was tall with curly blond hair, a high forehead, and a ruddy complexion. When he had taken the stand he'd described himself as owner of three Ford-Datsun dealerships in the Berkshires, father of four, chairman of the Lyle Chamber of Commerce, and vice president of Pittsfield's Veterans of Foreign Wars.

"I vote Republican," he'd said, leaning toward the journalists in the front row.

"We were friends at college. We'd go to Red Sox games, have a few beers. We went to classes together," he told the court.

The prosecutor's voice took on an edge. "Were you members of any organizations?"

He shifted uncomfortably in his seat. "Students for a Better America."

Juror number seven, the retired clockmaker, started, leaned forward, and stared at the auto dealer.

James Henry paused to let the name sink in. "Students for a Better America," he repeated. "What was Students for a Better America?"

"I know what a lot of people think, and it wasn't that way, not at all."

Henry said, "Why don't you tell us what it was."

At first, Stahlhaber had carried himself with the easy confidence of a well-to-do businessman; but on the stand his anxiety was reflected in a tendency to lean forward and answer quickly. "A community organization. We helped people, old people. We invited speakers to the school."

Henry moved closer. "Like Joe Pride, chairman of the national Communist party?"

"Ye-es."

"And Frank Quesada? Author of *Share Our Nuclear Secrets?*

"I don't have anything to do with this anymore. That was a long time ago."

Henry nodded, understanding. "Answer yes or no, please. Mr. Stahlhaber, one month after Mr. Pride addressed Students for a Better America, did your chapter receive an invitation from the Soviet government? To send a representative to Moscow, *all expenses paid?"*

The courtroom stirred. Murtaugh looked sternly around. Stahlhaber said, "Mr. Henry, I sell cars. I was young."

Henry patted the railing. "I'm sure you're very patriotic. Lots of people are rash in their youth." He glanced at Madden. "Most get over it. Tell us about the invitation you received."

"Well, the Russians were interested in sympathetic . . . I mean, they thought students might be sympathetic to them, their way of life. I was elected to the delegation. We saw factories there, farms. Those big farms, collectives. We talked to military men. The Russians kept telling us they wanted peace."

"And when you returned from the Soviet Union, did you talk with the defendant about your trip?"

Stahlhaber ran his hand through his curly hair. "Sure I did. He wanted to know everything about it, about the trip. Even after I talked to the group as a whole, Bill wanted to go out for a beer. He had more questions. He asked if they would risk blowing up the whole planet in nuclear war. He said he didn't see how anyone could start a nuclear war."

Henry strolled to his table, which was bare except for a water pitcher and a single manila folder. The defense table, in contrast, was ringed by lawyers and piled with cardboard boxes of evidence.

More boxes lined a side wall behind a free-standing blackboard. One reporter wrote, "Madden's table looks under siege."

"What else did you talk about that day?" Henry said.

"Bill said sometimes he thought anything would be better than another war. He said when he saw what villages in Korea looked like after the army went through he'd asked himself what he was fighting for. He said he didn't think there was such a big difference between the two governments, the Communist north and the south. He said anything would be better than all that suffering."

Stahlhaber spread his palms. "I said, 'You don't mean *anything,* do you? You wouldn't just want to give up if they attacked here!' He snapped at me. He said, "I said 'anything,' didn't I? Giving up is anything."

A voice among the spectators said, "Oh, wow!" Henry waited for the hubbub to die down. His practice when switching subjects was to visit his table. He produced a sheaf of papers from the manila folder. He said, returning to the stand, "One more little point. I know how unpleasant it must be to recall these old associations."

He kept the papers in front of him almost absentmindedly, but the effect was to keep them in the public eye. Instead of mentioning them he said, "Can you tell us about the arrest of some group members a week after your discussion with the defendant?"

"Objection!" Medaglia was on her feet. "These arrests are irrelevant. My client was not arrested. This has nothing to do with this case!"

"Oh no, no," Henry replied, unperturbed. "These incidents have every bearing on the case. They relate to the defendant's frame of mind, as I will show."

Murtaugh unwrapped a candy. "I'll allow it."

Stahlhaber seemed a bit more relaxed. "Can I give a little background?"

"By all means."

Stahlhaber leaned back. "You have to understand the climate then. The year before, the Russians had exploded their first hydrogen bomb. The papers were saying we had a bomb a hundred times more powerful than the one we'd dropped on Japan. People were scared. You might say some Students for a Better America were the first nuclear protesters." He added quickly, "Not that I'm saying they were right.

"They were arrested in Boston. A company there made parts for the bomb. Then more people from the organization protested. They wanted Eisenhower to share secrets, how our bombs worked, with the Russians." Stahlhaber was blushing. "They thought if everybody shared, the tests would stop. There would be peace."

Madden scribbled to Medaglia, *not a bad idea.*

Henry said, "What were the effects of these arrests on Students for a Better America?"

"It fell apart. People started getting out. They'd joined to do community service and listen to speakers. Most of us thought the country would be crazy to give away secrets. We'd just lost thirty thousand men fighting Communists in Korea."

Henry finally handed the papers to Stahlhaber. "Can you identify this list?"

"It's the roster of SBA. I kept it as secretary."

"If Your Honor pleases, let these papers be marked Exhibit A. Mr. Stahlhaber, can you read the name beside fourteen?"

"William Madden."

"I see some of these other names are crossed out. Like number six, William Brannigan, is crossed out. And numbers thirteen and twenty. What does it mean to be crossed out?"

"It means that person asked for his name to be removed. Like I said, lots of people got out when the arrests started. I took my name off the following year. You can see a line through my name if you turn to number forty-two."

"Is there a line through Mr. Madden's name?"

"No, sir."

"Did Mr. Madden ever ask you to strike his name off the rolls?"

"No."

"But it was common knowledge in the organization that those who disagreed with the violently antigovernment policies of Students for a Better America could easily disassociate themselves by merely asking for their name to be crossed off the list?"

"Members knew that, yes."

James Henry turned to Diane Medaglia. "Your witness."

Diane Medaglia rolled the pencil in her hand as she walked in front of the jury. "Mr. Stahlhaber, you said you were President Madden's friend. Were you invited to dinner at President Madden's house on many occasions?"

"Not many," Stahlhaber said, in the same helpful tone he'd used with Henry.

"On any occasion you can recall?"

"I don't believe I ever actually went to the Madden house," Stahlhaber said.

"Oh, then I guess the Maddens spent social evenings at your home."

"I was a bachelor then. I had a little apartment. I didn't invite friends over."

Medaglia looked puzzled. "Mr. Stahlhaber, did you ever meet Mrs. Madden?"

"You can be someone's friend without meeting his wife," Stahlhaber said. "We were campus friends."

"I'm just trying to establish how much of a friend you were, since you certainly weren't acting like . . ."

"Objection."

"Sustained."

"All these incidents you've been describing took place over thirty years ago," Medaglia said. "Your memory was faulty on the nature of your 'friendship' with President Madden. Isn't it possible, with the passage of time, that you don't remember what the President said to you as well?"

"Some things stay with you, excuse me. We didn't have any other Purple Heart winners at school. And besides, he went into politics soon after that. It isn't like I haven't thought about him since then."

Diane Medaglia switched topics. "You told us Joe Pride spoke to Students for a Better America. Was another speaker Lucius Stone, senator from Massachusetts?"

"Yeah, he was good too. A real anticommunist. Fiery."

"Were other speakers members of the House of Representatives? Officers from the armed forces? Even a White House lawyer? Didn't Students for a Better America exist to promote debate by inviting speakers from the whole political spectrum? And wasn't President Madden present at these other speeches as well?"

Stahlhaber seemed relieved. "That's what I said. I'm not trying to get anyone in trouble. I'm just telling what happened."

"Didn't President Madden ask numerous questions of most guests?"

"He always seemed to ask lots of questions."

"In your friendship with the President, did you ever hear him utter statements in *support* of the United States military?"

Stahlhaber shook his head. "I'm sorry. I have a general impression he might have but I just don't remember any special thing."

As she sat down, Henry indicated that the witness should remain in the box. From his seat the prosecutor said, "I just want to clarify your testimony. You've been saying the defendant might have voiced both opinions at different times, when it suited him. That the country should defend itself if attacked, and that it shouldn't."

"I guess . . . if you put it . . . I guess so."

"And which did he do when the opportunity came to make a choice?"

The gavel sounded. Diane Medaglia was on her feet, shouting. In the jury box, the chemist glared at Madden.

Professor Frederick J. Venir mounted the stand with a slight dragging of the right foot. The smell of mothballs and cologne lingered behind him. He was a thin old man with a salt-and-pepper beard, thick wire rimmed glasses, and a corduroy suit. He took time settling into his seat.

"Professor Venir, could you tell us what your job was at St. Anselm's College?"

The voice was high, but strong and clear. "I was chairman of the speech department and advisor of the debate club." He smiled. "They kicked me out last year, when I turned eighty."

"Can you tell us your recollection of Bill Madden?"

The old man's watery eyes flickered to the defense table. "He was president of the debate club in 1956. I looked it up when you called."

"Did he win any honors from the club?"

The professor nodded. "I only remember the good ones. He won

the Chair of Argument. That's the top award." The professor turned
to the jury. "In '56 he was best debater, top man. Third best debate
I ever heard."

"And who decides who wins?"

"A panel of students and teachers. Nine people."

"Do you recall the title of the prize-winning debate?"

"Sure, I keep the winners. 'Why the United States and the Soviet
Union Should Destroy All Nuclear Weapons.' "

A collective sigh went through the court. When Henry pulled
out the worn, brown pages, every neck craned. His manila folder
had been emptied for the last witness so these new sheets seemed to
have appeared by magic. Henry's voice filled the court as he read
portions of the debate. " 'Nuclear weapons must never be used . . . New
means must be found for resolving conflict . . . Even if attacked by
nuclear weapons, each side must exercise the greatest restraint . . .' "

Murtaugh looked around sternly. Henry was doing his trick with
the papers again, holding them high enough so they were always
visible to the court. "Can you tell us why the defendant was assigned
this topic?"

"That was the interesting part to me, Mr. Henry. He asked
for it."

"Isn't it possible the President requested a harder topic because he
wanted to improve his skills as a debater?" Diane Medaglia asked.

"Objection!" Henry rose, the papers still in hand. "I'm sorry to
bring this up again, but I must protest the continued use of the word
'President.' The defendant was not President when these events occurred thirty-two years ago. He was twenty-six years old."

Diane Medaglia said, "He was President of the debating club."
The room burst into laughter.

Murtaugh said, "If you want to make jokes, Miss Medaglia, there's
a club on Connecticut Avenue for aspiring comedians. Mr. Henry,
I explained before. 'President' is allowable."

Medaglia repeated the question and Venir said, "It's possible he
might have wanted to hone his skills."

"Your memory seems clear on certain details and foggy on other
ones."

He laughed. "Miss Medaglia. If you're trying to say the brain cells are dying, sorry. You know how many thousands of students I had in fifty-two years? I remember winners, lots of things about winners. When we get away from winners, well, you wouldn't want me to say I remember something I don't, would you?"

"Of course not. But, Professor, didn't President Madden also choose as a topic 'Why the Constitution Is the Greatest Government Document Ever Written'? And 'Why President Truman Was Right to Use the Atomic Bomb in Japan'?"

Venir smiled. "Maybe. But I told you, I remember the winners. You could look it up in the records."

She had. She introduced into evidence college records and newspaper clippings. She said, "Wasn't it the purpose of the debating club, as stated in this old brochure, to promote skills, not to espouse points of view? Didn't you ask club members to choose topics in which they did not believe to polish their skills as debaters?"

"Absolutely. Especially the ones who wanted to be lawyers."

Someone laughed in the back. Medaglia said more earnestly, "Excuse me, Professor, but didn't President Madden tell you *he* planned to be a lawyer and preferred more difficult topics?"

The professor held up both hands. "I'm sorry. It was a long time ago."

Diane Medaglia had no more questions. James Henry stood. "By the way, Professor," he said, hands in his pockets, "counsel for the defense has been kind enough to supply a list of topics on which the defendant spoke. Did he win prizes for these other debates?"

"Oh no, I would remember if he did. Or have it in the file."

"Why is it that he only won the argument on the United States exercising restraint if attacked?"

The old man beamed. "He was at his best that day. Carried away, I would say."

The grandfather clock ticked thickly in the judge's chambers. Madden, Medaglia, and Catherine ate lunch. In twenty minutes the afternoon session would begin.

"Two to nothing, first inning," Madden said. Commentators had loved his baseball metaphors when he'd been President. The Russians had "hit a Texas leaguer" in Afghanistan. The French were "sending in a pinch hitter" in Chad.

Madden perched on the edge of the oak desk, half a roast beef on rye in one hand and a 7-Up in the other. His left foot swung back and forth. He didn't seem worried.

Leaning back in the swivel chair behind the desk, Diane Medaglia speared a miniature tomato from a Styrofoam container. She said, "How many sentences do you think a human being says in a lifetime? A million? Twenty million? Trust James Henry to come up with the fifteen most damaging remarks."

She sipped iced tea. He said, "I don't even remember Carl Stahlhaber."

"Sure you do." Catherine cradled the telephone receiver between chin and shoulder. She stood two feet away. "He used to date that beatnik girl." She made a drumming motion with her hands. "She played the bongos."

"I don't remember her either." Madden grinned. "Some politician's memory!" Catherine leaned into the phone. "Josh! Have you heard from her?" She pulled anxiously at her red cashmere sweater. The narrow skirt fell below the knees. "Stephanie's all right. I'm sure you'll hear from her soon."

Madden could not make out his son's words, but the familiar angry tone depressed him more than the trial. The note Stephanie had left on the refrigerator had read, "Going to Washington." "She hasn't called us either," Catherine said. The room was all dark leather and wood, loaned by a sympathetic judge on vacation.

Catherine bit into her turkey on wheat but did not taste it. Of the three of them, she was in the worst mood. She was going crazy sitting hour after hour with her hands in her lap while strangers attacked her husband. She could not join Madden at the defense table. The CBS sketch artist always seemed to be watching her. Twice this morning she'd turned jokingly to the woman, whom she knew, and stuck out her tongue. They'd both smiled. But she knew the instant she showed real fear or anxiety, the image would be captured for the evening news.

Last night she'd talked to Danny on the phone and the boy had kept asking for his mother. Catherine flashed back to Stephanie the first time Josh had brought her home. A plump, cheery girl, tongue-tied at dinner when politics came up, who'd watched Josh all evening with adoring brown eyes. Catherine tried to imagine Stephanie in jeans and down parka, wandering in the tent city that had sprung up near the Lincoln Memorial. Ringed by police sawhorses. Heated by fires. Fed by donors who drove in with trucks of food.

My family is falling apart.

"Why can't you come to Washington, even for a day?" she'd begged Josh. "Your father needs you. Sit in the court, he'd appreciate it."

"I'd like to come." A lie. "I'm stuck grading midterms. Put Dad on, he'll be fine, he'll beat 'em." That had been Josh at his best, polite on the phone.

Ten minutes until the afternoon session. Dress up, sit up, and shut up, Catherine thought. Fold your hands. Nod once in a while so you won't look stiff like Pat Nixon. Remember how Maureen Dean had helped John during Watergate by looking supportive?

She put the rest of the sandwich beside an uneaten pickle. Mayonnaise squeezed out between the crusts of the bread. She did not want to go back to court. She wanted to walk to the Lincoln Memorial and find Stephanie and get her to go home or phone Josh. At least she wanted to know Stephanie was safe. If Catherine were still first lady, a simple call would release hundreds of police into the mall to find her daughter-in-law.

Medaglia frowned between bites. "Mr. President, we can't bring up what happened among you three when you were in London, so how do we explain why she turned against you? Did you call St. Johns last night? Can't he stop Nicki from testifying?"

Madden finished the last bite of sandwich. "They're not exactly getting along," he said.

Tension was going up and they were going over old ground anyway. *Distract him*, Catherine thought. She switched to her hostess voice. "Were you really in SDS, Diane?"

Sunlight spilled in between the half-open slats at the windows. Motes of dust rose against the law books lining the shelves.

Medaglia laughed, a harsh, masculine burst. "Those old student associations are hurting the good guys today."

Lightly, to show support for the lawyer, Catherine said, "And what were the 'cockeyed causes' he talked about?"

Medaglia leaned back, swiveled right and crossed her legs, so her gaze stayed on a painting of deer near a lake. She said, "I'll tell you about the first one. My father was a biologist at the University of Wisconsin." Her voice remained distant and dry. "A scientist. He never paid attention to politics. He never even ate unless you put food in front of him."

With a light, quick motion she sent the cup spinning into the wastebasket. There was a silver Model T on the desk blotter. The inscription read, "Worst Driver Award, love Doris." A framed comic on the wall beside the Yale law degree showed a furry animal walking on two legs in front of the jury. The caption read, "Stop badgering the witness!"

Medaglia said, "He didn't even know who McCarthy was and then they called him for the hearings. He wasn't worried, he was mad because they were interrupting some experiment. He'd issued a joint statement a couple of years earlier with a Russian biologist. Cheese preservatives or some earth shattering secret like that. They kept asking about his 'communist connections.' They couldn't possibly be serious, he thought. He laughed at them. He kept saying, 'It was only cheese.' "

Madden came around the desk and laid his hand on her shoulder. "What happened to him?"

Her voice had no tone. "He worked as a night watchman at first. During the day he did experiments in the house. After a couple of months he hanged himself. I found him."

A bailiff stuck his head in the door. "Two minutes," he said.

In a clear, ringing voice James Henry announced, "Nicole St. Johns!"

Catherine sucked in her breath. She was shocked at the change in her old friend. Eyes hidden by a black wide-brimmed hat, Nicki moved with the side-to-side gait of an old woman. The skin sagged on her forearms. Touring Greece with Madden once, Catherine had been struck by the widows in black she'd seen in the countryside. They'd seemed dried out, used up.

The prosecutor approached the witness box with delicacy. He cleared his throat.

"How long have you known the defendant?"

"Almost forty years." The natural hoarseness of her voice had deepened.

"Were you friends?"

"Can I have a drink of water? I need a drink of water."

Henry poured from the pitcher that had been in front of her all along. Her hand shook as she drank. She nodded. "Friends."

Henry leaned against the witness box, close, calming. "Did you attend a party with Congressman and Mrs. Madden on the night of February ninth, 1968? At the home of Abigail Cook in Boston?"

Catherine shut her eyes. What had Diane Medaglia said? "James Henry strings together the worst moments"?

Catherine saw the three-story Louisburg Square mansion of Abigail Cook. Socialite and widow of the governor. She saw the bay windows of the dining room. An oil portrait of Cotton Mather glared out from above the crackling fireplace.

Nicki listed the guests. "Waldo Fay, the painter. His date, I don't remember her name, a stewardness or nurse. A French diplomat, Antoine Suplee. He's in Ottawa now, the French ambassador. And his wife."

The courtroom seemed hotter. How can Nicki testify against him? Catherine thought. Against all of us?

James Henry pressed the tips of his fingers together. "Do you recall a conversation that took place that night concerning nuclear war between the United States and the Soviet Union?"

Nicki had been such a fluent, easy talker before Weber's death. Now her words came out choked. "Waldo Fay started it," Nicki said. "He'd been in the Lincoln Brigade in the Spanish Civil War, fighting Franco."

Catherine tried to imagine how she would feel if Josh had died instead of Weber. A wave of faintness refocused her attention on the stand.

"Fay was flamboyant," Nicki said. "He used to wear a beret, even in the house. He was drinking. A lot. He kept talking about Hiroshima." She imitated him. *"The only way to keep the planet from blowing up is world government!"*

"Go on."

"He kept saying it. Waving his arms around, and he was smoking those awful black cigars." Nicki's voice was growing stronger with conviction. "Antoine was annoyed. He said, 'How do we *get* this world government?' Waldo started making predictions." She drank more water. "The superpowers would combine. Communists were becoming more capitalist and vice versa anyway. Soon little countries would have the bomb, and world government would be the only way out." No more water came out of the pitcher. "It's empty," she said.

"Did the defendant take part in the conversation?" Henry prompted after getting more water.

"Oh, he liked it. Sided with Waldo. He said we could have a world government easily, if we surrendered to the Russians. He said it wouldn't be so bad."

Murtaugh had to use the gavel. A reporter rushed for the door.

After a pause Henry said, slightly more softly, "Those were his exact words? 'Surrender'?"

Nicki talked more quickly. "I was shocked. I remember it clearly. He said how it could be done. He said we could call the Russians or meet with them and tell them we wouldn't fight. He said we'd explain we were doing it for peace. It would be hard at first, we would have to make sacrifices. But it would be for the greater good. After a while both countries would mesh. You wouldn't be able to tell Russians and Americans apart. It made me sick."

Catherine squeezed her eyes closed. The preposterousness of the testimony was making her ill. She wanted to cry out, *You're twisting everything!* How could the jury believe what Nicki was saying? How could Nicki believe it?

In her mind, Catherine saw Waldo Fay that night in his blue beret and leather vest. He had delicate wrists, like a girl's. He waved them in the air when he spoke. She saw her husband looking into his glass as Fay went on and on. Growing angrier. All of them. Madden had been pretty drunk himself. Finally he'd burst out, "Sure! All we have to do is surrender! It'll be great. We'll eat borscht and black bread under pictures of Engels. We'll rename monuments in Washington! The Lenin Memorial." He'd started calling everyone at the table comrade. "More wine, please, comrade butler!"

Could Nicki really have taken him seriously?

Catherine thought. What's happening to us?

Henry had stationed himself between the witness and jury box. The chemist's fists were clenched on his knees. "I want to make sure I heard you correctly," Henry said. "Forgive me for asking so many questions, it must be hard to talk about an old friend. But the defendant said the surrender would come when we called the Russians?"

"Yes."

"On the telephone?"

With unexpected humor, Nicki said, "How else do you call people?" A smattering of laughter rippled through the audience, and even Henry smiled, his point scored.

Dizzy, Catherine saw Diane Medaglia in the living room last night, in the house they'd rented in Potomac for the duration of the trial. The lawyer had looked somber. "Fay died seven years ago. Nobody remembers the stewardess. Abigail Cook says she was in the kitchen with the butler during the conversation. The Frenchman remembers, I'm sure of it, but he says he doesn't. Diplomats," she said with disgust. "He's probably under orders. That leaves St. Johns, but we have to wait until I can call witnesses."

There were places in your body where painful thoughts collected. They were a physical presence in the back of her mouth and between her eyes. She wanted to weep but held it in. What amazed her most was that she could not be angry. Once at Cape Cod she'd stayed up all night with Nicki, walking on the beach. The men had been in the cottage, asleep. The moon had been a yellow funnel of light on the water. The shore had smelled of wild sea grass that grew behind the dunes. Nicki had told her about growing up in Manhattan on the East Side. About the coming-out parties at sixteen and the private girls' schools and her first meeting with Mark St. Johns. She'd met him at a fundraiser at the Metropolitan Museum of Art. He'd still been at Columbia but had been sent as representative of the bank. He didn't talk much but there was something solid about him. Confidence. Nicki had said, "I liked his eyes." Later, the library at the White House had featured a special shelf of oversized children's books by Nicki, with pastel covers. The little boys in the drawings wore glasses like Weber's.

The pain spread to the back of Catherine's head.

Diane Medaglia was cross-examining now. "Didn't you attend other dinner parties with the Maddens, over the years?" she asked. "Did you ever hear the President utter opinions like that again?"

To a whole series of questions inferring faulty memory, Nicki stuck to her story with strengthening conviction. Medaglia was not making inroads against the testimony. To Catherine it was obvious Nicki's emotional delivery was overpowering Medaglia's dry, chipping-away style.

Medaglia seemed to realize it too. A light sheen had broken out on her forehead. Henry had brought out Weber's death and she knew she should go easy, but Nicki was beating her. She strolled to the desk and stared down. She didn't seem to be reading anything. Catherine guessed she was coming to a decision.

"Mrs. St. Johns," Medaglia resumed, with an odd quietness in her voice. "What if I were to tell you," she paused and her voice rose, "that on the night of that dinner party President Madden was a *paid agent of the Soviets?*"

The uproar drowned out the gavel. Reporters leaned forward, writing frantically. Murtaugh swiveled and stared, dumbfounded. James Henry was half out of his chair.

Catherine understood what was about to happen. She prayed the gamble would work.

"That's right," Medaglia confirmed, talking faster, nodding. "A spy. They paid him in rubles. He'd been working for them for years, since he was a boy." Henry figured it out and he was up and objecting. This was irrelevant, he said. If the defense had this information, the prosecution should have been supplied with it. At the bench Medaglia, Henry, and Murtaugh whispered, and Medaglia must have been allowed to keep going because she said, ". . . since he was a boy." She began to wave her arms a little. "In fact, the butler worked for the KGB. So did Abigail Cook. The President had bank accounts in Switzerland. Big bank accounts. And every night he got on the ham radio in his basement and personally reported to Mr. Khrushchev. *Do you believe that, Mrs. St. Johns?*"

"No, you're making fun . . ."

Nicki's mouth opened and closed as the trap became obvious. Catherine sank back with relief.

Medaglia suggested, "Making fun of you?" She turned to the jury but addressed Nicki. The dryness was gone from her voice. "You mean it's possible to say something and not believe it? Mrs. St. Johns, haven't you ever been at a party, haven't *you* ever engaged in conversation on a facetious basis? Isn't it a fact that you hear things from people that are so ridiculous sometimes you join in with them, tongue in cheek, to make them appear *more* ridiculous?"

"I know what I heard."

"Oh, come on. Isn't that exactly the mood President Madden was in that night, goaded by Mr. Fay? Isn't it possible that when the President made his wild remarks that night, words you never heard him repeat in later years, that his point was *not* that he wished those things to happen but that he was trying to make a point exactly the opposite of the one you claim to remember?"

Nicki looked directly into Diane Medaglia's eyes. "No."

James Henry followed up. "Mrs. St. Johns, do you know the difference between a joke and a frank and true statement of belief?"

"I certainly do."

She did not look at Catherine as she left the court.

Madden wanted to drive past the mall before going home. The tents seemed to have multiplied since last week. Smoke from wood fires hung in the freezing dusk, rising to half obscure the middle of the Washington Monument a quarter mile away. Police walking German shepherds shooed men in a pickup truck away from the curb. Catherine saw a shotgun rack in back, empty. A sign on the truck read HANG HIM.

She rolled down the window, catching a glimpse of curly blond hair. The woman turned. She wasn't Stephanie. Catherine kept seeing Nicki's face, eyes red, skin sallow as if she were sick. She saw the fingers gripping the stand.

At home, after Madden went to sleep early, Catherine rummaged in her study desk. Her appointment calendar had been a gift from the Speaker of the House. A gold-leaf cover opened in on expensive color prints of her favorite parts of the country. The Rocky Mountains. New England in the fall. After a while she realized she'd been flipping pages for two hours, reliving the speeches, meetings, and trips.

The phone had remained silent all evening. No word from Stephanie or Josh. In her mind, Catherine saw Nicki's face again, only younger, fuller. Smiling and framed by the sea.

In the back of the book, in neatly looped script penned by Catherine's secretary, she found a list of organizations to which she'd spoken. A Sierra Club chapter in Omaha. A working mothers' cooperative in Providence. Hospitals. Orphanages. High schools. Clubs.

Catherine knew what she had to do. The clock chimed nine. She turned to the list of phone numbers, to the very first A. She felt like she was back in the White House for the first time in months. Stephanie and Nicki had shown her what to do. She reached for the phone.

15

In the dark the men leaned forward, concentrating. The slide projector clicked and a voice breathed, "Dear God." The screen showed a bay from high up, and an aircraft carrier. A voice with an Eastern European accent said, "Yak-36s on deck."

President Rittenhouse's hideaway office in the Executive Office Building smelled of coffee and cigarettes. There was no conference table, so his senior cabinet advisors sat on armchairs or a couch. As the slides changed, the accented voice drove at them, flat and businesslike, from behind the projector's light.

The screen showed a close-up of the Yaks, their wings gleaming as they launched off the carrier. "Vertical takeoff and landing. They carry ATOLL missiles." The projector clicked. The voice said, "The T-72 is the most powerful tank in Africa south of the Sahara. The ones you're looking at are equipped with one-hundred-and-twenty-millimeter guns."

Grim nods met the words, and muttering. They saw Russian troops on gangplanks, disembarking. They saw ground-to-air missile complexes, and more being built. "We estimate eight thousand new Soviet airborne troops arrived in the Ogaden last week."

When the lights came on, there was a pained, troubled silence. Rittenhouse sat in a leather club chair set slightly off from the others.

He looked over the men he had summoned. The secretary of defense, Harold Sonnenfeld, made notes with a gold pen, sitting on the couch. He was a fastidious man with a soldierly bearing. His nails were buffed. Secretary of State Warren Pell sat beside him. A holdover from the Madden administration, his recent bout with cancer left a lingering cough. Before the slide show he'd reported on Soviet successes in Europe in arranging an upcoming conference to discuss limitations in nuclear arms.

Also present were the head of the Joint Chiefs of Staff, the CIA chief, and a businessman friend of Rittenhouse's who often attended high-level meetings and whose advice the President frequently sought.

The man who had been speaking sauntered back to his chair. He was a stocky, broad-featured Slav with ginger hair and sandy eyebrows. Richard Szokan was chairman of the National Security Council, a former Princeton professor who had come to the United States from Czechoslovakia in 1951.

He lit a pipe and smoke curled upward. The furniture was sparse, Finnish whitewood. The rugs were Scandinavian, cream colored and expensive. A portrait of Andrew Jackson hung over the desk.

Szokan turned to Rittenhouse, who sat diagonally across the room with his hands hanging over the arms of his chair. He said, "May I be blunt, Mr. President? I believe we should deploy the Beasley in the Mehta Valley."

A collective intaking of breath. The Beasley was a tactical nuclear weapon designed for use on the battlefield. It could be fired in a common artillery shell. It had long been used by NATO in Germany.

Szokan counted arguments on his fingers as the pipe smoked. "Strong action on our part will lessen escalation. We must raise the Soviet estimate of the cost of their aggression." He addressed himself to Rittenhouse. He reasoned, "Africa is the perfect place to deploy these weapons. The valley holds little importance to Moscow. They are only testing us. They will back off if they believe we are serious. Conventional escalation doesn't appear to be doing the trick. The problem is, the Russians don't believe we will risk a full-scale encounter. They must understand we'd prefer strategic exchange to surrender."

"Strategic exchange" meant nuclear exchange. All the men felt Madden's presence in the room.

Rittenhouse leaned sideways and nodded. He meant he'd heard the argument, not that he agreed.

The chairman of the Joint Chiefs of Staff, Admiral Jeb Tunney, pushed himself to the edge of the couch. He'd been a first lieutenant on the *California*, which the Japanese had sunk in the surprise attack on Pearl Harbor in 1941. He said gruffly, "It makes no sense to use nuclear in a valley. Use nuclear in a valley and you kill everyone, the way the radiation spreads. Your own men too."

"I don't mean to be callous, but that is the ideal threat for us to make," Szokan pressed in his dry academic voice. "Soviet moves are always probing at first. If we do not resist them early and cause them to back down, their commitment grows." He relit the pipe. Rittenhouse had been replacing Madden's old staff with his own, and Szokan had chaired the NSC for only a month.

"We've already let the initial stages go by," he said. He turned to the President. "The Russians test us regularly. President Truman defied them when he airlifted supplies to Berlin. Kennedy stopped them when he blockaded Cuba." His argument implied, if you want to be great like them, you have to take risks.

Tunney nodded with annoyance. "The Russians didn't have the same kind of nuclear arsenal they have now."

Szokan continued as if no interruption had taken place. His accent was like a secret credential. I know how people think behind the Iron Curtain, it seemed to say. "Unilateral American restraint has never elicited a positive Soviet response," he said. Tunney snorted. "Restraint? You call nine thousand troops restraint?"

Rittenhouse seemed lost in meditation, but they all knew he was listening.

The argument spread among the others. Szokan suggested that Moscow be apprised of the deployment quietly. "That will make it easier for them to withdraw," he said. Hal Sonnenfeld thought the threat of deployment would be enough. "There's no reason to actually move the stuff there," he said. Tunney asked for more conventional troops and fighter planes. Pell, the last cabinet holdover from the Madden administration, shook his head. "We don't want to regret wild moves later," he said. "The Soviets are ready to solidify gains instead of gambling for more. They've already squeezed all advantages out of the Somali-Ethiopian border dispute." He coughed into his hand. "They don't want to fight us, it's a gamble, Mr. Szokan is right. But I think an offer of compensatory gains elsewhere might achieve compromise without fighting. I really don't think any new troops will be dispatched to the region."

Muldea from the CIA reported more Russian ships heading for the Red Sea.

Szokan kept relighting his pipe. The President's friend, Arthur Luchs, was a millionaire businessman whose company made parts for oil rigs. He talked about erosion of American strength. He thought the European allies perceived a loss of nerve in the United States.

Szokan wrapped up with a prediction. "If we do not stand up to them now we will be forced to come to the same decision in a year or two, but in a place closer to home." He leaned forward and uttered a word that shook them all. "Mexico," he said.

Rittenhouse said, "Thank you, gentlemen." In the silence he rose and paced for some minutes. When he concentrated, he closed one eye and tilted his head and looked with the other toward the ceiling. He stood brooding in front of the window. They could hear traffic noises from Pennsylvania Avenue outside.

Rittenhouse frowned, he exhaled noisily. "I think Dr. Szokan has a point," he said.

His days were different now. Sometimes Mark St. Johns could not believe only four months had passed since Madden's messenger had visited him in the bank. On Tuesdays and Thursdays he went for therapy for the prosthetic hand at Columbia Presbyterian. On Wednesdays he played squash, learning the game from scratch with his left hand. The cook lived full-time in the apartment. Most nights when he came home late, having stayed at the office, throwing himself into work again, he still expected to see Nicki in the chair by the window, writing.

"I understand you need a loan." Mark St. Johns handed his card to the priest, who did not look at it.

The man was bitter. "Your bank already turned me down. What do you want now?"

St. Johns knew why Nicki had testified against Madden but that didn't make it easier. "I didn't want Weber to fly planes and you did and he died," she'd said. "I didn't want you to go to London. This time I'm not going to be the quiet wife. James Henry came to see me. I told him about that dinner party. You'll hate me for it, but I'd rather live with that than a dead husband."

Mark St. Johns told the priest, "Don't be so angry. Let's start fresh. Why do you want the loan?"

St. Johns wore a winter overcoat and narrow-brimmed hat. Even inside the warehouse their breath frosted. He heard boat whistles from the river outside. Men loaded boxes of food from rows of crates into a truck near the sliding door.

The priest repeated, "Why?" He was a young man and his mouth was hard. "You know why. We've always paid our loans before. No collateral! That's not the reason! It's because this food is for strikers. For Ohio and for Washington! We feed the Maddenites so no one will give us money!"

Maddenites, St. Johns thought, amused. I've never heard that term, Maddenites.

At first Nicki had called from Massachusetts once a week. Remember to get your shirts to the laundry, Mark, she'd say. Remember to tell Hilma to cook without MSG, it gives you a headache."

But you couldn't maintain the little rhythms of marriage in a vacuum. He'd gone to see her once, to bring her back, and had been shocked at her appearance. He could still hear her in his mind, screaming at him. In forty years of marriage she'd never done that until that day. "You didn't come here to get me! You came to talk me out of testifying!"

"What's wrong with you, baby?"

"No, not 'baby.' Nicki. I'm not letting you make decisions for me anymore. Bill said those things at that party, people have to know what he's really like."

"But you know he didn't mean them. You're not remembering it right."

Crying, she'd turned so her back was to the gray winter sea past the picture window. "*My* memory? Oh God, can he do that too? Make you forget things he did?"

The priest said, "I don't know why you came here anyway. Gloating, is that it, Mr. . . . ." The priest looked at the business card. His mouth dropped open. "Mark St. Johns?" he said.

St. Johns wrapped the gray overcoat tighter. From the back of a truck a man yelled, "Watch it, watch it, Eddy! For chrissakes, you'll drop it."

St. Johns said, "You'll get the money now but there are some conditions."

The priest's knowing smile changed, but it did not get nicer. He sneered, "You want the deed to the warehouse? You want to foreclose on our trucks?"

"Shut up and stop whining and pay attention," St. Johns snapped, finally fed up. "First, I don't want you to tell anyone I visited you. If word gets out, I'll see the loan gets revoked. Second, nobody is to find out the bank made the loan."

"And third?" the priest mocked, anger in the corners of his blue eyes. "I know that's not all of it. What's third? Your loan officer explained how you work." He imitated whomever he had spoken to at the bank. " 'I'm so sorry, Father. I'd like to loan money for a humanitarian endeavor but how could I justify it to my boss?' That's you, isn't it, Mr. St. Johns! What's the third condition?"

"You're a pushy, unpleasant man. The third condition is all the money must be used for the Food for Tent City program. A bank examiner will be here and I hope he doesn't have a bad temper, because I wouldn't blame him if he smacked a little courtesy into you. If one penny goes anywhere else we'll pull the loan. I'm only using you because I made inquiries. You run the best program in Washington despite your big mouth. No interest on the loan. Four years to pay. You'd better pay."

He'd tried to get her to come home with him one more time before he'd left. They'd been outside, he on the gravel driveway that came up to the house, she on the porch, in the rain. He could see past her, through the house and out the other end to where the

Atlantic moved, slow and white capped. He'd worn the same blue-gray hat he had on now. After the cacophony of New York streets, the Cape in winter had been bathed in unreal silence.

He'd told her, "You're out here, making yourself sick, brooding." He'd been gentle-voiced but inside metals moved in his stomach. Iron. Tungsten. He'd said, "Come back home at least. Your friends are there. People you can talk to. Nicki?"

She'd shielded her eyes in the rain, as if the sun were strong or she were trying to make out his features from far away. Her hand had looked so bony.

"Are you still working for him?" she'd said.

Now the priest raised his eyes slowly from the floor, and to St. Johns's surprise they were glistening. "I'd given up hope," the man said.

St. Johns walked in the afternoon, back toward his office. He spent more time walking these days than he had in the past. In the old days, when he'd gone home earlier he'd used cabs in the daytime. Now he would just stay late in the bank again tonight. "Where do you *go*, Chief?" said Willa when he got back. "Drink this coffee, you're shivering."

"This steel hand picks up the cold, that's all," he said.

"Well, let it pick up heat from the coffee. Mr. Lea has been waiting ten minutes."

Mr. Lea was an Englishman who held a UN post for the British government. Its title in no way described his real security job. He was a cheery, mustachioed man who wore neat black suits and shiny shoes like a policeman's. He'd been reporting regularly to Mark St. Johns on the bombing. He'd already settled into the big chair by the corner picture windows. He put down the *Times*.

"Mr. St. Johns, I'll never get over this view. Quite a view, quite a scene. Why, that's a big semi truck down there, the size of a crumb, sir. I'll never get over the steam off the Hudson. We caught the people who blew up your car, Mr. St. Johns."

He looked proud and efficient. The bombing had been the work of terrorists, men who targeted American businessmen since the surrender. "The Mideast Red Army Faction," Mr. Lea said in his crisp all-in-a-day's-work voice. "They don't like some loans you chaps made in Israel. Arms or something like that. They know the bank kept an apartment at the St. Regis. A bellboy kept them informed of visitors. They put the bomb under the car in the garage. They blew it up by remote control." Mr. Lea said cheerily, "Not to worry about them, Mr. St. Johns. I don't know if they have friends here, though. How's your security in the States?"

"I'll beef it up, thanks."

Weber's picture was gone from the desk. So was Nicki's. A squash racket lay in a corner, by a potted palm. When Lea left, John Gillespie entered, resplendent in an Italian suit. St. Johns approved loans for a new Navy missile and submergible battle vehicle to be deployed in Europe. Gillespie scratched his head. "Sometimes I don't understand you, Chief. Sneaking around and making loans to peace groups, then approving this."

St. Johns laughed. "Madden's the genius, not me," he said. "One thing at a time."

The squash was improving rapidly. When he was finished playing he was sweating. His partner said, "What vitamins do you use?" He was getting good at eating too. "Like chopsticks in reverse," laughed a waitress on Fifth Avenue where he ate dinner. "How do you hold a fork like that?"

Sometimes his wrist ached when the weather was bad. At home the phone was ringing as he came in the door. Hilma was probably asleep. His pulse quickened when he heard Catherine Madden's voice. He fought off the sadness and with growing excitement listened.

"They don't have any organization," she was saying. "There are so many of them, they can help him."

She told him what she needed. He was amazed.

Later, he sprawled in the king-size bed. Sometimes he could smell Nicki no matter how often Hilma washed the sheets. There was an oil portrait of her by the curtains, and the moonlight made her throat luminous. He was falling asleep. He was a one-woman man. He was straightforward in his loyalties and they did not change. The pillows were bunched against the wooden headboard. The sound of a plane came to him in the night. When Weber was a teenager, he used to like to lie on the big bed and watch "Star Trek" on the color TV. Flying shows. Show with pilots. If there's one thing I can do, St. Johns thought, it's raise money.

She was going to save the world. She didn't care how simple or unsophisticated or inflated that sounded. In the mornings she ran off posters on a Xerox machine, announcing rallies and protests in Washington. She stood vigil on silent lines along roadways. She held up signs that read, NO NUKES. She buttonholed tourists under the statue at the Jefferson Memorial. She passed out leaflets at churches and supermarkets. She carried a candle past the White House at night, a speck of light in a river of people. It was all for Danny, all for peace.

"I'm certainly glad to see so many interested people coming to Washington," the congressman said.

She showered in houses donated around the city. She ate bean soup and bread arriving in semi trucks. She slept in a tent within view of the monuments. Her clothes got clammy and the nights were cold. You never knew which contact might tip the balance. You had to talk to everybody. You couldn't give up.

"Will you or won't you vote for the freeze?" she said.

She'd known she'd done the right thing as soon as the plane landed at National. The sun had been rising over the Potomac. Josh was probably still asleep. She'd pinned the note to him under the refrigerator magnet shaped like a pineapple. All she could think was, Why did I wait so long?

"Slow down, let's get this in perspective," Congressman Dancer said. He smiled broadly but Stephanie wasn't fooled. He chaired the House Armed Services Committee, and at Tent City she'd picked up his voting record. A glance around the office confirmed his violent inclinations. Military influence lay all over the place. Models of fighter planes topped the oak cabinets. Pictures of battleships lined the far wall. Even the paperweight was a glass-encased bayonet. To Stephanie, the plush, sunny office advertised war.

Surrounded by protesters, Dancer perched on the arm of a chair. He looked over the Stanford students on the carpet, the Omaha lawyers by the door. An aide passed a silver tray of grapefruit juice

in Dixie Cups to the actor and farmers on the couch. "I don't agree
with you, I'll tell you right out," he said. The Capitol dome was
visible through half-open blinds. "I'd get rid of nuclear weapons too
if it were possible. But in ten years fifty countries will have the bomb,
or at least the capability. That's what the CIA says, fifty! Those
missiles won't go away even if we tear down every weapon we have."

For months she'd been arguing in Evanston. At stores with housewives. At churches with priests. She had a vision of Josh leaning
toward her at a faculty luncheon, squeezing her knee under the table.
"Can't you stop talking about it for a minute? You're embarrassing me."

"But what do we *do*?" Dancer said. He had a sincere, confident
voice and he looked crisp in a blue pinstripe suit. "It's a very tough
question. You want to limit arms?" He threw up his hands. "Me too,
but how? You have to do it right. Do we start with long-range missiles
or midrange? Do we keep MIRVs? Do we bargain away our Polaris
or cruise missiles? And for what?" Dancer reminded her of a magician
she'd seen in a movie who hypnotized victims just by talking to them.
He stood. For some reason he concentrated his argument on the
surgeon from San Francisco. "For example, take the Soviet SS-19
and SS-20 versus our Minuteman missile with 12A-type warheads . . ."

"No!" All the faces swung to her. Her anger propelled her to her
feet. "Experts!" she cried. "Numbers!" She was sick of the logical
arguments. The careful massing of stupefying information. "Who
cares what you call the missiles?" she said.

Calmly, he said, "You can't just simplify . . ."

She wanted to laugh. Once she'd been at a White House dinner
next to a French writer. The writer had told her, "My job is to make
simple subjects complicated so intellectuals can appreciate them."
She snapped, "You have to simplify!" Dancer's soothing smile remained fixed. She said, "You only see little pieces of it your way!"
He nodded like he knew what she was talking about, but he didn't
at all. Danny's face swam in her mind. She pleaded with them. "I
have a little boy. He's four." The eyes of the mothers were shining.
There was a photo of Dancer in a Marine uniform on the wall, with
jungle in the background. "He got the flu this fall. I got up every

night, four times a night. I made him better with medicine. There's nothing I can do for him if there's war."

Dancer held his hands up to stop her, but she advanced toward him, weaving around people on the floor. "I used to think, even if you had war you'd have people and trees. I used to think, even if there's war Danny could be one of the lucky ones."

Dancer said, "Whoa, hold it! I'm not starting any wars."

"Do you have kids?" She saw the color photo of Dancer and two girls beside a pile of paper. They were pretty blond girls in yellow sun dresses. She thrust the photo at him. "They're your kids, aren't they? It's like they have cancer, the whole world has cancer. If Danny had cancer, I wouldn't need to know statistics before I tried to help."

The applause seemed thunderous, but he just shook his head. "I wish it was that easy," he said. He quoted Churchill. "It is the greatest mistake to mix up disarmament with peace. When you have peace you will have disarmament."

Outside in the hall people gathered around her. A woman was crying. "Stephanie, that was great," she said. "If enough people argue with him, he'll change."

A man in a gray suit and long hair came down the hall joyously. "We just met with Harrigan," he said, naming a senator from New York. "He'll vote for the freeze! Did you hear about Frankfurt? *Ninety thousand* marchers! And it's in Russia too! I heard it on the news!"

"Marchers in Russia?" someone said, amazed.

"Well, only five people, but they were arrested outside the Kremlin. Russia! It's starting!"

The congressman from Alabama said they were inspiring. The congresswoman from Kentucky asked shrewdly, "Who do you think *provides* you with our voting records?" She seemed to think it was the Soviets. The Indiana representative fed them bacon-and-cheese hors d'oeuvres. "I'll give this lots of thought," he promised. It was dusk. The lawyer said, "Eat with us, Stephanie, you haven't eaten all day."

"I have to do something first."

She waited in line to use a pay phone a block from Tent City and the mall. Across Seventeenth Street, beyond parked charter buses and police sawhorses, the whole rolling area east-west from the Vietnam Memorial to the Washington Monument was covered with tents. *The Washington Times* had called it "the camp of the Mongols." She heard rock music muffled by distance. She smelled cooking fires as plumes of smoke curled toward the sky. During a cold April like this the mall area was generally deserted. But the streets were filled with people tonight. People coming back from marches. From leafleting, visiting senators, showering, touring, seeing old friends. Three old men walked toward camp wearing blue Veterans for Peace caps. Five or six college-age boys and girls sang while they strolled, as one played guitar.

> Oh-ho-ho, I want to know-ho
> When Dunkirk Camp will go . . .

Gulls circled in the darkening skies over the tents, come from the Potomac looking for food. A man carrying a black medical bag, his raincoat collar turned up, strode briskly away from camp, toward downtown. Volunteer doctors had set up Red Cross tents.

The woman in front of Stephanie said, into the phone, "Chuck, it's like college. A party. You have to come down."

Stephanie imagined Josh at a faculty party in Scott Hall, in a corduroy jacket with a scotch in his hand. "Stephanie's aunt is sick," he was lying. "She went to take care of her. In Detroit."

The receiver warmed her ear as she punched the numbers. Josh picked up midway through the first ring. "What am I supposed to tell people?" he demanded. "I can understand you leaving me, but how can you do this to Danny? You didn't even talk to me about this, sneaking out in the night. I don't even believe in what you're doing."

Across the street college boys played Frisbee with a black Labrador retriever wearing a red scarf around its neck. Her hands felt clammy in her gloves. The old, whiny voice clutched at her. "Don't do this to me," she said. "Try to understand."

"Understand what? You'll hang up and everything will be fine for you. He's going to cry all night."

You won't pull me down, she thought. "Put Danny on." But when she heard the frantic little voice her heart opened up.

"My Friar Tuck costume wasn't sewed," he said. "Everyone else brought their costumes to school." At this hour he'd be in pajamas, smelling of talcum powder. She put it on him every night after his bath. It gave him white patches on his chest above his nipples. "I'm sorry, Danny. I'm doing very important work." The words sounded hollow even to her. "Tell Daddy to take your costume to a tailor. I love you. I'll be home soon."

Danny didn't say anything at first. Then he said, "I want you home yesterday."

When he was trying to keep from crying, he lowered his head so his chin touched his chest. His voice grew tighter like he was squeezing his larynx.

He changed the subject, more sensitive than Josh. "I found a bug in the basement."

"Really? What kind of bug?"

But he couldn't hold it in. "I want you to see my bug! I want you to see it right now!"

After she hung up she didn't move. His pajamas had little Civil War soldiers on them, with muskets and bayonets. An arm came around her shoulders. She looked into a woman's plump face, brown eyes magnified by glasses. The woman steered her away from the phone. She said, "I was going to bring my Laura from Florida but it's too cold here for a child. You did the right thing."

Stephanie thought, I can't even make peace in my own home.

She was exhausted and hungry. Inside Tent City the noise grew. People played music on radios or guitars. They cooked dinner in pots on open fires. There was a smoky, gritty quality to the air. Men hammered wooden-plank sidewalks together between clumps of tents. A thaw was forecast, which would turn the ground soft. "Good night, Stephanie," called two teenage girls in sleeping bags. She smelled frying sausages. Near a MINNESOTA sign by a cluster of old army tents, a television newsman's breath frosted as he spoke into a mike. The spotlight formed a halo over his head. "More protesters pour into Tent City every day. In ones and twos. On buses. In cars. They hitchhike here, they ride the trains. Housewives and building contractors and retired people and children. An army without a leader. A sprawling, grass-roots crusade . . ."

As she approached her own area, she heard men and women singing. An old civil rights song.

Inside a larger circle of tents a smaller group of men, women, and children sat around a bonfire. She took her place with them. She was thinking that when she was first married, Josh had loved to tell her stories of his old Vietnam War protest days in Chicago. They'd sit in their cramped Evanston apartment and look out at Lake Michigan and drink Gallo wine. "There were thousands of us parading on Michigan Avenue," he'd say dreamily. "We stopped that war." Now he said, "Let's face it, honey. We marched because we were afraid we'd be sent to fight. As soon as the draft ended, the protests stopped."

Someone put a hot tin of soup in her hand. The warmth spread to her stomach, delicious. A man in a John Deere hat gave her a cup of wine. Cheese and a pocket knife were coming around the circle.

He has bad luck, that's all, she thought. He should have gotten that job.

At the far end of the circle, tacked to a tent, she saw a glossy color photo of Madden from *Time* magazine. The fire leaped high. In the photo Madden looked younger, like Josh, especially the high forehead and hint of a smile. Would Danny really cry all night? She started to sing with the others. Sometimes she sang with Danny at night. He liked to sing "Frère Jacques" before he went to sleep.

She missed him so badly. It was the strongest moment of doubt. A voice on her left said, "That man's like Jesus." It was the Colorado grandmother who'd driven here alone. She was wrapped in a combination of gray wool coat, scarves, and a blanket. She said reverently, "He took the sins on himself."

When Stephanie looked again, Madden's face resembled an icon. All pale white ovals beneath huge brown eyes. She shivered, but not from the cold. Every time Josh talked with her she wished someone could make the hurt go away. Tonight was Saturday night, she remembered. Sometimes he liked to read to her after Danny went to sleep. Shakespeare was his favorite; he had all the leatherbound books. "Love is not love which alters when it alteration finds." She blew out long breaths of air. The heaviness lodged in her throat and shoulders. In the days before the surrender she'd cooked him treats. Indonesian beef sate or sweet crispy noodles. She'd light candles in the bedroom and turn up the heat.

The photo of Madden seemed kinder, bigger. The singing was like the beating of a great common heart. She looked around the circle, felt warmth from the people. She did not know their names but felt like she'd known them for years. They were working together to save Danny. She couldn't believe so many people felt like she did. And then she was singing. Her passion was rising, embracing them all. The fire leaped high, its heat warmed her face. A man several feet off told her, "He'd know what to do." The food made her feel better, she could pass out more leaflets. Lots of people would be downtown on Saturday night.

"He gave up everything for us," said a lean man in ear muffs. "That's why they're trying to kill him."

A woman wept. "Bastards! Leave him alone."

Honeymooning with Josh, she'd visited Notre Dame. Inside, it had been so beautiful, holy, and right. The photo of Madden was like that. The grandmother wrapped her scarves tighter. "When I look at his eyes, I swear I'm looking at the family Bible," she said. Stephanie had seen on the news that each morning as Madden walked to court his followers outside chanted his name over and over. Now the chant began. The grandmother started it; others joined in. The man in the John Deere hat repeated, eyes closed, "Mad-den." The name sounded new to Stephanie, powerful like she had never heard it before. It was not her name, or even Josh's, but the name of the face in the photograph. She felt her lips moving. His eyes glowed in the photos. Save my family, she prayed. The fire leaped high; the chanting grew louder. "Madden," Stephanie mouthed, in a frenzy of hope.

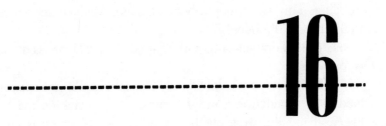

16

"**S**tate your name, please."

"Otis Monterey."

He'd been a senator from the great state of New Mexico for thirty-one years, he told the court. He was a rancher and a father. He'd been a Navy pilot in World War Two. He was deeply saddened by the story he was about to tell. He had a rolling voice which gathered strength at the end of each sentence, making it into a pronouncement. His thick white hair was famous. At sixty-four his face was angular but softening beneath the jaw and jowls. His ruddy color marked him as an outdoorsman or a drinker.

"We were on the Armed Services Committee together," announced Otis Monterey.

A tremor of unease ran through the court, an almost physical ripple. They were coming more steadily, as if disturbances in the outside world were beating against the doors. A beleaguered quality marked the faces of the jurors. A grim silence emanated from spectators who had access to outside news.

A *Times* columnist in the first row wrote, "No matter how logical Diane Medaglia's arguments, they sound smaller and less effective with each witness. James Henry is only the face of the prosecution. The people of the country are the heart."

Monterey tended to shift his gaze, like a speechmaker, from one part of the court to another as he talked. Now the jury. Now the press.

"He and I had just left a committee meeting. Funding for the Air Force. I'm not sorry to say we should give them everything they want. We'd had a disagreement. We were in the hall in the Rayburn Building. This was a month before Senator Madden announced he would run for President."

He paused dramatically. Grim-jawed, James Henry said, "Please go on."

"Well, I don't know how to say it nicely, so I'll just tell you out loud. Mr. Madden told me if there were an attack on the United States, if missiles were on their way, he would seriously consider surrender instead of fighting."

The tumult went on for five minutes, drowning out Murtaugh's gavel. Madden sat absolutely straight, looking neither right nor left. Medaglia was unbuckling her briefcase; no one could see her face.

Monterey spread his hands as if to share the shock. The *Times* man wrote, "With the situation in Africa worsening, this courtroom is becoming the focus of the nation's will."

The memory robbed Monterey's voice of its natural tenor. "He seemed very disturbed over the lives that would be lost in a war. I said, 'How can you run for President knowing we are subject to a first strike?'" The note Madden slipped to Medaglia said, "Not the way it was." Monterey said, "I told him by definition war kills innocent people. I didn't like it any more than he did. He said he could not countenance a war in which millions would die." Monterey's voice went up a notch. "He insisted surrender was a viable solution."

Monterey swung toward the *Times* man. "I told him the entire tenor of our defense was that although we deplore the possibility of war, we have to protect our people, save as many as possible with retaliation. I told him the one thing the country would not tolerate, could not understand, would not accept, was a surrender. Why, our very way of life, our Constitution, the Declaration of Independence; *everything we hold dear* would be destroyed." A murmur was rising in the court. "All the wars we had engaged in to preserve our democracy would be meaningless. But he didn't care. He said . . ."

"Objection. 'He didn't care,' " Medaglia remarked over the buzz, as if to dismiss the entire testimony.

"Sustained."

In the lower tier of the jury, the secretary from HUD had turned on Madden. Her lips were drawn back in a rictus of rage. She had told the judge when the jury was chosen that a dead son in Vietnam would not affect her decision.

Monterey's booming voice held them in thrall. "He said the factors I mentioned were secondary to the lives. He said the Japanese emporer had surrendered after the atomic attack on Hiroshima and look what happened to Japan. It wasn't destroyed at all. It became a major nation. He said he thought even under a different political system this country could survive and grow again."

Still he wasn't finished. The note Medaglia passed back to Madden said "bad." Monterey shook his head as if to clear his memory. "I was flabbergasted. Horrified. I told him we would not survive. As a people. As a spirit. As an institution." He quavered with indignation. "I reminded him the President took an oath when he was sworn in, to be commander-in-chief of the armies, to protect the Constitution. I told him if he did run he should make his position clear so the people would make the choice, not him. Whether to surrender or not."

James Henry backed away from the stand. His hand swept low in a gesture of respect. "No further questions," he said.

To give the emotion time to settle, Diane Medaglia took her time shuffling papers, putting on glasses and taking them off, whispering with Madden. When she reached the podium, the jury regarded her coldly. James Henry had scored big with Otis Monterey.

She had one hand in the pocket of her wool flannel jumper. She wore a white poet's blouse with a black crepe bow. Oddly, even after Monterey's testimony she seemed more at ease. She was one of those people whom adversity relaxes. She always expected trouble, so when it finally came she had a focus.

She started off mildly. "I'm not clear on one thing, Senator. You told us President Madden revealed to you an intent to surrender. This horrified you, troubled you. Is that correct?"

Monterey sat back, hands on his lap. He breathed heavily from emotion. "Yes."

"Then why didn't you tell anyone until now?"

The noise in the room told her she had made an impression. She said, "A man like you, a public servant. Why didn't you alert the country during the primary or the election that year, before Mr. Madden could become President?"

Without hesitating, Monterey named the senator who had run against Madden in the primary. "I advised him of Mr. Madden's remarks," he countered.

"But why," Medaglia pushed, coming out from behind the podium, moving toward him, "weren't President Madden's 'plans' ever brought out in the campaign, if they were so serious?"

James Henry started to object, but the senator waved him down. "I don't mind answering that. I'd heard him say it, so had my aide, but there wasn't any record. He never repeated it. Using it in a campaign could have backfired. Voters would think it was mudslinging, making it up."

Medaglia said, "I see. But I still don't understand." She was a foot away from Monterey. "After President Madden won the nomination, when he was running for the White House, about to plunge the country into the gravest peril, according to you, why didn't you speak up?"

Henry said, standing up; "We're getting off the track here. Who's on trial, Mr. Madden or Mr. Monterey?"

Medaglia gave Henry the tiniest smile. "Senator Monterey's motivation is crucial to our argument."

The question was allowed. Monterey sagged a little, and strain came into his voice. "I suppose I was too loyal to the party," he admitted. "More concerned with my own position. I was running myself, for the Senate." He finished with one of those rising sentences that ended in an exclamation. "That does not change what he said!"

One or two jurors nodded in understanding but Medaglia struck a skeptical pose, pencil at her lip, unswayed. She returned to the defense table. She picked a folder from the top of a pile. The court craned to see. In a softer tone, coming at him from a different direction, she said, "Or maybe you had another reason, the same one you had in coming here today. Senator, you and President Madden were on the Armed Services Committee five years prior to the comment you say he made. How would you describe your relationship?"

He shrugged. "Normal. We disagreed sometimes. Everybody does."

"Did any of those disagreements result in violent arguments?"

"We had political discussions, that's all."

Her eyebrows rose. "I have in my hand a transcript of a committee meeting, marked Exhibit F, which occurred two years before the night you've been telling us about. Do you recall being present at the meeting?" He did. She quoted him. " '*I don't care what you want, Senator Madden, I'm here to stop you!*' "

Wryly, she said, "Isn't it true the two of you had a reputation for hating each other?"

Henry's objection was overruled. A moment later she said, "Isn't it true that in every single instance his name appeared on a bill, you voted against it?"

"I don't remember."

"Would you like to look at your voting record?"

"I guess I did vote against him."

"Let me show you a bill that supports increasing the budget for ranch aid, Senator. You come from a ranching state. Isn't it true you voted against this bill because Senator Madden co-sponsored it?"

"I wouldn't say that." Monterey recrossed his legs.

She pursed her lips. "You wouldn't say you voted against it?"

"I did vote against it," Monterey told the jury. "But it wasn't *enough* for ranchers. Recheck the record. You'll find I co-sponsored a different bill, which was passed, giving ranchers more."

She drove at him. "Three hundred dollars more? Three . . . hundred . . . dollars. Would you like to check the mathematics?" She flipped through pages, each one a bill; each, she seemed to say, an argument. "Hmmmm. Widows and orphans of veterans? Farm aid?"

Monterey was growing annoyed. "I'm perfectly willing to go over each and every bill you bring up and explain why I voted against it."

"I'm glad of that, Senator, because we will do just that. We have plenty of time and we want to get at the truth. And I suggest the truth is that you are here today doing what you have been doing for over seventeen years; attacking the President out of some personal vendetta."

"*I* suggest," said James Henry, getting to his feet, "that counsel for the defense is doing a skillful job trying to switch the focus from treason to politics. I don't think the jury will be fooled. Objection."

"I don't think they'll be fooled either," Medaglia shot back.

Murtaugh waved them to the bench. "I told you," he lectured Henry, "that Senator Monterey's motivation is relevant. And you," he turned to Medaglia. "I thought you learned self-control somewhere along the line."

The prosecutor said, "Miss Medaglia has made her little point without going over every single bill. Senator Monterey's aide is testifying next. He heard Madden's remark too. Will we go through this again?"

Fritz Scott, the secretary of defense before Madden came into office, had been known as the worst dresser in Washington. Reporters recognized the oversized, rumpled brown suit even before they saw the face. He was short and wideshouldered with a steel colored crew cut. His brown scuffed shoes needed new heels. The hand that rested on the Bible was rough and beefy. After starting off as a sixteen-year-old laborer in an Ohio steel plant, he had risen to become the millionaire chairman of a California insurance company.

He'd been testifying for forty minutes, listing weapons programs Madden had cancelled when he came into office.

"We'd been working on the space defense system for three years, even before I came to be secretary," he said with reverence. "It was a new kind of weapon. A quantum leap in what we could do."

To a *Post* Style section reporter who had once suggested he hire a clothing consultant, he had snapped, "Which branch of the armed forces should I take the time from to do it?"

He frowned. "President Madden dismantled the program. He said, what was the point of spending billions for a system that might not be technically feasible and that could become outdated soon after coming into existence."

"Did you make any effort to change his thinking?"

"Sure. Use his logic and the space program never would have started. The atomic bomb never would have been invented. I told him in everyday life we purchase insurance not because we expect fires to occur, or accidents, but because of the possibilities. We may never cash in on the policies, but the money is well spent. Defense is the same. I told him he should reevaluate his thinking." His voice grew more urgent. "Those programs are important. We've got to have them, got to stay ahead."

"Did he respond?"

"He told me that having been secretary of defense he would expect me to think that way, but he had to consider the social welfare of the people." He snorted. "As if defense isn't included in that."

"In your professional opinion, how would you say President Madden maintained the defense capabilities of the United States?" Henry asked.

"He systematically weakened them."

Henry smiled with disarming candor. "Was that because he intended never to use them?"

"Objection!"

"Sustained."

"No further questions."

Diane Medaglia had spent a long time going through her cardboard boxes during Scott's testimony, arranging papers. "Secretary Scott," she started, "while you were in the cabinet didn't Senator Madden vote to fund the Hermes missile and the new Stealth bomber?"

Scott grew monosyllabic when he addressed her, although whether it was because she was a woman or because she was the defense attorney was unclear. "Yes."

"Both of these are nuclear weapons?"

"Well, the bomber carries nuclear weapons."

"And during President Madden's administration didn't he maintain an existing arsenal of thousands of MX missiles, cruise missiles, Polaris missiles, Minuteman missiles, midgetman missiles, intercontinental ballistic missiles, and antiballistic missiles?"

"He did."

"Wouldn't you say he did believe in insurance, then?"

Doggedly, Scott said; "The space program is crucial."

Medaglia considered the jury. She'd made her point and she moved on, walking back and forth in front of the box. "In the course of your work as secretary of defense, did you ever review a budget?"

"Of course. I always reviewed budgets."

Medaglia leaned against the railing of the jury box. "And when you looked over these budgets, did you ever have occasion to add something here, subtract something there?"

Scott fidgeted. "Everybody does."

Medaglia seemed fascinated. "Tell me something. When you subtract from the budget, or add something, what prompts you to do that?"

Scott saw where the argument was leading and shifted in his seat. "Everybody knows you're only given a limited amount of money. You have to exercise priorities."

"Oh, so you recognize priorities play a role in determining where you spend funds. And sir, you were a military man, so you thought military expenditures had a high priority. Would you say that is true?"

"Military matters should have a high priority."

Medaglia nodded. "Would you say because of military expenditures the welfare of poor and sick people should be ignored?"

"I never said that."

Medaglia's voice quickened. "Did you ever sit down and attempt to figure out how much money should be allocated to other government activities? Roads? Bridges? Research for food and drugs?"

Scott said briskly, "That wasn't my field."

"But you recognize the President has to make those determinations."

"Yes, yes, of course."

"And will you admit, Mr. Secretary, that reasonable people may differ with respect to how much money should be spent on a particular project?"

Scott reared back and let out a deep breath. "Within limits."

"And when the President decided not to go forward with the defense project you recommended, did you think him a traitor at the time?"

"I thought he was encouraging the Russians. I thought one day there might not be enough hospitals to accommodate all the people who could be hurt because of him. If we're strong we won't have to go to war."

It was the longest speech he had given. She said triumphantly, "But you did not think him a traitor."

The witness hesitated, thinking of an answer. "I didn't know then what I know now," he said.

Despite the uniform, the general resembled a boyish monk, with a smooth white face and a fringe of tiny blond curls around his otherwise bald head.

Henry, in his bow tie and vest sweater beneath a jacket of black tweed, urged, "Go on."

The general grunted, as if the memory he was about to relate gave him a twinge of pain. "The war plans section was meeting with the President that day. We were discussing how to respond to attack. Mr. Madden asked, out of the blue, 'How can we *stop* our men from fighting?' "

The courtroom grew still. General Hacker was less inclined to look around the room than other witnesses. He spoke solely to the prosecutor. "I asked the President, 'What do you mean, stop?' He said, 'Well, suppose the situation were so dire the only alternative was giving up?' "

The *Times* man wrote, "Diane Medaglia looks surprised and distressed; so does Catherine Madden." Hacker explained to the fascinated jury, "He was concerned about communication. You see, if a one-hundred-megaton bomb is exploded in the upper atmosphere, radio and telephone signals go out."

The *Times* reporter wrote, "In two days Madden seemed to have aged. With each revelation the court seems less shocked, more accepting, as if coming to the conclusion the President is guilty."

Hacker said, "Admiral Tunney, who was present, interjected that he had never considered surrender. The policy has always been after a first strike we would retaliate. That's why we've deployed missiles all over the world. But the President persisted. He asked if I would draw up a memo on how to restrain our forces from fighting. I and my staff did so."

"Is this that memo?" Henry asked, displaying the booklet.
Murtaugh glanced at the clock. "Recess for lunch," he said.

They hardly spoke as they ate. Once, looking up from the Defense
Department reports she was reading, Medaglia said, "For every one
of his witnesses we have three." But she seemed far away. Madden
gazed out the window at Constitution Avenue. His sandwich remained untouched. Medaglia ate her salad as she went over her
notes, up to the last minute. Catherine read *Time* magazine.

Madden said; "That's not the way it was, what he said." Medaglia
glanced at him sideways. "Of course."

Madden was the only one who saw her wipe her hands on her
dress under the table before she began her cross-examination.

"General Hacker," she said, browsing through the papers in her
hand and sounding curious, nothing more, "would you tell us the
number of nuclear warheads the United States has stockpiled all over
the world?"

"Over seven thousand warheads."

There was a gasp in the back.

"And the Russians?"

"The same," he said. "More or less."

She paused to let the number sink in. On the lower tier of the
jury, the hat-shop owner half raised her hand to her mouth. The
TASS man, who really worked for the KGB, wrote furiously. Medaglia picked up a pencil, rolled it in her hand. "If a single one of
those weapons were to be detonated in, say, a city, say, New York
City, what would the result be?"

Hacker swallowed, showing the kind of discomfort professional
military men display when discussing war with emotional civilians.
He sidestepped a graphic answer. "A great deal of death and destruction." He added, "I hope it never happens."

"Me too. We all hope it never happens." With her thumb, Me-
daglia pressed and rolled the eraser on the pencil. She read from the
Defense Department report on the result of nuclear blasts in cities.
She lowered her voice so people had to strain to hear.

" 'Winds would be whipped up to five-hundred miles an hour.
Windows would blow out at a hundred miles an hour, decapitating

people. Eyes would melt close to the blast. Millions would die in the most intense agony. Clothes would instantaneously ignite up to twenty miles from the explosion. Fires would suck oxygen out of fallout shelters and turn them into crematoriums.' "

In the back of the court, a woman began crying. Marshals gently led her out. Medaglia kept reading. The sobs were audible but muffled in the hallway. The court had gone dead silent. Hacker acknowledged the quote as true.

Medaglia grew thoughtful. "That was a description of a single nuclear blast," she reminded the jury, voice up a notch. "General, what would the effect be were all fifteen thousand warheads to be detonated?"

The general sighed heavily. "It is not automatic that all missiles would be fired if hostilities broke out."

"But *if* they were launched?"

The general ran his hand over his face. "Annihilation."

Medaglia half pivoted toward the jury. "General, would you agree that were a nuclear exchange to erupt, a prudent course might be to stop it before all the warheads were launched?"

"Of course."

"But how could such a disaster be stopped? You've just testified our communications systems would go out right away."

Hacker brightened. "That's in my report."

The tension had been so thick the laughter erupted hysterically, sweeping through the court in waves. Murtaugh tried to suppress a smile as he banged the gavel.

When the noise had dropped to sporadic chuckles, Diane Medaglia said, "Then isn't it possible the reason President Madden asked for your memo was not that he was planning surrender but that he was interested in being able to control a nuclear exchange were one to begin?"

General Hacker looked at James Henry. "I guess so," he said. "But he did say 'give up.' "

James Henry called to the stand the White House translator, Professor Shinitzky, who described Madden's surrender. "He ordered me to say it. *'Tell him we will not fight. Don't launch any more missiles!'* "

The Joint Chiefs of Staff chairman, Admiral Tunney, detailed how a surrender would have taken place, how it would have meant handing over the whole nuclear arsenal to the Russians. Tight-faced, he depicted Soviet troops entering United States military bases, Soviet pilots taking over U.S. jets. As he spoke, the court imagined American nuclear submarines docking in Russian ports, the sailors filing onto land, giving up. "They'd rule the world," the admiral said.

To Medaglia's question "What would have happened if the President had listened to your advice and launched?" he said, "Lots of people would be dead but we'd still be a country. He could have waited, he didn't have to give up. Let me turn it around, counselor. Suppose the Russians *had* been launching and he'd surrendered. Would you try him for treason then? You're damn right you would!"

It was mid afternoon. Under Henry's skillful questioning a State Department economist reported on the deteriorating condition of U.S. investments abroad because of the surrender. "The dollar is dropping. The Saudis have withdrawn money from our banks and deposited it in Switzerland. In Africa and South America our companies' mines are being nationalized and so are their factories. Nobody thinks we'll fight."

The bailiff kept emptying wrappers from Murtaugh's ashtray. The judge popped another peppermint candy into his mouth. "Do you have many more witnesses, Mr. Henry?" he asked, looking at the clock.

"Only one, Your Honor."

Some of the jurors stretched, yawned. But their eyes burned with concentration. A kind of intimacy had settled onto the court. Like the feeling in a commuter train at the end of the day. There was a warm, smoky odor, bodies and cigarettes. The court reporter kept rotating her head side to side to relax her muscles. The bus driver in the jury exhaled when he saw who was mounting the stand. Ariel Levy wore an indigo blue cardigan over a gold abstract-print blouse. Her skirt was of soft blue lamb suede. The men leaned forward and the women settled back. Levy was the premier expert on U.S.-Soviet relations at the Brookings Institution.

"He couldn't have helped them more if they'd paid him," Levy said. Medaglia objected and Murtaugh remarked; "Stick to facts, not speculation." But the damage showed in the jurors' faces. Some glanced to the back of the court as if they felt Russian troops outside in the hall. James Henry had to show the surrender had aided the enemy. Levy listed problems. "The French and Germans are exploring new treaties with Moscow. That would weaken NATO. The Russians have stepped up shipments to guerrillas in Central America. It wouldn't have been so blatant before. Terrorists are more active. And I don't think Premier Menkes would have risked troops in Ethiopia before the surrender."

Up until now her prim academic expertise had masked her fear but suddenly she looked afraid. "Just because war hasn't broken out in the last few months doesn't mean it won't happen any day."

A heavy sign of recognition went through the court. Everyone knew it. Levy had told them nothing new.

Diane Medaglia asked only one question. "You say these countries don't think we would fight. What do you think their attitude would be had President Madden launched missiles instead of refraining?"

For the first time humor came into Levy's voice. "You mean if countries still existed?" she said.

Outside, the storm had thickened. Snow fell hard and continuously, a freak April storm. Because of the weather only a few Madden supporters were present, but they broke into their chant when he appeared with Medaglia at the top step. He buttoned his overcoat.

The high-pitched whir of tires spinning on ice cut the air. Headlights crawled on Constitution Avenue, past the east wing of the National Gallery, shrouded in storm.

Medaglia jerked her head toward the courtroom upstairs. "Bring on the men in the white coats," she said. She wore a blue wool pullover hat that covered all her hair and made her misshapen nose look gigantic. Her forehead was damp with perspiration even in the cold. She'd been fine in court, but the afternoon had been hard on her.

Madden linked arms with her. He said, "You were very good."

"Well, at least our side starts tomorrow."

Catherine had passed up the strategy dinner. "I'll go on home," she'd said. "I have calls to make." Medaglia extended her bare palm and watched flakes melt into the creases of her lifeline. Stretching down the steps, across the plaza and up to the waiting limousine, the police linked arms. "He makes everything so obscure," she said. They started down the steps. Even though only a few dozen protestors were present, the police remained wary under their snow dusted helmets. The pattern of trampled snow on the ground gave it a gauzy appearance, like a bandage over the earth.

Madden dug a thumb in her direction. "Sometimes when I'm sitting in there pieces of speeches go through my head. I can't even remember who said them. When Levy was testifying I heard . . ." He deepened his voice. ". . . We shall join hands with our friends south of the border . . ." His laugh bubbled out, sparkling and innocent. "That's what I said when we opened the gas pipeline with Mexico. Why should I be thinking of that?"

The clouds lay massed, purplish. Through the falling flakes they saw twin red lights blinking atop the Washington Monument, the highest structure in the city. The lights looked like eyes of a two-hundred-foot-high Ku Klux Klansman.

"Scallops," he said, getting into the car, knowing foods she liked by now, trying to cheer her up. "Bay scallops. Fresh raspberries for dessert."

As they pulled away from the curb, the driver switched on the radio. Madden liked the all-news channel. An announcer's voice was saying, "The Madden case has been filled with strange twists, but none as shocking as this death and the NORAD cover-up. More on this later as it comes in . . ."

Medaglia shot out of her reverie. "What was that all about? Get another station," she ordered the driver. "Quick!" Madden fell back in his seat, numb with horror. He could see over the front seat to where the fingers rotated the dial. Jazz music merged into static merged into a voice saying, "No more acne." He knew what had happened. The car accelerated into traffic. He could smell Medaglia's perfume, it seemed to grow stronger when something roused her. The pain started up in his temples. The wipers made screeching noises as they moved. Huff turned and said, "Sir, are you all right?" "Diane," Madden said, "there's something I'd better tell you." He was thinking, What did the announcer mean, *the death*? He repeated her name. She waved a hand for him to be silent. The driver had found more news. An announcer with a Latin accent was saying, "Robert Gardner, the reporter who found the story . . ." The pain grew, encompassing his whole skull. It was the low point, the worst point. He had tried to avoid this moment for months.

17

He's late, Robert Gardner thought. He checked his watch again. Eleven-thirty. The cold made his teeth ache and lodged in his knees. He was too anxious to wait in the car, so he stamped in the snow to keep warm.

But an electric tingle gripped him, a lust that came over him when a story was near. All his senses were roaring.

It was two days before James Henry called his last witness in the Madden trial. The gas station hugged a bend in the two lane Rocky Mountain highway. It was a honey colored log cabin dwarfed by three immense pines and snow-covered peaks, which rose on all sides and leaned inward, almost blotting out the sky. The stars seemed closer this high up. The twenty-year-old pumps were the color of fire engines. The old Mobil sign, a red Pegasus on a field of white, creaked in the wind. The only light flickered in the back of the lot, ten feet over a blue trash dumpster.

HOT COFFEE, taunted the sign in the window of the locked building.

"If you're going alone, at least call your editor," Susan had said. "You don't know who left you that note." He saw her in the hotel room as he pulled on his hiking boots. "I'm not calling Edelstein for another wild goose chase," he'd said. The plowed snow lining the highway came up to his neck. He'd said, "The problem is, how do I get up there without Jankerelli knowing?" He'd smiled when the idea came. "What would you say to a delicious romantic dinner; good wine, wonderful food?" She'd said terrific and he'd said, "I'll go get your escort." When he'd explained it all to the hotel handyman, a bearded ski bum named Chrobersky, the man had said, "A hundred dollars, huh? You sure it's nothing illegal?"

Gardner had left the hotel and driven his rented Subaru back to the entrance. He figured if anyone was watching, it would look like he was picking up Susan. Inside he'd switched coats, hats, and car keys with Chrobersky. "Man, you're crazy to leave a beautiful lady like her," the ski bum had said. And to Susan he had said, "Baby, run away with me to Meh-he-co."

The pines crowded up to the station, the spaces between them yawning black. As far as Gardner knew, nobody had followed him here.

He spun at a sudden *whump* in the forest. Probably a tree dumping snow.

High above, in the brief space between cliffs, a red pin prick of light glided across the moon. Satellite.

Where the hell are you?

"Yo!" Gardner whirled to see a soldier stepping out of the pines, in a long military greatcoat and fur hat. The man stamped snow from his boots and continued forward with the jaunty side-to-side stride of a Harlem street hustler. His hands were thrust deep in his pockets. There was no road up there. No path. "Switched cars, eh?" the man called. "Not bad!" He came up to Gardner. "Co-ho-ld!"

Beneath the heavy fur army hat, Gardner looked into a young face, maybe twenty-three. Neat, thin mustache. Boyish smile. Double dimple near the right side of the mouth.

"Hot coffee coming up!" The soldier withdrew a short, fat Thermos from his pocket. "You want a cigarette? Something to eat? I got a sandwich and chocolate. I got gum."

Gardner could only force out, "Where did you come from?"

The finger wagged back and forth in his face. "Whaddaya think, I'm tellin' my secrets?" The soldier popped Juicy Fruit into his mouth, delighted with the effect of his mysterious appearance. He stepped back, threw his arms wide. He looked like a Las Vegas performer acknowledging a big hand. "So?" he said expectantly. "Recognize me?"

This was the timid letter writer who had been contacting Gardner for months? Gardner experienced a sick, sinking feeling. The mercury had dropped off the foot-high thermometer on the side of the cabin. The soldier was grinning, waiting for a reaction. Gardner thought, Great. A nut.

The smile widened. The soldier cried, "It's Bobby L!"

He yanked the hat off. "What'samatta, you don't remember nuthin'? The Stickball King!"

Gardner looked up slowly. His face went blank, then he started to laugh. He laughed so hard tears collected in his eyes and he felt the sting of them freezing. The soldier pumped Gardner's hand. Powerful grip. Gardner thought back to 126th Street in Harlem on a summer day. A teenage boy in denim shorts swung a stickball bat between two lines of parked cars. A rubber Pensy Pinkie ball flew high over Amsterdam Avenue. Screaming teammates rounded makehift bases. Gardner's first story in the *Daily News*, ten years ago, had been beadlined HARLEM BOY NAMED STICKBALL KING.

You worked for years in Washington, cultivating sources. You took senators to dinner, bought lobbyists drinks. You spent months poring over federal reports, searching for leads. Then the big break of your life came from the Stickball King.

Bobby L stepped back, looked him over. "Hey, you got older," he said. "Your hair's different, whattaya, losin' it? Why don't we move back to the trees. I don't think nobody's watchin', but you ever see that infrared shit they use? Clear as noon at midnight. Sure you don't want chocolate? Chocolate keeps you warm 'cause there's energy in it."

They might have been standing at 126th Street, with the Spanish music blasting and the Mr. Softee ice cream truck honking and the drug pushers leaning against the brick walls, waiting for customers to drive by. Bobby L made the Colorado mountains seem unreal. There was a crash behind them.

A raccoon scurried out of an overturned trash can by the dumpster.

Gardner thought, *Test him.* "What was the first letter you sent me?" he asked. When Bobby L answered correctly he said, "And the last?"

It was darker inside the tree line. There was a dense, sappy odor, more moisture in the air. He didn't remember Bobby L's last name. Moonlight made purple patches in the snow where it penetrated. Gardner couldn't tell if the numbness in his legs was excitement or cold.

In his mind he saw Bobby L as a skinny kid in a Satan's Disciples jacket, trying to sell him stolen Gucci shoes, two sizes too small, in front of a bodega.

Gardner said, "*You* went into the Air Force?"

Bobby L bounced on his toes. His movements seemed synchronized to salsa music only he could hear. "Food's good, I get time off. I'll tell ya how it happened. I got this thing about computers." He popped half a Hershey bar in his mouth. "I mean, history, it goes outta my head. Like who's the first President? Don't ask me. Kennedy? But I'm some kinda genius with computers. They tested me."

He licked chocolate from his front teeth. "You like the way I typed those letters? I got that idea from a movie. Kidnappers did it." He poked his index finger into Gardner's chest, head weaving like a boxer's. "But where I'm gonna get computers in Harlem, steal 'em? So I'm watchin' TV. You seen those Armed Forces commercials. '*Be all that you can be.*' Helicopters flyin' and guys shootin' and puttin' their arms around girls in France. But all I see are the computers. Man!" His voice was heavy with admiration. Suddenly he stopped. Gardner heard the faint growl of a car engine, the slap of chains on tarmac. Bobby pulled him into the trees.

"Assholes," he whispered.

An old white Cadillac clunked into view, slowed, as if the driver were eyeing the gas station, and accelerated around the bend.

Bobby L took a step into the half-light. He cocked his head and listened. After a moment he said, "They use old cars, everything. Anyway, somethin' came over me when I saw those computers. I had to get at those computers! And I like it here, ya know? The hours stink and I can't tell anyone what my job is, so what am I doing with you, right? But I love those machines!"

Bobby L blew out a long funnel of breath. When he frowned, his eyebrows dipped past the bridge of his nose. "But I got limits, and that general crossed my limits. I didn't sign on to do *that* kind of shit."

"What kind?" Gardner's blood was roaring. *Finally*, he thought. His hand came out of his pocket with the mini-recorder. As the blue light blinked on, Bobby's hand closed around Gardner's wrist. He pulled away the machine. He whispered, "No pad, no recorder. They'll put me in prison for life. It's worse than regular jail, they warned us. It's Air Force jail. You didn't get it from me. Promise."

"I promise."

Bobby L licked his lips.

"We started to launch," he said.

Gardner frowned. He waited for more, but nothing came. "That's it?" he said. The disappointment was coming back. "But I know we almost launched, everybody knows. I came halfway across the country for that?"

"No, not *almost* launched. *Started* to launch. I'm telling you, DeLavery disobeyed Madden. After the President said give up, he kept going. He ordered us to attack! We were counting down when we found out meteors were coming, not missiles. We were three friggin' seconds from the big boom. The only thing the President did was delay it, delay the launch. It was mutiny!"

The enormity of the revelation stunned Gardner silent. Bobby L looked nervous now, glancing this way and that. The night had the fragile, crystalline quality of glass. Three seconds, Gardner thought. The wind was moaning. He timed it in his mind. In three seconds he could put toothpaste on a toothbrush. In three seconds he couldn't even lace up one shoe.

He shuddered. Even thinking his last two thoughts had taken more than three seconds.

There was a harsh sucking sound from the direction of the dumpster. The raccoon had returned with two cubs.

Bobby L picked an imaginary pine needle off his chest. He seemed embarrassed now that he'd told his story to Gardner. He'd broken some code, the old gang code. "I never told on nobody before," he said. The cheeriness was gone from his voice. Gardner realized all the chatter had been delay. Bobby L looked at the ground and said, "Everybody, man." It took a moment for Gardner to realize he meant all the people who would have died.

He saw the soldier would never feel good about what he had done.

"I had to tell you," said Bobby L. He crumpled the Hershey wrapper, let it fall to the snow. "It isn't right. You wrote good things about the President." He was looking at his feet. "Hey," he said, the bounce coming back, "you ever get to the old neighborhood? See those guys?"

Gardner squeezed the muscled shoulder. "You did right, Bobby. You did an important thing. I'll get the story somewhere else. I didn't get it from you."

Already a plan formed in Gardner's head.

Bobby L's breath came in quick, smoky bursts. "I liked that story you wrote on me. I got it home in a book." He looked at the trees. "A young Mickey Mantle," he said. Half in shadow, half in moonlight, he swung the imaginary bat in his gloved hands. He put his palm to his eyes as if watching the ball sail away.

"Things were easy those days," he said. "Home run."

The van's owner was a freelance photographer named Marshall. He sold pictures of the protesters at NORAD to newspapers and wire services. Gardner, who had worked with him two months ago, kept banging until the back door swung open. "It's six in the damn morning, what the . . . ? Gardner!" Marshall said.

"A thousand dollar bonus," Gardner said. "Can I come in?"

He had a last glimpse of his surroundings as he climbed into the Ford: the ring of camper trucks and thermal tents pitched two hundred yards from NORAD, off the road. The line of sign carrying demonstrators chanting even at this hour, parting to let the bakery truck pass.

The sweet, stale reek of marijuana enveloped him inside. Cameras and lens bags hung from hooks. Marshall's sleeping bag was half-open on top of an air mattress. Bumble Bee tuna and Heinz baked bean cans were piled neatly on a shelf near a dirty pot.

"How can you live here?" Gardner said. Marshall grinned through his stubbly orange beard. He was a small man and he moved in the van with ease. "Beats sitting in an office."

Gardner handed him the three sealed, addressed envelopes. He'd spent hours driving to find an all-night 7-11 store, buying the stationery, writing the letters. "You'll have to get the stamps yourself," he said. He'd not wanted to risk going back to the hotel, where Jankerelli could start following him again. "I know I don't have to say this, but I'll feel better if I do. Tell anyone what we're doing today and you'll never work for the *News* again."

Marshall nodded, squatting on the air mattress in his long johns, counting money in his head, grinning. "I'm a believer, I'm on your side," he said. "No worries."

Gardner looked over the lens cases on the wall. "We'll need your most powerful one," he said.

At eight he was forty-five miles away, back at the 7-11, which had the closest public phone to NORAD. After four cups of coffee he still felt the cold in his bones. The phone was outside, by the air pump.

DeLavery's secretary turned frosty when she recognized his voice.

"Mr. Gardner, I've told you a hundred times . . ."

He cut her off. "Give him a message," he said. "Tell him we're going to press with my story. It's already written. It's about what the general did the night of the surrender. I know he started to launch, you hear?" From the intake of breath, he knew she did. He said, "I'm running the story whether he talks to me or not. I know about the three seconds. Please repeat that. *Three* . . . right. This is his last chance to talk to me before the story runs, to tell his side. I'll wait at this number thirty minutes."

He hung up.

The truth was, he did not have enough verifiable information to write even a paragraph.

Five minutes went by.

Seven.

Fourteen minutes. The phone rang.

An olive colored Army Ford met him at the front gate of NORAD. The demonstrators receded in the rearview mirror. In the backseat, Gardner was flanked by two MPs. Deep inside him a shivering started. He was not cold anymore, and his breathing was steady, but the shivering grew. It grew as they passed fields of snow and pines; a bobcat leaped across the two lane road. A hawk. On the earth's surface NORAD looked like a national park, not a military installation. Nobody would guess what lay three quarters of a mile below. The car was silent. The shivering was in his throat as they plunged into the big tunnel, going deeper beneath the reinforced concrete roof and bright lights, passing jeeps and troop carriers, heading for the heart of NORAD.

As Gardner wrote in his reporter's notebook, he didn't care that the MPs looked over his shoulders. He used a shorthand only he understood. "I feel the missiles, not only around me but spread over thousands of miles. In Kansas and Minnesota. In silos. Hibernating. Ticking like great clocks."

He felt a sense of culmination, of crescendo. They drove through the thirty-foot-high arched steel vault door that could seal NORAD for years. Gardner wrote; "Last time I was here the reporters were joking. Today I feel the awesome might." On foot the MPs led him through bare halls and down steel stairways. He felt in his pocket for extra batteries for the recorder. When they broke into the control room, he gasped in amazement. The shivering was in his head now, he felt it behind his eyes. The words "three seconds" kept beating at him. The MPs shifted impatiently as he wrote. "Nothing has changed here. The same men bend studiously by the same rows of consoles. The same seagreen glow comes from the huge screens in front. I don't know what I expected to feel, but it was not sameness. All over the world people have changed, but not in this room."

He was not surprised when DeLavery did not appear. They brought him into a small, cramped office, bare of decorations, containing only a steel desk and two chairs. Soundproofed. The MPs left and closed the door behind them. Jankerelli, you bastard, come on in, Gardner thought.

He put his hands behind his head and his feet up on the desk.

He was the picture of relaxation when the big man strode into the room. Jankerelli was in uniform, with captain's bars, pudgier-looking in a tailored shirt, larger-looking in the small space. Beneath the cropped blond hair the eyes glowed with the familiar malevolence. He was probably in big trouble for letting Gardner get away last night.

"You look tired," Gardner said, stretching. "Didn't sleep?"

The flame color began creeping up from Jankerelli's collar. He looked like a surfer who'd just washed out in front of his girl. He wasn't going to make an issue over Gardner's taking the good seat, so he sat in the smaller chair, squeezing his knees.

"You told the general's secretary you were writing a story," he said.

Gardner's brows rose. He placed the recorder on the desk and switched it on. He said with excessive pleasantness, "You're not the one I'm here to see. The story is written. It's running tomorrow. It's gone to five papers, not only the *News*, so a court order won't stop it. If the general won't see me, you can take me back. One more thing. Our photographer took pictures of your MPs taking me in here. If you have any idea of locking me up again, the photos will run."

He leaned further back to indicate he'd finished talking. The crimson was up to Jankerelli's cheeks. His neck swelled like an oboe player's. When he forced himself to laugh, he made a hollow, barking sound. "What a sense of humor," Jankerelli snorted. "A prisoner. What an imagination. Who do you think we are?"

Gardner suppressed the whoop of triumph as Jankerelli reached for the phone. A moment later the captain said, "The general will see you now." He coughed on the last word. "Sir."

The house was Victorian style, built on a high knoll at the end of a suburban street. But the rows of fine homes were inside NORAD, a mile from the tunnel and set into the woods. Beyond the porch railing and the snow covered lawn DeLavery had a gorgeous view of the mountains. Gardner rang the doorbell, the shivering deep in his chest.

"Mr. Gardner," the general said, opening the door himself. "Come in."

Gardner felt as if he'd never left the man's presence. The general wore his uniform even at home. He spoke with the same clipped consonants Gardner remembered. The black hair, like an Indian's, shone blue in the half light of the foyer. The wedge shaped face was all angles; even the eyebrows had sharp points.

But now that he was with DeLavery, Gardner's mood changed again. He channeled his attention so that his heart slowed. He did not want to miss a nuance, a phrase. He was taking in everything. He noted the vast quiet in the house as DeLavery led him toward the study. He concluded no one else was home. He glimpsed evidence of the military life abroad; deep blue Oriental vases in the living room, Asian masks on the wall.

But mostly, in those early moments, he took in the change in DeLavery. There was something flawed and hurt in the man. Nothing overt, but an edge was missing. Gardner had interviewed many successful men. They shared a sheen of accomplishment. There was a lack of the crispness that had formerly marked DeLavery. There was effort in the lines beneath the eyes and around the mouth. The gait was slower. The scrubbed look of power was gone.

In the study DeLavery sat behind his mahogany desk and waved Gardner into a chair. The wall to Gardner's right had been turned into a private military museum. A shiny saber, razor sharp, arced upward in its long rectangular case. A Mauser, all blued steel, hung from a peg beneath a torn Army cap. There was a glass case with an Air Force tunic and another with a compass. Each case was labeled, but Gardner was too far away to make out the words.

To the left were birds, exquisite watercolor paintings. He admired the boreal owl, brown and white, eyes hooded. He noted the curved, sharp beak of the osprey as it dove for a fish, and the deep blue of the water. Gardner thought they were Audubon prints, but when he looked closer, the signature read "DeLavery."

In his study the general took on some of the old formidableness. Behind the desk his posture grew. He steepled his hands and his eyes traveled over Gardner. With soldiers he had probably been master of the intimidating stare. Gardner merely made notes in his head. *The shaving nick is recent. Why is he at home?*

DeLavery saw the stare wasn't working. "You're to be congratulated on your persistence," he said. "Perhaps I should have let you stay in the room that night. It would have saved us both trouble."

Gardner supposed this was the closest thing he would receive to a compliment. He switched on the recorder in his pocket, where DeLavery could not see. He spoke carefully, politely. "General, since I learned you would meet with me I've been trying to think how I would ask my question. But I guess I can say it in two words."

DeLavery cocked his head and gave a dignified nod. "What are those words, Mr. Gardner?"

"Three seconds."

A plaque on the desk, beside a small greeting card lying on its side, read, "Honor. Duty. Sacrifice." DeLavery chuckled. He seemed genuinely amused. "You would concentrate on that," he said. He uncoiled himself from the chair and strolled to a bar in a hutch near the osprey. "Orange juice?" he said. There was a pleasant tinkling sound of ice against glass when he poured. Gardner thought, his color is bad.

"Three seconds," DeLavery repeated, more to himself than to Gardner, musing as if he'd heard an idea that he had never thought about before. "You know, Mr. Gardner, back in the beginning, forty years ago, those bombs were a miracle." He was gazing at the shades even though they were drawn. "Hitler was trying to get them first. Stalin. It was a miracle. It saved so many lives. It was God, that we got it." DeLavery's hair had grown slightly longer so that the edges curled, Gardner saw. "And not only weapons but engines, power," DeLavery said. "You never had to refuel. Ships could go so fast."

DeLavery came out of his reverie. He pressed his lips together when he smiled. "You want to know about the three seconds. Do you mind if I take up a little time, turn it around, ask you a question?"

He's lost weight, Gardner thought. "Ask."

The general sipped juice. "Your opinion, Mr. Gardner. If this terrible bomb had never been invented, if it was still an idea on a scientist's drawing board and we were making do with tanks and infantry, when do you think World War Three would have broken out?"

"World War Three, General?"

DeLavery was drifting across the room, toward the artifacts in the glass cases. "1948?" he asked. "When the Russians blockaded Berlin? 1968? The Czechoslovakian invasion? Israel? Cuba?" He looked surprised. "Don't tell me you think we wouldn't have fought the Russians? You'd probably be a military man yourself. Intelligence, I imagine. With your penchant for ferreting out information."

"I don't have all the answers. I don't know."

DeLavery seemed delighted. "You don't want to talk about 1948 or 1968. You don't want to talk about history." A slight disdain came into his voice. "You're just an expert on the three seconds."

"All I know is, the man who saved the country is being tried for treason and you almost destroyed it. Here you are, comfortable at home. That's why I'm here."

DeLavery nodded dryly. "Yes," he said. "Comfortable." Bitterness tinged his voice. DeLavery drained his orange juice, reached for a humidor but decided against a cigar. There was the thump of a snowball against the house, and boys yelled at each other outside, high and muffled, "Missed me, dirty Russian!" Gardner realized the general's questions were not idle but he was unsure where they might lead.

DeLavery had reached the saber in its shiny case. He glanced toward the plaque on the desk. "Duty. Honor," he said. "That's what they taught at West Point. Do you know what duty is, Mr. Gardner? Do you ever think about honor? What *do* you think about honor?"

Keep talking, Gardner thought, feeling the vibration of the spinning tape recorder in his pocket. *Dig your own grave.*

But he felt the force of the man's will. DeLavery rested his fingers lightly against the top of the biggest glass case. "This cavalry sword. My great-great-grandfather fought in Texas with it. Mexican-American war." With his fingers trailing across the glass, DeLavery gave the tour. "My grandfather used this sword at Antietam. My great-uncle fought the Huks on horseback in the Philippines with this gun. My father was a pilot. This was his cap."

Gardner noted the military ring on the fourth finger of the hand resting atop the case. DeLavery's voice softened. "Duty. Honor. In my family we always sought the cutting edge of warfare. My grandfather taught my father. My father taught me. Take the most difficult, the most challenging positions!" His voice rose. "No freedom without sacrifice!"

You don't have to tell me about sacrifice, Gardner thought, irritated at the sanctimonious condescension. My father died for nothing.

He asked, "What will you leave in your glass case, General? A hydrogen bomb?"

DeLavery shrugged. "Someone has to watch over it. Or would you rather we forget it, pretend it doesn't exist? Leave it in a hole and assume the Russians are doing the same? The man of duty seeks out his task, no matter how difficult. I'm proud of what I did. There was no launch, Mr. Gardner. The system worked, we were warned in time. We did not falter!"

Gardner realized he detected a smell in the room. It had been there all along, but it was so subtle he only now noticed it. A dampness. It cast him back. He was standing in front of a white house on Long Island, twenty-four, a reporter on his first investigation, about to interview a lawyer he would send to jail. On a spring morning he eyed the peeling paint on the home, the unmowed lawn. The man inside had stolen thirty thousand dollars from a client, an eighty-three-year-old widow whose money he'd been hired to manage. The district attorney had shown Gardner the cancelled checks. There was no doubt about the lawyer's guilt.

Gardner saw the door open slightly. He saw the pale, frightened face emerge. "I have cancer," the lawyer had croaked through a ravaged throat. "I didn't mean to use her money. I'll get it back. Please don't write the story."

The same smell had seeped from the house that day. Now Gardner realized it had not been the odor of disease, but ruin.

DeLavery leaned back in his chair. "You train for years to be strong enough to use the weapon if you have to. You hope you will never have to, but you have to be strong. I have sons in New York, grandchildren. What makes you think I'm eager to destroy them?"

DeLavery saw reason wasn't working. He snapped, "If you're not ready to die for your country, you don't deserve to live in it!"

"Oh, I would die for it," Gardner said. "But I won't see it in ashes. General, you didn't answer my question. Why did you disobey the President that night?"

The greeting card on the desk showed an old man and a young boy in a rowboat on a lake hazy with mist. The upside-down caption read, "Happy Birthday, Grandpa."

Quite calmly, DeLavery said, "I had met the President on several occasions. He was always aware of what needed to be done if we were attacked. When he gave the order to give up I . . . I'm still convinced he suffered a breakdown. Pressure."

"Did he say anything to give you that impression?"

DeLavery laughed. "He said give up! I've served under four Presidents. Good men, patriots, God knows I could never do their job. But when we brief them at NORAD they just don't like to talk about the worst case scenarios. They're not any different from most people. They'll go on for hours about money for arms or SALT talks. But try to talk about the final order, what will happen when the button is pushed, you have to strap them down in a chair like a boy at the dentist. They don't want to talk about it. You're lucky if you get ten minutes with them. I told him when I took command from him, 'Mr. President, *you're not ready . . .*'"

Gardner was half out of the chair. "Madden *knows*? But, why doesn't he bring it out in court?"

"I told you. He's a patriot. He knows what has to be done. He won't save himself with sordid revelations that would drag down the military. Honor, Mr. Gardner." Apparently DeLavery judged the time right for his pitch. The hands steepled again. The voice became reasonable, delicate. "You said you would die for your country but would you suppress a news story for it?"

Gardner stared back at him. "You want me to flush the story?"

DeLavery was up, hands behind his back. Addressing the troops. Speaking at a luncheon. Passion came into his voice and made it resonant. "Mr. Gardner, this country is facing the gravest danger." He was standing by the .45, the sword, the cap. "The military can police itself. You're an observant man. Look at me. I'm home, not at my post." The bitterness came back. "Post? I have no post! Colonel

Choyke is in charge. I'm broken, finished. It'll be official in six months. Don't you see? The general who disobeyed can't be allowed to command troops."

Gardner said, "General, people need to know what happened."

In the birthday card on the desk, the grandfather did the rowing and the little boy held a fishing rod. DeLavery came closer, his hands upraised, his fingers splayed in appeal. "Need?" he laughed. "Who are you to know what they need? Do you know what will happen if you publish? Hearings! Investigations! They'll strip NORAD and make it a husk. When we need it most. Remember what happened to the CIA? A vibrant agency dismembered by Congress. Is that what people need, a sniveling, weak, broken military, an army that can't even make decisions for itself? You can stop it!"

With a loud click, the tape recorder in Gardner's pocket switched off.

Gardner watched the general's reflection freeze in the glass case containing the .45.

In a half whisper, shock turning to rage, DeLavery said, "A tape."

Gardner casually removed the machine from his pocket and flipped the tape to the unused side, as if both of them had known all along it was in operation. The blue light blinked on. He said, easily, "Everything's on the record, General."

But he knew people never talked as freely when a recorder was present. He watched a wave of almost physical violence come over DeLavery, stiffen his wide shoulders, deepen the lines on his face. Once in a Chicago bar a thug from the Teamsters Union had tried to grab Gardner's tape recorder. Gardner had smashed a beer stein in the man's face and run. In NORAD there was no place to run. The snow outside was deep, the MPs seconds away if DeLavery called them.

Gardner said, "I have a pretty good memory anyway." As suddenly as the anger had risen, it subsided. DeLavery's eyes dulled over. He was surrendering to more than just the presence of a tape recorder. Gardner wondered what his life had been like for the past few months, the proud man stripped of authority, confined to the house? He had the sense of blocks of support slipping out from beneath DeLavery, first the military, then the secret. Where was his family anyway?

"Somehow I always knew you would be the one to come," DeLavery said. "What good would it do to take the machine away from you? I'm not even supposed to be talking to you. You might say I disobeyed instructions twice." Enfolded between the arms of the chair, he seemed diminished and his voice dropped, softer. "You have your pint of blood. You're young, Mr. Gardner. You'll write lots of stories. You'll fill our prisons with felons, I'm sure. If you really care for your country, pass up this opportunity. The Air Force is finished for me. Honor, Mr. Gardner. Show that you have it. I can live with what I did. Don't make me the man who destroyed the Air Force."

Gardner had an image of DeLavery placing the family artifacts in their cases with reverence. He wondered where DeLavery would live when the Air Force made him leave NORAD. He wondered what the next occupant would do with the glass cases. He wondered if DeLavery would keep his pension. He would check with the Pentagon later, on the phone. But the brightness was gone from his feeling of triumph.

"I'm sorry," Gardner said, rising. "Don't exaggerate. The Air Force will survive." To his left the osprey's beak hung an inch from the water. A trout's tail was visible, the fish fleeing in vain. The osprey's eye was bright with hunger. Gardner left the man standing by his desk.

Outside, the morning air was fresh and sparkling. The MPs warmed themselves with the motor running in the Ford. Exhaust came from the tailpipe, dissipated. He heard muffled rock music from the next house. The mountains rose beyond the woods, glacial and white. He had thought he would feel wonderful leaving the general. The tape recorder rested snugly against his thigh. He wondered things about DeLavery he'd never thought about before. Did the man have a wife? Had she left him? Was he alone?

As he started down the steps, toward the car, he heard DeLavery's shot, clear and resonant in the morning air.

Gardner sat in the Subaru with the engine running and the heater on. The hotel was across the street. He could not bring himself to go in yet. From the spinning tape recorder on the seat, DeLavery's voice said, "I told that prosecutor to leave it alone." Gardner smashed his fist into the dashboard. The pain sliced through his wrist and up his arm. He remembered flinging DeLavery's door open. He heard the MPs' pounding footsteps behind. No sight of DeLavery at first. Just blue smoke rising. The thick, acrid odor made him want to sneeze. Maybe I didn't hear a gun, he thought. Maybe it was a car backfiring. But then he saw the ruby drop sliding down the print of the osprey, smearing a trail on the glass.

A voice outside snapped him back to the present. "Oh my God, Todd asked me for a date!" Two college girls were passing on the sidewalk, laughing, skis over their shoulders, blond hair blowing in the breeze. The normalcy of Midas Gulch seemed unreal after DeLavery. All along Main Street, merchants shoveled last night's snowfall from the sidewalks.

On the evening news James Henry had stood in court near Madden. His hand had been in his pocket, and he had had that superior, sharklike smile on his face. The tape said, "I'm asking you, please, don't write the piece." Gardner took a deep breath and shut it off violently. She'd be upstairs, across the street.

He was barely aware of the lobby and stairway. In the room she was sleeping with her jeans and shirt on, sprawled on top of the bed. The TV was droning, a weatherman said, "Fifteen inches on the mountain last night." She'd probably waited up into the early hours, worrying about him.

Sbe murmured something he could not hear and her hand slid across his pillow. Gardner felt as if he had been away from her for years. He remembered her at that first dinner party at Mark St. Johns's. She had worn the black dress with the low front that he liked so much. And an Italian watch with a thin golden band. That night he'd been conscious of her slightest movement. He remembered how she had gently changed the conversation when it upset Nicki St. Johns. That was the moment when he'd started to love her. He'd wanted her from the first, but the kindness had been a surprise.

Gardner pulled a chair close and watched her breathing. In her apartment he'd seen a photograph of her at fourteen. Her hair was cut short, thicker on the right side. She had no breasts at all. She was sprawled on a beach doing a bad imitation of Veronica Lake. You could tell from the way she smiled that she knew she looked pretty gawky. He'd felt jealous looking at the picture. Jealous of a time when she'd been a stranger to him.

And then her eyes popped open as if she had known he was there. The red nails reached his knees, squeezed. She said with a drowsy, happy relief, "Oh, it's really you."

Gardner heard himself say when she asked what was wrong. "He shot himself. I got the story but DeLavery killed himself."

She was up, her arms around his shoulders. She was kissing him and saying, "I'm so sorry, so sorry." But it wasn't over. He had to write the story and include her father. Her father, whom she loved fiercely, who might go to jail now for suppressing evidence. Who had Henry been kidding all these months, coming on so tough about Madden? James Henry was a cheat masquerading as a respectable lawyer. He was an opportunist looking for the supreme trophy for his basement wall. But he was her father, the father of the woman Gardner wanted to marry.

He kept seeing the top of DeLavery's head blown off, the bits of blood-covered bone on the side of the desk, the fingers twitching and going still. He heard the sirens. He saw Jankerelli's face in the car on the way back to the gate, nobody talking, driving so fast they might have been in an ambulance taking the general to a hospital, as if speed could change anything. Jankerelli had cried out, "What the hell did you say to him in there?" The big man had been crying. "I've been with DeLavery thirteen years."

He hadn't told Susan the James Henry part. With her arms around him he felt dirty and low. But through the shock and pain a voice kept insisting, You have to write about him. I told you he was involved all along. People have to know what he did.

Who are you to say what people have to know? DeLavery had said on the tape.

It's my job, Gardner answered. Who were *you* to almost blow up the fucking planet.

Madden will stay on trial no matter what happens to me, James Henry had said. Take me off the case and another lawyer will step in.

Gardner's mind jumped from one image to another. He'd sent men to prison, but no one had killed himself before. In a minute he would get on the phone and call Edelstein and Washington. He'd get more quotes, round out the piece. For a flash he saw his old girlfriend Julia in their Manhattan apartment. Sitting in a black body suit on Manhattan's West Side, legs folded beneath her in a yoga position. Ferns rising behind her from a dozen pots on the floor. They were calmly discussing the baby she was carrying. They were reasonable and businesslike; in a half hour they were scheduled to go to a movie with friends. Gardner was saying, "My career is too important." Julia was saying, "How can I go to law school with a child?"

"Bob?" Susan said to him.

He kept seeing DeLavery's fingers. All that talk about duty and honor on the tape.

"Bob?" Colder now. Frightened. He could tell she knew. She had said to him, "I'm not afraid to go with you to Colorado. My father's not involved."

But Gardner was frozen. All that talk about duty and honor, and in the end DeLavery was as lost as everybody else.

In wonder he repeated, out loud, "Everybody else . . ."

With the words he felt lighter. He felt the tiredness streaming away, leaving him as if it had never existed. He stood up and squeezed her shoulders and headed for the typewriter near the TV. He kept the paper in the drawer with the Bible, next to the postcards saying HOWDY FROM MIDAS GULCH! When a column came to him, power surged into his hands.

He pounded the keys; the words emerged.

"In a private study in Colorado, a United States general shot and killed himself today. A man who met the challenges of a new age with the values of the old. This will be a column about two men, both victims. Proud men who faced the same decision four months ago. One lies dead, the other is on trial. Both were helpless against the nuclear age."

As he worked he felt her come up behind him. He saw her in the mirror, the red shirt hanging loose. Her hand rested on his shoulder, soft and warm.

Susan said, "It's more than DeLavery. Tell me the rest."

She seemed to glow, her lips were so beautiful. He didn't have to be like everybody else. He could hide the tape in his safe deposit box. He could record over the James Henry part if Edelstein wanted to hear it. The plaque on DeLavery's desk meant something after all. For Susan he made his voice surly and gruff.

"I can't be right all the time. He had nothing to do with it, okay? Okay, let me finish. I didn't even eat last night."

The piece would punch holes through James Henry's case anyway. It would help Madden. It had to. When the happiness broke over her face, he felt a kind of freedom he had never before experienced. He felt light and good in a way DeLavery would not change. Her relief showed in the way her body relaxed.

He saw his father in his mind. In wonder Gardner thought, So that's what you meant.

"I'll order breakfast," she said, but she paused before lifting the receiver. She was feeling so good she was going to do one of her little acts. She clasped her hands to her breast in a parody of a silent film actress. Mary Pickford, maybe. "My hero," she said.

Gardner pounded the typewriter. She could be such a goofball sometimes.

18

Diane Medaglia caught sight of James Henry across the cafeteria, at a table by himself. It was seven-thirty a.m. She rubbed her eyes, not having slept last night, worrying. She paid for her coffee and headed for his spot.

Henry nodded hello but concentrated on his eggs and paper. She glimpsed the top-left headline, SOVIETS INSTALL NUKES IN MEHTA, and it made her shiver. She eyed the prosecutor more speculatively at another headline: WHO WAS IN ON COVERUP?

"Who do you think knew about it?" she asked idly, unwrapping a plain danish. The coffee was weak, but at least it was hot. Henry's blue eyes were watery, he coughed like he'd picked up a flu. She glimpsed the Harris tweed through the half-open raincoat.

The smile was pleasant, as usual. "I thought this was a social visit," he said, mopping up egg with a sesame roll. At nearby tables courthouse workers sat in silent clusters beneath banks of lights. Tracked-in snow melted on the linoleum. He flicked his wrists, casting an imaginary fishing rod. "What are we after today?" he asked. "Perch? Trout?"

But he seemed flattered and that gave her a thought. *He wants me to know he was involved.* Her heart beat faster. Probably everyone in the country knew about the mutiny at NORAD this morning except the jury, which was sequestered. That's the way it would stay unless either attorney brought it up in court. Her nightmare last night had started off pleasantly enough. She'd imagined herself calling experts to the stand and getting them to admit the coverup hurt the country as much as the surrender. But what had kept her awake was a vision of James Henry gleefully bringing general after general to the stand. "Why did you disobey the President?" he kept asking.

Because he committed treason, they would say.

He blew his nose on a monogrammed handkerchief. His nose was the color of his maroon bow tie. "Try the pineapple danish tomorrow," he advised.

He trundled off with the briefcase he never let the jury see. Medaglia thought he looked like an old man. She'd admired Gardner's work for months. If only he'd linked Henry to the coverup. That would get the case thrown out, she thought. Henry had said nothing directly, but she'd felt like he was teasing her. She wouldn't touch the NORAD disclosure; it was too risky. She hoped she was doing the right thing.

At nine she was rising to address her first witness and there was no time for second thoughts. Medaglia moved through her case chronologically. She called seven members of Madden's old squad, who recalled his courage under fire in Korea. College friends and veterans recounted years of patriotic speeches. By the time the third congressman was praising Madden's weapons bills Henry rose, coughing into his hand. "Why are we listening to one more person saying the same thing?"

Medaglia always felt stronger presenting her own witnesses. "Your Honor," she said in a bench conference, "Mr. Henry has claimed a handful of random remarks made over the years constitute treason. To prove how ridiculous that is, I want to show the vast number of times the President acted true to character."

Murtaugh signaled the bailiff to bring more mints. "Not so many occasions," he sighed.

A grim, gritty quality entered the proceedings. Trench warfare going into the second week. Medaglia introduced reports, memos, studies. "The President signed military treaties with Chile, France,

India, Australia to strengthen the country against the Russians," reported a former secretary of state. "He courted dictators, men he despised, because the alliances would make us more powerful." A former speechwriter read portions of Madden's State of the Union addresses. The chairman of the Yale department of nuclear physics testified, "Life would end on earth if a full-scale war were to erupt. Not a plant. Not a fish. Not a beam of sunlight."

Henry asked witnesses who praised Madden's weapons programs, "Did he use those weapons the night he gave up?"

He paced back and forth in front of the Yale scientist. "Isn't it true your theory is all speculation? Isn't it true many experts believe nuclear war survivable?"

When Mark St. Johns took the stand, a hush descended over the room. All eyes went to the steel hand raised out of his gray woolen sleeve as he swore to tell the whole truth. He'd lost none of the power of his appearance, with his football player's shoulders and massive bald pate. If anyone should have a grudge against Madden, the hook seemed to say, shouldn't it be this witness?

"He saved my life in Korea," St. Johns said, "when other men wanted to give up. He showed the same spirit throughout his years as President." In the jury box, the bus driver leaned back and pursed his lips. He seemed to regard Madden with more softness. The women, especially the milliner, smiled often as the banker spoke.

St. Johns brought the jury back to the dinner party Nicki had described. "Madden joked about surrender, he didn't promote it," St. Johns said. He did a parody of Madden drunk. He waved his arms and slurred, " 'We'll hand ourselves to the Russians.' " Normally he was so formal that good-natured laughter swept the court.

Medaglia leaned close. There were dark circles under her eyes. "In all your years of knowing the President, did you ever hear him advocate surrender?"

Mark St. Johns sat up straight and looked directly at the jury.

"Never," he said.

Unfazed, the prosecutor started off respectfully, his voice hoarser from the flu. He sipped water from a plastic cup, returning to the table to drink every few minutes.

"Mr. St. Johns," said Henry, "you've testified that you are a close, intimate friend of the defendant's, is that true?"

"Close" and "intimate" sounded dirty the way he said them. "It is."

"And your business is banking?"

"Yes." St. Johns tended to sound pompous under cross-examination.

Henry nodded to himself as if he had confirmed a suspicion. "Mr. St. Johns, isn't it a fact that since your friend William Madden came to reside in the White House, the assets of your bank have risen substantially, by several billion dollars, in fact?"

A hum broke out in the back of the court. St. Johns snapped, "Oh, for chrissake."

Murtaugh ordered him to answer. "Our assets grew by several billion dollars even before he became President."

James Henry approached the stand, one of his ubiquitous papers seeming to have materialized in his hand. "I'm holding several annual reports from Global American Bank. We can go over them if you wish. Isn't it true, Mr. St. Johns, that the *rate* of growth *doubled* after Mr. Madden took office?"

The friendly expression on the bus driver's face was replaced by something more sour. "Yes," St. Johns admitted.

Henry coughed into his handkerchief, a hard, racking sound. He looked over more papers on the prosecution table. "Mr. St. Johns, do you recall being visited by Mr. Madden at London Anglican Hospital on or about December twenty-first?"

To the hat shop owner, who sat closest in the jury box, it seemed the color drained from St. Johns's face.

"Your wife, from whom you are separated, was present," Henry continued. "You notice her in the audience, do you not?"

St. Johns said more softly, "Yes." She was in the fifth row, where Henry had asked her to sit. She wore a beige wool sweater and matching wide-brimmed hat which obscured the top half of her face. When St. Johns glanced in her direction, the chemist in the jury looked at the accountant. His brows went up.

Henry seemed to be saying, if you lie she will catch you.

Mildly, Henry asked, "During the conversation, do you recall Mr. Madden saying he was glad he had surrendered?"

A gasp broke from the room. St. Johns's steel hook grated against the witness box, as if he had tried to grab the railing and forgotten he had no hand. "You have to take it in context."

"Yes? Or no?"

St. Johns banged the railing with his real hand. "He meant he was glad everything hadn't gone up!"

Murtaugh took a dim view of outbursts in his courtroom. He advised levelly, "This is not your bank, Mr. St. Johns. This is a court of law. Answer simply and respectfully or I will find you in contempt."

Henry seemed pleased at St. Johns's explosion. He continued, "But Mr. Madden's *words* were, he was glad he surrendered?"

"His words were, he was glad how things turned out."

"No further questions."

"WILLIAM SHOW MADDEN," boomed the bailiff's voice.

And then, finally, Madden was in front of them, blinking out into the room. From the witness box he could see the details of the jurors' faces. The black, triangular beauty mark on the secretary's chin. The shaving nick near the chemist's sideburns. The shell-shocked look of weariness, interest, and responsibility they all shared after two weeks of trial.

"Keep it simple," Medaglia had warned. But what was simple about it? On stand he experienced the feeling of unreality again. But there was more. A change that had started when he'd read Gardner's article. All the elements inside jolted, realigning.

Medaglia came to a stop one step from the witness box.

"In your own words, Mr. President, tell us what happened?"

"I was asleep in the White House," he began. He'd practiced the words so often they came by themselves. In his mind he played a montage of images. Iowa in summer. He saw himself stepping from a train caboose festooned with red and blue streamers. The rich, loamy smell of farmland came. The humid earthiness. Goldman's voice saying, "An old-fashioned campaign."

He pictured a boy in kneehigh shorts by an overturned tricycle. His father's face bending down, amused. "You broke it, son. Can you fix it?"

An unconscious riffling of images for a pattern that made sense.

Madden told the court, "I instructed Dr. Shinitzky to contact the Russians. At that point I hoped the alert was a mistake."

He felt the violence in the courtroom, the immensity of the need. But in his mind he went back to the limousine as the news erupted over the radio. He'd been stuck in traffic, in a storm.

Medaglia had sat motionless. When the truth had registered, she'd uncoiled toward him on the seat, her face a hardened mask. "You knew about this!"

Inside he'd been screaming. Who let DeLavery talk to reporters? The car smelled of leather and cologne. He'd reached for the phone to give orders. To Admiral Tunney to announce the Joint Chiefs' investigation. To the press office to . . . *I'm not President,* he'd suddenly realized. He was powerless. He could do nothing. He'd grown dizzy with rage.

Outside the limousine, the horns and shouts had grown louder. "Congressional leaders are calling for hearings," the radio had said. Madden had snapped at Medaglia, "You told me you wanted to try the case. I told you what you needed to know. This has nothing to do with you." When he'd been President, that tone had sent aides scurrying from the office. Medaglia did not customarily use the limousine bar, but she'd reached into the cluster of shiny miniature bottles. The announcer had said, "Pentagon officials refuse to say how high the mutiny went."

Mutiny, he'd thought. The press was after the Army already.

He'd asked for Rittenhouse when the White House operator answered. The two of them had agreed on the coverup the night of the surrender.

Medaglia had spoken up while he waited to talk to the President. She'd forced her words, calmly. "You'd better tell me everything."

In the corner of the backseat she'd looked younger, less experienced. Wisps of black hair frizzed out above her ears. The storm blew louder outside; snow beat at the slashing wipers. Her fingers had been interlaced around her glass of gin. "Oh, you have a marvelous view of the world," he'd said. "Give any problem to a jury and it comes out fixed. The magical religion of attorneys. Those twelve people set me free and it's over, is it?" Her pupils had looked enormous. "Do you really believe what you're saying?" he'd said.

His face had told her the rest. *You know what will happen to me in the end.*

In court, Madden told the jury, "Premier Menkes came on the line with two minutes to go."

Nicki lifted her face so that Madden saw her eyes, sad and luminous. He felt a sudden pang of loss. He wished Josh were here: he missed his son.

He went on talking but he was saying nothing they had not already heard. On TV or radio. In arguments in private homes. Madden gave the facts veracity. He brought them back. Each person present heard the same words but saw a different picture. In the jury box the accountant was back in the bedroom of his northwest side home. Headlights swept the ceiling when cars rounded the corner outside. He had insomnia and barely slept. His wife had left him a month before the surrender. The secretary beside him imagined a lush basement in a Chevy Chase club. She did not know the names of the two naked men on top of her. The cushions all over the floor had crazy zigzag patterns in purple and black. Spectators saw mothers, husbands, daughters, sons. The thrill of their escape was palpable in the courtroom. The horror of the near miss was a collective drawing of breath.

Madden kept talking. "The premier was being advised to launch. His aides insisted we were trying to keep him occupied while we attacked."

In his mind he went back to the limousine. Rittenhouse had come on the line. Madden's anger had hardened to a cold, effective resolve. "I'll do whatever you want," he had told Rittenhouse. "I'll tell them I authorized it, withheld it from you. I'll take the whole responsibility."

He'd always had to watch his tone with Rittenhouse, remind himself the man was no longer the compromise candidate he had picked for his number two spot. Rittenhouse had kept repeating, "That sonofabitch DeLavery." With only months until the primaries, he was watching his chances for reelection plunge.

Rittenhouse had grown conciliatory. "I'll handle it, I appreciate the call." Which meant, stay out of it. Rittenhouse had said, "It's good to know you're always there." *You've done enough damage.*

When he'd been President Madden had been briefed each morning at six. He'd looked over topographical maps of the Mehta Valley. "These are the Ethiopians," the voice would say, fingers tracing blue arrows. "These red ones are the Russians." On the two occasions when Rittenhouse had been present they'd argued. "You're not tough enough," Rittenhouse had said.

In the limousine, before they hung up, Rittenhouse had said, "I don't understand you. One minute you're tearing everything apart and the next you're making this offer."

In court, James Henry nodded from his seat, satisfied with Madden's testimony. How the jury was taking it remained unclear. For Madden, the dreamlike quality intensified. He was saying, "I decided I would stay in the White House until the end." But he was remembering the strange thing that had happened after Rittenhouse had hung up. He'd gotten out of the car to see why traffic wasn't moving, unable to stand sitting anymore.

Outside, the storm had thickened. The snow had seeped into his shoes and blown into the sleeves of his coat. Fifty yards ahead a Metrobus had slid into a Wagoneer in an intersection. A broken traffic light rocked in the wind. Rush hour traffic battled to inch through behind the bus, but cars were wedged in so tightly no one could move. Amid the honking and shouting a man's voice had yelled, "Step on the fucking accelerator! That's how you do it!" A woman's voice with a French Canadian accent shouted, "Get out of ze way!"

With Huff beside him Madden had approached the shouting, gesticulating mass. The side of the Wagoneer had caved in. Sad looking kids wiped condensation off the windows in back. Someone had grabbed the Secret Service man's elbow and was complaining in a high pitched whine, "Where are the police when you need . . ." when Madden turned around.

The man's mouth had snapped shut. "Oh," he'd said. He'd backed a step. The wind had risen. Madden had realized the silence was extending out from him, in a wave. The honking was stopping, the shouting too. The storm had been so thick it obscured the buildings. No rooftops. Airplanes. Lights. Sky.

Everyone had turned to stare at him.

Once, in the White House, Madden had seen ten minutes of a movie called *Rise from the Dead.* The attorney general had showed it to him because it had been banned for violence in Mississippi. In the film dead people walked like zombies through a Southern town. The dead people all wore the same blank expression. In the snowy intersection Madden had been tempted to laugh, because for an instant he felt like he was in the movie. The drivers in the cars had turned toward him, faces half obscured by the wet and dark.

Madden had walked behind the bus and seen how easy it would be to get traffic moving. One car at a time ought to do it, he'd thought. He'd picked out a woman standing with one foot in her station wagon, the other in the snow. The car's overhead light had shown a baby in a carseat waving its arms. Snow had collected on the woman's glasses. "Why don't you go first?" he'd said. When he'd gotten back to the limousine Huff had joked, "There's a new job for you, Mr. President. Traffic cop."

In court the twinge subsided again. He was saying, "There was no doubt in my mind, none at all. Once we responded, all the missiles would go off. Fifteen thousand warheads. Fifteen thousand warheads," he repeated.

But he kept going back and forth in his mind. Now he was at home with Catherine. "Love, you can be mad as you want about that article but I'm celebrating, Gardner's a genius." She'd blown the *Daily News* a kiss, it lay on the corner of the bed. "Let's invite him here, throw him a party." She'd been giddy with delight. "Sourpuss. You should have seen the audience tonight. They were wild." She'd come in at midnight, her flight delayed from New York, where she'd been speaking. Beneath his pajama tops her long fingers had kneaded his upper back. She'd worn one of his old shirts and nothing else.

"Here's a meeting," she'd said. She called bunched muscles meetings. She'd pushed down on the muscles. "Meeting adjourned."

But Madden had gotten up, pacing like a wild man, furious at Gardner. "DeLavery tried to talk him out of it! Journalists!" At the window he'd said, "You should have seen the way those drivers looked at me. Like I was some kind of freak. Monster. Maybe Rittenhouse is right. I feel like two people. Maybe I don't belong here any-more."

That was when she'd finally gotten mad. "Stop feeling sorry for yourself." She'd taken him by the hand, like a boy, and brought him to her upstairs workroom. He'd been thinking after all these months he still felt the awful responsibility. He had to do something but had no idea what. Once again he'd felt his frustration with a violence of suppressed passion grinding at his insides. It made no difference how often he turned the thing over in his mind. It was more than just the surrender. There had always been all those easy victories for him and the sense that someday he would have to pay. He'd suppressed that New England fear for years. All that time he'd piously accepted award until he expected it. And then demanded it. And all the while that suppressed gnawing New England voice, the voice of his uncle in the Lyle, Massachusetts, pulpit. That voice from somewhere above. Cotton Mather. John Calvin. As a politician he knew there was no perfection, only compromise. But why wasn't compromise enough now? The heaviness never went away, the feeling that he must do something. Withdrawal and reckoning. All mixed up.

He missed the power. Not love, just energy. A beast leaping, alive.

Robert Gardner's article had dislodged it all. Wildly careening fragments of thought collided and realigned. As he testified, he watched Medaglia's fingers playing with her pencil. He remembered the time he had tried to teach Josh to swing a baseball bat. Josh hadn't been able to hold it right; he'd kept putting his thumb up along the shaft. He had started to cry. *"Put down the damn thumb!"* Madden had always lost patience with him. Why was he feeling bad about that now? Why hadn't he come out publicly for the boy during his college marijuana arrest? Sure, he'd made arrangements in private, but he'd never told Josh. Build that character! Why was that bothering him now? He didn't understand the things he was thinking. He was think-ing he needed to do something for his son. Something . . . no . . . they never even . . . something big.

His mind shifted back to Catherine's workroom. A small square room in pastel yellows and blues. The furniture had been drawing room French, skinny, sickly legs on an expensive desk with too small a surface for him. RALLY ROUND CATHERINE, the *News* headline had announced. MRS. AMERICA FOR PEACE.

She'd whispered, "Not belong here? Look what you started." She'd let the pile of unopened telegrams rain down through her fingers, fall in unruly mounds on the desk and slip down to the powder blue carpet. "It's you they really want to hear from. I'm just the substitute. After only five days! Look at all of it!" In her excitement she'd picked up telegram after telegram, announcing the return addresses. "A teachers' group. High schools. A Nebraska Sierra Club chapter. A truck drivers' local in Charleston. A farmers' cooperative in Eugene. 'Dear Mrs. Madden, We've been reading about your success forming a permanent antinuclear lobby in Washington. How can we help?' "

That ticking, that feeling of impending breakthrough, had been strong as he listened to her.

" 'Dear Mrs. Madden, Do you think the President or you might address our university on . . .' 'Dear Mrs . . .' It's *you* they want," she'd said. "Millions of people! You could be elected again, yes you could! That little prosecutor knows it, that's why they're ramming you through the court! They're afraid! You're bigger than they are! All you have to do is say yes to these people, that's why they looked at you that way in the intersection. That's why they listened when you told them to go."

Her eyes had been shining. Madden had looked over at two bulky gray mail sacks, filled to the brim, leaning against the far wall. They had not been opened yet.

Madden had looked at the San Diego Headline: HIDING BEHIND HER SKIRTS! It had all kept going around inside him. That feeling of being millions of miles away had come back, but at the same time he had never felt closer to his answer.

She'd kept it up, behind him. "You've never been stronger. You can't see it in the court. Come with me tomorrow night, look at the crowds. You can feel them reaching for you. They're going to be with you when you testify tomorrow."

He'd felt like she'd touched the germ of it. Something fundamental. He was staring at the envelopes and telegrams all over the floor. He'd said, more to himself than to her, "Why is it whenever you go against these weapons you seem to be attacking your own side?"

Madden had looked up.

That was when the ticking had started inside his head. The feeling of oppression dropping away. The sense of certainty. He'd recognized it.

It's coming, he thought now, in court.

He finished his testimony with a story he and Medaglia had agreed upon. "I served under General MacArthur in Korea, I believed in him." Madden sat straight, invoking the respected name. "I heard the speech he made when he retired. I want to tell it to you because it's how I feel."

He raised his voice. "In war at the turn of the century, the target was one enemy casualty at the end of a rifle or bayonet. Then came the machine gun designed to kill by the dozens. After that, the heavy artillery raining death by the hundreds, the atomic explosion reached hundreds of thousands." Madden saw the hat shop owner in the jury lick her lips, wet them. In the fifth row, Nicki had tilted her head slightly left to hear better. He continued quoting MacArthur. "The very triumph of scientific annihilation destroyed the possibility of war as a practical settlement. If you lose, you are annihilated. If you win, you stand to lose. No longer does war possess the chance of a winner. It contains the germ of double suicide."

Medaglia stepped briskly into the silence. "Mr. President, did you plan to surrender this country if attacked?"

"Never."

"Why did you choose not to fight when you could have launched missiles?"

"I made a choice to save lives."

"Are you a Communist, have you ever been a Communist? Do you harbor sympathy for the Communist form of government?"

"I have loathing for it."

Medaglia looked at the jury. She asked, "Did you think you were committing treason when you advised our troops not to fight?"

Madden looked up at her. Even though they had planned the question, he was surprised to hear it.

"I love this country," he said.

James Henry seemed oddly subdued as he rose for his final cross-examination. The blatant skepticism was gone, at least as he began. The predatory undertone was wiped from the voice. He conveyed respect, but the courtesy seemed directed at the office, not the man.

"We seem to have a problem of semantics," he started. "Counsel for the defense has said you advised our soldiers not to fight. But you ordered them to surrender, is that not so?"

"It is." The sureness was close. The acuteness of Madden's calm was delicious, meaningful. It lay over him like a blanket in a dark room. He could not see it but he felt its warmth.

"Wouldn't you say there's a big difference between not fighting and turning over all your assets to the enemy?"

"I was trying to stop a second wave of missiles from being launched."

Madden met the prosecutor's gaze. He pictured the Soviet premier across a long table at the start of their second summit meeting. A large Ukrainian in a European suit, leading off the meeting with a blistering, angry diatribe against Madden's missile program. Chain smoking and drinking mineral water in huge gulps. Menkes would have launched if Madden hadn't surrendered. He was certain of it.

Henry said, "As a former military man, would you say you knew before you became President that a commander in chief must plan options against Soviet attack? That it would be a dereliction of duty not to do so?"

"We had many contingencies."

"Surrender? Was that one?"

Madden repeated, "I did not plan to surrender."

Henry looked puzzled. He flourished his handkerchief and blew his nose. He was standing in front of the cab driver as if to reclaim his allegiance. "Then when did the surrender become an option?" he asked.

"I did what I thought best at the time."

Henry turned from Madden to face the jury. The edges of his

mouth had crept up. The weary skepticism was back in the tone. "Are you seriously suggesting in all your years as a *congressman* and *senator* and *President*, with all the time you spent on defense, you never considered giving up until you did so?"

"That's a pretty fair description of it," Madden said.

Henry started walking faster. "What made you change your mind?" Madden observed the prosecutor with utter clarity. The bantam cock walk. The way the hands never moved unless they had a purpose. The two small eruptions, pimples, below the right eye. Someone coughed in the back of the room.

Henry said, "What new factors influenced you? Tell us, share your thoughts. We all want to know, *every American* wants to know why you surrendered."

"Objection." Medaglia spoke without standing up. "If Mr. Henry wants an answer he merely has to consult the record."

The prosecutor's brows went up. "I'm trying to understand what *prompted* him to change his mind."

"Proceed, Mr. Henry."

Madden answered, "It was real." There was a thick, lustful sensation in his throat.

Henry grunted, bringing the scorn into the open. He walked a little and repeated the word as if turning its aspects over in his mind. " 'Real,' " he said. "Then are you telling us that even if you had had *ten* minutes to make a decision you would have surrendered? Even if you had had a *whole hour* to . . ."

"Objection!" Medaglia was up this time. "This is all speculative."

Henry looked astounded. "But, Your Honor, it is based on the defendant's own answers."

Murtaugh allowed the question and Madden said, "Well, if I had had more time I would have reviewed the options, the facts."

"But if the facts were that the attack was real? Are you telling us you would have surrendered no matter how much time you had?"

The question pierced Madden. He heard himself say, "I guess I would have done the same thing."

The courtroom erupted. Murtaugh banged the gavel again and again. Reporters ran for the door. Medaglia, stunned, was shaking her head. She had just watched Madden destroy her case. For an instant Madden saw DeLavery as he must have looked lying on the carpet. He sat oblivious to the tumult. The sensation in his throat was growing. He had known he was doing grave damage by telling the truth. He flashed to himself shaking the hand of a Minnesota congressman: "I'll damn well think about voting for that farm bill." But he had had no intention of doing so.

Medaglia slid a few inches lower in her seat, her famous poise having deserted her.

When Madden started talking again he accomplished what the gavel had failed to do: he quieted the court. "You want to know when I came to my realization," he said softly. Medaglia was sliding up, fast, shaking her head. *Don't make things worse.* Madden felt the ticking getting louder in his head. He said, "I saw something at that moment I'd never seen before. Presidents had been diminished." The ticking became a steady booming. He said, "I wasn't supposed to make a decision. Don't you see? It had been made a long time before. Forty years of refining the missiles had made Presidents into stewards. We weren't masters of our own weapons. I'm on trial *because* I made a decision." The reporters had stopped writing. A weight was lifting off him. He said, "I wish I could show you what I saw. I looked into our open grave."

At that moment something burst inside him. He saw that the excruciating humiliation he had suffered had led him here. The pounding in his head crescendoed. All the cells of his body were flooded by a sudden violent charge, gripping him and flowing upward, everywhere at the same moment, exploding forward in a sureness so passionate and clear and beautiful and obvious he was in awe that he had never seen the truth before.

Madden sat in wonder, not moving, not talking.

Africa, he thought.

James Henry said, "Mr. Madden, are you all right?"

Murtaugh echoed, "Mr. Madden?"

All the facets merged. Men had callings. They sought omnipotence through leadership. They struggled to survive. They believed the world would die when they did. They fought for their families.

The *Times* reporter, writing in his notebook without taking his eyes off the transfixed figure on the stand, scribbled, "Breakdown?"

Medaglia was calling to Murtaugh, "Recess, Your Honor, please!"

Only Catherine recognized what was happening. She felt tears of joy on her cheeks.

Madden saw by telling the truth he had brought on the answer, but he had also sabotaged his chances of getting out of the court free. The jury was regarding him almost uniformly with shock mixed with horror. He told Murtaugh, "I'm fine."

The thought of being locked away was suddenly intolerable. He needed desperately to get free of this court. He saw what the trial was, the last gasp of a powerful opposition. He saw the forces he had cheated reaching to constrain him. He was up before a religious tribunal. A missile in a black hood with a fire burning in a dark basement and a voice intoning "Heresy." He did not want to die in a cell with the bars melting on the floor.

Madden had seen a place without people or green or water. Scoured, baking earth, brown and dead. He saw a few troops watching over ragged survivors. It might have been a city once, or a farm, or a road. It was the worst thing he had ever imagined. It was even the end of the future. How do you bear witness to nuclear war, Catherine had said. Go there?

Yes. Before it is too late.

Murtaugh called the recess anyway. "Be prepared to sum up when we convene," he told the lawyers. "I need an airplane," Madden told St. Johns in the corridor. The banker looked lost and miserable leaning against a wall. "Sorry I lost my temper with him," he said. "And Diane told me what he would say, too."

Madden led him toward the judge's chambers he had been using. "You were terrific, the jury was with you," he said. When St. Johns brightened a little, Madden told the banker what he needed. "Clearances. Passports. Shots. For a hundred people. Use Catherine's contacts, they send relief there every day. And Robert Gardner. I want to talk to Robert Gardner."

His troops were all mangled. Medaglia came into the room when St. Johns left. "Don't say anything, don't say one thing," she said to Madden. She fell into a chair, bowed and defeated. "I'm going into tax law after this," she said. "A normal life with normal clients. People who want to win. How different that will be!"

He could hear reporters on the phones outside: "He admitted he'd give up no matter what!"

Madden crossed the room to her. This was one campaign he wasn't going to lose. She was going to have to go into the court and win the jury back. The afternoon sun blazed through the blinds and formed bars across her face. He gripped her shoulders. "Diane, I know I hurt myself out there, but I want to win this. Ah ha! I'm just a big old pain in the butt sometimes! That's why I need good people around and you're it!" She pursed her lips. At least she was listening. He said, "I believe in you, so does Catherine. I bet James Henry's worried too, never mind his phony smile."

The old pep talk, the presidential treatment. Her eyes were red; she'd been up working late last night. She was responding, unbending. She mistook his new mood for remorse, but that made no difference.

"Get on that ledge with that bullhorn," he told her.

The beginning of a smile showed on her face.

"Recess is over," called the bailiff's voice.

19

James Henry stepped up to the jury box.

"Ladies and gentlemen of the jury," he began, "it is a painful and difficult thing to accept that a President of the United States could baldly and calculatingly betray his country. Yet that is the conclusion you must reach.

"You have heard shocking testimony proving beyond the shadow of a doubt that William Madden committed treason. Voluntarily and of his own free will, he attempted to turn over the country to an enemy."

Henry moved along the box, trailing his fingers on the railing. "You heard how even in college William Madden gave speeches advocating sharing our nuclear secrets with the Russians, how even thirty years ago he told friends he believed in surrender. You heard how he worked to weaken the armed forces of the United States in Congress and the Senate. You even heard the defendant's own words, under oath, admitting he would have surrendered no matter how much time he had to make the decision."

Robert Gardner and Susan Henry had arrived for the last session. They sat in the second row, Gardner looking severe and making copious notes. Catherine looked emotionless, hands in her lap. For the first time during the trial Nicki St. Johns had taken off her hat, so that her face was visible.

Madden sat upright, never taking his eyes off the prosecutor.

Henry spun toward the defense table. "He weakened the power of the country to resist enemies. He gave aid and comfort to the foe. His act was designed to defeat our armies, to prevent them from fighting back. He attempted to subvert the Constitution, and when I say that sacred word '*Constitution*,' I don't mean the piece of paper which would have remained intact after the surrender, I mean our way of life which would have been destroyed. The peril in which William Madden placed our country still exists today because of his treason. Only your courage stands between us and the ruination he sought."

Henry coughed and cleared his throat. At his table he sipped water. He said more softly, returning to the jury box, "The defense has claimed William Madden made a choice, but *it was not a choice, it was a philosophy*! Arrived at in Korea, where he turned against war. Nurtured in private for years, while he vetoed bills that would have kept our country strong. Hidden from voters and put into effect when the opportunity presented itself. If surrendering your country without a fight is not treason, what is?"

Henry was seized by a fit of coughing that doubled him over. He wiped his mouth with his handkerchief. He leaned into the jury box, weight on his forearms, voice loud enough so that it carried as he changed tack.

"The defense has gone back again and again to two words during this trial, and those words are 'what if.' *What if* he had launched," Henry cried out. "*What if* he had started a war and killed millions. *What if* we in this room today were dead because of that?"

Henry surveyed the court. "Well, I can use 'what if' too. What if missiles had really been coming that night? What if they had hit and we had never fought back? What if the Russians had accepted William Madden's surrender, and our cities lay in ruins and your loved ones were dead? What if, ladies and gentlemen, you were one of the survivors, crawling in the wreckage, envying the dead, watching Soviet troops occupy the homes that were not destroyed? And what if, under those circumstances, you caught William Madden, still alive? *Would you try him for treason then? Of course you would!"*

Henry looked as if he were about to have another coughing fit but his shoulders jerked once, and he didn't. "So you see, 'what if' has no place in this trial. *What was* is important. What happened after the surrender is of no consequence. I am reminded of a story. It happened during the closing days of the American Revolution. A lieutenant in George Washington's Continental Army went over to the British enemy. He sold the British plans which indicated the route Washington would take. When the British got hold of these plans, they canceled an order to attack and positioned themselves along a forest road where they could ambush Washington's troops. But before the battle could occur, the British received word the war had ended.

"Ladies and gentlemen. The battle never occurred and lives were saved. Did that lieutenant commit treason when he sold the British American plans? Or was he a hero because he prevented a battle?

"He committed treason, I think you will agree."

Henry's hand crashed down on the railing. "The defense is arguing William Madden is like that lieutenant. The defense is saying because of an accident of circumstance following the surrender the defendant saved millions of lives! Why," Henry said in disgust, "here is a man ready to destroy the presidency of the United States, and now he tries to hide behind the privilege of the office he tried to abandon. A choice! The defense claims the President saved millions of lives around the world, that his motivation in fact was to *save* the world." Henry blew his nose. He removed a plastic vial from an inside jacket pocket and swallowed a red pill.

"I say to you, it was not this man's job to give allegiance to other countries. I say to you, allegiance to other countries is treason. Maybe someday, some glorious day in the future that we have prayed for and read about in the Bible, maybe one day in a time of profound safety for those we love, there will be no more countries as we know them. Only one glorious country under God. I don't know if it's possible. Maybe it's possible. I don't know how it could happen. The point is, it has not happened yet. No one asked Mr. Madden to become President. No one made him put his name on the ballot. He sought out the office. He took an oath to protect and defend the people of this country, not the people of the world. Not the people of Canada or France, or any other countries which might have been damaged in a thermonuclear war.

"To the United States! To the survival, and continuance, and prosperity of the United States. Mr. Madden's motivation was to serve the peoples of the world? He was not elected President of the world. His mandate did not come from the world. As long as a single chance of survival exists for the people of this country, it is treason for a President to throw it away. His mandate came from us!"

Hands in his pockets, Henry strolled toward Murtaugh, turned quickly, and returned to the lectern. He was letting his words sink in. Suddenly he said, softer, "I have been a prosecutor for thirty-nine years. Whenever I try a case, those people close to the accused— mothers, neighbors, friends—have a hard time accepting the fact that a man they love could have perpetrated a crime. It is a hard and painful realization they come to. I do not envy them. I feel sorry for them.

"Now each of you finds himself in that painful position. A President is a member of all our families, in a way. He is someone we invite into our homes each night, someone to whom we grant our allegiance, whom we trust, look up to, who we believe must epitomize the best and finest humankind has to offer. A President symbolizes all that is good and strong in our country. I beg you to separate the man from the office. I beg you to have the strength and courage to do what must be done.

"Because the whole world is watching what happens in this court today. Our country stands on the brink of war. Every American must show our enemy we are a strong and resilient people who will fight if attacked. Not only our patriotic soldiers in faraway lands but each citizen at home. I ask you to speak with the collective voice of the American people. I ask you not to perpetuate the message William Madden treasonably tried to send. I ask you to tell the enemies of freedom everywhere that what this man did will not be countenanced.

"Will you send William Madden home to his comfortable cabin in the woods? Free to choose between book contracts and movie options? Will you teach your children that surrender is a way of life?

What kind of future do you think this country has if traitors are rewarded as heroes?"

Henry's face had gone red with effort; his breathing was hard. "Some say patriotism is old fashioned, that there are bigger issues at stake than the survival of the United States. I am proud to be the biggest patriot on the block. I love this country, and I assume you do too.

"I ask you to return a verdict of guilty so that every man, woman, and child in the United States can sleep easier tonight!"

Why, he's just a little boy, thought Mark St. Johns. The third Russian to emerge from the embassy across the street clutched his mother's blue wool coat with one hand and with the other lugged a suitcase so heavy it dragged on the ground. The crowd in the street roared again. St. Johns saw the mother was crying. The boy had to stop to catch his breath. The father, who led the family, reached the end of the twenty-foot walkway that led from the front door to the iron-grille gate. A guard swung it open. An angry shout went up from the crowd pressed against police sawhorses on Sixteenth Street.

"GET OUT GET OUT GET OUT!"

"Good news," said a hoarse voice behind St. Johns.

The man joining him at the window was tall, fiftyish, and dressed well in a dark conservative suit. Lloyd Hood was legislative liaison for Congress from the American Red Cross. His thinning dirty blond hair had been brushed back to expose a half moon shaped area of pinkish skin between hairline and forehead. His pale blue eyes radiated benign good humor.

He swept aside the brocade curtain. The new Red Cross headquarters lay across Sixteenth Street from *The Washington Post* and Soviet embassy. As they watched, the Russian father hurried his family into a Fiat-shaped, mustard colored Lada. A Soviet security agent stood nearby, hands in the pockets of his coat, surveying the crowd. Uniformed American Secret Service men lined the sawhorses with regular D.C. police, blank faced, assigned to protect the Russians.

A brick flew out of the mob and clattered in the courtyard.

"I never thought the board would go for it, but they did," said Hood admiringly. "For ten years my job has been, keep politics out of it. Now you come along." He had the hoarse voice of a smoker, a Marlboro Light smoldered between the second and third fingers of his left hand. There were lots of potted palms around the office. A glass coffee table displayed Red Cross magazines. Glossy color photos of relief operations hung on all four walls. Men with shovels dug at the wreckage of collapsed homes. Nurses in white held emaciated infants while doctors positioned syringes.

Outside, the chanting quickened. "OUT OUT OUT OUT!"

More Russians were emerging into the sunlight. A van squeezed through the crowd and stopped in front of the embassy. The evacuees looked like a country western dance line, moving in two lines, but the backs were bent, the suitcases stuffed. One little girl in a red coat spun around and around, looking at the screaming crowd, clutching a blond doll dressed in green chiffon.

"We're giving you three planes," Hood said. "Sponsors all over, thanks to Mrs. Madden. Schools. Sierra Club. Nursing homes even. They'll be regularly scheduled relief flights. So if anyone tries to stop them it will look like they're shutting down the Red Cross. Mark, the board never would have done anything like this a year ago. It's that NORAD news. They're shook up, scared. And Mrs. Madden. I heard her last night at the Kennedy Center." He quoted her. " *The people want peace so badly governments better get out of the way!* "

"The boy dropped his truck," St. Johns said. Across the street one of the Russian adults pulled the Russian boy into the van. The security man waved as it pulled off.

St. Johns exhaled. "Closing the embassy."

"And our diplomats coming home. What's going to happen?"

Outside, a long, low wail filled the air, growing louder. A single rising note.

People began breaking away from the perimeter of the crowd, glancing up, hurrying in all directions, ducking into buildings. The next van to pull up was purple. Two Russians in sheepskin coats carried wooden crates out of the embassy.

Hood checked his watch. "Never saw people move like that for air-raid sirens in the old days, eh?" He crossed the room and flicked on a small clock radio on the desk, beside a photo of two boys in a kayak running rapids. A somber voice from the speaker said, "This is a test, only a . . ."

Hood said, shutting it off, "Just checking. I told the board your people would be picking the volunteers, not us."

St. Johns was gathering his coat from the couch. Hood lit another Marlboro. He had not left the desk and he sucked in his rubbery lips as if considering how to convey bad news.

St. Johns said, "Lloyd, thanks. The President will be happy to hear this."

"Er, one thing. The flights will be canceled if he loses," Hood said. "The board was adamant. I'm sorry. They won't stick their necks out unless he wins."

St. Johns gritted his teeth with an intensity that hurt his jaw. "He'll win."

Diane Medaglia approached the lectern with a confidence that surprised the spectators. The last they had seen her she had sat emotionless at the defense table during Henry's summation.

"James Henry has told you he is asking you to do a hard thing, and I don't doubt it is hard because it is wrong," she said. "To vote guilty in this case would be to go against everything we believe in in this country. The prosecution has not proved its case. President Madden made a choice he was legally empowered to make. It was not a treasonous choice. It saved the lives of each and every person in this court. Your families. Your loved ones."

She seemed to float a foot from the jury box, addressing the whole jury. "Witness after witness has testified to the President's loyalty to this country. Congressmen. Generals. Prominent Americans from all walks of life. I could spend hours going back over their words. But instead I would like to ask *you* to make the choice the President faced that night. Put yourself in his shoes. As of right now missiles are hurtling toward this country. Look at the clock. You have three minutes to decide what to do. When the minute hand hits the six, sixty nuclear weapons will go off around the United States."

Everyone spun to the clock. Medaglia retreated a step but kept facing the jury. People could hear themselves breathing.

"You could listen to your generals urging you to attack," she said softly. "You could unleash an arsenal of over seven thousand nuclear warheads at the enemy, who could fire an equal number of megatons back. But let me remind you. You heard the chairman of the World Health Organization testify one billion people would die in *the first hour* of a thermonuclear war. You heard scientists predict only one thousand nuclear explosions could cause the extinction of God's creation. One thousand warheads are *one seventh* of the combined arsenals of the two countries. To push the button will begin not a battle but a change in the front of the universe.

"Two minutes," she said.

Medaglia moved closer to face the chemist. He was twisting his hands.

"You could wait. James Henry charged the President acted prematurely. But if you wait, Soviet missiles will destroy Washington in two minutes, maximum. Your generals have assured you this is true. The Generals will take over then and will launch. Besides, while you spend time vacillating, the Soviets are probably preparing a second wave of missiles.

"Fifty seconds," she said.

The second hand was thin and red, and it seemed to move more quickly than usual. Medaglia's fist slid along the railing. Now she stood before the bus driver, who had a light sheen of perspiration on his forehead. His right hand was draped over the back of the accountant's chair in front of him.

Nobody said anything.

The minute hand hit the six.

"Or you could surrender," she said softly.

She stepped back. Her voice rose as she addressed the whole jury. "William Madden entered the Situation Room that night as a President empowered by the people to make a choice for which nothing in human history had prepared him. Not just conventional war faced him, with its hideous destructive potential, but nuclear war, a new kind of war. If the attack that night had been a conventional one, with ships bombarding our ports or enemy troops disembarking, you heard the President testify he would have fought back with all his might."

She squeezed a pencil between thumb and forefinger. "Who here would like to have faced this choice? No human being should ever have to be faced with it, and I don't know how events developed to the point that this man was. Do you think it was easy for a President who had worked all his life to strengthen the United States to make the choice he made? Imagine the torment he must have suffered in those three minutes. President Madden had grown up during a war for freedom, World War Two. He won medals fighting Communists in Korea. He watched Communist troops kill his friends. He was in the Congress and the Senate when the Russians marched into Hungary and Afghanistan. He had no illusions about the nature of the foe, no love for the system he surrendered to that night.

"But his love for his country was greater than his personal desire to strike back. He was willing to forego the momentary satisfaction of revenge in order that someday this nation might grow strong again. He knew a long period of hardship would follow his act. But he knew something else too. He knew what the result of a nuclear war would be. He knew that when the last individual of a race of living things dies, another heaven and another earth must pass before a race can live again."

She moved to the hat shop owner, who was rubbing in hand cream. "Maybe when you think about it you will opt for a different choice. But we are not here to decide which choice was best. We are here to confirm that by making the choice the President acted legally."

In the second row, Gardner squeezed Susan Henry's hand. He mouthed, "She's good."

Medaglia was back at the lectern, hands upright and fingers splayed, as if each were an exclamation point.

"Treason," she said harshly, loud and clear. "Benedict Arnold committed treason. He foully betrayed his country for money. Aaron Burr committed treason. He tried to get the western United States to break away and form another nation. He sought power. Self-aggrandizement. Did the defendant have any chance of receiving money or power from the choice he made? No. He had no motivation to commit treason."

Medaglia lowered her voice, glanced at Henry. "The prosecution has suggested that the President didn't make a choice at all, that he acted in accordance with some 'secret philosophy,' some 'secret plan.' Well, if it was secret, it was so secret even the President didn't know about it." Laughter erupted from the row of reporters. "Would the prosecution have us believe the President orchestrated the arrival of the meteors that set off the early warning system that night? Is he suggesting the computer malfunction at NORAD was caused by the President? Perhaps, Mr. Henry, President Madden *snuck into* NORAD and sabotaged the equipment. Was that part of his 'secret philosophy,' his 'secret plan'?"

Medaglia's shoulders squared, her voice became soothing. "Isn't a much more likely explanation that the President is like all of us, like you or me, that he is subject to moments of personal revelation? Haven't we all experienced moments in our lives when we've come to realizations about our relationships or our jobs? And haven't those moments of clarity caused us to act, to quit the jobs, ask for raises, to improve relationships with people we love?

"When the President testified that he would have surrendered no matter how much time he had to consider the question, he did not mean he always planned to surrender. He meant he supposed he always would have come to the same realization. Nothing secret or insidious was going on. I am describing an ordinary human way of coming to a decision applied to an extraordinary circumstance, an alleged attack on the United States."

In the jury box, the accountant's face, which had been blank during much of the speech, hardened, as if he had come to a decision. Shaking her head with passion, Medaglia kept driving at them. "He. Made. A. Choice. I'll say it a million times if I have to. God help us if juries take away a President's right to make a choice. Is the prosecution's aim to tell future Presidents that any unpopular policies will be construed as treason? What happens the next time a President vetoes a grant for the Pentagon? Embarks upon an economic path that weakens the dollar? Will he find himself in a court of law too? Accused and branded a traitor? Because that is what the prosecution is asking. Not just a verdict of guilt against an innocent man but a fundamental subversion of our free system of government. A vote that from now on presidential decisions will be reviewed by juries."

Her voice grew hushed, adamant and outraged. "And he is asking more. The world is watching, you've been told. What should that matter to a jury in a free country? Send the Russians a message, the prosecution asked. Are we actually being advised to let the opinion of a foreign government determine how we vote in a court of law?"

She returned to her table. Her thumb pressed white against the shaft of the pencil. She said, "If we are so weak and fearful that we would allow such a thing to happen, then it is we in this court who have surrendered to the other side, who have thrown away our right to make independent decisions."

She charged the jury, "Ladies and gentlemen, set this man free!"

It was well past dark, six hours later. The jury still had not reached a verdict. The spectators had dispersed to the cafeteria or nearby bars, where they made bets on who would win. In the empty courtroom, Diane Medaglia sat slumped and immobile at her table, eyes closed, not asleep. Only one other person was present: Robert Gardner, two rows back, a glazed, fixed expression on his face. Occasionally he would rise, walk to the railing, and stare thoughtfully at the seat of a particular juror, or at the prosecution table. He was planning a column.

Diane Medaglia's eyes opened and she swung her head toward Gardner. "Too bad you couldn't tie Henry in," she said.

In the lawyers' lounge James Henry read a Ludlum novel. Unconsciously, he hummed to himself. No particular song, just a hum. His gray-suited associate approached, clutching a sheaf of papers. "About her closing argument, Mr. Henry . . ." Henry waved the man away without looking up. He went back to *The Bourne Identity*.

The jury sent a note to Murtaugh asking to see the memo Madden had ordered drawn up by General Hacker, which detailed how to stop troops from fighting in a nuclear war.

Nicki St. Johns sat in a window seat of an Eastern Airlines 727 banking into Boston's Logan Airport, looking at the lights below. She couldn't wait to get back to the beach house, but she was struck by the thought that once she got there she'd have nothing particular to do.

The jury's second note, delivered at nine-thirty, read, "Can we have Italian food tonight?"

Susan Henry had returned to her Watergate studio after two hours of waiting in court. The stereo played a soft Chopin nocturne. She kept the radio on in case the jury came back. She stood in a frock coated with marble dust, surveying the statue she was about to complete. Madden's bust stood three feet high, the skull cleaved violently in two as if by an ax. The sides of the head were out of proportion. One eye was higher than the other, both wide with terror. The mouth was severed in mid-cry. Susan peered at the nose. She leaned forward with a piece of sandpaper.

In the Russian port of Vladivostok, the Soviet troop carrier *Andropov* and the brig *Lenin* steamed under armed escort toward the Pacific, where they would turn south toward Africa. A band on the *Andropov*'s deck played "The Internationale." Tarps covered five Soviet SS-20 nuclear missiles.

In the judge's chambers Madden had been using as a lounge, he and Catherine sat on the couch together, not talking, fingers touching lightly. The way they'd sat on the swing on Catherine's father's porch in Lyle when they were sixteen. The heat was on too high. The window was open, and traffic noise came in from Constitution Avenue. Outside, the spring thaw had begun.

They'd finished the dinner she'd ordered from Chinatown. It was their election meal, the one they'd eaten in Boston's Parker House the night Madden won the presidency. Open cardboard containers sat on the desk, filled with the remains of cold noodles with peanut sauce, moo shu pork, fried dumplings, and Szechuan chicken. Three empty bottles of San Miguel beer stood nearby.

Madden's fortune cookie had read, "You are popular."

Madden was remembering the presidential election night. He envisioned the big three-room suite at the Parker House. He heard Tom Brokaw on TV saying, "We have a projection. Kentucky for Governor Amos." Goldman had been the only aide present. He'd been sunk in gloom in an armchair. "What about California," he'd kept saying.

Catherine had sat on the couch in a tweed skirt and pale blue sweater, four feet from the big TV. Stephanie had curled in front of her on the carpet with Danny, who lay on a blue blanket and cooed or played with his fingers. Stephanie had gotten the most excited each time a state went to Madden, "Pennsylvania! Wow, Dad! Pennsylvania! All those people!"

Danny, who was seven months old, had chirped "Gup!" whenever Madden came close, "He knows you," Stephanie had laughed. "He's voting for you!"

Josh had remained by the window for much of the evening, smoking his pipe. He'd showed the beginning of a smile when Georgia went for Madden.

Madden remembered how the corner of the living room had been filled by a four-by-six black and white map of the United States. Each time a candidate won a state, Goldman would change the color by placing a magnetic sticker over it: bright patriotic blue for Madden, sickly yellow for Jack Amos, the three-hundred-pound Republican governor of Nevada, whose slogan, "The business of America is still business," had attracted massive support.

The country had turned into a patchwork of yellow and blue by nine p.m. in the closely fought election. New York, blue. Pennsylvania, blue. Ohio and Michigan and Florida, yellow. Texas by a hair to Madden, because of Rittenhouse. Tennessee and Connecticut, yellow.

"Early returns from California show Jack Amos with a big lead," Brokaw had said. "Illinois looks closer than we anticipated. With 80 percent of the vote we still have no winner."

The screen had switched to a chorus line of Madden supporters in paper hats in the hotel ballroom fifteen stories below. Drunk and singing:

> We're MAD about MAD-DEN
> Tough luck to Fat Jack.

Madden had risen and walked to the window. He'd stood in silence beside Josh. Outside, the Prudential Building seemed to float in the sky. He'd imagined he could feel the celebrants below through the girders of the Parker House. The vibration of the bands. The cries of the crowd glued to the video screens.

What will I do if I lose? he'd thought.

A sharp pain had traveled from his chest to his testicles.

It occurred to him that he'd never lost an election.

Goldman's gasp had pulled Madden's attention back to the TV. The lawyer had bolted up in his chair. "Damn, damn, California went for Amos."

Now a knocking at the door called Madden back from election night. Goldman's voice called, "Jury's ready."

They filed in slowly. The bus driver glanced at Madden, then quickly away, mouth a tight line. The chemist looked neither right nor left, shoulders slumped. The secretary peered eagerly around the room, as if memorizing the final scene to tell someone else.

Murtaugh leaned sideways. "The foreman will rise. Have you reached a verdict?"

The hat shop owner stood. She licked her lips. "We have, Your Honor."

"The defendant will rise." Madden's head was buzzing. Murtaugh said, "What is your verdict?"

"Not guilty, Your Honor."

A roar went up from the court, the spectators surging into the aisles. Murtaugh didn't bother to use the gavel. It was like a convention. Madden was swept up by the cry, borne on it along the aisle as it grew louder. Catherine was fighting her way past reporters to reach him. Goldman started to cry. Madden caught sight of Robert Gardner standing alone in the stands, clapping. Medaglia pumped his hand, then stopped and threw her arms around him. Camera flashes were exploding everywhere until the room looked to him like black and yellow spots. As he was carried by the tide of celebrants into the hall, he saw James Henry at the prosecution table, expressionless.

There was a high shout of triumph in his head. A beat of freedom. The reporters fought at his heels, transformed back from jurors into journalists. Following him again. Shouting questions.

"How do you feel, Mr. President? Did Medaglia's summation win it?" "Mr. President! Mr. President!"

"I feel good." Laughter. "I don't care how she won it, she won."

More laughter. He felt the old easy power, the control. Someone yelled, "Why'd the jury take so long to decide?" Another voice shouted through the din, "What are you going to do now?"

Madden stopped. He was in the hallway outside courtroom number two. This was the question he had been waiting for. He looked out over the reporters. Their smiling, eager faces seemed utterly at his disposal.

"Well, I've been thinking, and I know exactly what I'm going to do, ah ha! And I guess I'll tell you about it."

A *Times* reporter scribbled, "Madden has a strange smile on his face, of radiance."

"I'm going to make a little salt," he said.

20

Six days after Madden's victory in court but less than twenty-four hours before the first nuclear weapon was ordered fired in war since 1945, three white helicopters left the highlands of Ethiopia and headed east across the Ogaden desert. The rising sun deepened the red of the crosses adorning the sides.

Inside the lead Chinook, men and women lay in sleeping bags amid sacks and crates stenciled BEANS, WHEAT, SYRINGES. A red beard poked from a green bedroll. Blue Magic Marker lettering on an old sheet suspended between penicillin boxes proclaimed IOWA PEACE MARCH. The copter pitched to a spatter of snores.

Madden and Gardner nursed steaming coffee mugs, elbows against crates piled near the lone porthole. Below, the creeping sun pushed shadows off an endless plain of dun-colored rubble which led in the distance to purplish peaks. Gardner wore a yellow windbreaker against the night chill. Madden wore a vest parka and blue flannel shirt.

Gardner felt the coffee's warmth spread inside him. "All these supplies and they'll last five days? Six?"

"Ah ha!" Madden grimaced at the taste. "We need lots more. Thousands of tons." He seemed cheery despite the hour. His hair was tousled, as if he'd been running his hands through it. He said,

"Leaving that beautiful fiancée of yours behind! I better give you a good story to make it worth your while, eh?"

Gardner pulled yesterday's *International Herald Tribune* from his back pocket. He spread the editorial page on a crate, smoothing it with his hands. He read, watching for reaction, " 'He's running away. He's won his case and he's not interested in the nuclear issue anymore.' "

Madden shrugged. "Of course people say that." The sun struck the porthole and shafted an orange beam of light into the face of a man in the sleeping bag, who moaned.

Madden said, "If we can show the miseries of the nuclear age as a human problem and not a political one, maybe people will soften when the subject of arms control comes up. That's my rhetoric limit for this early in the morning. Fighters coming out there, Bob."

Gardner caught his breath. Trailing white, two vicious-looking Tupolev jets screamed down from above, silver, streamlined. Gardner knew there were no arms on the copters. The fighters leveled off less than two hundred feet away. Pain shot through Gardner's chest. He could see the smile on the face of the Ethiopian pilot.

The lead fighter wagged wing tips and they both shot away.

Gardner heard himself exhale.

As the peaks grew closer, the rubbly earth softened to whitish sand. The copters flew low over a meandering series of S-curves in the earth which normally would have marked a river. But they were brown and not blue. A cluster of rectangular huts hugged a bank, but no smoke rose from the village. No people moved.

Gardner tapped the porthole to the east. A line of refugees trudged single-file in the same direction the copters were flying. Black faces turned up as the copters' shadows cut the line. Some people walked with hands stretched forward on others' shoulders. Gardner muttered, "Malnutrition blind."

Madden said, "Everything will look like this the day after."

Gardner shivered, the coffee was finished. He'd never even met the President until the trial was over. Then Madden had astounded him in the hallway outside the court, invited him to the private victory party and then on this trip, the only journalist allowed.

"The business about making salt," he said. "I'm still not sure I understand it."

Madden squeezed Gardner's shoulder, and Gardner felt the strength in the man, the will and utter concentration. Madden said, "Oh. Gandhi. Gandhi dismantled a whole military system by rallying people. Salt was his symbol. He announced he was going to march to the sea and defy the British law and make salt."

"And you're Gandhi?"

Madden laughed. "Dr. Freud, you're falling back on your natural journalist's suspicion."

"You brought up Gandhi, not me."

Twenty feet back, the loudest snoring stopped abruptly. The bearded man raised his head off a sack of wheat. He looked around wildly. "Where the . . . Oh," he said.

Madden turned back to Gardner. "If you're asking whether I like leading people, I do." He shrugged. "I know you'll see what we want to do. The column of yours about the professor. I liked it. About people who do good deeds. I knew when I read it you were the one I should bring with me."

Gardner remembered himself yelling at his editor Edelstein on the phone: *"Take me off this story!"* Astonished, he said, "That's the piece you liked? Not the NORAD story?"

They had to grab crates for balance as the helicopter jolted and angled down for descent. The peaks seemed to pass inches from the copter. Suddenly Gardner's heart beat fast. He was looking at the Mehta Valley, unmistakable from the air with its funnel shape narrowing in the brown distance. The rising sun was striking the base of the sandstone cliffs and banding them crimson and gold. The rear of the American lines were dotted with parked tanks and troop carriers. A lone jeep threw up dust. At the front, a line of trenches sealed the wide end of the valley. Soldiers waved.

Gardner asked, "Your daughter-in-law, how come she was the only member of the family to come along?"

Madden stiffened. Coming up a mile ahead, occupying two-thirds of the width of the brown, rutted valley, dwarfed by the cliffs, sprawling, amoeba shaped, was the camp. Madden announced to the volunteers, "Home sweet home." They crowded around to get a look.

Gardner saw a crazy jumble of tents and tin roofs and running people.

"There was another reason I wanted you along," Madden said. Their cheeks were an inch apart, near the glass. The copter lowered toward a rectangular landing area surrounded by refugees, with more coming. They all seemed dressed in the same sulphur colored rags.

Gardner caught sight of one of the volunteers gazing at Madden. A young blonde with braided hair and an upturned nose. She stood near Huff. Her lips were parted and her blue eyes glowed. She reminded him of people he'd seen in St. Peter's Square watching the Pope.

Madden said, "In your NORAD articles, I was surprised a man with your instincts had such capacity for compassion."

Gardner looked at him sharply, but there was no rancor in Madden's face. Gardner would never forget DeLavery's hand quivering on the carpet, before it went still. A dull throbbing came into his head. He said quietly, "Were you a friend of the general's?"

"I'm not talking about General DeLavery." The heat was starting to seep through the steel body. Madden unzipped his vest as they hit the ground. He wore khaki shorts; his legs looked thin and old. Behind them the volunteers rolled their sleeping bags. Trucks with flatbeds were backing through the crowds outside, toward the copters.

Madden winked. "I was talking about James Henry," he said. "You protected him, didn't you?"

As Madden stepped out into the sunlight, two miles east Sergeant Dewey Beech stood at ease in an air conditioned underground room, sweating with tension. He had never been summoned to a personal audience with a general before.

Although his attention remained fixed on General Ishmael Macy, he was taking in the comfortable looking headquarters: the refrigerator purring near the two-cushion couch. The real bed. The drafting tables and the red and blue phones.

Macy advised, "Relax, Sergeant." Fat chance.

Beech was thinking of a county judge in Oklahoma who had granted his first wife Lucille's divorce request and awarded her a big alimony allowance too. The judge had been a crewcut, bullnecked man who'd watched Beech with half-closed eyes for what seemed like hours as Lucille did her crying trick, complete with heaving shoulders beneath her best midnight blue dress. She'd blubbered, "And then, then he said . . . he said I was a bitch, Your Honor."

General Macy looked at him like the judge had.

To Macy's right, Mr. Square Jaw drummed his fingers against his chin, glared at Beech as if he had an opinion on the line here, and Beech had better confirm it. He wore a captain's bars.

The major on the left, hovering near the topographical map of the valley on the draftsman's table, was a dead ringer for Beech's brother-in-law Wynn, currently doing five to nine in the Oklahoma State Penitentiary for dynamiting the truck of a driver stupid enough to bed down with Beech's sister Wanda. Every time Beech thought about it he was amazed. Wanda had a great personality and all that, but she was the fattest woman he'd ever seen. The driver must have been drunk.

General Macy's smile never left his mouth or extended beyond it either. "In your own words," he said in his gravelly voice, "tell us what's going on on the Russian side at night."

Even though the valley was between Ethiopia and Somalia the far side was considered "Russian." Beech, ready, rapped out, "Yes, sir! There's more of them out there every night, sir. Observation posts! It's getting thicker out there, all right." In a matter-of-fact, uncomplaining voice he listed the men who had been wounded in the nightly skirmishes between scouting parties. "We've engaged them four out of the last five times."

The captain looked as if he'd just swallowed a bad oyster. But Wynn's look-alike brightened. Beech thought, a little older. Grayer, too. But definitely Wynn, even to the cheek scar.

With a lazy gesture Macy waved Beech to the map. All three officers clustered around him. One of them wore after-shave that smelled like perfume. "Show me where you made contact," Macy ordered.

Beech indicated swirls and ridges on the black and white map with a sure hand. "Here. Here." They all knew neither side's patrols were supposed to be in the valley, the valley was off limits by treaty, but you couldn't just sit back when the enemy was crawling out there every night, planning and watching you. Beech leaned closer and indicated a small dark hump on the map between a dry well and a twelve-foot escarpment. "Sir, this isn't a hill, someone made a mistake. It's a ditch."

The Wynn look-alike told Macy, "Sir, it's just as I suggested. They're planning something. We've got to nip it, nip it. If we don't nip it, it will get out of hand."

In his head, Beech imitated the faggy officer who looked like his brother-in-law. "Nip it!"

The captain shook his head violently. "Sir, we're talking about a significant escalation! Without Washington's knowledge."

The general raised both hands like a southern belle being courted by two overeager boys at the same time. It was clear he did not want significant strategic factors being discussed in the presence of a lowly peon like Beech. Pursing his thick lips shrewdly, he asked, "Sergeant, your opinion. Do you think the men's morale might rise a bit if we did something to lessen the . . . er . . . enemy's enthusiasm?"

Beech said, "Mine would."

"A little recon in force?"

A thrill of anticipation and fear went through Beech. Recon in force meant four or five tanks and a couple of armored troop carriers bursting into the Soviet side of the valley. The tanks would drive around, battle flags flying, showing off, engaging any small Russian parties they found in no-man's-land, leaving the main Soviet line alone.

Beech met the eyes of the captain, who disapproved of the idea. He told the general, "Teach them a lesson, sir."

"Prisoners," whispered the major, sweetening the lure.

Macy retreated to the plush couch, one boot tip swinging idly, leg over knee. The great man was starting to muse. "Hmmmmm," he said. "Mmmmmmmmmm." Beech, forgotten, was ushered toward the door by the major, who slapped him on the back the way management manuals said to do. "Thanks, soldier," he told Beech.

As he left, Beech was aware of the captain's gaze resting on him sourly. He thought, Up yours too, pal.

He hurried back to the squad, filled with excitement and nervousness. He had a pretty good idea which men would have to guide the recon in force into the valley if Macy decided to go ahead.

The men were lying around in undershirts in the sun, stuffing powdered eggs into their faces. With the sun up, all semblance of color had been driven from the cliffs. The air out beyond them shimmered and danced.

Grady, the bigmouth, was the first to tell him the news.

"Guess who's in the camp! Fucking Madden!"

It was eleven-fifteen.

Madden heard the camp as a vibration that never went away. Babies crying. Gasoline generators roaring. Six thousand people arguing, wailing, squabbling over rations. The camp was so big he held it in his mind as a montage of images.

The young girl beneath the dry water tap on the back of an empty truck, hands wrapped around the tap, head between her knees, a cruel, naked parody of a child's body. The V shape of the hipbone jutting, pointing to the ridgy spine. The spine curving up to the bird's-wing-shaped shoulder bones. The moisture on the back of her wrists drying.

The two women in blue shrouds washing the body of a boy in a shack for the dead. One woman pouring a trickle of silvery water from a kettle, the other wiping a rag across the sunken chest.

The thousands of wispy comma shaped marks he had seen in the sand everywhere, brief, odd indentations that would not have been made by wind.

"The children make them poking in the dirt, looking for grains that might have fallen from a bag," the director had said.

The tin-roofed sheds that were the "hospitals." The shacks that housed the terminally ill. The brushy lean-tos made of thorn bushes, half covering hand clawed holes in the flinty earth, where new arrivals lived until tents could be supplied. The sweetening smell of decay as the day grew hotter. But mostly, wherever he went, the hundreds of people just sitting, hands over their skulls or faces, maybe waiting, maybe dreaming, purple or pink or beige wrist bands fastened snugly, worn to indicate when they could eat.

"We have seven, eight tribes here," the director had said, showing them the camp before putting them to work. He was a soft spoken thirty-five-year-old Canadian with silver wire-rimmed glasses and an African necklace of blue shells.

"We started out the size of a football field. Ten rows of the green tents. But more people kept coming." The director had shaken his head. "Now there's no shape to the place. Tents. Lean-tos. Tin sheds. Whatever comes in, we put up. That smell's from the latrine trenches, which some of you will be digging more of today."

Headquarters were two tin shacks in the northeast corner of the amoeba, a hundred yards from the helicopter landing area. Food distribution points lay along all four perimeters of the camp, linked by narrow footpaths through the crazy maze of makeshift living quarters.

"Plenty to do," the director had said, assigning jobs. Unload food. Guard supplies. Supervise ration distribution. Delousing department. Clean away the human feces from the spattered earth.

Madden lifted another boy, amazed at his lightness. He was somewhere in the center of camp, surrounded by what seemed like hundreds of children squatting in the dust, hands over their heads against the sun, flies on their faces. The earth covered with bodies every two feet. Madden dabbed the stringy upper arm with alcohol, talking softly to the boy.

"Hold him tighter," Dr. Tamhane said.

The boy's wedge shaped, oversized head rested against Madden's chest. The five-year-old's torso had shrunk to the size of an infant's. Madden was afraid to press too hard.

Dr. Tamhane was a slight Indian in khaki shorts, knee socks, and an oversized pith helmet. He looked like a New Delhi traffic patrolman. He had come out from Geneva two months ago.

As Tamhane plunged in the needle, Madden said, "What's your name? Joe? I knew a Joe in Lyle." The boy shifted, responding to the tone, not the English words. Madden said, "He was about your age. He was a champion skier. Whoosh," Madden said. "Snow. Cold. White, wet snow."

The boy imitated the sound he liked: "Whoosh."

Flies dropped onto the moist area on his arm as soon as Madden put him down.

The only color in the camp came from donated items. Bright red plastic bowls for milk. Orange Tupperware scoopers for grain spread on burlap sacking and measured out carefully to staring crowds. Blue Xs stood out on the foreheads of tribesmen who had come from other camps, where so little food remained doctors marked hardier subjects for survival.

As Madden worked, he thought back to the night of the victory party, at Goldman's house on Foxhall Road. Just a small gathering. Catherine and Mark and the Goldmans and Medaglia. And Gardner, whom Madden had picked out of the crowd at the courthouse on a hunch. Madden remembered the phone ringing every five minutes with congratulations from people who had not wanted to talk to him a week before. He had not heard Diane Medaglia laugh until that night. She had a crystalline laugh, musical, surprisingly carefree.

She'd sprawled like Cleopatra on the couch, high heels on the carpet. In a nasal parody of Queen Victoria she'd kept extending her glass to Goldman, saying, "We require more champagne."

Madden had entertained them with his favorite stories about the East German premier's troublesome drinking habits. "I bet James Henry's not holding court at Joe and Mo's tonight," Jill Goldman had said. They'd recounted stories about the trial. "That bus driver on the jury never smiled," Medaglia had said, and Goldman had quipped, "Republican."

When the hour had grown late, Madden had found himself alone looking at the books in Goldman's well stocked library. Nixon's *Six Crises*. *The Jefferson Papers*.

In Kennedy's *Profiles in Courage* he had opened to a passage quoting columnist Walter Lippmann. "With exceptions so rare they are regarded as miracles of nature, successful democratic politicians are insecure and intimidated men. They advance politically only as they placate, appease, bribe, seduce, bamboozle or otherwise manage to manipulate the demanding threatening elements in their constituencies . . ."

"Oh, buddy, we beat 'em. We beat 'em."

Mark St. Johns had lurched into the room, tie loosened, white sleeves rolled up. He held a glass filled with straight Chivas. He fell into a leather chair beneath the floor to ceiling rows of books. The big shoulders had been hunched, the old end ready to play offense. "What are you doing here alone? There's a party."

"Thinking."

St. Johns had lifted the Chivas in a toast. "Well, whatever it is, I'm in on it." After he took a long drink an inch of liquor remained in the glass. He leaned back. The hand holding the glass dangled over the arm of the chair. He said, "For a long time nothing's meant anything to me. I feel better now, whole again." He grinned and displayed the steel hook. "Well, almost whole." Madden thought he looked exhausted.

More seriously, St. Johns had said, "I've decided to leave the bank. I was thinking about it before any of this anyway. I want to work with you full time. Hell! I travel all over the world and I've never even been in Africa. Bill, I felt great walking out of that Red Cross building." He shrugged. "The bank?" He let out a long breath. "Forty-two years," he said.

Madden had nodded thoughtfully. "I can understand that, sure makes sense to me!" At the bookcase he'd pulled out a worn, thin volume in leather. "Listen to this," he'd said. "Lincoln was always my favorite."

"I made up my mind," St. Johns had said.

"He didn't even have a speechwriter. Ready? 'Fellow citizens, we cannot escape history! No personal significance or insignificance can spare one or another of us. We shall nobly save, or meanly lose, the last best hope of earth.' "

Madden had beamed. St. Johns had groaned. "Lincoln. Spare me Lincoln."

Madden had run his fingers along the spines of Goldman's books. "Hey, remember that little sidestep you used to do?" Madden had faked left with his shoulders, like an athlete about to run right. "I could hit you deep every time. Turner couldn't do it. McMahon couldn't do it, he couldn't get downfield fast enough. What a play! Only you could do it."

"You never stop pushing, damn you. What about what I want?"

Madden had said, "I need your help. The chairman of Global American can do plenty for us. Stay there. I'm asking you."

"I'll think about it." But from the grudging tone Madden had known he would decide to stay. He was struck again by how old his friend looked. "Mark, you've been working so hard to bring all these people together in another country. Maybe there's someone you ought to talk to at home."

"Anything else you want me to do? Polish your shoes? Paint your house?"

Afterwards, Madden had reached for the phone, dialed a number in Massachusetts. "Nicki, I just wanted to tell you, I understand why you testified. I'm not angry, if it makes any difference. If you ever want to call us, don't hesitate." He'd envisioned Weber St. Johns as a curly-haired ten-year-old charging from the surf on Cape Cod, with Josh lumbering behind. Two boys screaming with delight. Madden had said, "You might have heard I'm going away. Mark won't be coming. I thought you'd like to know."

She'd never said anything, but her breathing had eased.

He'd fought off a premonition after hanging up. He would never be in the same house with all these people again.

Catherine had come into the room, beautiful in a plain black dress and single strand of pearls. The color had been bright on her cheeks. "Wooooo, champagne," she'd said, raising the quarter empty Dom Pérignon bottle and two longstemmed glasses. From downstairs, he heard the first crashing note of a Beach Boys record. "Good Vibrations." Goldman's normally sedate voice had howled, "Do the twist!"

She'd beamed at him. "Josh called to congratulate you. Thrilled. And sorry he couldn't be here." Madden had not heard the phone ring. The champagne had fizzed when she poured. Premier Menkes, awed at her ability to drink, had remarked during a break in the Paris summit, "Is she consuming it or pouring it somewhere?"

The house vibrated from the music.

She'd said, making herself comfortable on the couch, "I have some old gardening dresses. They ought to do in the heat. The hat from Caracas." She'd laughed. They'd been pelted with eggs as their motorcade went under an overpass on that trip, and she'd saved the straw hat as a "war souvenir."

"What did you say to Mark, anyway?" she'd asked gaily. "He positively looked like the grim reaper stomping out of here?"

She'd caught herself, seeing the hardness on his face.

"Oh, Bill," she'd said, leaning forward. "But I want to come."

Downstairs, the music had turned low, as if someone had snatched off the Beach Boys. The soft strains of Debussy's *La Mer* started up, violins. They'd heard Medaglia's laughter. "So the law student says, 'Where's my lemon cookie?' "

On the couch, Catherine had looked straight ahead when he talked to her. He could see the whiteness of her knees. "Who'll talk to the governors if you go? Who'll coordinate the flights to other camps?"

Now, in the camp, Dr. Tamhane give the last injection and dropped the used syringe into a wooden crate carried by an aide. Madden felt the sunburn on the back of his arms and legs. He'd better get long pants, he thought. "Finished?" he asked Dr. Tamhane.

The small, serious face of the Indian broke into a dazzling smile. "Oh, oh, oh," Dr. Tamhane said. He sounded like he was hiccuping, but Madden realized he was laughing. "Finished? Finished?"

The heat came at them in one long wave. A desert heat of age and exhaustion. The dust filled Madden's nostrils and scratched his ears. He thought a shower would be great and then he smiled, because there wouldn't be any shower. This was what his life would be like from now on, he thought. Lines of people needing shots every day.

Dr. Tamhane led him briskly and expertly through the maze of thorn bush lean-tos. He caught sight of Stephanie in long pants, carrying a bucket, disappearing into a tent. You could lose yourself in the camp and forget the desert. Madden saw another line of men and women snaking out from a four-posted, thatch roofed structure. Robert Gardner was prying open another crate on a table in the shaded area. Dr. Tamhane was frowning at the aide. "We *did* cholera with this group. Typhoid! Get me typhoid!"

It was four p.m.

One more task had remained before Madden left for Africa. He remembered how the cab had left him at Josh's door at seven-thirty a.m. In Evanston snow had still been piled high in April. His son's eyes had widened when he opened the door. Josh was wearing his orange terrycloth bathrobe, an unlit Meerschaum in his mouth. He'd looked over Madden's shoulder as if expecting to see Catherine or press aides or photographers. He'd mumbled, "Danny left for school."

In the fern filled kitchen Madden had sat silently while Josh made coffee. A faint smell of brackish water had come from the sink, and pot handles protruded above the edge. Even from across the room Madden had made out Danny's smudge marks on the lower part of the refrigerator. Stephanie's geraniums on the windowsill were withering. Madden had not been alone with his son in years.

"I was working on papers," Josh had mumbled as he banged the cups on the table. Half sullen. Half antagonistic. They'd looked more at Danny's three wheel plastic charge-a-cycle blocking the doorway to the den than at each other. Madden had let Josh cook up some eggs, even though he'd eaten on the plane. They'd tried small talk about the Cubs. "So I invited Mike Russell to the White House and I told him, *'Get Haney to bunt!'* What do you think happens! Haney bunts, Friday. He pops out and the game's over. What a bum! What do I know!"

He'd had a vision while sitting there, a headmaster's office at a private high school in Pittsfield, Massachusetts. A young headmaster behind a mahogany desk, blond hair slightly long, blinking behind round tortoiseshell glasses.

"Congressman, Josh tries, but he doesn't have the ability. We like him here, he fits in and he's popular and I'm only telling you this because I get the feeling some pressure has been exerted on . . ."

Madden remembered shaking his head, furious. *Doesn't have the ability?* "He doesn't work hard enough!"

In the kitchen, finally even the feeble attempts at small talk had lapsed into silence. There was no graceful way to bring up what he had come to say. He didn't know what he had expected to find. "I wanted to tell you," he had said, "when you were arrested, at Northwestern, I called the chief. The chief of police." Josh had stiffened slightly and his eyes had narrowed. Madden had always hated the beard. Madden had said, "I know you think I never did anything."

"You mean I didn't even win that case by myself?" Josh had said bitterly.

In the camp Dr. Tamhane said, "If you're tired you can stop now. There's not much left to do."

"I'm fine," Madden said, wiping his brow with his sleeve. "It's the heat. Okay, mister! Step right up! Next!"

It was six p.m.

As Madden made his way to his tent an hour later, Robert Gardner was writing in his tent to the hiss of a kerosene lamp. At night the noise level seemed to rise in the camp. Someone nearby was playing a radio. What passed for music sounded like cats fighting in a trash can. At least a breeze had sprung up.

"I understand what Madden was talking about," Gardner wrote. His fingers were swollen and stiff from carrying crates all afternoon. Every joint hurt. He scribbled: "With each passing moment I am more aware that this valley is the problem in a nutshell. There is a stupefying discrepancy between the sleek oiled machines of war several miles away and the awful human want all around me. The gruesome feeling haunts me. The near-starving people are ghosts of our future. I feel as if war has already happened. I see no green, no water, no trees. People are dying as two armies see only each other. This afternoon I watched a mother bathe her dead son, readying him for burial. But I saw mothers in Detroit and Tulsa and San Francisco who may be doing the same thing. Madden came to show us this. Madden came to reveal the future."

Gardner rolled on his back, laid his hands across his chest, and looked at the shadows dancing on the roof of the tent. Susan's face came into his mind, white and oval and lovely. He smelled the perfume she wore. He saw her in a bridal gown, with her jet black hair. *We'll have children right away. No one's going to hurt my children.*

It was morning in Washington. She was probably working in her studio right now. See you in three weeks, he had told her.

He wondered what was happening on the Russian side of the valley.

He brightened. Good idea for tomorrow's column.

It was one a.m.

21

As Robert Gardner lay on his cot, two miles away the whole Soviet line was on the move. Company size strings of troops moved single file into the valley, threading gullies or keeping behind hills, all the while heading east. When they reached new positions, they sent runners back to call up the next wave. Radio messages were chancy, because they might be overheard.

Tank after tank emerged through the Mehta Pass and chugged in low gear toward the refugee camp. With commanders' heads sticking out of turrets, and engines in low gear to decrease noise, they followed guides on foot wearing neon green strips of tape on the back of their helmets. At ravine crossroads, soldiers directed them right or left with hooded flashlights. Over a thousand men had crossed into no-man's-land.

Like his American counterpart, the Russian general was taking a calculated risk. If he could advance to a new front by dawn, and finish digging in, the Americans would see he was not attacking. They would call Washington for instructions, like they'd always done in Vietnam. They would complain to Moscow and raise a fuss in the UN. But in the end they would accept the new Russian position.

In the darkness, Russian troops used entrenching tools to dig in. They positioned tripod-mounted antitank missiles behind rocks. They set up machine guns for intersecting fire to rip attackers apart. They dug slots in the earth for tanks. They readied camouflage netting.

It was three a.m. A single Russian tank company missed its stopping point in the dark. It went blundering farther into the valley, toward the refugee camp.

At the same time, four miles east, an American lieutenant hit a switch in the recreation shack behind American lines and flooded the room with bare-bulb light. Soldiers lay snoring on the carpeted floor, against prefab walls, under the ping-pong table, and beneath glossy color posters of Christie Brinkley and Paulina in bathing suits. The girls' smiles were radiant. Men coughed and snorted, groaning as they woke.

Sergeant Dewey Beech shouted, "Move it, move it!"

Beech bent quietly over Private Grady, who snored inches from Christie Brinkley's toe. She seemed about to nudge him. Beech kicked Grady's boot and cooed, in his mama's-boy voice, "Schoooooooool."

Exiting the shack into the chilly purple gloom, the forty soldiers felt the cold and tension drive the grogginess away. Four M-1 tanks and two Bradley armored fighting vehicles idled by the motor pool. The night was cloudy, no stars or moon. Beech eyed the cluster of rockets and the bristling 25mm chain gun on the box shaped Bradley with respect. But he was glad he wasn't going to have to ride inside. Steel coffin, he thought.

With the lieutenant riding on the lead tank and Beech, Grady, and two others on the next, the recon group moved out toward the cliffs on the south side of the valley, staying parallel to and behind American lines. When the lead tank reached fifty feet from the mushroom-shaped sandstone rumps, it plunged down an eight-foot escarpment through thorn scrub that tore at Beech, and turned west in a dry riverbed where the heavy steel tread ground flint shards to dust. Beech could just make out the wind-eroded shelves and pinnacles looming above.

They passed through the front in low gear, using the concealed dead river as cover. They headed into no-man's-land toward the refugee camp. Gasoline fumes washed back into Beech's face. He sniffed a tantalizing humid smell in the air, but he knew no rain would come. In four months he'd never seen rain here.

The recon was scheduled for first light. None of them wanted to die stupidly in the dark.

The riverbed curved away from the cliffs, meandering into the center of the valley. Beech watched a startled hyena lope away, disappearing over the edge of the river's embankment. He had scouted this route. He marked progress with a little rhythm in his head, his way of memorizing landmarks. Heart rock. Little holes. Dead bush.

The tank jolted his kidneys.

Finally they stopped at the north end of an inverted U-shaped bend in the river. Beech scrambled up the side of the embankment. A scarce fifty yards north, he saw flickering fires from the camp. He heard the low drone of gasoline generators for light in the intensive feeding unit. He could even make out the tin-roofed unit, the south-ernmost building in camp. He'd visited the children inside as Santa Claus at Christmas.

The plan was to charge around the side of the ravine, up the embankment, out onto the surface of the valley in forty minutes. They would roar past the tip of the camp, which now concealed them. Battle flags flying to impress the enemy and the natives, they would engage Russian scouting groups illegally in no-man's-land.

Grady had fallen back asleep against the engine-warmed side of the turret. Jackson the radio operator, had a deck of cards out. No one was allowed to talk. Beech squatted with the men and smelled the alkaline odor of the dead river and watched as Jackson dealt the first hand. He picked up the cards. He suppressed a smile. Not bad. Full house.

Stephanie Madden wriggled from her sleeping bag, swung her heavy legs over the side of the cot, and checked the luminous green dial of her Timex. Five-fifteen. Her head felt heavy, stuffed. She'd been unable to sleep. Every time she'd closed her eyes last night the children's faces had swum in at her. The fly-specked eyes. The con-centration camp limbs.

Even when she'd nursed in a hospital, bad cases could send her home in tears. She told herself she'd seen photographs of drought victims at home, in *Newsweek*. She might have been better prepared. But she realized the pictures had been only eight and a half by eleven inches. And she'd looked them over at the kitchen counter, an arm's reach from the fruit bowl with its juicy pears and oranges. The television, which had shown her larger, moving pictures, had wedged them into a mélange of news between home-run predictions and divorce announcements of Hollywood movie stars.

She touched her toes a few times. No Jane Fonda exercises in this valley.

Her tent mates, a blond Denver freelance writer and a neurotic New York tax lawyer who "wanted to do something for others for a change," slept soundly despite odd scraping noises outside. Babies were always crying somewhere in camp. She pulled on smelly trousers and the dusty shirt she'd worn yesterday. She thought, *I've got to get back to them.* She shook out her desert boots because the director had warned scorpions might crawl inside them at night. A purple Northwestern windbreaker was protection against the predawn chill.

Outside, the sky had lightened to a sullen gray. Stepping from the tent, she looked around, surprised. So that was where the scraping noises came from. Yesterday, when they'd pitched tents in the teardrop-shaped clearing, around rocky columns and hillocks, this part of camp had been empty. But during the night hundreds of refugees had moved in. They were digging holes everywhere with old tin cans. They lay wrapped in blankets on the ground. They held bony, imploring hands to her for food. "I'm sorry," Stephanie said. She opened her palms as she walked to show she had nothing. A healthy-looking boy ran up to her, grinned dazzlingly, and asked a question. Stephanie smiled back. "Sorry. What's your name?"

The boy hissed, "Ferenj!" He kicked her in the ankle and walked proudly away, shoulders straight.

Wincing at the sting, she walked south. The volunteers had been assigned to the newest part of camp, a Florida-shaped area jutting into the desert, near an old dead river. She walked to the intensive feeding unit. The children inside had lost 70 percent of their body weight.

She passed her father-in-law's tent and her face twisted in concern. He'd looked wan and exhausted at their bean-and-bread dinner. She hoped he'd slept. The heat had been brutal on him.

Thinking of Madden made her flash back to the victory celebration in Tent City the night he'd won his trial. Stephanie smiled. The singing and guitar playing had gone on into the early morning. It was like their leafletting and arguing had helped him win, even though the jury had been locked away. It was like they'd won a contest of wills with an invisible foe. *They* had won the trial.

Stephanie remembered how word had spread that Madden needed volunteers for Africa. She'd been among the first to apply. As she picked her way around newly erected lean-tos and boulders, she remembered the cramped office in DuPont Circle where she had been interviewed. The Save the Children poster and the astonished look of the woman behind the desk as Stephanie had given her real name. No way she could hurt Madden now that the trial was over. She'd checked the "nurse" box with a surge of pride. Josh hadn't even tried to argue her out of it when she'd called.

She'd told Danny, "Remember I showed you pictures of boys and girls in Africa who don't have any food?"

"Yes."

"I'm taking a trip with Grandpa, to help them."

"I'll go to Aperca too," Danny had said.

Stephanie remembered Madden when he addressed the volunteers two nights before they left. She pictured the banquet room at Red Cross headquarters, the volunteers at round tables eating baked chicken and soggy string beans on plastic plates. The banner that read, simply, PEACE, suspended over Madden's podium in the center of the stage.

"The world is ready to starve Africans so it can blow itself up," he'd said. "I admire your patriotism. Your love of your country."

Stephanie remembered toasting Madden and loving him. That was why she had been so shocked the next night when he tried to talk her out of coming. She'd gone to a family dinner at the Goldmans' house. Somehow Madden had gotten her alone in the impressive library. First he'd told her funny stories, and then he'd reminisced about Danny and Josh. He'd read quotes from Presidents in Goldman's books. All the Presidents seemed to be urging her to go home to her family.

Closing the leatherbound Roosevelt, he'd said, "Steph, I'm happy you want to go, but they need you. I'm an old man. What's an ex-

President supposed to do? Write memoirs? Ah ha, I hate writing. Steph. Even the Army doesn't send two members of the same family to the same posting. A little peace of mind. You think you can give your old father-in-law that?"

She remembered her face burning with embarrassment. She'd never argued with him before. She'd said, falteringly, "Sometimes I think back to my life before. Shopping or reading books with Josh, or playing with Danny. That's what I want in the end. It's what I love. I suppose it's funny, because all I have to do is get on a plane and I'll have it. But you want to know how I feel here, every day?"

She'd come so close to him she could see the pores on his face. She worried about him, because the lines around his mouth and eyes had deepened so much during the trial. She'd been wearing the only good dress she'd taken to Washington, purple cotton with lace on the sleeves. She'd said, fervently, "Like I'm saving the world. I know it sounds crazy, but I keep thinking. Maybe if I talk to one more person. Give out one more leaflet or make one more call . . . maybe *that* will make the difference." She'd laid her hand over his so that she could feel the old man's cartilage beneath his skin and hair. She'd glanced at the rows of books. "I believe in you so much," she'd said. "I can't explain myself as well as all these Presidents, but I know what I feel. If you say it's important to go somewhere I won't do less."

Madden had stood eyeing her in his tuxedo. Elegant. Defeated. "Who would have thought you'd be the one I couldn't convince?" he'd said.

The intensive feeding unit was a low, rectangular tin-roofed shack that leaned in on itself like dilapidated abandoned barns in Carolina. Through cracks in the walls she saw stark orange light glowing inside from overhead bulbs. The door was nothing more than sticks tied together. She pushed it open and an errie, painful silence enveloped her. She saw row after row of tiny cots, evenly spaced, all occupied. Tubes hung from suspended plastic bags of nutrient mix for intravenous feeding. There was a slight alcohol smell to the place, which made her feel at home.

In the rear of the shack, beyond the last row of patients, a Danakil mother leaned against the wall, rocking on the straw matting covering the earth floor, cradling in her lap the shrunken body of her baby. The child's face pressed into the woman's parchmentlike breast, but Stephanie was too far away to see if the lips were moving.

The only other nurse present was a heavy blond Swede in khaki. Stephanie had met her when the shifts changed last night. From across the room she greeted Stephanie with a nod. She went back to singing a Swedish nursery rhyme to a boy nestled in the crook of her arm.

It was five-forty-five. Stephanie saw dawn's oncoming bleakness through gaps in the walls. Josh would be brewing his Medaglia d'Oro at home, eating his two jelly donut breakfast and scanning notes for his eight o'clock class on Henry James.

She washed in a ceramic basin with hot water from a kettle heated over a hotplate. The intensive feeding unit always had plenty of water, stored in old oil drums lining one wall. The medicines were in padlocked trunks. Paper was short for medical charts this week, so the nurses had cut up cardboard cartons with scissors, but the pens were donated, gold-tipped Swiss ballpoints.

She had always intended to go back to the hospital when Danny started school. Her hands throbbed pleasantly from the heat of the water. She started rounds with the boy closest to the basin, a three-year-old whose woolly hair had fallen out in patches, as if he had undergone chemotherapy. He slept with his hands tucked under him in a powder blue snap-up pajama suit from America with a smiling yellow kitten emblazoned on the arm. The brand-new blanket had slid past his knees. A white tag on the suit read, "Ages six months to a year."

Stephanie heard the growl of engines starting up somewhere nearby. Probably the expected water trucks moving close. She scanned the cardboard chart and bent quietly, without disturbing the boy's sleep, to check the facial bandage holding a blue translucent tube in place for nostril feeding. He would receive a mix of grain and water.

Abruptly the cot slid three inches right.

A plasma bottle shattered on the ground.

Stephanie heard a roar like thunder. When she looked up, blinking, the stakes in the east wall seemed to be caving in. Her last thought was that the feeding tube needed adjustment. The tank shell came through the hut and tore her face away. Across the ward the Swedish nurse held the baby in her arms and saw Stephanie pitch forward, dead already, spraying blood from her neck.

Dewey Beech slithered backwards on his belly and fired off another round. He yelled, "Into the gully!" The desert ahead quivered like a mirage with advancing Russian soldiers and tanks, coming from behind small hills and out of ravines. A mushroom of dirt burst in front of him. Private Ogolnick clutched his forehead, rolled left, and toppled to the earth. Beech roared, "Cover fire!"

The recon group had charged from the dry river at first light. They'd roared north around the Florida-shaped southern tip of the camp, battle flags flapping. They'd run into Russian tanks, the spearhead of the group they were now fighting, fifty yards ahead.

Everything had seemed to stop. The Russians had appeared as dumbfounded as the Americans. Beech had seen two Russian officers on a rocky knoll, frozen over a map. And behind them three of the huge, sand-colored, red-starred T-72s atop hillocks, with at least one cannon protruding from behind another hill and Soviet infantry looking back.

The lead American tank's cannon had started to hum and swivel.

Beech had yelled, "Off the tank!"

The first Russian shot had gone wide, into the refugee camp. As the Americans began firing, Beech had seen a Soviet Spandrel missile strike the lead M-1 just below the turret. The hatch had blown off, but only flames had come out.

With the tank commander and Beech's lieutenant killed, pieces of the American force fought on their own. As Beech fell back toward the riverbed, where he could establish a battle line, he saw the developing firefight in segments. One Bradley on the ridge of the dry river, unleashing its missiles with a whoosh as the 25mm chain gun roared. He didn't see the other. Two M-1s backing west, around the tip of the refugee camp and away from the Russians, either for concealment or as part of a circling maneuver. The third tank advanced alone. It stopped. There was a boom, and yellow smoke balled out from the turret.

Russian tanks were disappearing into the refugee camp, trying to cut off the M-1s.

Beech heard the screech of an incoming shell. He ducked, felt the force of the blast sweep over his head. Fountains of earth pelted him. The Russians were twenty yards away, dropping to the ground, crawling forward and firing. Jackson grunted, slapped his cheek and dropped his M-16, which rolled down the ravine to the dead river. Beech heard the spattering of the Bradley's machine gun. He fired, and a running Russian threw out his arms and danced sideways, like a fighter, before collapsing in a heap.

Beech fell back over the embankment, poked his head up and kept firing. All around him men were doing the same. "Radio!" Beech barked. Grady slid down two feet and wrestled the machine off Jackson's back. Jackson fell back against the embankment, leaning casually as if on a break, except his eyes were too wide and the helmet strap clenched a rigid jaw.

Grady held the receiver to Beech. He'd made contact.

Those bastards aren't going to force us back, Beech decided.

As he reached for the receiver, the burning lead M-1 blew up in a series of mad, roaring volleys as the fire reached its ammunition.

Black smoke swirled upward inside the refugee camp. Tank fight.

Beech yelled into the radio, "We can hold but we need reinforcements. They ambushed us!"

At the top of the embankment again Beech emptied his clip. The Russians seemed to be faltering, slowing. Some of their men were crawling backwards now, toward the protection of their own hills or ravines. A T-72 burned. The turret was upside down, and soldiers lay on the ground beneath the open hatch.

Someone moaned, "Mary, Mary."

He heard more fire from inside the refugee camp.

On the ground, a lizard ran back and forth, terrified, scattering spent shell casings.

Beech shouted, "On the right! Fire!" Grady was still talking urgently on the radio. He cried up to Beech, an awed look on his face, "They're everywhere, not just here! Attacking all over the valley!"

Grady had a talent for bringing up the worst questions at bad times. "Sarge!" He jerked his brows toward the sky. "The nukes. You think they'll use 'em?"

"I don't know."

"Well, if there are nukes shouldn't we pull back or something?"

"They'll tell us what we need to know."

But the nukes had bothered him when he'd learned they were here. The Army never told you anything. To the Army, you were a bullet to be fired.

Beech broke off the thought and looked left, by instinct, along the riverbed. Unaware he had detected a vibration from that direction. A hundred yards up, red star gleaming, a T-72 was edging its way into the ravine.

With the first explosion, Madden fought his way out of deep sleep. Dreamless, exhausted unconsciousness. His leg muscles burned, his neck throbbed. The rocking ground cleared the sleep out of him. He heard the cries of terror outside. In his pajamas, Madden yanked back the flap of his tent.

Africans and volunteers were shouting, running in all directions. Trampling lean-tos. Charging from tents in bathrobes or underwear. An African staggered toward him holding a stump where a hand had been. A volunteer lurched past in the other direction, hands out, blood pumping from the side of her head.

Madden had seen plenty of arms demonstrations, and he recognized the boom of M-1 tank shells, as well as heavier, thick explosions from Russian T-72s.

Stephanie, he thought.

Madden ran north, weaving past tents and rocky columns, a sixty-five-year-old man in pajamas and a white steel helmet bearing a red cross. The earth seemed like it was exploding. A geyser of dirt boomed up and fell back, crushing a tent. He'd kept Huff elsewhere in the camp, not wanting to have a bodyguard in front of the other volunteers, so he was alone now. The firing seemed to be coming from all directions simultaneously.

To the west, at the periphery of the tent area, he saw tanks firing at each other. American and Russian.

Her tent was empty. There was one neatly made-up cot and two that were rumpled and had been left in haste. Her pink suitcase lay open, with folded T-shirts on top. The partly visible logo said PEPSI. There was a gold rimmed, glass-covered photo of Josh and Danny in bathing suits in the tent on top of an empty penicillin crate.

Madden's chest felt like it was expanding. An iron poker had been inserted between his ribs. He gripped his side as he ran for the intensive feeding unit. He crashed into people running the other way, toward the helicopter pad, but kept going. He prayed she'd stayed away from the ward.

As he ran he saw a tent scooped into the air, gliding gently, bursting into flame. He threw himself on the ground when he heard the screech of a tank shell. Dirt rained down on his shoulders. Across a clearing he caught sight of Robert Gardner helping a wounded man, supporting him, heading the other way. There was the spatter of machine gun fire to the west. It thickened as he crawled forward. He passed a burning T-72, its buglike turret half-severed from the main part of the tank. Now he was passing bodies. He fought down the horror to keep his thinking clear. A line of bullets tore the earth, and Madden rolled right. He kept calling her name.

He thought, *don't be there.*

Then he was out of the clearing and he saw the intensive feeding unit and his heart turned over. The tin roof had been blown off sideways and leaned against the only remaining wall. Cots and bodies had been blown all over a seventy-yard radius. A baby's fist lay severed, thumb twitching, an inch from his face. He groaned and kept going. Crazed with pain, a little girl rolled on her back and screamed and tore at her ankles.

Maybe Stephanie hadn't been here when the shooting started. Maybe she was back at the helicopter pad and a copter would take her away. *What will I tell Josh?*

The poker in his ribs grew hot. He remembered the first time he had seen her in her nurse's whites, before she and Josh were married. She'd introduced him to all her patients in Evanston Hospital. He clutched at his chest, but the pain subsided. The day heat was coming quickly now. He tasted sweat. The sky was clearing, going blue; soon planes would join in the fray. Beyond the intensive feeding unit he caught sight of a bare area of desert and men firing from a ditch. He could not tell whether they were Russian or American.

He was crawling diagonally south, into the hottest area of fighting. He saw that behind him men were shooting from behind stubby-looking mounds. The carnage was thickest within the actual boundaries of the intensive feeding unit. Blankets and clumps of straw burned. Water spurted into the ground from holes blasted in old oil drums. An African woman in blue rags lay sprawled over an overturned cot, by a broken plasma bottle.

Overhead he heard the thin, high whine of long distance artillery, arcing east to west.

Madden saw Stephanie's purple slicker.

He stopped and forced himself to crawl forward. The world reduced itself to that flapping piece of purple. Maybe it wasn't her slicker. With so many people in camp, wouldn't at least one other person have a purple slicker? A surge of hope flashed through him.

The face was turned away from him.

He turned her over and gagged.

Six inches above the circular Northwestern motto, white bits of bloodied bone poked through tendon and muscle.

"Oh Jesus, Stephanie. Oh God!"

Madden cradled the body, oblivious to the whining bullets. In an agony of self-blame he said, "Why didn't you listen to me?" He saw how useless his efforts had been all along. He thought it was impossible this awful corpse had been the mother of his grandchild. Maybe Stephanie had loaned the slicker to someone else, someone her size, with her curly hair. He wondered if the fighting had started here or spread to Africa from somewhere else. He wondered if Washington was gone yet. He saw Catherine as a fifteen-year-old girl swinging on a country porch.

He spoke out loud to Rittenhouse, six thousand miles away. "I would have done it too a year ago. Just a little one, to scare them. Just a calculated risk." Madden said to Stephanie, "I could have stopped it. I had the chance."

Through the horror he was aware of a grotesque weary relief that the end had come.

Madden's heart thundered louder than all the artillery. The world seemed to be blowing apart. The pain spread in waves that intensified in his chest. And then he heard something that distracted him, a vague crying over the sound of the gunfire. It was children weeping. Somewhere nearby.

Madden looked around but saw only corpses. Smoke and flame swirled and the firing increased. He realized the wailing came from the dark triangular crawl space between the fallen roof and the wall. When he reached it on hands and knees, he saw four or five shadowy forms inside, in a row.

"Don't be afraid. Come on, this is the worst place. We can get out of here."

They didn't look up. Or seem to hear. His eyes adjusted slightly to the darkness and he saw they'd buried their heads in their knees or covered their faces with their hands. The wailing was louder in the confined space. The open mouths were black caves.

Madden scooped out the first child, a girl whose fragile weight finally worked to her advantage. She didn't fight him, but she didn't acknowledge him either. Then the hands went around his neck. Her limbs were so shrunken. He clasped her to his chest and ran, zig-zagging like a soldier, toward the open desert. A ravine, he thought. Anywhere to get the kids out of the line of fire.

Madden's running feet hit the desert. The bomb would be exploding soon, he thought, but he would not just give up.

Then hot pain spiked through the back of his thigh, propelling him forward. He heard his own grunt as if it were far away and came from another man. He pulled the child closer to protect her as he went down. He was truly surprised he had been shot.

Dewey Beech let out his breath. The old man in the red cross helmet was moving again, slower but still alive. The man had gathered up the child and used his free hand to crawl out of the line of fire. He must have succeeded, because both of them disappeared off the surface of the desert, into a ravine, Beech supposed.

"He made it!" Grady cried, taking pleasure in little things, celebrating by firing off a long burst at the Russians.

The fighting had settled down, at least for the moment. The T-72 that had tried to get into the ravine lay on its side sixty yards west, tread blown off by a TOW missile that had killed the crew. The Russians out in front of them were probably waiting for reinforcements too. The artillery was getting thicker in other parts of the valley.

Grady cried suddenly, "He's going back! Hey! Get out of there!"

The old man was alone now, crawling toward the intensive feeding unit again. Moving sideways, face to the Russians, sort of dragging his left leg as if it had been hit. He dropped flat to the ground and grabbed his helmet in place when a shell boomed overhead.

The old guy reached the clumps of burning straw that marked the boundary of the unit.

He clutched his back and arced and pitched forward. The helmet tipped away, rolling like an eggshell with a red cross on the side.

Beech fired at the Russians.

He couldn't believe it. The old man's hand was groping forward.

Looking west, toward American lines, Beech saw a long file of dust coming. Tanks!

The old guy's hand located the helmet and dragged it back, put it on his head, but he was moving jerkily, in pain. He'd lost coordination.

The firing picked up. Grady said, "There he goes."

Beech was filled with admiration for the old guy, even though he thought the man was crazy.

The old man disappeared behind the tumbled-down tin roof. He emerged seconds later clutching another child, half pulling, half dragging the terrified kid. Christ, the kid was making it harder for him! Beech filled with pride. That old man was American, he knew it. He fought the urge to run out there and help. Who would lead the men if he did that?

The old man rolled over sideways, started to get up and dropped back again. The helmet fell off.

The boy must have figured out what the old man wanted, because he crawled away from his would-be benefactor toward the ravine.

"Go for it, kid!" Grady yelled.

Beech was furious. He fired off a burst at the Russians. He found a pair of binoculars. He felt terrible, as if the old man had been a friend.

He focused.

"My God," he whispered. "It's the President."

The shock rippled through the line. The face was unmistakable. Beech had a crazy thought: *His legs are so skinny.* They didn't look like a President's legs. They looked like old guys' legs at the beach. The men faltered, but Beech snapped, "Keep firing." He was operating by rote. A vision came to him from Vietnam. He'd led his squad up a dirt road toward a village. As they neared the huts, a line of Vietnamese women had come toward them, unarmed and stretched in a line across the road. The Vietcong had been behind with their Chinese machine guns. Beech remembered screaming at the women, *"Get down,"* but they'd kept coming. One of them had been so beautiful, maybe seventeen, in a bright red sarong. She'd pressed her palms over her stomach as if she might stop the bullets that way. She hadn't been saying anything, but Beech had seen tears streaming down her cheeks.

He'd ordered his men to fire. What else could he do?

Beech couldn't fire and he couldn't take his eyes off the President. He filled with awe. He wanted to scream at Madden that he shouldn't have been there in the first place, that it wasn't Beech's fault he'd been killed. His head hurt. It was like George Washington was lying there. Or the flag. Even without field glasses anyone could see blood streaming down his leg and forehead.

Beech had voted for Madden. He'd railed at him for cowardice after the surrender. He'd cursed him, like every soldier here, blaming him for their rotten assignment. Up until this moment he'd viewed Madden with conflicting feelings. With distance, as if Madden were unreal, like a movie star you never met and who lived only on TV. Contempt, for giving up. Relief, for saving Beech's life and the lives of his wife and daughter, although the relief made Beech slightly ashamed of himself. Mockery, over the theatrical switch from politics to gentle phony spiritualism, like death row murderers who say they found Christ. And since this morning, when he'd found out Madden was here, with a reluctant pride that the President had come, made Beech's valley more important, touched his life personally.

Beech rubbed his eyes. It was impossible. Madden couldn't be moving. He couldn't be, it was an illusion, the only thing moving was smoke. He was dead. He was not pulling his arms back, tucking them under his chest. He was not dragging his legs up and down, as if painfully pedaling a bicycle. He was not trying to push himself off the ground. Even if he was conscious, he'd been too badly hurt. He couldn't have the strength. He was an old guy.

Madden stood up.

He stood there swaying. First Beech thought he was going to walk right, then left. The firing let up a bit all along the line. He wondered if the Russians had recognized him too.

Blindly, Madden took one step forward.

His hands dropped to his sides.

His head fell sideways onto his left shoulder.

He crashed forward, into the dust.

Now all along the line the firing was stopping. The last bullet was fired. There were artillery sounds from far away, but Beech realized, with wonder, that the only hand-to-hand had been here.

In the lull Beech heard flames crackling and the cries of the wounded. A hand raised through the smoke, clutched at the air, and dropped back. There was a high undulating sound like the screaming of a horse. Amid static on the radio a voice was saying, "Sergeant? Sergeant Beech!"

Looking out at the wreckage, Beech grew aware of more. He saw the dead children and the nurses, really saw them for the first time. A feeling of profound horror seized him. They were the children he had taken toys to as Santa Claus.

On both sides of the fight, soldiers were thinking, *Here's my chance to live.*

"Sergeant," the radio instructed him. "Tell your men to cover themselves, take cover. We're going to be sending them a nuke. Just one."

Beech got on the radio, dazed, still staring. "President Madden was here. He's dead. He's lying out there. The fighting has stopped."

Twenty minutes later he saw a T-72 pull back from behind a hillock. The Soviet soldiers trailed after it. They were going back to their lines.

The radio instructed him to stay put. "Don't fire. We're getting you back here, Sergeant, so relax."

22

It was very, very sunny but there was no heat in the air. Robert Gardner left the rented Cimarron a quarter-mile from the cemetery in the back row of a slick, muddy field, between a blue Ford pickup and a stretch limousine from New York. As he and Susan joined the people streaming along the soft earth track to the two-lane highway, he saw license plates from Massachusetts, New Mexico, Oregon, Canada. In the Berkshires it was springtime. The police had blocked the road to vehicles. Mourners stood shoulder to shoulder. The eerie quiet was punctuated by the chirping of birds.

Gardner saw no houses or barns or fences or cattle. Just a long wooded curve by a two lane blacktop.

It was two weeks after the battle of the Mehta Valley. Where the crowd ended and the path to the cemetery began, more police guarded wooden sawhorses. A trooper signaled Gardner to stay back, but Madden's old bodyguard, Huff, materialized in a black suit.

"Mr. Gardner's a friend."

He walked up worn granite steps set into the hillside. The cemetery was small, surrounded by a New England stone wall fence. The headstones had been worn thin over two centuries. Small rounded slabs leaned forward with age, rubbed by rain and wind, many of the inscriptions barely visible.

COLONEL JOSEPH MADDEN

1741–1801

COLONEL OF THE MILITIA.

The Lyle Board of Selectmen had voted to admit one last burial in the old cemetery.

Gardner saw President Rittenhouse inside the fence with his hat off, and the Vice-President and the chief justice of the Supreme Court. He saw the presidents of France and Egypt and the Prince of Wales. He still could not believe sometimes that he was alive, that he had returned home to Susan. Despite his numbness he tasted the overturned earth smell and the vegetation. Loamy. Lush.

By the grave, Catherine and Josh Madden talked quietly with Mark St. Johns and Nicki. St. Johns had his hand pressed lovingly in the small of Nicki's back.

Catherine broke off when she saw Gardner. She squeezed his hands. "That was a beautiful story. Thank you," she said. A May breeze came through the gap in the brown, budding trees and made the black veil over her face quiver. Josh Madden's skin was gray, he had black circles under his eyes and looked like he'd been sobbing. As Gardner turned away, he heard Josh say to Catherine, "I never told him I loved him."

Below, the people seemed to stretch away. Thousands of people.

"Yea, though I walk through the valley of the shadow," spoke the preacher, a tall, emaciated Madden, stooped with age, topped by the familiar gray thatch. The uncle, Gardner guessed. An old man with a young man's voice. The words cast Gardner back. His knees weakened at the memory. In the camp he'd helped a wounded man to the doctor and run to look for Madden by the helicopter pad. The ground had rocked with explosions. Against restraining hands he'd run back through camp, past burning tanks and bodies on the ground.

He'd reached the intensive feeding unit to see Madden ahead, through yellow drifting smoke, an outline at first, swaying. He'd watched Madden fall.

As Catherine Madden approached the microphone, the silence was like the quiet when Madden had gone down. Her voice boomed out from loudspeakers in the trees, startling blue jays and robins into the air. "I have something to read to you," she said. "A press release dated this morning." Her voice trembled and grew strong. Gardner saw that Josh Madden, beside her, had started to quietly cry.

Catherine said, " 'This morning the United States and the Soviet Union began historic talks which will hopefully lessen the possibility of accidental nuclear war. The two countries will explore opening a nuclear monitoring center to supplement the hotline, staffed by scientists and military personnel from the United States and Russia, equipped with the most modern tracking devices and communications technology, operating twenty-four hours a day. In the event of false alarms, instant communication and cooperation will be possible.

" 'In addition, the hotline telephone will be updated to a video link-up, so that the President and Russian Premier will be able to talk face to face in the event of emergency.' "

One person started clapping below. Others joined in and the applause grew long and thunderous.

Gardner squeezed Susan's arm. One blue jay had landed on the rock wall near Catherine. Gardner remembered how the U.S. and Soviet forces had pulled back from the Mehta Valley days after the battle. How airlifts had begun taking most of the troops home. In his mind he glimpsed the wooden side of a boathouse near Washington, on the banks of the Potomac, at eleven at night. A white haired man in a conservative suit whispered to Gardner, ". . . Szokan told Rittenhouse to launch, one Beasley to seal the pass and show the Russians we meant business. Muldea said negotiate or warn them at least. After Rittenhouse gave Macy the order, he got on the hotline. Menkes was willing to pull back, but he said if we went nuclear he'd respond in kind. Bob, I tell you. If that sergeant hadn't called Macy from the fighting and stopped the . . ."

Maybe it was true and maybe it wasn't. Maybe the Russians had recalled their general for acting without orders, as Moscow had announced. Maybe the general had just failed. Gardner would spend the days to come tracking down the story, but since being with Madden the specific chain of events that had led to the fight interested him less. Madden had said, "If it doesn't happen one way, it will happen another." Madden had said, "All great cataclysms in the world have been preceded by the words 'It'll never happen.' "

Catherine's voice boomed out of the trees and snapped Gardner back to attention. " 'The courage of life is often less dramatic than the courage of the final moment. A man does what he must, in spite of personal consequences, in spite of obstacles and dangers and pressures, and that is the basis of all human morality.' "

He knew she was smiling under the veil. "I hope President Kennedy will forgive me for using his words," she said. "My husband loved to read the Presidents. Wives can say grand things about their husbands. My husband saved the world." She paused, and Gardner saw her smile faltering. Still strong, she said, "That's why services are being held now all over the world. In London and Jakarta. Tokyo. Peking. In Ottawa and Paris. In millions of homes people are mourning William Madden."

At his name her voice caught. She bent and straightened.

"I hope this service is more than just a funeral, a goodbye. I hope our grief will bring together millions of voices, here and in the Soviet Union and in all countries. The people he reached out to. You. We must make ourselves heard over and over again as we build a common conscience to end the arms race. Your participation at the grass roots level won a battle, but the power of nuclear war continues to increase, threatening our children, our community, our country, and our world. I pledge myself . . . I pledge . . . I . . ."

Josh Madden came up to Catherine and led her away.

Heading back to the car, in the silent mass of people, Gardner and Susan held each other tight.

He didn't speak for a while, driving.

"I want to make a baby," he said. There was fierceness in his voice.

And two thousand miles south Sergeant Dewey Beech groaned, "Grady, hump it. Move it."

He pushed forward up the muddy ravine in the mountain, cursing to himself. Fuckin' Army never gives you a rest. If it isn't one thing it's another. The better you do, the worse duty you get.

The flies buzzed everywhere. He could feel leeches sucking on his ankles after fording that last stream. The mosquitos were the size of babies' fists. A banded red and yellow snake slithered into an upright rotting tree trunk.

First the desert. Now the jungle.

Christ. The leaves are big as jeeps.

They stopped behind a rotted, fallen log, a great, wide specimen caked with greenish mold, breaking off in damp rust-colored segments. Some kind of gigantic orange mushrooms grew on top, with purplish specks at the edges and red ants all over the place. He didn't know if the actual temperature was as hot here as in the Mehta Valley, already becoming a dry, hot memory, but you felt like you were covered with wet rags after thirty seconds outside.

Ahead, they heard the muted but unmistakable sound of footfalls. One man? Three?

The small dark soldier at Beech's side grunted knowingly and threw up his M-16 and aimed at an opening in the trail ahead, between ferns and a large blue rock. The man was the local military liaison and guide for Beech. The insects buzzed. The treetops blotted out the sun except for gold patches, and dust danced in the long sunbeams arcing down from two hundred feet above.

Someone was coming into view ahead. One man with a machine gun.

The soldier beside Beech nudged him and held his breath. He mouthed one word.

"Russian."